Y0-DWL-989

Wedding Day . . .

"You look beautiful," Ajani said, shutting the door. I lifted the hem of my gown and backed away. I was deeply, helplessly conflicted. I wanted Ajani, needed him, but it wasn't right. My relationship with him had already cost me so much. "I'm getting married, Ajani. You shouldn't be here," I told him, my voice shaking uncontrollably.

"No, Yvette," Ajani interrupted, his voice thick with anger and desperation. "You're the one who shouldn't be here. We both know that you don't want to marry Terrence." Ajani's toffee-hued features were as perfect as I remembered. I envisaged running my hands along the contours of his classic cheekbones, kissing his smooth neck . . .

"That's not true," I said, shaking my head to stop the fantasizing. "I've planned for this a long time; everyone is waiting."

"So what we had meant nothing to you?" Ajani spoke as if he were in physical pain. His normally clear eyes were bloodshot; his voice sounded raspy and tired. He sat on the corner of the bed I'd slept in the night before. It seemed so familiar, so natural; it took me back to a time when I was truly happy.

THINGS FORBIDDEN

MARYAM DIAAB

Genesis Press, Inc.

INDIGO

An imprint of Genesis Press, Inc.
Publishing Company

Genesis Press, Inc.
P.O. Box 101
Columbus, MS 39703

ISBN: 13 DIGIT : 978-1-58571-327-1
ISBN: 10 DIGIT : 1-58571-327-9
Manufactured in the United States of America

First Edition

Visit us at www.genesis-press.com
or call at 1-888-Indigo-1-4-0

DEDICATION

To my husband Damon.
My heart belongs to only you.

PROLOGUE

A vision in white silk, I thought ruefully, studying my reflection in the full-length mirror. The hotel suite, elegantly decorated perfectly for the "happy" occasion, was itself a vision. Bouquets of Casablanca lilies and red roses covered nearly every surface; their scent perfumed the air. Someone had placed a small-framed photograph of me and my bridegroom, Dr. Terrence Hall, on the bedside table. We looked the perfect couple; our arms were wrapped around each other, our smiles relaxed, expectant, genuine. But that seemed like eons ago; so much had happened since the day we happily posed for that photo.

"What am I doing?" I asked myself. "What am I *doing*?" I asked again, turning back to the mirror. The V-neck, spaghetti-strapped wedding gown cost more than my car, but seven months ago when I watched Terrence hand over his Visa to the sales clerk, I hadn't thought about the cost. But then again, seven months ago marrying Terrence was all I thought about. I thought a ring would keep him at home, keep him from wandering. Now my mind was crowded with conflicting emotions, and uncertainty had become a constant, terrifying presence.

"I really can't get over how beautiful you look," Wendy said, standing behind me and looking at my reflection in the mirror. "Like a princess, even more so than we dreamed, remember?" Our eyes met in the mirror, and I forced a slight smile. "What's with the phony smile, Yvette? Aren't you excited?"

"Of course I'm excited," I replied halfheartedly, lifting my gown and going over to the bed. "It's just . . . just maybe everything is moving too fast. I wish everything would slow down."

"Slow down? You and Terrence have been together since college. Fifteen minutes before you're supposed to say 'I do' isn't the time to suddenly get cold feet."

"I'm not getting cold feet. I—"

"A lot of women would kill to be in your shoes right now." And with those few words, Wendy's demeanor changed. In maybe ten seconds, she had gone from concerned, supportive friend to something else, something I didn't recognize. Maybe *she* was one of those women who would kill to be standing in my shoes.

"I know. I get it, but don't forget Terrence and I have been through a lot. He's not what everyone thinks he is," I said, looking at Wendy with pleading eyes. Right now, I needed Wendy to be on my side; I needed her to show me that she was still my best friend. But since my return that seemed like more than Wendy could handle.

"Yeah, well . . ." Wendy began, a hint of bitterness in her voice. She walked over to the mirror and dabbed at a bit of extra lipstick on her upper lip. "Let's not pretend that you're innocent in all this. You've done your share, too."

I held my head between my hands, inhaling deep before standing. It was painfully obvious that I couldn't talk to Wendy; she had her own agenda, although I wasn't quite sure what it was. "Okay, I'm fine, I'm fine. Let's just get this over with."

"That's the spirit, Yvette!" Wendy said sarcastically, giving me a thumbs up. In return, I gave her the middle finger.

Wendy handed me a bouquet of lilies tied with a red silk ribbon that matched her dress perfectly.

I wrapped my fingers around the bouquet and immediately felt my eyes well with tears. Wendy's expression softened.

"I'm not trying to upset you," Wendy said, hugging me stiffly. Her words were unconvincing but nonetheless comforted me. "I just think that you need to make a decision, because all this back and forth is—"

"I know, and I made my decision," I responded quickly, hoping to shut her up. "Thirty minutes from now, I will be Mrs. Terrence Hall, and then I'll be able to put the last few months behind me," I said with a conviction I didn't feel.

"Just take a deep breath, and as you walk down the aisle, think about the wonderful man you're about to marry," Wendy urged, her voice sounding slightly and unaccountably sad as we headed for the door.

"You're right, as usual." I forced a laugh, following Wendy into the hallway. And then I came face-to-face with the memory that I had tried so desperately to suppress. All composure vanished as I looked into his eyes, and before I could retreat to the room and close myself off to him, Ajani stepped close, so close I could smell his cologne, so close I could practically taste him.

"What are you doing here?" I whispered, panic filling every fiber of my body. A deep longing I thought I'd banished forever resurfaced and made me weak in the knees.

"I—I needed to talk to you. I've been calling and calling but . . ." He stopped when he saw Wendy staring at us. Then he turned back to me.

"I can't do this, Ajani. I *won't* do this, not here, not now," I said adamantly, my eyes again filling with tears. I knew what he wanted, what he'd always wanted and I wasn't prepared to give in to him. I looked away, unable to bear the look of love in his eyes. I looked to Wendy for support, but she was smirking, amused and a strange kind of satisfaction marring her pretty face.

"Just give me ten minutes," Ajani pleaded, moving closer to me. "That's all the time I'll need to say what I have to say. Afterward, if you still want me to leave, then I'll go."

"Yvette, I think you should listen to him," Wendy interrupted, inching further and further away. "Maybe you two should go back inside the suite. I'll be right outside if you need me."

Giving Wendy a tiny smile of gratitude, Ajani came all the way into the bridal suite, leaving me with no choice but to follow.

"You look beautiful," Ajani said, shutting the door.

I lifted the hem of my gown and backed away. I was deeply, helplessly, conflicted. I wanted Ajani, needed him, but it wasn't right. My relationship with him had already cost me so much. "I'm getting married, Ajani. You shouldn't be here," I told him, my voice shaking uncontrollably.

"No, Yvette," Ajani interrupted, his voice thick with anger and desperation. "You're the one who shouldn't be here. We both know that you don't want to marry Terrence." Ajani's toffee-hued features were as perfect as I remembered. I envisaged running my hands along the contours of classic cheekbones, kissing his smooth neck . . .

"That's not true," I said, shaking my head to stop fantasizing. "I've planned for this a long time; everyone is waiting."

"So what we had meant nothing to you?" Ajani spoke as if he were in physical pain. His normally clear eyes were bloodshot; his voice sounded raspy and tired. He sat on the corner of the bed I'd slept in the night before. It seemed so familiar, so natural; it took me back to a time when I was truly happy.

"That's not what I'm saying, Ajani. What we had was special, and I'll remember it for a very long time," I whispered, unable to look away from him.

"Be honest with me. You and I, were we some kind of experiment? Were you using me?" Ajani's voice rose higher and became more desperate with every word. His heart was breaking.

"Well, in the beginning I was out to get back at Terrence and have a good time, but then something changed," I admitted reluctantly. "But I never hid the fact that I was getting married. I never once misled you."

"But you just said yourself that something changed. Our relationship wasn't just about sex; you told me you loved me and I told you the same. I don't play with that, Yvette; those feelings were real!"

"You're young, Ajani. Other women will come along and make you forget all about me."

"You're missing the point, Yvette. I don't want to forget. And I really wish that you would stop with all the May/December shit! Okay, so you're thirty-four and I'm twenty-one. Yvette, age never mattered when we were together, so it shouldn't matter now."

"Life is complicated. People depend on me to do the right thing, to be responsible. I plan to have a life here with Terrence, and I can't throw all that away for a couple of months of good sex with someone barely out of high school."

"So you're telling me to my face that you don't love me?"

Hot tears poured unchecked from my eyes. I loved Ajani; I couldn't deny it. But sometimes love just isn't enough.

"I do love you, Ajani, but—"

"Do you love him?" The confident, sexy, irresistible Ajani was taking charge again, refusing to give up.

"I've built twelve years with Terrence. Twelve years is a long time," I replied, desperate for him to understand.

"I'm ready to build a life with you." Ajani stood and walked towards me, his handsome face pained but determined. As he advanced, I knew I wanted Ajani to touch me, to kiss me, to take me back with him. But that wasn't reality, wasn't an option.

"Ajani, you really don't know what you're saying," I told him, shaking my head sternly as if I were talking to one of my students.

"I'm not a little kid! I know what I want. Come back with me and let's work this out, Yvette."

My heart screamed yes, but my head was on a more realistic plane. "I can't, Ajani. Marrying Terrence is just something I have to do." Before I could turn away, Ajani took me into his arms and planted his mouth on mine. My mind spun crazily as our tongues became one. I remembered the first time I'd seen him, remembered the way he had made my body feel every moment we were together. As the kiss deepened, Ajani's hands began exploring places that he knew so well.

"Don't marry him," Ajani whispered, his lips still pressed against mine. "Come with me. Let me take care of you."

A torrent of blinding tears poured forth as I tried unsuccessfully to pull away. "Ajani, please," I begged as his mouth traveled down to my collarbone.

"We're not over, Yvette," he breathed, his tongue on my tingling skin. "I love you." Ajani held on tightly as if his entire future was at stake.

"Yvette, Yvette, it's time," Wendy called through the closed door.

My breathing heavy and erratic, I pushed Ajani away and looked at the closed door.

"I know that you love me, Yvette. Don't do this. Don't fuck up your life because you're too scared to follow your heart. Do what's going to make you happy."

I looked into his eyes and withdrew my hand from his grasp. "I think it's time for you to go." My voice had become steady, sure.

Ajani stood silently, watching the tears of utter confusion fall from my eyes. "I'm not leaving, Yvette," Ajani told me after what seemed like an eternity. "I'm going downstairs to that ballroom, and I'm going to watch you make the biggest mistake of your life. I want to see it for myself." And with that Ajani opened the door, thrust his hands into his trouser pockets and slowly walked past Wendy and out of my life.

"Oh, look at your makeup," Wendy said, hurrying into the suite and handing me a handkerchief. "Are you okay?"

"I'm fine!" I responded harshly, but I wasn't. My body shook and my heart beat hard and fast against my chest. I could still feel Ajani's lips on mine and I could still feel the beat of his heart. "Ajani and I just had some unfinished business to attend to."

"Well, let me help you get your face together." Wendy tossed her flowers onto the bed and dabbed at my running makeup.

"No!" I said a little too loudly. "I mean, no, I'm okay. I need you to go downstairs and tell everyone that I'm on my way. I'll compose myself and be down in a second," I said, attempting to reassure my friend.

"Are you sure?" Wendy asked skeptically.

"Of course," I said, squeezing her hand. "I'll be about five minutes." Wendy grabbed her bouquet and headed for the door, a bemused look on her face.

Turning to the mirror, I took a hard look at myself. I could not believe what had just happened. "I can't," I said, shaking my head. "I can't."

Not wanting to waste another second, I frantically searched for my purse, finally locating it on the recliner in the corner. I was focused on getting to the elevator and out of the hotel without anyone noticing that I had become a runaway bride. My mind was cloudy, my thoughts scattered, and I was consumed by a sense of confusion and sadness unlike any I had ever known. Marrying Terrence was supposed to give me clarity, take me back to the things that were really important. I thought marriage would help me get my life back on track. But after seeing Ajani, all that I was clear on was that I had fucked up. Big time.

When I finally reached the lobby, my entire bridal party—six of my closest friends, waiting in height order and wearing the red gowns it had taken me four months to choose, stood outside the ballroom entrance—but none of that mattered now. I didn't know where I was going or how I was going to get there, but I did know that I couldn't marry Terrence.

"Yvette! Yvette! Where are you going?" someone shouted as I ran to the revolving door to freedom. "Yvette!"

Hurrying footsteps clicked toward me as I slipped through the exit and into the blinding sunshine.

"I'm on a break, ma'am," the cab driver told me as I slid into the backseat of his car.

"Please," I pleaded, looking over my shoulder at my bridal party heading toward me in a collective state of panic. Wendy, however, stood on the sidelines, her smile so big it looked as if she'd just won the lottery. Putting aside my best friend's baffling behavior for now, I turned back to the cab driver. "I'm supposed to be getting married right now, but I can't. Do you see those people? If you don't go—" I was shrill, hysterical, not recognizing my own voice.

The cab driver turned in his seat to get a closer look at me in my wedding dress, and then he looked at the mob rushing toward us. "Where to?" he chuckled, starting his engine.

With a sigh of relief, I leaned back against the cool leather and closed my eyes. "The airport."

PART 1

Six Months Prenuptial

Yvette

1

"Yvette? Yvette? Did you hear what Mr. Cochran just said?" an excited Mrs. King asked, poking me in the ribs with her red ink pen.

"Since when have I listened to anything Mr. Cochran says in staff meetings?" I answered, not looking up from the mountain of papers I should have checked days ago.

"Well, I really think you should listen to this."

Sighing, I reluctantly looked up from the writing assignment I'd just marked up in red ink. The entire faculty of Detroit Preparatory was looking at me. While some smiled encouragingly, others did not even try to hide their disgust. Something big was happening, and I had just missed whatever it was.

"Ms. Brooks, why don't you stand up and tell us how you feel," Principal Cochran suggested, laughing heartily.

"How do I feel about what exactly?" I asked, feeling my face burning with embarrassment. I laughed nervously, hating that I had put myself into this situation, especially in front of my colleagues.

"I just announced that the board has chosen you as the new assistant principal of Nashville Prep!" Mr.

Cochran said, applauding enthusiastically and prompting others to follow suit.

Still clueless, I sat staring at my fellow teachers. I racked my brain, hoping to remember when I had applied for a new position, let alone one at Nashville Prep. "What assistant principal position?" I asked stupidly.

Mr. Cochran chuckled and looked amused. "The one you applied for a year ago. Remember the Monday morning you rushed into my office and asked to be relocated? The board said you were perfect for the position." Mr. Cochran's puffy pink features were lit up. He was obviously very proud of himself. "Everyone wish Ms. Brooks well on her appointment," he urged, looking like a proud papa. A few of my colleagues murmured congratulations, while other muttered something indistinct. Was that a 'fuck you' I heard? It was difficult for me to tell, but it was something profane. "Now get out there and have a great weekend!"

Looking at some of the unhappy faces in the cafeteria, I was almost certain that some of them had placed their names into the same administration-relocation pool and had been with the district longer than I had. It was like déjà vu. The exact same thing happened when I was promoted to lead teacher five years ago, just after my twenty-ninth birthday. Back then, some smartass on staff started a rumor that I'd gotten the job by providing early-morning head and a cup of Starbucks latte to Mr. Cochran on a daily basis. I wondered what the rumor would be this time.

"Congratulations, girl!" Monique King said, pulling me into a warm bear hug. "I can't believe that you applied for the position without telling me! That doctor you're getting ready to marry must be the most supportive man in the world to let you go all the way down to Tennessee without him. Will he be relocating as well?"

"He doesn't know anything about this. Hell, I don't know anything about this—" And then it all hit me at once.

The red lacy panties stuffed between the couch cushions. The crystal vase in pieces on the bathroom floor.

Crying. Screaming. Finally, the assistant-principal relocation pool with openings several states away.

I sat down at one of the long lunch tables and held my head in my hands.

"Well, I guess you'll have some explaining to do when you get home," Monique said, patting me on the shoulder before lumbering her wide frame across the room.

"Ms. Brooks, I'm confused as to why this seems to be such a shock to you," Mr. Cochran said, concern in his voice. "Last year you seemed quite determined to move up the career ladder and to relocate, so I just naturally assumed that this news would make you happy." He gathered his notes off the center table and walked over to me slowly. "I know that Nashville may not be your ideal city, but it really is a wonderful place to live."

He stood about five feet six inches, but pretended that he was larger than life. He had a smile on his plump, pink face, but I saw confusion in his blue eyes. "Mr.

Cochran, please don't get me wrong. I am flattered and really appreciate that the board selected me for the position, but when I applied last year, things in my life were different. Now—" I took a deep breath to calm my pounding heart. "I'm getting married in six months and—" Another deep breath. *Relax, girl.* "This just isn't coming at a good time. I have a lot of things going on in my life right now, and for me to pick up and move five hundred miles to Tennessee, of all places, is impossible."

"I'm sure it's not that serious, Yvette. This is the opportunity of a lifetime. Do you know how many people applied for this same position? The board received résumés from at least ten of our own faculty members, not to mention over two hundred from across the country. You would be crazy to pass this up."

"Mr. Cochran, my fiancé can't even wash his own socks, let alone run an entire household while I'm gone." That was a lie; Terrence was perfectly capable of cooking, cleaning and taking care of himself while I was gone. What I really wanted to say was that my fiancé was a cheating dog who couldn't be trusted to piss on his own, but I thought providing Mr. Cochran with that little tidbit may have been unprofessional. I hoped Mr. Cochran would understand that, while I would have given my right arm for the job, I didn't think it would be a good idea to give up Terrence or abandon all the relationship rebuilding we had done in the past few months.

"Yvette, I don't want this difference of opinion to get in the way of our professional relationship, but I know you. You want this. There is nothing you would like more than seeing an administrative title after your name. I'm sure your fiancé would understand if you simply explained what a wonderful opportunity this is. I've known many professional couples who have made long-distance marriages work. It can be done, Yvette. Take some time to think about what you would be giving up. Sleep on it and let me know tomorrow."

"Making a decision by tomorrow doesn't give me a big window. When does this position begin?" I stood up and walked with Mr. Cochran to the door with what I was sure was desperation on my face.

"You would assume the position of assistant principal in a week's time. Mrs. Kelper, the former AP, didn't give notice when she resigned, so they need someone right away. They have offered to pay all moving expenses and have a two-bedroom, two-bathroom courtesy apartment that's ready and waiting. All you have to do is give the word."

"This is a lot to digest in such a short time," I responded, still unconvinced.

"Yes, it is. But I can guarantee that if you decide to accept this position, you will not be sorry. It pays nearly twenty-five thousand dollars a year above your current salary, and relocating to Nashville will change your life in ways you never expected."

"Mr. Cochran," I said, looking directly into his watery blue eyes, "to be completely honest with you, that is exactly what I'm afraid of."

Yvette

2

Before leaving this earth, my grandmother passed down many pieces of advice. The one that I kept closest to my heart, however, was to never judge a book by its cover. Those words of wisdom explained my relationship with Terrence perfectly. Everyone I knew thought that we were the gold standard of black relationships, with Terrence being the successful doctor and me the focused and driven thirty-four-year-old woman on the fast tack in educational administration. *The Huxtables.*

Terrence and I had been together nearly twelve years, including a two-year engagement. In the beginning, I, too, thought we were the perfect couple, but as time passed, things began to get rocky. Trust issues, work issues and inattentiveness plagued us from year seven on. Our relationship could be best described as a roller-coaster ride—exciting highs, chilling lows, spins, flips, turns and near-disasters. But Terrence and I never failed to come out in one piece, always opting to get back on and ride again, year after year. Just eleven months ago, however, it seemed the ride was finally over: I learned that Terrence had been unfaithful.

In the months leading up to my discovery, I had been completely oblivious to any significant change in our relationship. Well, maybe not entirely oblivious, but definitely unconcerned. Work, my grandmother's illness, my mother's recovery and wedding plans all intersected to keep me clueless about what was going on at home. All the signs were there, and my first mistake was choosing to ignore the red flags: whispered conversations and late nights 'working'. After a couple of months of the lies, Terrence became cold and unfeeling toward me; all his free time was spent out with 'the boys' and most nights I found myself falling asleep long before he would slip discreetly into bed.

"Terrence, I think we need to talk," I told him two days before my grandmother's surgery. I'd found the panties several days before but couldn't bring myself to show them to him, deciding instead to put the evidence into a Zip-loc bag, CSI style, and stuff it into an empty shoebox at the back of my closet. I wasn't ready to let go yet. I guess I wanted to wait for more signs, more proof that he had stepped out on me. I quickly got it that same afternoon when he hurried past me smelling like some cheap-ass drugstore perfume counter.

I stood in the middle of our massive bathroom, gingerly dangling the pair of red panties between two fingers. The empty zip-loc bag lay at my feet. I waited, holding back the tears that threatened to break down my defenses.

"Can't you just wait until after I finish showering?" he asked, scrubbing his cream-colored body furiously behind the transparent shower curtain.

"Don't want me to smell her?" I sneered. I watched his reaction closely, my eyes intent, focused-like a lion stalking its pray. He paused warily. *Gotcha, bitch.*

My grandmother—the only real parent I'd ever known—was battling cancer, and Terrence was less than supportive. I was fed up with his bullshit, and it was confrontation time. There was no backing out; enough was enough.

"Smell who? What are you talking about?" he asked, sounding nervous. He squirted more soap onto his washcloth and scrubbed even harder, his butter-pecan skin beginning to turn a rosy shade of pink.

"I'm talking about the way you practically sprinted past me reeking of some other woman's cheap-ass perfume. Not to mention the fact that I found these," I stomped closer to him, snatching back the shower curtain so forcefully the entire rod fell to the floor in a heap. With an anger and hatred that I had never felt, I threw the panties, hitting Terrence square in the face. "Now don't lie to me, Terrence; I know something is going on. How long have you been seeing her?"

Terrence removed the underwear from his face and looked at me before sitting down on the small shower bench. "Alaina and I have been seeing each other for about three months," Terrence admitted, obviously realizing that there was no sense in lying, especially with the evidence clogging up the shower drain.

With Terrence's admission, my heart felt as if it had been ripped in two, but still I refused to cry. I didn't want to give him the satisfaction. "Okay," I began, not quite sure where I was supposed to go from there, "do you love her?" The words flew from my mouth; each word a dagger that I hoped would pierce Terrence in the heart.

"No, no. There is no love between Alaina and me, just sex."

"Oh?" I laughed bitterly, my eyes wild in the mirror. "Just sex! Well, isn't that comforting? Where did you meet her?" *This must be the calm before the storm.*

"At work. She's one of the nurses in the labor and delivery unit," he admitted hesitantly, hanging his head low in shame. He was disgusting. I screamed at the top of my lungs, took the heavy ceramic vase filled with fresh flowers from the bathroom counter and hurled it into the shower. It slammed into Terrence's shoulder; a bright-red bruise immediately appeared on his pale skin. The vase hit the shower floor and broke into a thousand little pieces, as if mimicking my own broken heart.

I hurried into the kitchen and grabbed the biggest, sharpest knife I could find. Then I calmly asked him to get out of the shower, out of the apartment, out of my life. The next day, I marched directly into Mr. Cochran's office and asked to be placed in the administration-relocation pool. "Anywhere," I told him. "I don't care where you send me. I just need to leave."

After that, Terrence kept calling, and often stopping by the apartment, banging on the door and begging for forgiveness. Despite his persistence, I refused to speak with him for a month and a half; door locks and cell-phone numbers were changed. I avoided him at all costs. Back then, Terrence Hall was worse than the plague.

Terrence Hall was like a slow, painful death. Returning to him would have been like committing suicide, and I wasn't ready to die.

As much as I loathed him for willfully destroying our relationship, slowly but surely nights were becoming lonely, and there's only so much *HBO's Real Sex* a person can watch without wanting some of her own.

"I don't know if I can take him back," I told my grandmother one morning after spending another night alone, watching *The Notebook* and sobbing uncontrollably into my pillow.

"Yvette, men make mistakes," Carrie Dupree told me, brushing the hair from my face. "Their flesh is weak."

My grandmother was old school and thought that it was a man's inalienable right to cheat on his woman. "Terrence taking up with another woman does not mean that he doesn't love you."

I could remember looking at Carrie as if she'd lost her mind. "You're right. It means that he doesn't respect me."

"You need to forgive that man and get on with those wedding plans so that I can have a great-grandbaby before I leave this world." My grandmother had a way of throwing a guilt trip unlike anyone I had ever known.

Spurred by my grandmother's plea and the constant throbbing between my legs, I called Terrence, having to dial three times before actually pushing send. "If you want to have any chance of moving back in, then there are some things you will have to agree to," I told him, still unsure if taking him back was the right thing to do.

"I'll do anything, Yvette. You just don't know how painful this time has been for me."

"Oh, I don't know how painful this has been for *you*?" I had laughed bitterly into the phone.

"I just meant that I truly regret what I've done to our relationship," he said. The sound of his sobs filled my ears and tugged at my heart.

"Well, I really regret what you've done to our relationship as well, and if you want what we had to continue, then I need you to find a position at another hospital. And we have to get into some kind of relationship counseling." I hated that I was willing to take him back, hated that I was so weak and predictable, but I felt as if I had no choice. Terrence was pretty much all I knew, and if I didn't have him, what did I have?

Yvette

3

That was one year, my grandmother's funeral and many counseling sessions ago. After about six months discussing our feelings and working out our problems, I decided it was time to take my engagement ring out of the nightstand drawer and place it back on my finger. With the help of my best friend, Wendy, I slowly resumed planning the wedding, though this time I wasn't so naïve. I decided to keep my ear to the ground and one eye on Terrence at all times.

Despite all our counseling sessions and his promises, I wasn't completely over Terrence's infidelity. I still found myself becoming angry at the pain he caused and often thought that marrying Terrence would be the worst mistake of my life. Sometimes I thought that I had allowed my grandmother to guilt-trip me into the mess my life had become; after all, her last dying wish was that I marry and be happy. Translated: marry Terrence and have lots of babies.

After Mr. Cochran's announcement, I stood just outside the school's cafeteria, where staff meetings were held, and was reminded of another saying my grandmother used frequently: Absence makes the heart grow fonder. She would whisper those words to me all those times when my mother would disappear for weeks at a time, barricading herself in some crack house, smoking her life away and destroying mine.

I leaned against the cafeteria door and closed my eyes, thinking about all that I'd been through with Terrence, and despite it all, I knew that he still didn't appreciate me the way he should. Maybe an absence like Nashville would make Terrence's heart grow fonder.

The minute I left the school grounds, I knew that I was going to accept the position. I had applied for that position for a reason, and the fact that I was chosen out of all the other applicants said something. This job in Nashville was meant for me.

The most compelling reason for my decision to up and leave, however, was the fact that I still wasn't sure that marrying Terrence was the best decision for me. One thing that I'd learned in counseling was that I, in all my fabulousness, had some major insecurity issues. The fact that I once thought Terrence was the center of my universe made me want to gag. This was turning into the opportunity I needed to prove to myself and everyone else that I could live without him and be happy at the same time. I didn't really want what Terrence and I had to end, but if what we had together could withstand me moving hundreds of miles away, then it could definitely withstand marriage. It may be just the thing to make him realize that my love was something special and I should be cherished.

All the way home I practiced the way I would drop the bomb. "Baby, guess what? I got promoted to assistant principal, but the school is really far away. No, sweetie, not on the east side of Detroit, on the east side of Nashville. Isn't that funny?" It was pretty sad, but that was the best I could come up with.

Some of my other choices were A) finding him a position at a hospital in Nashville before I told him my news or B) coming home, cooking him a gourmet meal Martha Stewart would envy, and sucking him like a Hoover until he was too exhausted to argue. Neither of those options appealed to me much. I despised cooking and dick sucking was not on my list of favorites, either. In the end, I would still be moving and he would still be left in Detroit until we worked out another arrangement.

When I pulled into the parking garage and saw Terrence's silver Mercedes, my heart began to race and my palms became sweaty.

"I love you and we can make this work," I practiced, pretending that Terrence was standing right in front of me. "It will be good for us, make our relationship stronger. Nashville isn't really that far way. An eight-hour drive or, better yet, an hour and a half by plane." My heels clicked loudly as I crossed the concrete lot and made my way to the elevator. I wanted the ride up to the twenty-eighth floor to take forever. I needed to finalize my attack plan, but it seemed as if only a couple of seconds went by before I was standing in front of my apartment door. The sweet and sultry sounds of Sade drifted into the hall, and the distinctive aroma of shrimp gumbo filled my nostrils. Terrence must have had a good day at work, which was rare. As a doctor of maternal fetal medicine dealing exclusively with high-risk patients, he was always complaining about the incompetence of some nurse, the laziness of a new resident or the way a desperate pregnant woman had faked contractions just to get admitted to the hospital. It was a wonder that I could ever get in anything about my day, and most times I didn't.

Taking a deep breath and saying a short prayer, I turned my key and pushed the door open. Before I could step one foot inside, Terrence enfolded me in his arms, planted a kiss on my lips and said, "I made dinner." He stood there in a Kiss the Cook apron and looked edible himself. Tall, creamy and handsome, Terrence stood six feet tall and spent his free time toning his slim body to perfection. His mustache and goatee were neatly trimmed and his wavy hair had been freshly cut. He was the late 1980s early 1990s pretty boy type.

"Thank you, baby. You just don't know how tired I am. Work was hectic and I have some news." I wanted to tell him immediately so that we could make some decisions. I was certain that he would try to talk me out of leaving, but my mind was made up. I was going. In fact, my bags were mentally packed already.

"I want to hear all about your day, but let me tell you about mine first," Terrence said, taking my black suede schoolbag and setting it down in the corner. As usual, his plan was to monopolize the conversation.

"Okay, but my news is really impor—"

"Mine will just take a minute," he said cutting me off mid-sentence. "Do you remember me telling you about the woman carrying the quads?" he asked excitedly.

"Vaguely." I sat down at the granite-topped island in the kitchen. Terrence poured two glasses of red wine.

"Well, anyway, the mom went in for an emergency C-section this morning, and all babies are healthy and doing great. You know that was my first delivery of quads? Everyone was taking pictures and congratulating me."

"That's wonderful, Terrence," I responded half-heartedly, throwing him a fake smile. "You'll have to get me a copy of the pictures. I would love to see that," I lied.

"Oh, don't worry, I will," he said, handing me a glass. He returned to stirring his gumbo, causing more of the delicious aroma to fill the air. "Now you tell me about your day."

"I got a promotion," I said, after nervously downing my wine in one gulp.

"What! That is excellent news, Yvette! So I guess we have two things to celebrate tonight. What are you going to be doing? When will you start?"

"They moved me up to assistant principal, and I start the Monday after next."

"What happened to Yost? Did she quit or something?" he asked, referring to the AP at Detroit Prep. I was absolutely shocked that he even remembered her name.

"No, no . . . she didn't quit. I won't be at Detroit Prep. They . . . they placed me at another school," I stuttered.

"Which one?" he asked, a genuine smile spreading across his face, making me feel slightly guilty about what I was about to announce.

I looked at how happy he seemed to be for me and felt a tug at my heart. I wanted to change my mind, but I couldn't. I wanted this position, and I wanted room to breathe to make sure that marrying Terrence wasn't a mistake that would last a lifetime. "I'll be at Nashville Prep."

Terrence

4

Yvette's pouty lips were moving but her words were not registering. Her honey-hued face was flushed and she was smiling widely, so I knew she had to be excited about something. Her green eyes sparkled, her arms were flapping, and the slight dimple in her chin faded in and out as her words tumbled out.

As I watched her, I became more and more annoyed. A lot of what Yvette did annoyed me—like the way she sang Luther in the shower and the way she would only drink her milk with three squirts of Hershey's Chocolate Syrup. At first, I wanted to wring her neck every time she reached for that brown bottle, but now I suppose I've gotten used to it. I even buy the mega-pack at Sam's Club just to make sure we never run out. Twelve years of repetitiveness in a relationship will do that to you. The same thing, the same conversations over and over again is enough to drive anyone insane.

"Did you hear me, Terrence? I said that I have to move."

"Move where? Is the school that far away?"

Her mouth started moving again, but I could not concentrate on a word she was saying, not with the way she was downing glass after glass of wine. I was almost guaranteed to get some tonight, because when she gets tipsy, the freak comes out.

I'll admit it. When it comes to beautiful women and sex, I'm weak. I have no self-control, and because I lack that specific, extremely important relationship skill, I almost ruined what Yvette and I have by sleeping with someone not half as fine as she.

". . . over five hundred miles away!" Her words finally began to penetrate my thoughts, but I was still distracted.

"What's over five hundred miles away?" My eyes traveled the length of her tall, lean frame, undressing her, my gaze lingering on her full breasts. I imagined undressing her right there in the kitchen. Or better yet, just pushing her skirt up around her waist and fucking her brains out right there on the kitchen counter. I hoped she was wearing a thong.

"The school, Terrence! What the hell is wrong with you?"

"Where did you say the school is again?" I knew I sounded ridiculous, but I couldn't concentrate. My dick was expanding just thinking about all the freaky things we would be doing in a few hours.

"Nashville, Tennessee. You know, south of the Mason-Dixon Line?"

I shook my head to clear my mind and blinked several times. The spread-eagled fantasy Yvette disappeared from my thoughts, and I finally understood what she had been trying to tell me. "Are you serious? You're moving to Nashville?"

"I just found out today."

I stared at her for a while, trying to process what she'd just said. "So you're just going to leave me here all by myself six months before our wedding? And after everything that's happened between us?" I was slowly becoming angry, and I had every right to be. The tingle in my dick diminished, and heat transferred to my head.

"This is the promotion I have been waiting for, Terrence. This doesn't mean the end of our relationship. We can do the long-distance thing, and the time apart will give us the space we need to make sure we're doing the right thing," she rationalized.

"The *long distance thing*? Are you crazy? You're just asking for disaster, Yvette. In our last session, Dr. Jop said that our relationship is still very fragile."

"So are you trying to tell me that if I leave you'll cheat? You really can't control yourself, can you?" Yvette stood and folded her arms across her ample chest. Her eyes flashed, and her mouth tightened.

I did come across untrustworthy, but my concerns were valid. Since Yvette and I had been working on our problems, I had been trying very hard to be an angel, but who was to say that if she wasn't around breathing down my neck every second of the day I wouldn't backslide?

"I didn't mean it to sound like that, but Yvette, I'm concerned."

"You'll be okay, baby. I'm sure of it," she said softly, although her glare was as fierce as ever.

"But what about the wedding and after we get married? What then? Will we have a long-distance marriage, too?"

"I can plan the wedding from Nashville; Wendy will help me. Let's cross the marriage bridge when we get to it, okay? And who's to say that you won't find a job in Nashville? They do have hospitals."

"Why would you apply for this position without even telling me? I thought we were a team," I said, almost not recognizing Yvette. The fiancée I thought I knew would never just abandon me like this, not without at least discussing it with me first.

"Terrence, I applied for the position after you slept with that slut," she retorted, her voice hard, uncompromising. "I didn't think we would be getting back together, and when we did, I forgot about it, okay?" she continued, her eyes flashing. "I remembered when Mr. Cochran announced it in the staff meeting."

Damn! This *was* my fault, but the fact that she'd forgotten about it gave me a glimmer of hope. "So you haven't accepted it yet. There's still time to say no."

Yvette walked over and wrapped her arms around my neck, although I could still feel her anger. "Terrence, I don't want to say no. I want this job, and I want you to support me."

"I am all for you being happy and fulfilling your dreams, but I really don't see why you can't do that right here in Detroit."

"Right now, there aren't any opportunities here. As soon as something opens up here in the city, I'll be on the first thing smoking out of Nashville. I promise."

"And what if nothing here becomes available? We're going to have phone sex for the rest of our lives!" I wailed, sounding more like a horny teenager than a grown man.

"As I said before, let's deal with some problems as they present themselves. And as far as the phone-sex thing goes, I can make trips to Detroit every weekend if the need arises. And of course, you can visit me. Terrence, I really don't believe that this arrangement will be as bad as you think."

"No, it will be worse."

Yvette rolled her eyes and took a deep breath. "You're not acting your age right now, Terrence. This is a wonderful opportunity for me, and the least you could do is be happy."

We sat there in the kitchen, picking at the gumbo, sipping wine, and staring at each other for a long time. I was thinking about all the pretty young things that would cross my path, tempting me when Yvette leaves and how much sleep I would miss trying to fend them off. There was this new X-ray technician who had been giving me some very seductive looks lately . . .

"Terrence, what are you thinking?" Yvette asked softly. As for me, I was mentally having sex with the new girl on one of her X-Ray machines. Legs parted, ankles up . . .

I shook my head to rid myself of the image. Sometimes I didn't know what was wrong with me. "How much I'm going to miss you. I know I'm not going to be able to sleep at night without you next to me," I lied.

"They say absence makes the heart grow fonder," she said, pressing her face against my neck. Her minty-fresh breath tickled my skin and succeeded in sending my fantasy from X-ray machines to Yvette bending over in a sexy red-and-white nurse's costume.

"I think we should make a commitment to stay true to each other no matter what happens or how far apart we are," I suggested, sounding completely out of character. But in all honesty, I *was* a bit insecure. Yvette was stunning, educated and had a great personality. And while I didn't consider myself too shabby, she could easily have any man she wanted. Living in Nashville would be the perfect opportunity for her to pay me back for my past indiscretions.

"I completely agree. Just because I'll be there and you will be here doesn't mean anything should change. We are still getting married in April; everything will be fine."

"And how can you be sure of that?" I asked.

"Terrence, what is this really about? Are you worried about me meeting someone else?"

"Why would you ask that? Are you planning to go down there and get with someone?"

"Of course not! Don't be ridiculous. I am not a teenager. *I* can control my hormones."

"Then why even mention it?" I asked, ignoring her intentional jab at my lack of self-control.

"Because I'm trying to figure out why you're acting this way!"

"You're my woman and I want you with me. Is that so crazy? I can't believe you're about to leave . . ." I couldn't finish my sentence, because I was amazed at her ability to see right through me. It was as if she could read my mind. I didn't appreciate it.

"I'm sorry, baby, but this is just something I have to do for me. You don't want me to stay here and end up resenting you for it in a few years, do you?"

"No, no," I quickly responded. "You have to do what you have to do, but that doesn't mean I can't be concerned."

"Terrence, the only thing that will change between us is our proximity."

She said the words and I wanted to believe her, but in the pit of my stomach, I had the sickening feeling that no good would come of this.

Yvette

5

"If this dress fits any differently, then we are going to have a serious problem," Wendy said to me from behind the pink curtain at the Bridal Boutique. This was the third fitting she had endured; I wanted to make sure her dress fit perfectly. I did not want her standing next to me in some frumpy, ill-fitting gown.

"It'll fit fine," I said, being optimistic. "I have something to tell you."

Wendy came out of the dressing room and stepped up on the pedestal. She looked amazing in the red full-length gown. But Wendy, with her clear, coffee-colored skin, bright onyx eyes and perfectly coifed, jet-black hair falling just above her shoulders, would look amazing in a pair of wrinkled sweats.

"What do you think?" she asked, doing what she did best—admiring herself in the mirror.

"I think it's perfect, but did you hear what I said? I have something to tell you."

"Okay, let's hear it," Wendy said, checking out her reflection in the mirror from all possible angles.

"I'm moving to Nashville later this week." I watched the mirror and Wendy's reflection as her eyes bulged and her mouth fell open. As a television news anchor in the city of Detroit, not a lot of things surprised her, but she was completely stunned by the news I'd just dropped. "I accepted an assistant principal position at Nashville Prep, and the job begins almost immediately."

"You didn't tell me that you were applying for any position in Nashville," Wendy said, turning away from the mirror and looking directly at me.

"I put my name in the administration-relocation pool after Terrence and I broke up, and I simply forgot about it after we reconciled. Mr. Cochran made the announcement yesterday at the staff meeting. I was totally surprised."

"You mean to tell me that you forgot about applying for a job in another state?" Wendy asked.

"Yes, that's what I'm telling you," I said, becoming a bit defensive.

"And you still accepted the job with a week's notice and your wedding, here in Detroit, only six months away? That is so typical, Yvette." Wendy stepped away from the mirror and entered the dressing room again to remove her gown.

"What's so typical?" I wondered, confused by the point she was trying to make.

"Always doing what people expect you to do. Your supervisor expected you to accept the job even though it's hundreds of miles away and your life is here. You've always been like that, Yvette; you can't help it, so why even try? It's actually one of the things that I love most about you, always trying to please."

"I do not always do what other people expect of me!"

"Yes, you do. I can list several times when you didn't do what you wanted because it went against your grandmother's grain. I'm only telling you this because you're my girl and I want you to be happy."

"Happy, schmappy." I laughed. "You think you know everything. What have I done only because people expected me to?" I was a little nervous about challenging her. Wendy and I had been friends since high school and, at times, I thought she knew me better than I knew myself.

"First of all, you went to Wayne State for college because it was what your grandmother wanted instead of going to a historically black college as you had been planning."

She had a point. It had always been my dream to attend an HBCU. I applied to Howard in Washington D.C., Tuskegee Institute and even Florida A&M, but when my grandmother found out my plans she was devastated. She told me that she had always envisioned that I would remain in Detroit, attend college, and live in her home. I couldn't bear to upset or disappoint her; after all, she had sacrificed to raise me after my mother took off. I didn't want to hurt her.

"Fine, what else?" I asked Wendy.

"One word: Terrence."

"What do you mean, *Terrence*?"

"Terrence was not your first choice. Remember Corey and how in love the two of you were?" Wendy came out of the dressing room wearing black slacks and a winter-white wrap around sweater. She would never be caught dead in jeans, not even on weekends.

Of course I remembered Corey, and as usual Wendy was right—we were very much in love. "Corey was high school and Terrence was college. There is a huge difference."

"The only difference is that Corey was broke, and Terrence comes from money. Corey wanted to be a writer, and Terrence wanted to be a doctor. Nobody expected you to continue things with Corey after graduation, and you didn't even though you both still loved each other. He has a new book out you know, an *Essence* bestseller."

I knew. I had followed Corey's literary career for years. He had become a success, just as he said he would. "I did not break things off with him because he wanted to be a writer or because that was what people expected me to do. Corey and I broke up because we grew apart. We ultimately wanted very different things," I said stoutly, trying to convince her.

"And your decision had absolutely nothing to do with your grandmother saying that she always dreamed of you marrying someone who was successful, someone who would allow you to stay home and be a housewife?"

"Let's just drop it, okay?"

"What about your mother?"

I glared at her. My mother was a very touchy subject. Untouchable, actually. Completely off limits, even for my best friend.

"Your grandmother didn't want you to have anything to do with her, so you don't."

"Now that is not true. Who do you think paid for my mother's three stints in rehab? Who do you think pays the mortgage on her house?"

"Just because you throw money at her doesn't mean she's in your life. Do you call her? Does she even know you're about to get married?"

"I didn't come here to talk about her," I snapped before she could give me a look that said she made her case. "I'm moving, and it's not because it's what anyone expects me to do. If anything it's the complete opposite. Are you forgetting the fact that the man cheated on me? I think it's fair that I take some time and get my head together. You and Terrence expect me to stay here and continue being his trophy."

"That's what you consider yourself? Terrence's trophy?"

"Maybe that came out wrong," I said, trying to clean up my comment. "I was simply saying that there are things that I want to do for me."

"How does Terrence feel about all this?"

"He's fine," I lied. "He was a little concerned at first, but we've made a commitment to each other. We will still be getting married, and everything will be fine."

"So you're going to leave Terrence alone, by himself? Aren't you just the slightest bit concerned that he will find someone else to occupy his time?"

"Yes, I am. But if that's what Terrence needs to do, then good, go ahead. I'll really have a reason not to trust him anymore. Terrence is an adult and is completely capable of controlling himself if he chooses to. And why are you getting so pissed? You're my friend, not Terrence's. You should be on my side."

Wendy threw the curtain back, the dress draped over her arm, and we headed for the sales desk. "I am on your side," she said. "I'm just concerned about the whole situation. You're my best friend and I am looking out for your best interests. I only want you to be happy."

Wendy

I have always had a thing for Terrence. Actually, I met him before Yvette did in Wayne State's student center the first week of our freshman year. Yvette and I were sitting at a table flipping through our books and eating Taco Bell burritos and tostadas. Then I saw him.

Terrence was tall and exuded confidence. There was something about him that made me want to jump his bones the second our eyes met. "Girl, look at him," I said, putting my food down and smiling in his direction.

"Who?" Yvette asked, looking up. "I know you aren't talking about that nerdy looking guy over there? He looks like a bootleg Al B. Sure," she said turning away and grimacing in disgust.

"He is not nerdy, he's an intellectual, and yellow guys are in, haven't you heard? I'm going over to talk to him," I declared, rising and straightening my skirt.

"You go right ahead, Wendy."

And I did. I strolled over to his table and stood right in front of him. "Hi, my name is Wendy Web," I said, dropping my given last name of Wilstink, and using the one I planned to adopt when I made it big in journalism.

"Terrence Hall." His voice was deep and sultry. I noticed his cellular biology book and smiled even wider.

"Premed?" I asked, running my fingertips over his brand-new textbook.

"I am. This is my third year. You're a freshman, right?"

My smile weakened slightly. "Yes. How could you tell?"

Terrence laughed lightly and glanced over at Yvette, who was looking very uninterested. "I can always tell the freshmen," he said, looking up at me then back to Yvette, who was now sloppily eating a bean burrito, taco sauce dripping onto the wrapper in front of her. "Who's your friend?"

With those three words, I was completely crushed but not surprised. This happened more often than not when it came to anything involving Yvette and me. We met our sophomore year of high school, and I had been in her shadow ever since. Yvette was among the best and the brightest, and I was the one always running behind her wishing that I were the one with a 4.0 GPA and the captain of the majorettes.

Men want to be with her and women want to be like her. Yvette had this aura that made people want to be around her. She's fun, friendly and kind. Sometimes I think that Yvette is everything I'm not. Don't get me wrong, I, Wendy Web, am definitely fabulous in my own way, but I struggle with the things that seem to come so naturally to Yvette. Her skin is clear and glowing, while I have to spend one hundred dollars a week to obtain the same healthy complexion. Yvette can eat any and everything she wants, and I have to work out three times a week to look half as good as she does.

I looked from Yvette to Terrence that day twelve years ago and wanted to cry. In my mind, things always came down to Yvette versus Wendy, and this was a prime example. What did she need Terrence for?

"Her name is Yvette, and she has a boyfriend," I said with the stankest attitude I could muster. What I told Terrence wasn't exactly the truth. Yvette and Corey were taking a break, seeing what was out there and exploring their options, but I didn't want Yvette exploring her options with Terrence. Though I didn't know much about him, I knew enough to realize that he was perfect for me.

"Okay, my fault. Just wanted to know," he said, keeping his eyes on Yvette.

Terrence and I did not exchange numbers that day. I could tell that he was into Yvette, and even though I was used to this scenario, I would not accept, under any circumstances, her rejects.

Three weeks later Yvette called and declared that she was in love with a premed student named Terrence Hall. I couldn't believe my ears and wanted to slam down the phone and never talk to her again. She was my friend, my best friend, and she was in love with a man who was meant for me. But I got over it quickly after I met the quarterback of the football team. And though I pretended to believe Yvette when she told me that she had no idea who Terrence was, I've never forgotten what happened so many years ago. When I was eighteen I thought of Terrence as Yvette's reject, but now I considered him an encore.

Because Yvette is so predictable and driven, she has now given me the perfect opportunity to take back what should rightfully be mine. I love Yvette, I really do, but I am sick and tired of being her sidekick, the Robin to her Batman. Her moving to Nashville and leaving Terrence behind, helpless, is just asking for trouble. What man can resist a home-cooked meal and an innocent massage when his woman has abandoned him?

Yvette

6

Nashville. It is the most beautiful, friendly, laid-back city I have ever seen. I've been here for three weeks and, aside from Terrence wanting me to come home every weekend to take care of his needs, my life couldn't be better.

The first time Terrence asked me to come home he had me believing he actually missed my company. "This is a big adjustment for me, Yvette," he told me during one of our nightly telephone conversations. "I think the transition would be much easier for both of us if you could visit on the weekends." Terrence offered to pay the plane fare, but I was still uncomfortable with the idea of visiting Detroit so frequently.

"Terrence, I just got here. Don't you think it would be a better idea if you came to see me? That way you could see my new apartment and meet some of my new colleagues."

The staff at Nashville Prep had been wonderful. Upon my arrival, the faculty welcomed me with open arms, hosting a luncheon in my honor. I had even been invited to a few after school events, happy hour and movie night, which shocked the shit out of me. It is very uncommon for members of the administration to socialize with teachers.

"I really don't have a problem with that, but I'm on call this weekend." So, like a lovesick fool, I quickly threw some necessities together and hightailed it to Detroit.

As it turned out he was at the hospital the entire weekend delivering babies and dealing with difficult patients, and I was stuck at home fluffing and folding, cooking and cleaning. When Terrence finally came home after sixteen hours at the hospital, he claimed that he couldn't go one more second without feeling my body next to his. We then had a whopping two minutes of the worst sex I'd ever experienced and then, predictably, he rolled over and fell asleep. I spent the remainder of that evening lying on the couch, tears rolling down my face. I was devastated and ready to go back to Nashville, but I wasn't surprised. This was typical Terrence, always thinking about himself. No one else was as important as he was. Ever.

The following weekend Terrence called, begging me to get on a plane and visit him. "I'm not on call because I found another doctor to cover for me. I've got reservations and I've planned a romantic evening out. If you don't come, everything will be ruined," he whined like a baby, causing me to wonder what I had ever seen in him in the first place.

"I am not coming to Detroit after that mess you pulled last weekend. If you want to see me, then you come here." He came and complained the entire time.

He didn't like the humidity, and he thought every white person who crossed his path was staring. "I cannot wait to get out of Hicksville," he said the night before his departure. "I know you won't be here for long. There is absolutely nothing to do unless you like country music, are one hundred years old or in college."

"That's what I like about it, Terrence. Everything is so slow and calm. I appreciate the opportunity to be with my thoughts."

"Are you serious?" he asked in disbelief. "You sound like one of those new age Bohemian chicks. A month from now, you're liable to cut off all your hair and stop wearing deodorant!"

Needless to say, this weekend we will both be at our separate places of residence. I was excited about finally being alone, beginning my journey to find myself; it is what I came to Nashville for. As Wendy so harshly pointed out a few weeks ago, I often chose to do what others expected of me. In Nashville I promised myself to begin concentrating on finding the real Yvette, and doing what makes me happy.

But as the school's twenty-two-year-old secretary came into my newly renovated office, I realized the weekend was still two days away and I still had work to do.

"Ms. Brooks, there is a guy in the office who says he's supposed to observe you. He goes to Tennessee State." Her eyes were bright and sparkling, her smile stretching from ear to ear. She ran her hand through her short Halle Berry-styled hair.

"Oh, right. I forgot all about that." Last week I agreed to have an honors education student shadow me one day a week for four weeks. The project was part of the university's methods requirements. "Now I'm going to have to create something exciting to do so he won't have to sit in my office for the next hour and watch me make phone calls. Maybe I can find someone to suspend. That's always interesting," I joked, looking up from my computer screen. I caught Jordan peeking around the door corner and back into the front office before jumping back, looking extremely guilty.

"What are you so excited about?" I asked, picking up a stack of unfinished teacher-evaluation forms and heading for the open door.

"Wait until you see this guy, Ms. Brooks!" she whispered excitedly. "He is, without a doubt, the best-looking man I have ever seen."

I looked at her skeptically. "How many men have you seen in your twenty-two years, Jordan?"

"Enough to know that he should be a model or something." Jordan led me into the front office, and with a grand sweep of her hand and a soft giggle, introduced me to my shadow for the next hour.

"Good morning," I said cheerfully without looking up. When I did, my breath caught in my throat, followed by a soft gasp. I realized that not only had Jordan been accurate in her assessment of his looks but she may have actually underplayed them a little. He introduced himself as Ajani Riley in a voice so deep and sexy that I almost wanted to scream. I felt as if I was standing before a god among men. His face was a golden bronze color, and he looked to be about six feet, three inches tall. Ajani wore his jet black, wavy hair faded to perfection. He wore a long-sleeved button-down shirt, slacks and shoes color coordinated in various shades of gray and blue. He was young, probably about nineteen or twenty, despite his neatly trimmed mustache and goatee. Ajani Riley took my breath away.

I was shocked and embarrassed when my heart started to beat faster and I felt my cheeks start to warm up. This was a child, a college student, and I was a thirty-four-year- old almost-married woman. I was not allowed to have this type of reaction, but I couldn't help myself. He was perfect.

I looked over at Jordan, who was now studiously filing papers. Our eyes met and she gave me a smile that said she knew that I was smitten by Mr. Riley as well. It was probably written all over my face.

"Should we get started? I'm going to evaluate a teacher today," I told Ajani, in a higher-than-normal voice. We left the office and walked to the school's English wing, our footsteps echoing on the freshly waxed linoleum floors. "I can give you a copy of the form I use so that you can do your own evaluation. If we finish a little early we can go back to my office to compare notes."

"How long have you been here?" Ajani asked me as we walked along. His voice traveled under my clothing and tugged at my underwear.

"I just arrived from Detroit Prep, our sister school. I was . . ." I stuttered, more nervous around him then I had ever been around any man. "I-I was a lead teacher there and received a promotion." He wasn't looking at me; he was looking through me, and the simple action sent chills up and down my spine.

"So you're new to Nashville. How do you like it so far?" We exited the main hallway and entered the English wing, with Ajani holding the door for me and, if I wasn't mistaken, guiding me through with his hand on the small of my back. His touch sent my mind reeling, making me wonder how quickly he could unsnap my bra.

"I'm really enjoying my time here. Everyone's very friendly and easygoing. Even though I do get lonely with my fiancé being back in Detroit, I like the laziness of the city." I was rambling and immediately regretted mentioning that I was engaged, although I wasn't sure why.

"Engaged, huh? I didn't notice a ring when we shook hands." His comment was innocent enough, but somewhere below the surface I detected a bit of disappointment in his voice.

"Sometimes it bothers my finger, so I don't wear it all the time." I didn't understand the need I felt to explain myself to him, but there it was; I didn't want any confusion between us.

"This town isn't as lazy as you think. Have you had a chance to go out at all?" He was obviously flirting with me and didn't seem to have any shame whatsoever. Didn't I just tell the child that I was a soon-to-be married woman?

"Not really." My mouth spoke even though my brain screamed 'Be quiet!' This was not the professional conversation that I was supposed to be having. I was supposed to be summarizing my duties as an assistant principal and giving him a rundown on what a typical school day for me was like. I needed to get back in control. Quickly.

I led Ajani into Mrs. Lawson's class, pulling a chair for him from the back of the room. As Mrs. Lawson began teaching her lesson on idioms, I felt Ajani's eyes on me. I became overly aware of what I was wearing, the length of my close-fitting black skirt and how low-cut my purple V-necked sweater was. Every time I looked up from the evaluation form, Ajani's eyes were boring into mine, a sly smile on his face. *Damn, he was sexy. Damn!*

I sat back and thought of the last time Terrence was in Nashville. He'd complained half the time and ignored me the other. I wondered what he would think of this young boy giving me all this attention.

Jotting down some notes regarding Mrs. Lawson's classroom-management style, I sneaked another look at Ajani. His gaze followed the length of my exposed leg, licking his lips on the way up.

An electric tingle shot through my body, causing me to shake my head and close my eyes. This was ridiculous.

Forty-five minutes later, Ajani and I left the classroom and headed down the hall back to my office. "So what did you think?" I asked, smiling professionally.

"I definitely like what I see."

"Excuse me?" I said, trying to keep my voice level.

"In the classroom. I like what I saw in Mrs. Lawson's room. She's an excellent teacher."

I relaxed a bit, though I was pretty sure there was a double meaning behind his comment. "She is an excellent teacher."

Ajani and I stood at the entrance to the main office face to face. He was at least six inches taller than I, and his lips looked so soft . . .

"So I guess I'll see you next week," Ajani said, flashing that perfect smile again.

"Right, next week," I answered, attempting to keep my composure intact, my tone light.

"I can't wait," he said. Winking, he smiled and walked away.

Something was seriously wrong with me. I woke up this morning all twisted in the covers and sweaty with thoughts not of my fiancé back in Detroit, but of Ajani. I dreamt of him all night, and in those dreams we were doing things to each other that would make a porn star blush. I woke up wondering if he would be as good in real life as he was in my dreams and then cussed myself out for wondering about him at all.

Since we met two days ago, I have thought of little else. I found out that Ajani was only twenty-one years old. That's an age difference of thirteen years, making my thoughts even more appalling. For a few hours after I met him, I thought that I was overreacting, that Terrence and I being apart, compounded by our still-unresolved relationship problems was causing me to completely lose my mind. But as those few hours turned into days and I couldn't stop thinking about him, I began to worry.

"Ms. Brooks, you have a surprise in your office," Jordan said, wearing her usual hundred-watt smile and bursting with energy, making me feel my thirty-four years that much more.

I stepped into my office and was greeted by the biggest, most beautiful bouquet of Casablanca lilies I had ever seen. I tossed my bag on the cream-colored chaise in the corner and grabbed the small card from the flowers. I expected to see an *I love you* with Terrence's name scrawled on the bottom, but after extracting the card from the envelope, I realized that my expectation was way off. Way, way off.

In case you would like a break from work or the lazy days of Nashville, give me a call.

555-1432

Ajani Riley

"Your fiancé is so sweet," Jordan said as she came into my office, clearly impressed. She went over to my desk and inhaled the bouquet's heady scent. "I really hope I can find someone like that when I'm ready to settle down," she gushed.

Staring at the card, I blinked rapidly, hoping that the signature on the bottom of the card would magically change.

"So I guess you're going to visit him this weekend?"

"Who?" I asked, by now distracted.

"Your fiancé. You know, the one who sent you the flowers."

I folded the card and palmed it. "No, I'm staying here for a change," I said, still in something of a fog.

"Well, call me if you want to do anything." Jordan left and closed the door behind her.

Opening my hand, I smoothed the card. Reading it over and over again, I found myself looking for any evidence that this was an innocent gesture from a young man with an obvious crush. I stared at the card for several minutes before reluctantly concluding that Ajani was hardly innocent. It was painfully obvious that he knew what he wanted and wasn't shy about going after it.

I couldn't deny my attraction to him, but I knew that what I felt wasn't okay. My wedding was now less than six months away, and if I gave into the feeling I was having then I wouldn't be any better than Terrence. Everyone loved Terrence. My grandmother. Wendy. Everyone. There was absolutely no way I was going to screw up my life because some delicious-looking college student sent me flowers.

I took the card and dropped it into the shredder, watching as the silver blades turned it into confetti.

Ajani

7

"I've met my future wife," I announced giddily to my brothers, who were at the kitchen at our father's home in Memphis. Both were eating massive bacon, lettuce and tomato sandwiches. Identical, in every sense of the word, Jabari and Dakari looked a lot like me. They had the same chiseled Riley chin, dark eyes, and wavy hair. At five feet, ten inches, they were several inches shorter than I was.

"Aren't you a little young to be talking marriage?" Dakari asked before gulping down half a glass of lemonade.

"And since when have you wanted to settle down with just one woman? Every time you come home, you have a different chick on your arm," Jabari added. My usual philosophy concerning women was 'variety is the spice of life.'

"You're right, but that was all before I met her."

"And who is she?" Dakari asked.

"The only woman I have known who can make me *want* to settle down. She is the end-all and be-all."

"What's her name?" Jabari asked, looking at me skeptically.

I hesitated for a moment trying to remember if I had come across her first name in the hour we were together.

"Yvette Brooks."

"And where did you meet her?" both asked simultaneously.

"She works at the school were I was doing some observation for class."

"Oh, so she's a first-year teacher? Did she just graduate from TSU?" Jabari asked.

"No, not exactly. She's the assistant principal."

Dakari and Jabari stared at me for a second, before looking at each other and chuckling. They shook their heads as if they couldn't believe my stupidity. "So I take it she's about fifty or sixty then?"

"Don't be an asshole," I said. "She's twenty-nine, thirty tops." I wasn't exactly sure how old she was, but I was sure my guess was not far off.

"Sounds like she's better suited for one of us," Jabari said. Two weeks ago my brothers celebrated their twenty-fifth birthday. Since then they had been tossing around unsolicited advice to anyone who would listen. Their advice, however, still sounded as if it was coming from horny sixteen-year-olds. It seemed as if Morehouse hadn't done much in raising their level of maturity.

"I met her first."

"You haven't been on a date with her, so in our opinion she's free game." My brothers always spoke for one another. What one said, the other believed. Sometimes I thought they shared one brain.

"I sent her flowers with a nice little invite, so I think I staked my claim."

"What did you put on the card?"

"Basically, I said that if she wanted to hang out, then she should give me a call."

"Did she call you?" Dakari asked knowingly.

I hesitated. "Not yet, but I think I'll give it a couple more days."

"She's not going to call. She's mature and does not want to be bothered by some twenty-one year old who doesn't know what he wants," Jabari said.

"I think she didn't call because she's engaged, and she doesn't want to be forced to cheat on her fiancé." I felt good enough about myself to assume that I was too much for her to handle.

"She's engaged?" they both asked incredulously.

"Yeah, but so what? I've dated a married woman, and she was all over me."

"Is this another one of your little rebellious stunts?" Dakari asked, getting up and putting his plate into the dishwasher.

"Rebellious?" I asked, playing dumb.

"Oh, don't act like you don't know what he's talking about. You have gone against the Riley grain ever since you hit puberty. First, the locks," Jabari said, referring to the way I wore my hair immediately after graduating high school. "Next, you decided to go to TSU when every man in our family since grandpa has gone to Morehouse. You are majoring in foreign languages and education instead of law like the rest of us. And now you want to date this engaged woman."

If you didn't know the facts, it did sound as if I lived to be different, but I saw it as more of wanting to be independent of my father and brothers, to be my own man and make my own way.

My family was steeped in tradition. Riley men went to Morehouse for undergrad, my brothers included, there were no exceptions. You can imagine the uproar I caused at my high-school graduation party when I announced that I had decided against attending Morehouse and majoring in political science and had instead accepted a scholarship to Tennessee State University and would be majoring in modern foreign languages. My father was so upset he even considered cutting me off. "No money, no car, no anything as long as you keep this up," he declared loudly, right in the middle of my opening my gifts. I understood his anger and wasn't the least bit surprised by his reaction. Thankfully, it didn't last very long. My grandparents talked to him and, shortly before I left for Nashville, he came around.

"You know how Dad is going to react when he hears about this," Dakari said.

"According to the two of you, there is nothing to hear about," I smugly reminded them.

"Are you doing this just to further piss him off?"

"This has nothing to do with Dad and everything to do with the fact that I am really interested in this woman."

"Whatever you say, little brother, but the last thing I'm going to say is this: Don't try to bite off more than you can chew."

"Never that, Jabari. I'm always in control when it comes to the ladies. Always."

Yvette

8

"Mr. Riley, before we begin the observation, I think there are some things we should discuss." As I led Ajani to my office, I sensed his eyes touring my body.

I slid into my desk chair and folded my hands. Ajani sat facing me, nervously biting his bottom lip. He was the best-looking thing I had ever seen. "First of all, I am very flattered by the flowers," I said, looking over at the slightly wilted lilies on a small table near the window.

"I hoped you would like them," he said, smiling.

"I do," I said, letting down my guard a little. I promised myself before work this morning that any contact between Ajani and me and would be kept strictly professional. I even wore a loose turtleneck sweater and slacks so that I wouldn't appear too sexy. "I like them, but I'm not exactly sure why you sent them."

Ajani hesitated for a moment before leaning forward in his chair. "I sent them because I wanted to invite you out sometime." He was confident; it showed in his voice and demeanor. And he seemed much older than his twenty-one years.

"Out?" I echoed, raising my recently arched eyebrow.

"Yes, out. You know, dinner, lunch, a movie or whatever you're into." He made the last option, *whatever you're into*, sound so enticing that I was tempted to clear off my desk and show him exactly what I was into.

"Didn't I mention that I'm engaged?" I asked, waving my engagement ring, newly cleaned and polished, in his face.

"Ms. Brooks, I'm not trying to take your fiancé's place. I just thought it would be nice if we hung out a little bit, got to know each other."

"Mr. Riley, Ajani, you're twenty-one and I'm thirty-four. I can't imagine that we have anything in common."

"You would be amazed, Ms. Brooks," he said, a naughty gleam in his eyes.

It was amazing how this young man was managing to make me actually consider his offer. I couldn't remember ever being this attracted to a man, especially after seeing him only twice. "This is very unprofessional," I said, uncomfortable and excited at the same time. "I'm sure the university has a rule forbidding this. What you're doing, or, rather, trying to do must be a violation of the student code of conduct." I dropped that line as a strong hint for him to back off, but the look on his face said he knew I did not have any plans to call the school.

"Why don't we do this," Ajani said, looking directly at me. His eyes gazed deep into my soul; I looked away, feeling my cheeks begin to redden. "Let's make plans to do something this weekend. We can hang out, do something fun and if you don't have a good time then I promise I won't bother you again."

This conversation had already gotten way out of hand, and I wanted to choose my words carefully. "And if I say yes and we do go out and I do have a good time, then what? What do you expect to happen then?" I knew I was on very thin ice here; I was falling into the trap Ajani had set for me. Right now, he was in control and that made him even sexier.

"I'm open, but at the very least, I would like your friendship." He seemed genuine, but deep down I knew his motives weren't strictly platonic.

It was time I put a stop to this and get back down to business. "Mr. Riley, I really don't think that would be a good idea." I stood up, picked up my clipboard and headed to the door. I had some students to meet and Ajani had some observing to do. This conversation was over.

The next morning I walked into my office and there on my desk was an amazing bouquet of red roses. "That man must love you," Jordan said, as I reached into the bouquet and extracted one rose for her.

I didn't need to read the card. I knew who sent them and, just as I had been the week before, I was intrigued despite my misgivings. Refusing to be caught up in thoughts of Ajani, I dialed Terrence's cellphone number. When the voicemail picked up, I left an urgent message to call me back. I planned to tell him that I wanted to come to Detroit for the weekend so that we could do something romantic, something that would take my mind off things I shouldn't be thinking about. Something to make me think about Terrence and not other men. I waited by the phone all morning and into the afternoon, but Terrence never called. The time was six-thirty, and my phone hadn't rung once. I sat at my desk, fearing the worst.

I dialed Wendy's cellphone, hoping she would answer. I needed someone to talk me off my ledge; I was ready to jump and knew that if I did, I'd fall right into Ajani's waiting arms. "Wendy Web," she said cheerfully after the second ring.

"Wendy, I'm having a crisis. I called Terrence this morning and left him an urgent message, but he still hasn't returned my call."

"Just so happens that I saw Mr. Hall and a cute hospital resident down at Southern Fires this very afternoon having a late lunch."

"What! You cannot be serious," I said, feeling as if my world was spinning out of control. Again. Stupid me.

"I am, but don't jump to any conclusions just yet; after all, it could have been a business lunch."

"Don't try to make me feel better. His little lunch date is the exact reason he hasn't called me back," I said, feeling a sickening sense of deja vu.

"Well, are you going to say anything to him? I really don't think you should, because I could have been wrong. I didn't exactly go up to their table and ask what was going on," Wendy said, trying to downplay the importance of the lunch she described.

"No, no, I won't say anything, but I will remember this next time he's acting funny or claiming he is too busy to have time for me. How stupid can I be sitting here thinking that he's in Detroit crying his eyes out when he's really getting drunk in the middle of the day with residents? You can't argue with history," I said, referring to his hospital love affair and the trashy red panties between my couch cushions.

"Relax, Yvette. As I said before, it was probably nothing."

"Yeah, right. Nothing. Let me call you back," I said, abruptly hanging up. I looked over at the roses. They were beautiful, and I wasn't married yet. Taking a deep breath, I slowly opened the card that was tucked deep into the roses.

> Will these make you change your mind? 555-1432.
> Ajani

Spurred by anger, loneliness and distrust, it was as if my fingers were working without direction from my brain. I dialed the first three numbers slowly, paused and then dialed the last four as if my life depended on it. On the fifth ring, just as I was about to hang up, Ajani answered. "Hello?" he said in a whisper.

"Um, hi, may I speak to Ajani, please?" My voice shook and I sounded more like a nervous fifteen-year-old schoolgirl than the confident thirty-four-year-old I thought I was.

"This is Ajani. Who is this?" he asked, still whispering. I could hear a lot of noise in the background.

"This is Yvette. Did I catch you at a bad time? I can call back." There was no way in the world I was going to call back. This was it; if he hung up the phone, then I was going to shred his number just as I had the first time. If he hung up, God was trying to tell me something.

"Yvette?" he asked confused. His voice became louder and the background noise had faded away.

"Um, Yvette Brooks, from Nashville Prep."

There was a pause, a laugh and then, "My fault, I was in class," he said, explaining the earlier background noise. "Calling to thank me for the flowers?"

"I am, and I wanted to let you know that I'm free on Saturday evening if the offer still stands." I held my breath and waited. If Terrence could go out and have a good time with someone of the opposite sex, then so could I. It would be completely platonic, just like Terrence's little lunch date. One little date wouldn't hurt anything. Right?

"Yeah, Saturday. My frat is having a party, so I have to do that. You can come with me or we could hang out after," Ajani suggested.

"A fraternity party? Are you serious?" I asked, feeling my age again. I would have rather chewed off my right arm than spend a Saturday night at a college fraternity party. Maybe this was God's way of telling me that I was moving too fast.

"It's going to be nice. But if you're not into that, we can always meet somewhere for drinks after."

"Maybe this isn't a good idea," I said, nervously switching the receiver from one shoulder to the other.

"No, no. It's a great idea. Why don't you meet me at the party, and we can go somewhere else if you want. That way you can drive your car, and if you're uncomfortable, you can drive yourself wherever you want to go."

I wanted to change my mind. I wanted to plead temporary insanity, hang up the phone and request a new student from TSU to observe me. But something was stopping me; something was preventing me from putting the receiver back on its cradle. It probably had something to do with the vision I had of Terrence feeding strawberries to his cute little resident and the warm, tingly feeling of Ajani's hand on my back.

"That sounds okay," I told him, grabbing a pen and sticky note before I lost my nerve. "What are the directions?" I wrote down the address and said good-bye, feeling as if I had just done something so wrong that it was right. Very right.

Wendy

9

"Wendy, what would you wear if you were going to a party?" Yvette asked.

"Well, what kind of party are we talking about? If it's a dinner party, I would suggest something really cute, like a skirt and top. But if it's a cocktail party then a little black dress."

"It's not exactly either one," she replied, sounding nervous and unsure of herself—definitely not the Yvette I thought I knew.

"What kind of party is it exactly?"

"A college party," she said in a voice so low I could barely hear her.

"I know you did not just say a college party!"

"Yes, I did. It's a college party," she said, her voice stronger, more determined.

"Why in the world would you voluntarily attend a college party?" I was confused. The Yvette I knew, the Detroit Yvette, the thirty-four-year-old Yvette, wouldn't be caught dead at a college party.

"I was invited. And I really don't plan to stay for very long," she asserted, probably hoping that the explanation would make sense.

"Invited by whom?"

"I met a guy," she quickly—maybe too quickly—answered.

"What are you talking about? You met a guy? You already have a guy, a doctor and fiancé and his name is Terrence."

"Well, aren't you the one who told me that Terrence was lunching with some other woman when he should have been returning my urgent call?"

Yvette was right. I had told her that that I had seen Terrence with another woman. The truth is, I hadn't seen him that day at all. "I was also the one who told you not to jump to any conclusions. I'm not exactly sure what I saw. You didn't mention it to him, did you?"

"Of course not, but I'm not going to sit up in Nashville doing nothing while he's living it up. He has a past, and it's not that hard to believe that he's at home doing something he's not supposed to be doing."

"Tell me more about the guy," I said, smiling to myself. My little plan was working better than I thought.

"He's young and cute and we're just friends—not really even friends yet. Acquaintances would be a better term," she explained.

"Yeah, right. I seriously doubt you guys are just acquaintances." I could barely keep the glee out of my voice. "So, how young is he?"

"Twenty-one."

"You have lost your mind! Why would you go out with a twenty-one-year-old college student when you have a rich, successful doctor waiting at home?"

"I'm not cheating on Terrence. I'm just having a little fun. I'm doing something unexpected for a change. Let Terrence sit at home and wonder what I'm doing and why I'm not returning his calls."

"Is this all because of what I told you the other day?" I was amazed that Yvette was so naïve, so gullible.

"No, not completely, although hearing that my fiancé was having lunch with another woman is a factor. But since I've been in Nashville, I have realized that I am too accommodating of what other people want. It's about time I started doing things because I want to do them."

"And cheating on Terrence is what you want to do?"

"Didn't I already tell you that I am not cheating on Terrence? I'm going out with Ajani to have a good time, and that's all!"

"How much of a good time?"

"Dancing, drinks and that's as far as it's going to go. He already knows that I'm engaged." Her tone was becoming defensive, but the more Yvette spoke, the more I realized that this little turn of events may prove to be more beneficial than I could have ever imagined.

"Since when has an engagement ring stopped a man?" I softened my voice to give her the impression that I was on her side. "So, how fine is he?"

"Girl," she said as if she had lost her breath just thinking about him. "He is a work of art, tall and muscular. Wendy, he is so confident and acts much older than his age."

"He does sound yummy, but what's going to happen when he makes a pass at you?"

"He won't." She answered so fast I knew she was lying.

"Sure, sure, whatever you say. Now back to reality. I saw Terrence yesterday," I said, this time telling the truth.

"Did you? Where?"

"Starbucks. He was alone, if you're wondering," I falsely reassured my best friend.

"I talked to him last night, and he didn't mention a thing," she said, her voice becoming slightly suspicious.

He wouldn't. After my broadcast yesterday morning, I knocked on Terrence's door armed with a breakfast of scrambled eggs and cheese, homemade biscuits, bacon, grits, and fresh fruit that my personal assistant had picked up a half an hour before. After talking to Yvette several days before, I had decided to put my plan into action sooner rather than later. I knew that a good meal was the fastest way into Terrence's bed. We ate, talked and even flirted a little. He was clearly appreciative of the meal, as well as the time I spent with him. As I was leaving, he kissed me on the cheek and asked if my morning visit was going to be a regular thing. With a seductive wink, I promised him it would be.

"Yvette, he probably just forgot to mention it. You know how hectic that man's schedule is."

"So you guys ran into each other?" I sensed her skepticism.

"No, I . . ." I paused a second. "Girl, my other line is clicking. Let me call you back," I lied, quickly hanging up. I didn't need Yvette asking too many questions, especially when my plan was taking shape so nicely.

Terrence

10

Yesterday something very strange happened. A knock at the door awakened me, and I almost didn't answer. But even with my head buried in the down pillow, I could still hear the insistent pounding on my door. Finally, I reluctantly I pulled myself out of bed and shuffled into the living room. I unlocked the deadbolts and was greeted by a smiling Wendy. My woman's best friend.

"Good morning, sleepy head," she said, sashaying past with a bag in each arm. The distinct sweet, smoky smell of bacon teased my senses. "I hope you're hungry because I made breakfast."

"Wendy, what are you doing here? It's only nine o'clock, and in case you didn't know, I like to spend my days off sleeping in."

Pouting suggestively, she put the bags on the kitchen counter. "Are you telling me that you don't want any grits, eggs and bacon? Did I drive all this way for nothing?"

I walked over to the counter and peered inside the bags. "You didn't have to drive very far. You work four blocks away," I reminded her.

"Okay, you're right. But I did have to delegate the purchase of this delicious meal to my assistant, and that took forever. She isn't that bright. Now I'm trying to do what Yvette asked me to do, so stop being so difficult."

"What did Yvette ask you to do?" I asked, taking a biscuit and going to the cupboard to get the syrup.

"She asked me, as her best friend, to take care of you and make sure that you weren't over here wasting away."

I know Yvette and I knew Wendy was lying.

She's always had a thing for me. When we first met back at Wayne State, she was offended that I showed interest in her best friend rather than her. Once Yvette and I became a couple, she gave me the cold shoulder for months.

"So how have you been?" she asked, setting the table for two.

"I've been okay. Work keeps me pretty busy, so I don't have much time to think about how much I miss Yvette." I saw a flicker of jealousy pass over her pretty face.

"Don't you two talk on the phone?"

"We try to every night, but it's not the same. There's nothing like having a warm body next to you at night," I said, enjoying the view inside her blouse as she bent over to pour orange juice into champagne flutes for mimosas.

"I know what you mean," she said. "I get so lonely over there in that big house all by myself. Yvette doesn't know what it's like to be alone, without a strong man to take care of her. She's always had you."

Wendy motioned for me to sit down at the table. I sat down and picked up a napkin, but before I could open it, Wendy took it from me and placed it in my lap, lightly touching my thigh. My skin tingled at her touch. The flesh is weak.

We ate in silence for a while, looking up only occasionally to exchange awkward smiles. "What are you doing for fun these days?" she asked me.

"Nothing much. I really don't have time for fun with my job being so hectic."

"Oh, come on now, Terrence. You have to get out and do something every once in a while. We should plan to hang out together sometime. Catch a movie or something."

I nearly fell out of my seat. "What do you mean hang out sometime?"

"Oh, Terrence, I think you know what I mean," she answered coyly, a sly smile on her face.

"No, Wendy, actually I don't know what you mean."

"Well, I was just suggesting that if you ever wanted to get out sometime, then I would be more than happy to be your company. We have known each other a long time, and there is no reason that we can't go out as friends."

"Friends?" I asked, raising a doubtful eyebrow.

"Of course, Terrence, what did you think I meant?" She sounded innocent, but the unmistakable look in her eyes was dangerous. I could tell that she had something up her sleeve, and though I knew it was wrong, I was nonetheless intrigued. At that moment, I wanted nothing more than to know what Wendy was hiding and how it would unfold.

Yvette

11

It took me almost three hours to get ready for my date with Ajani. My hands kept shaking, and I couldn't find a single thing to wear, though my closet was bursting with outfits with the price tags still attached. The first outfit, jeans and a baby tee, made me look like a sixteen-year-old trying to pass for twenty-one. I went through at least five outfits before I slipped on the first pair of jeans I had tried on and a black top, sexy and mature at the same time.

Styling my hair and applying my makeup was an adventure in itself. My hands shook as though I was having a seizure, and every time I tried to pick up the comb, it would slip right through my fingers. And when lining my eyes, I poked myself twice. But by the time eleven-thirty rolled around, I looked completely fabulous and there were no signs that I had nearly blinded myself.

On the drive to the party, my heart was beating so fast I was sure I was going into cardiac arrest. I dialed Ajani's cellphone number seven times but didn't push send once. I wanted to tell him that just the thought of meeting up with him was wrecking havoc on my health, so I wouldn't be able to make it. I wanted to but I couldn't; something was whispering softly into my ear, urging me to relax, to go out and have a good time. I needed to live a little. I decided to listen to that voice, so with sweaty, slippery palms, I drove across town to meet a man thirteen years my junior.

I heard the party from two blocks away. I pulled into the parking lot, turned the engine off, and rested my head on the steering wheel. I was unsure about what I was doing, but I knew for sure I would stick out like a sore thumb as soon as I stepped out of the car and into the party.

As a group of men walked by and peered inside my car, I saw my cellphone vibrating in the cup holder. Ajani's number blinked across the screen until the voicemail symbol appeared. "Yvette, this is Ajani. It's getting late and you're not here yet, so I'm wondering if you're still coming. Give me a call when you get this message." He sounded so sweet and worried that I decided to put my insecurities aside and get out of the car.

"Hi," I said to the handsome young man dressed in a purple and gold t-shirt, and fatigued army pants blocking the door. "I'm looking for Ajani Riley."

He looked me up and down and then licked his lips and smiled. "Well, I don't see him right now, but I'm sure I can fulfill all your needs."

I showed him my identification and paid the five-dollar cover charge. "No, thank you. I think I'll just find Ajani." I walked past him and into the building. The bass was thumping, throngs of bodies were clumped together dancing, and the thick, suffocating smell of marijuana filled the air.

In the middle of the dance floor, about twenty men dressed like the doorman formed a large circle. I spotted Ajani almost immediately. His fatigue hat was pulled down low over his eyes, and his smile lit up the entire dark space. The women who stood on the perimeter of the group were practically swooning over him. It was easy to see that among his peers Ajani Riley was a very hot commodity.

I stood on the outer edge of the dance floor watching for about five minutes before Ajani spun around and our eyes met. A huge smile spread across his face, while he hurried to pull a towel from his back pocket. "You made it," Ajani said, leaning down and kissing my cheek, causing a jolt of electricity to run through my body unlike anything I had ever felt before, not even in the early years with Terrence.

"Yeah," I said, trying to collect my thoughts. His hand was still resting on my waist, and the tingling I felt was making it difficult to focus. "I'm sorry, I was running a little late." I looked around the room and noticed that about fifteen pairs of angry eyes were on Ajani and me.

"No problem, no problem. I'm just glad you made it. Can I get you a drink?"

I surveyed the room again; the women who were glaring minutes before were now whispering and pointing in our direction. "A strong drink sounds good."

"Okay, cool. Why don't you sit right here," Ajani suggested, guiding me to an empty table near the dance floor. "I'll be right back."

I sat down and began tapping my foot to David Banner. Everyone seemed to be having such a good time, and their excitement was infectious. "Here you go," Ajani said, handing me a pink drink in a purple plastic cup. If Wendy was here, she would die. "It's a Long Island punch. I asked the bartender to make it extra strong."

"Thank you." I smiled at him and gulped half of the potent drink down. The fiery liquid burned my throat and boiled my insides, but it was worth the immediate feeling of calm and relaxation I felt.

"So are you ready to go? I know this quiet little lounge that stays open late—" Ajani was cut off by a pretty young thing wearing what looked like little more than a bathing suit.

"Hey, baby," she said, slithering up to him and planting a wet kiss on his neck. "I haven't seen you in a while, Ajani. Don't you miss me?" She spoke to him but looked directly at me, and the smirk on her face and the fire in her eyes said it all. I was invading her territory.

"Lisa, how many times have I told you that we're over?" Ajani said angrily. He seemed embarrassed by her behavior and gave me an apologetic look. As for me, I swallowed the last of my drink and signaled the bartender for another.

"So how does your aunt like the party so far?" Lisa asked, ignoring Ajani's rejection and taking a jab at our obvious age difference. "It's so sweet of you to bring her here to relive her youth."

"I'm not his aunt," I said, shifting in my seat uncomfortably.

"Older cousin?" she asked, smiling sweetly.

"She's a friend," Ajani said. Then he took my hand and led me onto the dance floor. I looked back and saw Lisa standing at the table looking embarrassed and confused.

"I'm sorry about that," Ajani whispered in my ear, his lips grazing my skin and lingering there.

I felt slightly dizzy and off balance, thanks to the Long Island punch. But when Ajani wrapped his arms around me, I became comfortable instantly. "I see that you're quite the ladies' man."

"Not really. Lisa's just kind of crazy. She doesn't like to take no for an answer, but we've been over for months."

"Ajani, you don't have to explain anything to me, I'm the one getting married in six months," I said, a bit of regret in my voice. As premature as it was, I was beginning to like Ajani. His touch made me shiver, and his voice made parts of my body ache. I wasn't sure if it was the alcohol or the fact that I was lonely, but I had a sudden, intense urge to kiss him.

"Now as I was saying about the lounge . . ." His lips moved so close to mine, I couldn't help myself. Placing my hand on the back of his neck, I stood on my tiptoes and moved in for the kill. It was as if the music had stopped and we were the only two people standing there. The room began spinning and all thoughts of Terrence and my life in Detroit disappeared. All I was conscious of was Ajani's hand on my back. He looked down at me as if he had the ability to read my mind. Just as our lips were about to become one, I saw Lisa moving through the crowd with the swiftness of a gazelle. With practically a running start, Ajani's ex bumped us from behind, causing my drink to splash on my jeans.

Yvette

12

"Are you heading to Detroit this weekend?" Jordan asked. I was at my desk admiring yet another bouquet of flowers from Ajani, this one a box of two dozen long-stemmed red roses with a card that read:

Can't wait to see you again.

"Yes, actually I am. I have let these wedding plans fall by the wayside too long. If I'm getting married, then I need to get on the ball," I added. She placed some papers on my desk and pulled up a chair. Jordan had been acting strangely all week. She hadn't been her usual bubbly, talkative self.

"We're friends, right?" she inquired, smiling slightly.

"Of course. You're pretty much the only friend I've got here in Nashville. Why?"

"Because there's something I need to ask you, and I want it to be off the record. It isn't job related, just one friend talking to another."

"Ok, let's hear it," I prompted, interest consuming me.

"You still plan on getting married?" she asked. It was almost as if I was being accused me of something, as if she knew what I had been doing a couple of days before.

"Of course I still plan to get married. What kind of question is that?" Jordan was the closest thing I had to a confidante in Nashville, but she was still my employee, and I wasn't sure I appreciated her overstepping her bounds.

"Well, I'm only asking because I saw you out on Saturday with Ajani, and the two of you looked extremely comfortable together. You did not look like a woman planning a wedding."

I stared at her, aware my mouth was slightly open. I was taken aback and embarrassed. "Are those flowers from Ajani or Terrence?" she asked, delving deeper.

There was no point in denying anything, so I answered her question. "The flowers are from Ajani. All the flowers have been from Ajani. And, yes, we did go out on one date, but that was it." I was baring the secret I had been unable to share until now. "We had fun, and I like him as a friend. And that's all. I really don't know what I'm doing; I'm so embarrassed." I was rambling on and on, not knowing how to stop.

"Yvette, you don't have to explain anything to me. I didn't come in here to accuse you of anything. I just thought you might want to talk about it, get an unbiased opinion on the situation."

"Okay, Jordan, let's hear it," I demanded, bracing myself. "You think I looked ridiculous with Ajani and that seeing him is going to ruin any plans I have for marrying Terrence. You think I'm just an old woman trying to relive my youth. I'm a *Stella*."

Laughing, Jordan jumped up and closed my office door. Mrs. Fisher, the principal at Nashville Prep, was insistent that all staff practice the highest level of professionalism at all times. Jordan and I knew that our conversation potentially could get us into a lot of trouble. "That is not what I think," she said, smiling at me. "I think you looked happy with him, and you seemed to be having the time of your life. I was on the opposite side of the room and, after watching you and Ajani for a while, I saw some definite sparks. Where there are sparks, a fire usually follows. I think you need to decide what you really want and go from there," she advised, sounding much older and wiser than her twenty-two years.

"I know what I want and whom I want. As I said before, Ajani is a friend and that's all."

"Okay, okay, whatever you say. But if you ever need someone to talk to or bounce ideas off, let me know. I know how confusing things can be when you have too many options."

Unlike Jordan, I did not consider Ajani an option. I did, however, consider him a distraction. He called me the day after our date and we talked for four hours. He told me about his brothers; his dad, who sounded rich and distinguished, perfect for Wendy; and school. I talked about my friends, job and grandmother. But whenever he asked me about Terrence, I changed the subject. I simply did not want to discuss him.

"So you had a good time last night, didn't you?" Ajani asked at one point.

"I did have a good time, despite your ex-girlfriend completely ruining a very expensive pair of jeans."

"You should feel flattered. It's not very often that Lisa feels threatened by another woman. She must know how much I like you."

"Is that right?" I asked, sounding like a smitten schoolgirl.

"That's exactly right, and since you had such a good time, does that mean you'll agree to another date?"

"You move quickly, don't you? It hasn't been a good twenty-four hours since we last saw each other."

"As I see it, Yvette, I need to work fast before my magic wears off and you go back to giving me the cold shoulder."

"No more cold shoulder, Ajani," I said. "But I do want to make something clear. We are just friends. Nothing else can happen between us."

"Who are you trying to convince here?"

"I'm not trying to convince anyone; I'm just telling you how it is."

"Um hmm, good, so dinner this Saturday then?" he asked confidently.

"I can't. I'm flying out to Detroit Saturday morning," I said with sincere regret.

"Okay. Friday night? I'll come by your place, cook dinner, help you pack . . ."

"You cook?" I asked, seriously considering the offer.

"Cook and pack a mean weekend bag. Southern fried chicken is my specialty."

My mouth began to water at the thought of authentic Southern fried chicken. My diet in Nashville has consisted of McDonald's and Taco Bell. I was grateful for my fast metabolism; without it, I would easily be over two hundred pounds. "I'll buy the groceries and you cook."

"Sounds like a plan."

"That it is," I said, excited at the prospect of seeing him again.

"And maybe while I'm there, I can convince you that you should stay."

Wendy

13

"I know they keep the key here somewhere," I said to myself, searching under the welcome mat outside Yvette and Terrence's apartment door for their spare key. Finally locating it under a potted plant in a corner, I slid into the keyhole and opened the door.

Signs of neglect were everywhere. In the kitchen, dishes were piled high in the sink. In the living room, covers were left on the floor from what must have been a late night of television watching. The funky smell of dirty socks filled the air. I picked up my bag of laundry and carried it to the Whirlpool washer and dryer in a corner of the kitchen. The laundry was merely a prop that would serve as my excuse for breaking into their apartment when Terrence walked through the door.

I began cleaning and straightening up the apartment. Dishes were scraped and loaded into dishwasher; blankets folded and returned to the linen closet. I moved quickly, realizing that Terrence would be home any minute. After getting that place into some semblance of order, I snatched off my clothes and threw them into the washing machine with the other darks. Then I stood in my best friend's kitchen in just my panties and bra, knowing what I was about to do was wrong and feeling slightly guilty . . . but only slightly.

I heard the key turn in the lock and the door opening; heavy footsteps followed. "Wendy! What are you doing here?" Terrence asked, throwing his keys into the basket on the kitchen counter. He took in my appearance from head to toe, his eyes moving slowly over my nearly naked body. All the while, he looked unreadable.

"I'm so sorry," I said, pretending I was looking for something to cover my body. "My washing machine is on the fritz, and I didn't think it would be a big deal to come over here and do some laundry. I thought you would be working the whole day."

"How did you get in?" he asked, walking toward me, never taking his eyes off my lacy bra and panties.

"The key under the mat outside. I'm really sorry about this. I'll leave," I said, gathering my pile of whites off the floor.

"Don't. It's cool. Go ahead and finish washing. I have some paperwork to finish up."

Then he went to the living room, sat down on the couch and turned on the television. He picked up some papers from the coffee table and began reading. Eyeing me over the island that separated the two spaces, he asked, "Forgot your clothes at home?"

"No. I didn't expect anyone to be here, so I just took off what I was wearing and threw it in with the rest of the clothes." I laughed nervously, hoping that he wasn't about to kick me out. I was taking a gamble, and if it didn't pay off I would be in serious trouble. "If you will lend me one of your shirts, I can cover up until my clothes are finished."

"You don't have to do that." He smiled slowly and placed his papers back on the coffee table. "As a matter of fact, I'm enjoying the view." The look in his eyes was unmistakable; he knew why I was there, and he wanted the same thing. Jackpot!

"What are you talking about?" I asked innocently.

"I'm talking about you prancing around here wearing a little bit of nothing."

"I offered to put on something of yours," I said, leaving the kitchen and walking towards him, my candy-apple red stilettos clicking across the ceramic tiled floor.

"What are you really doing here?" he asked, leaning forward.

Taking a deep breath, I looked into Terrence's eyes and decided it was all or nothing. "I'm here to do what Yvette won't."

Terrence

The moment I walked into the apartment and saw Wendy bent over the washing machine half naked, I knew what she was looking for. At first, I told myself that there was absolutely no way that anything would happen between her and me, but after seeing her breasts practically fall out of her bra as she pranced around and with the words, *I'm here to do what Yvette won't*, everything began spinning out of control. I grabbed Wendy's nearly naked body and kissed her vanilla-scented skin. She tasted so good and smelled so sweet that I couldn't stop myself. I picked her up, and she wrapped her shapely legs around my torso. I carried her from the living room to the kitchen and sat her on top of the washing machine, barely able to catch my breath. "Is this what you want?"

Instead of answering, she quickly unzipped my pants. I knew I should put a stop to what was happening, ask her to leave and get on a plane to Nashville, but I couldn't. Having Wendy had always been a fantasy of mine. Granted, I always saw Yvette somewhere in the mix. You know, a nice three-way situation, but what was happening now was the next best thing. What man could turn down hot sex during the spin cycle?

I kissed, sucked, and rubbed Wendy's body until she screamed. Then, when she reached a point of unbearable pleasure, I pushed her panties to the side and entered her wetness. With every thrust in and out of my fiancée's best friend, the guilt grew. I thought about Yvette being lonely in Nashville; saw her walking down the aisle towards me in a beautiful wedding dress. I even thought about her reaction if she was to ever find out what Wendy and I were doing at that very moment. But as guilty as I felt about the situation, it still wasn't enough for me to stop and ask Wendy to leave. It had been almost two weeks since Yvette and I made love; I was in need and Wendy was gladly accommodating.

Three hours later, Wendy dressed, folded her laundry and went home. No words were spoken about what had happened or if it would ever happen again. The way she made me feel spoke volumes. I couldn't get enough of her. She was like the forbidden fruit I had always wanted to taste, and the way she kept screaming my name and clawing at my back, I knew she couldn't get enough of me. And even though what we had just done was completely wrong, it felt so right—so right, in fact, that it was obvious this would not be our last time meeting like this.

Yvette

14

He was early. Thirty minutes early, and here I was a mess in pajama pants and a tank top. When I heard the first knock, I hurried to my bedroom, snatching off my ponytail holder and letting my hair fall loosely to my shoulders. "Just a minute," I called out when the knocking become insistent. Grabbing a tube of lip gloss from the dresser, I swiped my lips, took a deep breath and ran to the door.

"I'm sorry I'm so early," Ajani said. Dressed casually in a black zippered jacket with 'Sean John' displayed in royal blue across the front and matching baggy pants, he looked good enough to eat.

"I look a mess," I said, laughing self-consciously as I stepped aside to let him in, but he had other plans. Holding me by my waist, he kissed my cheek softly, sending shock waves through my body.

"You look great." Those three simple words and the way he looked at me when said them had me wondering if my invitation had been a bit premature, perhaps even foolhardy. Despite my second thoughts, I couldn't deny the obvious: I wanted him. Having him in my space while I wore my pajamas could be very, very dangerous.

"I wouldn't have come this early normally, and I know this sounds lame, but my barber is right around the corner, and I—" Ajani explained, walking past me.

"It's okay. I'll just go change now—if you don't mind waiting."

"You don't have to change on my account. I think you look sexy in your pj's. Definitely less intimidating than your power suits, Ms. Brooks," he teased, taking a seat on the living room couch.

"Well, that is something I probably shouldn't be. I am engaged, after all."

"I won't tell if you don't," he said, smiling brightly.

He sat on the couch as if this was exactly where he belonged. Watching him, my heart began beating erratically, and I could hardly get my next words out. "I shopped this morning and got everything you'll need to cook dinner," I said, walking to the kitchen. I thought it was wise to keep my distance, at least until the urge to kiss him wore off.

"So you're going to put me right to work?" Ajani asked, following me into the kitchen, his sleeves already rolled up, revealing well-defined, caramel colored forearms.

"Isn't that what you're here for? To cook?" I asked, handing him the bag of flour.

"Among other things."

"Ajani," I warned.

"What? I'm talking about helping you pack. Would you please get your mind out of the gutter?"

"What else will we have with the chicken?" I asked, changing the subject. The kitchen was becoming unbearably hot, and it had nothing to do with the oil heating on the stove.

"I don't know. I'm in charge of the chicken. It's my specialty, remember?"

I remembered, so I decided to make a tossed salad, and I got busy rinsing the romaine lettuce and other ingredients, but wasn't too busy to notice how adorably domestic Ajani looked seasoning the chicken.

"How was your day, Yvette?" he asked, breaking the easy silence and interrupting my wayward thoughts.

"Pretty uneventful. I mostly sat around here and watched TV reruns."

When the food was ready, we took everything into the living room and ate on the floor.

"I've been forgetting to ask you the meaning of your name," I said, finishing off a piece of perfectly seasoned chicken.

"Ajani means 'young man who likes an engaged woman.' "

I smiled at his stab at humor. "Well, if you're not going to be serious about that, then you tell me where you learned to cook. Did your mother teach you everything you know?" I asked, taking our plates to the kitchen.

"Actually, my mother died when I was three days old. She had complications during my birth and never recovered. I grew up living with my dad and brothers, but my grandmother taught me all I know about Southern fried chicken."

"Oh, Ajani, I am so sorry," I said. "I had no idea."

"No, it's okay. You can't miss what you've never had," Ajani said, taking a few logs and throwing them into the fireplace, causing orange flames to jump and dance in front of us.

"I can relate to the *can't miss* part. My mother is still alive, but my grandmother raised me. My mother has been in and out of rehab for as long as I can remember," I revealed, sipping my wine and staring at the fire. I was amazed at how comfortable I felt with Ajani. It took me almost six months to relate that same story to Terrence.

"Where is she now?" he asked.

"Around. I send her money for her bills and living expenses once a month, but we don't talk much."

"Everybody has demons," Ajani said gently, tucking a few strands of hair behind my ear. "What are yours?"

"Besides the fact that I'm here with you when I'm getting married five months from now?" He kept running his fingers up and down my bare arm, and it was making me nervous.

"You're getting married, Yvette, but you're not dead. You are still entitled to a little fun every now and then."

"But the problem is, Ajani, I'm not sure what kind of fun you have in mind." He touched me and I became weak. And the look in his eyes made me wet.

"Why don't we just see where this takes us?" Ajani asked, lifting the hair off my neck and nuzzling his face against my skin. He brushed his lips against my neck, not quite kissing, more like teasing.

"Ajani?" I whispered, wanting him to continue but knowing I should make him stop.

"Yeah, baby?" he answered. His lips left my neck and headed to my jawline. His face was so close to mine that all I had to do was move a fraction of an inch and our lips would meet.

"I think maybe you should go," I said, without much conviction. In my heart, I knew that was the last thing I wanted to do.

"You really want me to leave?" he asked, running his hands through my hair.

I closed my eyes, loving the way he was making me feel. "I don't know what I want, Ajani. I feel so good, so relaxed around you, but what about Terrence?"

"I can respect your concern," Ajani whispered, his hands nonetheless leaving my hair and going straight to my thighs.

I found myself responding pleasurably to the way he caressed me. How amazing that this man, this boy, made me feel better and more special than Terrence ever had. Then it abruptly ended.

"I'm going to go," Ajani said, pulling his hands away and clapping them together. "I really want to kiss you. I mean, I *really* want to kiss you." He clapped his hands together again, as if only that kept him from touching me.

"Ajani I—"

He rose quickly and looked down at me. "It's cool, Yvette. You don't have to say anything. I would hate for you to do something that you'll regret in the morning." Ajani held his hand out and helped me up.

"I guess I'll see you in a couple of days; I need to finish my observations." We walked hand in hand to the door.

"Yes, I know."

Ajani slowly came closer, gently pushing my nervous body against the doorframe.

"You know I don't want to leave, and I really don't think you want me to," Ajani breathed, pressing his hard body against mine, causing an involuntary gasp to escape my lips. Then he leaned down and planted a trail of kisses from my jawline to my lips.

His mouth felt even better than what I had imagined. His lips were soft, and they met mine with an urgency that produced an intense throbbing between my legs. His tongue explored my mouth and he wrapped his arms around my waist, holding me as if he never wanted to let me go.

What was happening was wrong, I knew that. I also knew that I should push him away, should tell him to stop, but I couldn't and didn't because I really didn't want him to.

Ajani pulled me close and deepened the kiss. He lifted my top slightly and touched my bare flesh. I wanted him to stop and keep going at the same time. Confusing images zoomed in and out my head, sometimes in blur, sometimes sharp—at the speed of light, Terrence, my wedding dress, my grandmother, Terrence, those lacy red panties. Terrence.

"My phone's ringing," I said, as Ajani's mouth left mine and kissed my chin. He was slowly making his way down to my breasts.

"So what?" he asked, slipping the strap off my shoulder.

"Ajani, I have to answer the phone. It might be important." I gently pushed him away and went to pick up the phone, not waiting to catch my breath before answering.

"Yvette?" he persisted, reaching for me again.

I pulled away and hurried to the other side of the room. "Hello?" I said, sounding as if I had just run a mile.

"Why are you out of breath? Are you okay?" Terrence asked, sounding genuinely alarmed.

"I'm fine, Terrence. I just got out of the shower and had to run through the apartment to answer the phone," I lied glibly.

Ajani just watched me, the expression on his face saying he was preparing to leave.

I turned my back to him.

"I was just calling to get your flight information."

"Terrence, can you hold on for a minute?" I pressed the mute button.

"Ajani, you don't have to leave."

"Yes, I do," he said, zipping up his jacket and checking his pockets for his car keys. "It's cool. Go handle your phone call." He took long quick strides across the room and leaned down. He kissed me softly on the lips. "Call me when you get back home."

It wasn't until Ajani left my apartment that I realized he had slipped a small piece of paper onto the coffee table.

Ajani means 'He who wins the struggle.'

Yvette

15

I couldn't stop thinking about Ajani. Even now, back in Detroit for a couple of days, I could still smell his cologne, taste his lips, and feel his hands.

I had looked his name up on the Internet, not because I didn't believe him but because *he who wins the struggle* seemed entirely too apt for the situation we were slowly creating for ourselves.

And he was still not letting up. He called me and left a voicemail as soon as my plane touched down. Walking through Detroit Metro Airport, I listened to his message over and over. I couldn't seem to get enough of his deep, sexy voice.

"Yvette, this is Ajani. I had a really nice time last night, and I'm looking forward to seeing you when you get back."

The mere sound of his voice aroused and scared me. I had never in my life felt so strongly about a man so soon. And one so young. Just thinking about him did things to my body that Terrence never had in twelve years of a relationship. And the more I thought about him, the more I wished I wasn't a thirty-four-year-old engaged woman.

Guilt kicked in the moment I saw Terrence waiting for me in the baggage claim area. Not only had I cheated on him, but I was also seriously considering letting it happen again. But the excited and happy feeling that I used to get after being apart from him for an extended time was missing. In a way, I wished he were more like Ajani.

"Everything is ready for tonight," Terrence said as we entered the apartment, the wide-open space of the loft reminding me of the huge hole in my heart.

"Great. Have you met Wendy's new boy toy?" I asked, checking the food Terrence had catered for tonight's get-together. I had invited Wendy and the guy she was seeing over because I missed her. I wanted to catch up and have a couples' evening at the same time.

"I haven't met him, but I'm sure he won't last very long," Terrence predicted.

"What are you talking about?"

"I'm just saying that Wendy is known for loving and leaving them. I don't think that you should start planning any couples' vacations," he said, his voice dripping with sarcasm and skepticism.

"Don't be like that. You have never met this guy. He could be the one."

Terrence didn't seem too convinced.

We spent the rest of the afternoon in bed. While Terrence was as inattentive and selfish as ever, I tried to make the time fly with thoughts of Ajani.

"How are the wedding plans coming?" Terrence asked as we dressed for the evening.

"Good. Everything is right on schedule," I lied, pulling on a green camisole with cream-colored lace trim. Jeans and pointy-toed heels finished the outfit.

"Good, good. Just let me know if there's anything I can help you with."

There was plenty he could help with. Since my relocation to Nashville, the wedding preparations had come to a standstill. My heart just wasn't in it.

"I think someone is knocking on the door, Terrence," I said, touching up my hair.

"Okay, I'll get it." After a few minutes of listening to voices and laughter in the living room, I made my entrance.

"It's so good to see you, 'Vette! I know it's only been a few weeks, but it feels like forever," Wendy said, walking over and hugging me.

She looked fabulous in her low-cut black dress and strappy sandals. "Let me introduce you to Alonzo Rivera," she said, turning to a tall, muscular man.

"Very nice to meet you," he said in a Latin accent. He shook my hand and held, shaking it a little too long. "I've heard a lot about you and it's a pleasure to finally meet you, Yvette." Alonzo's eyes traveled the length of my body and lingered on my cleavage before stopping at my face. I shifted uncomfortably but smiled politely.

"Anyway, Yvette," Wendy said, "we have a lot to catch up on so why don't we leave the boys so they can talk about sports or whatever." She had noticed Alonzo noticing me and wanted to deflect his attention. She linked her arm through mine and we went into the bedroom.

"You look great, as always," I said, sitting down on the bed.

"So do you. You're actually glowing. You and Terrence must have had a hell of an afternoon."

"No, not exactly."

"Trouble in paradise?"

"No, everything is okay for the most part. I'll tell you what I've been up to after you tell me about Alonzo."

"He's cool. I met him at a fundraiser for the mayor a few weeks ago. He pitches for the Tigers."

"He's cute."

Wendy raised an eyebrow. "Don't you have enough on your plate? Should you really be trying to eat off mine?"

"What's that supposed to mean? Please don't think that I'm interested in Alonzo. I have my own issues."

"That's exactly what I'm talking about. You have Terrence and the frat guy you're seeing," she laughed, probably trying to lighten the tense mood she had just created. "How's that going?"

"We had dinner last night. He came over to my apartment and cooked for me."

"This sounds like it's becoming a lot more than a harmless friendship."

"Wendy, I can't lie; I do like him. I like him a lot. I know I shouldn't, but I do. The whole idea is completely absurd. I mean, I'm engaged and he's twenty-one years old."

"This guy must be Morris Chestnut, Taye Diggs and LL Cool J all rolled into one," Wendy joked.

"I have honestly never met anyone like him."

"Your eyes are sparkling, Yvette. Are you sure that the two of you only had dinner?"

"He kissed me." I could feel myself blushing.

"He kissed you, and you didn't tell him to stop?"

"I didn't ask him to stop, because I didn't want him to. Wendy, I can't stop thinking about him."

"This relationship you have with Terrence is doomed. I think you need to call off the wedding. Terrence might be seeing someone from the hospital, and you're in Nashville kissing a high-school student."

"He is not in high school, and I am not calling off the wedding. Not now, anyway. I just think that Ajani is something that I have to get out of my system before I walk down the aisle."

"So you're planning to sleep with him?"

"I'm not *planning* to do anything. I just can't stop thinking about him, and if something happens naturally, then I'm not going to try to stop it."

"I'm positive that when you get back to Nashville you are going to meet up with Ajani and sow your oats."

"Do you think that's wrong?" I asked her. "After all Terrence has put me through, don't you think I should do something for myself?"

"I think you have some decisions to make, Yvette. Maybe you should talk to Terrence."

"I don't recall him discussing his little fling with me! I don't even remember him telling me he was lunching with some tramp at Flood's the other day!"

With that, she and I left the room and joined the men for dinner. For the next several hours, I tried to ignore Alonzo's inappropriate looks, but at the same time I sensed a strange vibe between Terrence and Wendy. I hoped that she wasn't planning to drop any hints about Ajani and me.

Around midnight, Wendy and Alonzo left and Terrence beckoned me to bed. Instead of joining him right away, I dashed to the guest bedroom and locked myself in, cellphone in hand.

"How are you, Ajani?"

"I'm good. How are you?" he answered.

"I'm fine. I got your message this morning."

"Yeah, I'm sorry I called so early, but you had been on my mind all night. Actually, you've been on my mind since the last time I saw you."

"Ajani, I'm nervous about what's happening with us."

"I feel you. You're getting married. I know I should back off, but I can't."

A knock at the door made me almost jump out of my skin. "Is everything okay, Yvette?" Terrence asked from the hallway.

"Yes. I was just freshening up. I'll be out in a second," I replied, disappointed that I had to cut my call short.

"You have to go?"

"Duty calls, but I'll be back in Nashville tomorrow evening."

"I want to see you," Ajani said. The urgency in his voice made me quiver.

"Tomorrow night?"

"Whenever. When you're free, I'm free."

I wanted to hear what he had to say. I needed to know where this was going. "My flight gets in at nine. I'll come by your place after that."

PART 2

4 months Pre-nuptial

Yvette

16

My intention was to meet Ajani at his house and engage in an evening of hot, butt-naked sex, but as I flew the five hundred miles back to Nashville, I chickened out. As badly as I wanted to push my boundaries and test the waters with a sexy young thing like Ajani, I could not bring myself to do it. Not yet, anyway.

After a long cellphone discussion with Wendy, I decided it would be best to put some distance between Ajani and me. The honest truth was that, at only twenty-one, he was literally more than I could handle. When we were together, he was like walking sex. And when I looked at him, when I talked to him on the phone, his hard body against mine was all I seemed to think about.

"Hi," I said, taking a deep breath, trying to strengthen my resolve.

"How are you? How was your flight? Are you on your way?" he asked, sounding adorable as ever.

"Ajani, I don't think I can come."

There was a pregnant pause, and I knew that he was thinking carefully about how to respond to my unexpected announcement.

"Why not? Is everything okay?" he finally asked, concern in his voice.

"That's the problem. I'm not sure if everything *is* okay."

"Yvette, I'm confused," Ajani said, sounding confident again. "I thought we enjoyed each other's company the last time we were together."

"We did. I enjoyed being with you very much, Ajani, but that's what I'm having issues with. What we're doing, what we're getting ourselves into is dangerous. I'm afraid that it's going to get out of hand."

"Yvette, I think you're putting too much thought into this. Just come over. We'll watch a movie, talk, whatever. I promise I'll keep my hands and my lips to myself."

"I can't. It's not right, Ajani." The battle between Terrence and Ajani—old standby versus fresh meat—was raging violently inside my heart, causing me to hesitate before continuing. "I think we need to put a little distance between the two of us."

"And what does that mean?"

"It means that I'll call you when I'm ready—if I'm ever ready."

"If you're ever ready?" Ajani asked, sounding completely thrown. "This is silly, Yvette. Okay, I get the fact that you don't want to come by my place, but this over-the-phone stuff just isn't working. There's a Starbucks near Vanderbilt University. Can you meet me there in twenty minutes? I want to hear what you have to say, but not over the phone."

I heard the urgency in Ajani's voice, and some of my resolve melted instantly. I was supposed to be concerned about the age difference between us, but *I* was the one behaving like a silly schoolgirl. "Okay, Ajani, but I can't stay long."

"Fifteen minutes is all I need," he said me before hanging up.

Navigating the streets of Nashville, my mind stayed fixed on Ajani, wondering what he would be wearing, what he would smell like, and whether our lips and tongues would meet again.

I saw him through the window of the coffee shop before I found a parking space in the crowded lot. He sat at a small table near the window, a baseball cap pulled low over his eyes.

"It took me a few minutes to find a parking spot," I said.

Ajani looked up from his *Slam* magazine and smiled slightly. "I'm glad you decided to show up."

"I can only stay for a little while. I have to go to work in the morning." I sat down and pulled my chair closer to the table. The place was pretty much empty, with only three or four people sitting in overstuffed armchairs sipping coffee, typing furiously on laptop computers or reading wrinkled newspapers.

"Now what's going on with you, Yvette? I understand that you're engaged and you're thirty-four, but none of that seemed to matter a couple of days ago," Ajani began, getting to the point.

"Ajani, things between us are moving very quickly, and they honestly shouldn't be moving at all."

"You shouldn't fight what feels right, Yvette. Make yourself happy; do what makes *you* feel good."

Looking at him from across the table, his cologne caressing my senses and making me senseless, I imagined *him* making me feel good over and over again. I had to shake my head several times to rid myself of the erotic fantasy.

"Yvette, what's the real reason you want to cut me out of your life? Is it that you won't admit that there's something between us?"

"If we had met years ago, before I met Terrence and if you were just a little older . . ."

"You can't turn back time, and I'm never going to be your age. We need to concentrate on the here and now, and you need to give us a chance." Ajani spoke with such conviction and determination that I almost let myself go there with him. Almost.

"What is it that you want from me? I can't just call Terrence and tell him that we're not getting married because I've kissed a college student. We've been alone together twice, Ajani, aside from your observation sessions. I can't leave someone I've spent twelve years with on a whim."

"Nobody is asking you to leave him. What I *am* asking you to do is explore the possibility of you and me."

"So cheat on him?" I asked, wanting to clarify his last comment.

"If necessary."

We looked at each other. His eyes bore into my soul, and it was impossible to hide from them. I wanted Ajani more than I'd ever wanted any man, but I knew the potential for trouble that could bring.

"Come back to my apartment with me." His voice gave me chills.

"I can't. Just give me some time, some space to sort out my thoughts . . ."

"How much time, Yvette?" Ajani asked, impatience evident in his voice.

"I'm not sure. Everything is happening so fast, and right now I just don't which way is up." My nervous laughter filled the coffee shop. "So no more flowers, okay? Or little notes. I just need some breathing room."

"Yvette, I'm not going to beg you. If what we have is meant to be, then you'll be back." Ajani leaned back in his chair and opened his magazine. The conversation was obviously over.

"Ajani, I've got to go," I whispered, standing up and grabbing my purse from the table.

He rose immediately and tucked his magazine under his arm. "At least let me walk you to your car," he said, holding the door for me and guiding me out with his hand on the small of my back.

"I guess I'll see you during my last observation then," he said when we reached my car. It was obvious that he was telling me in so many words that there was no way he was going to give up so easily. The intensity of his stare caused me to drop my car keys on the pavement.

Ajani, always the gentleman, bent down to retrieve the keys. On his way up, he placed both hands on my car, trapping me in between. He was so close I could feel the electricity of our attraction jump from him to me. He slowly removed his left hand from the car and placed it low on my hip, sending tremors through my body.

"Yvette, you know it's not over between us, don't you?" he whispered, his mouth dangerously close to my skin.

"I'm taken, Ajani."

"I don't care, and deep down, neither do you." He used his other hand to pull me close, so close that I felt his heart beating.

"I want you to let me go home," I responded weakly, attempting to block out the feeling I'd be giving up what really made me happy if I let Ajani go.

With a soft, seductive nibble on my earlobe, Ajani backed away silently. A faint smile graced his face as he handed the keys over and walked away.

I drove home as if my life depended on it. Taking deep breaths along the way, I tried to suppress my growing sense of regret for turning around and not going after what I wanted. After explaining to Ajani that I needed things to cool off between us, I thought I would feel relieved. Instead, I wanted to call him back and tell him how strong my feelings for him were becoming. Since the night Ajani and I kissed, I'd been caught in a mind-numbing place between extreme guilt and suffocating desire. And with what just happened in the parking lot, desire seemed to be winning out. I could still feel his touch; hear his whispered words in my ear. If I didn't regain control of my hormones immediately, I knew without a doubt that I was going to end up drowning.

Ajani

I wanted to tell her what I felt. I wanted to say that she was the most amazing woman I had ever known, but even to me my feelings seemed a bit premature. I followed her lead and pretended that this distance she wanted didn't faze me, because I knew—we both knew—that it wouldn't last long.

After arriving at my apartment, I sat in silence on my black leather couch for hours. I looked around the room at the flowers, candles, and the champagne—all in anticipation of Yvette's visit, and I became angry and hurt all at the same time. A month ago, I would not have gone to all this trouble for a woman, but Yvette Brooks did something to me I couldn't explain. She made me want to settle down, take care of her, have a house, picket fence and a couple of kids . . . the whole nine yards. It was scary realizing that I was losing control of both my heart and my head faster than I wanted to.

"Dakari, I need to talk to you," I said quietly into the phone, trying to disguise my hurt and anxiety over Yvette's rejection.

"Not at one o'clock in the morning you don't. Call me back around noon, Ajani."

"It's important. Yvette was supposed to come over here after her flight got in, but she called and told me she couldn't come. Then we met at a neutral place, and she goes into this big thing."

"Why? Did she give you a reason?" Dakari asked, yawning loudly into the phone.

"Some bullshit about needing to put some space between the two of us."

"Oohh . . . Are you over there getting a little too serious about her?" he laughed, sounding slightly more awake. "Could it be that Ajani Riley is letting a woman get the best of him?"

"No, I'm not mistreating her if that's what you mean. That's not what I'm about," I said, looking at the chocolate-covered strawberries on the coffee table.

"Since when?"

"Since I met her. She's not like the rest of the women I've dated, Dakari."

"You're right. She's old and engaged."

"I'm serious. I like her. I more than like her, and I'm not trying to fuck this up."

"Ajani, you're living in a fantasy. There is nothing to fuck up, because the two of you don't have a relationship."

"She likes me, too, why else would she say she needed to put some distance between us?"

"That's just a nice way of telling your ugly ass to beat it." Dakari laughed loudly at his own attempt at humor.

"She wants me, and it's driving her crazy." Maybe all hope wasn't lost; I just needed to figure out how to turn things around.

"In my opinion, you're going to end up getting your heart broken," Dakari warned. "I think you should call that chick Lisa and let her take your mind off 'Granny' Brooks."

"I don't know what possessed me to call your ignorant ass. Why don't *you* call Lisa? That bitch is crazy, anyway. Do you know she's been calling here ever since she ruined Yvette's jeans at that party? She showed up outside of my educational law class offering to suck my dick."

"Damn!" Dakari exclaimed jealously.

"I'll give her your number. I'm sure she'll be more than happy to do whatever you want."

"And what are you going to do about Yvette?"

"I'm going to give her all the space she wants, but it won't last very long. We have a connection; there's no denying that."

Wendy

17

I rolled over and grabbed my cellphone from the nightstand and pushed the silent button before it could ring again. "Hello?" I said, grogginess in my normally smooth and silky voice.

"Wendy, I think I just made a huge mistake," Yvette whined into the phone. My alarm clock showed I only had forty minutes to sleep before I had to start getting ready for work. Yvette's little crisis would have to wait.

"I'm sure whatever you've done isn't that bad. Call me tomorrow. I get off at noon," I whispered, feeling the figure next to me stirring.

"I have to talk to someone, and calling Terrence is out of the question. Wendy, my life is falling apart."

"Is this about him?" I asked, referring to her little boy toy back in Nashville. This conversation may prove to be worth losing a few minutes of sleep.

"Yes, and . . ."

"What happened? Did you go over there?"

"I couldn't. I had planned to but the closer I got to Nashville, the more the guilt began to eat away at me. I couldn't stop thinking about Terrence and what he would do if he ever found out about Ajani. I mean, if I had sex with someone other than Terrence, I wouldn't be any better than he is."

"But what about the lunch at Floods? Did you ask him about that?" I got out of the bed and tiptoed into the bathroom. I was hoping Yvette wasn't losing interest in her college guy. All I needed was for her to come to her senses and move back to Detroit. My hard work in and out of the bedroom would be wasted. Terrence and I had been practically living together since our laundry-room romp, sex day in and day out, but I needed more time and I needed Yvette to continue seeing Ajani.

"I don't want to ask him until I have more proof. Nothing makes Terrence angrier than being accused of something that he's not doing. But I didn't call to talk about him. I called to talk about Ajani. Wendy, this is serious. I'm falling for him, and I don't know what to do about it."

"You need to follow your heart. If it makes you happy, then go for it."

"Well, you've had a change of heart since last night. When we were at my apartment, you were totally against me seeing Ajani without breaking things off with Terrence first."

"I've had the chance to think about it, and I've decided that you only live once and true happiness doesn't come around often. I want you to live the life you want, but I still think you should break things off with Terrence before things get out of hand," I urged, not only for Yvette's benefit but my own as well.

"What can a twenty-one year old do for me? I want to live well, have kids, a house. Ajani is still a child; he can't give me an adult life."

"He can vote and buy liquor, so that makes him an adult. Stop stressing over everything; get over there and let that young man fuck your brains out. It sounds to me like you need some, anyway."

"Wendy, stop being so crass. I told Ajani that I needed to put some space between the two of us, but after I said it, I immediately wanted to take it back. I'm talking about my life here, my future! I want to know what I should do."

"Yvette, I can't make your decisions for you. I gave you my honest opinion, but that's the best I can do. Everything else is up to you." We hung up a few minutes later.

"Was that your boy Alonzo on the phone?" Terrence asked as I climbed back into bed and snuggled up next to his warm body. "Trying to get in a little phone bone before dawn?"

"As a matter of fact, it was Yvette, and why do you keep bringing up Alonzo? I told you he's just a friend. I had to bring a decoy to dinner so Yvette wouldn't get suspicious. It would be totally out of character for me to come to a party without an escort. I am Wendy Web, after all," I joked, allowing my hand to rest comfortably on his manhood.

"Why is Yvette calling you this early in the morning? Is she okay?" his voice turned from quiet with sleep to loud, worried and frantic in the blink of an eye.

"She's fine, Terrence. Would you calm down? She's having some job issues, and we always discuss things with each other, no matter what time of day it is." I removed my hand from his body and rolled over, my back to him. It seemed no matter how hard I tried there was no breaking the bond that Yvette and Terrence shared.

"Don't be mad, baby," Terrence said, drawing my body closer to his. He grabbed me around the waist and thrust his midsection against me. I felt him stiffen and hot, sticky moisture seeped from my body immediately.

"I just wish that when we're together, it was really just *us*. It feels like Yvette is always here, watching, listening, and you like it that way."

"Wendy, you always have my undivided attention. You know that. I can't worry about Yvette. She's hundreds of miles away all alone and . . ."

"Well, you'd be surprised how much company she has down in Nashville," I blurted out before I could stop myself.

"What the hell is that supposed to mean? Who's keeping Yvette company? She doesn't have any friends or family down there."

"Nobody, Terrence. Forget it! I was just trying to make you mad," I said, hoping that dismissing my comment as one as coming from a bitter, jealous woman would be enough to get him to forget what I'd just said.

"Is she cheating on me?" his voice was quiet, not loud and angry as it had been moments before. "She's seeing someone, isn't she?" Pain filled his eyes and sickened me.

"Terrence, don't you think I would tell you if she was seeing some other guy? The last thing I would do is keep something like that from you," I lied, guiding his hands up and down my body. I needed to get his mind off Yvette, and an early-morning quickie always did the trick.

Terrence

I didn't believe Wendy when she told me that Yvette wasn't seeing anyone. Something in her voice told me that Yvette was down in Nashville being just as "faithful" as I was in Detroit, and that was a problem, considering I've been having mind-blowing sex with her best friend night after night.

Every morning I woke up with Wendy lying naked next to me, I would promise myself that it would be the last time. I didn't want to hurt Yvette, but I just couldn't let Wendy go. In the few weeks that we'd been seeing each other, she'd made me feel like more of a man than Yvette ever had. When we weren't together I felt myself thinking about her, wishing that she was around, wishing that I was inside her. Things were getting crazy, and I needed a way out.

After that stressful conversation with Wendy, I booked myself a plane ticket and planned a little surprise visit to Nashville. I needed to see for myself what was going on with my fiancée. I wanted to catch her before she caught me.

"Hi, my name is Dr. Terrence Hall, and I'm here to see Yvette Brooks," I told the sexy little thing behind the desk at Nashville Prep. She was tiny, and as she smiled at me, I imagined throwing her on top of the office counter and having my way with her.

It's official, I have a serious problem. Maybe I should look up that doctor who treated Eric Benet for his sex addiction, I thought to myself as cutie pie leaned over, giving me a nice full helping of supple brown breast down her shirt.

"Oh, you must be Ms. Brooks' fiancé. My name is Jordan; it's a pleasure to finally meet you. Ms. Brooks talks about you all the time."

"It's very nice to meet you as well, Jordan. Is Yvette here?"

"Um . . ." Jordan began, a nervous look replacing her bright smile. "She is here but she's in a meeting right now. You see, an honor student from Tennessee State observes her as apart of his course work. He's in there with her right now—"

"He?" I asked, my eyebrows rising involuntarily.

"Yes, it's part of his pre-teaching requirement. I'm sure she'll be finishing up shortly. I'll go in and tell her that you're here."

I watched as Jordan hurried from behind the tall counter to an office door. "Jordan, I would love to surprise her," I said, rushing to the door, my hand reaching the knob before hers. "I'm sure she won't mind." I knocked once and pushed open the door before Jordan had another opportunity to object. I wanted to see what was going on for myself.

Yvette

18

"I need you to fill this out for my class," Ajani said, standing in my office after his final observation. It was a week and a half after our good-bye at Starbucks and we hadn't spoken since that night. Ajani and I had succeeded in maintaining our professionalism for the entire time he'd been at the school. But as he followed me into my office and the door snapped shut behind us, I became nervous.

"What is it?" I asked. He handed me the green form and our fingers touched. I felt a familiar tingle.

"You have to score me. Did I come on time, was I dressed appropriately. Things like that." His tone was dry and unfamiliar, as if we were strangers.

"You did an excellent job and I enjoyed having you here," I said in a low voice. Looking into his eyes, I searched for some sign that he was still interested in me. I didn't want him to stay, but I didn't want him to leave, either.

"You can just sign right there, Ms. Brooks," Ajani said, pointing to the signature line, "and I'll be on my way."

He stood before me, his arms crossed over his chest and his face expressionless. The smile I had come to expect was missing.

"Ajani, what are you doing?" I asked, pushing the form to the side and giving him a slight smile.

"I'm giving you space. Isn't that what you wanted?"

"I did. I mean, I do but I didn't think it would be like this. You barely spoke to me the entire time you were here."

"And what did you want me to say, Ms. Brooks? I've said and done all I can; the rest is up to you."

"Stop calling me Ms. Brooks, Ajani, it sounds ridiculous."

"Okay, what would you prefer I call you?" he asked sarcastically.

"Yvette. I want you to call me Yvette, and I don't want to argue."

"We're not arguing."

"How have you been?" I sat down behind my desk and motioned for Ajani to sit opposite me.

"Okay. Busy with school, and the frat, mentoring at the Boys and Girls Club. I visited my family in Memphis a couple of days ago," Ajani answered, softening a little, although he remained standing by the door.

I took a deep breath and folded my hands in my lap. "I've missed you Ajani. I didn't think that I would but I do . . ."

"Yvette, you already know that I don't want things to end. Besides telling you that, I have nothing else to say."

"This is crazy, I can't stop thinking about you and—" I was cut off mid-confession by a knock at the door and a commotion outside.

"Surprise!" Terrence said, walking into my office and slamming the door in Jordan's face. I stared at my fiancé in total shock. I looked from Terrence to Ajani and back again. My heart began beating fast and my palms practically dripped sweat. My fiancé and Ajani in the same room, face to face. This was not going to turn out well.

"Terrence, what are you doing here?" I asked trying to appear cool and collected while I prayed silently that my face didn't betray the guilt I was feeling.

"I wanted to see you. I missed you, baby."

Ajani stared at Terrence with loathing, disgust and jealousy written all over his handsome face.

"I'm working, Terrence."

"I know, I know. And your secretary made that perfectly clear, but I just couldn't wait. I had to see you," Terrence explained and then turned to look at Ajani. "I'm Dr. Terrence Hall, Yvette's fiancé. And you are?" He spoke in a condescending tone I barely recognized.

Ajani looked at me before he spoke, as if trying to read me. His eyes bore into mine, and I knew he would do everything in his power to make me feel as comfortable as possible in this very uncomfortable situation.

"My name is Ajani Riley, and I was just leaving."

"Ajani has been assigned to this school for one of his teaching methods courses. He's been following me around for about a month, and I've been trying to keep him entertained," I said, a nervous laugh escaping my lips.

"Not too entertained, I hope," Terrence responded, looking Ajani up and down as if readying for a fight.

"Terrence! What is that supposed to mean?"

"Nothing, nothing. Just making a little joke, that's all. It was nice to meet you, young man."

"Yeah, sure," Ajani said, looking at Terrence with hatred before turning back to me. "Thank you, Ms. Brooks, for *everything*," he emphasized seductively, obviously intending to rile Terrence. "I'm sure we'll see each other again soon." Ajani winked before turning the knob and walking out.

"What the hell was that about?" Terrence demanded after the door closed and the office grew quiet.

It took a tremendous effort to hold back the smile that tugged at the corners of my mouth after Ajani's departure. His subtle wink let me know that he knew I was about to tell him something important before Terrence interrupted.

"What are you talking about?" I asked, walking behind my desk and slopping down in my chair.

"That asshole winked at you!"

"He did not. Stop being ridiculous."

"Oh, yes, he did. 'Thanks for everything. I'm sure we'll see each other again soon,' " Terrence mocked, making a sad attempt to match the bass in Ajani's voice.

"What's the matter? Are you jealous of a twenty-one-year-old?" I asked, eyeing him.

"I don't know what you're down here in Nashville doing, and with the icy reception you've given me so far, I can't help but wonder."

"Look, Terrence, I just don't like being interrupted at work. You barging in here makes me look unprofessional.

Suppose I had been meeting with the principal, or even worse, a parent? Are you trying to cause me to lose my job?"

"Lucky for both of us you were only meeting with a college student then," Terrence said, coming over to me and pulling me into a standing position.

His lips met mine and I felt nothing. Not a spark, not even a flicker. As Terrence's hands moved up and down my back, my mind wandered to all the work still piled high on my desk, what I would be eating for dinner and finally, predictably, to Ajani.

Ajani

19

Two days after I ran into Yvette's fiancé, I sat across from my father and said, "I need a favor."

He folded his newspaper and looked at me. Asking my father for a favor of any kind was like pulling teeth, and I was certain that this time would be no different.

"What do you need this time, Ajani? A kidney? A million dollars? What can I help you with today?" my father said sarcastically, giving me his undivided attention.

"I'm looking to get away next weekend, and I was wondering if you had any plans for the Gorham's Bluff house?"

Three years ago, my father came home with a brochure and a huge smile on his face. He showed my brothers and me a beautiful, three-story yellow-and-white house that was situated on the bluff of the Tennessee River Valley in Alabama. It had three bedrooms, three bathrooms with Jacuzzi tubs and a gorgeous view. My father bought the house from an older couple, expecting to use it to entertain clients and the occasional overnight female guest. Instead, the place had become more of a love shack for Dakari and Jabari. I had never invited a woman there; I always considered it too romantic to take someone for just a quick bone. No woman I'd ever known had been special enough—until now.

"No, can't say that I do, but that doesn't mean that I'm giving you the keys, especially without knowing why you want to go down there." My father opened the newspaper again and hid his face from view. It was as if he got a high from making my life difficult.

"I don't know if you know, but I met someone—"

"Of course I know, Ajani. I know everything that happens with my sons, even if they refuse to confide in me themselves. I'm just wondering why I haven't met this young woman yet. Dakari and Jabari tell me that you consider her to be very special."

"What else have they told you?" I asked, wanting to know if Yvette's age or engagement had been discussed as well.

"Not much. It seems that no one has met her. Why are you hiding her, Ajani?"

"I'm not hiding anyone. Things between Yvette and me are complicated. She asked for some space, but . . ."

"So your idea of space is inviting her to the most romantic spot in the South? Are you really respecting her wishes, son?"

"As I just said, it's complicated. I want her and she wants me, but there are issues in the way," I attempted to explain without going into too much detail.

"Issues such as?" my father prodded. He had a way of pulling all kinds of information out of a person; it must be the lawyer in him.

I sighed loudly, knowing that I would never be able to leave his office without telling him everything he wanted to know. "She's a little older than me."

"How much older?" He placed his newspaper back on the desk, finally seeming interested.

"Thirteen years."

My father's eyes widened, but his demeanor remained cool as a cucumber. "Is that all?"

"She's engaged to a doctor. She's supposed to be getting married in a few months."

"Ajani, what's wrong with you?"

I looked at him as if there was something wrong with *him*. "What?"

"Is there something I did wrong when you were growing up? Why do you insist on doing things ass-backward? Getting involved with a woman like that will cause you nothing but trouble."

"I didn't come in here for a lecture. I'm a grown man and I can decide whom I become involved with." I could feel my anger rising.

"But a thirty-four-year-old engaged woman, Ajani? What do you expect to gain from this relationship? Are you just seeing her for a good time?"

"She makes me happy, okay?" I said, feeling silly revealing something so personal to my overly macho father. "I want to be with her."

"Do you honestly think she's going to leave her fiancé for a twenty-one-year-old undergraduate student who can't even pay his own rent without reaching into his father's pockets once a month?" he asked skeptically.

"I really don't know what's going to happen with all this, but I think she's the one and I just can't let her go, not yet."

My father stared at me for a long time, silently evaluating everything I'd just told him. "I worry about you, Ajani; you're reckless. You remind me so much of your mother, following your heart and not your head," he said finally, smiling at me slightly.

"I don't know what to do, but I can't stop now. My heart is too into what I've started."

"I hope you know what you're doing, Ajani," my father said, taking the keys from his desk and handing them to me.

It took a couple of hours to drive from Memphis back to Nashville, and in that time I considered the possibility that I may have gone to all this trouble for nothing. What if Yvette wouldn't agree to spend the weekend with me?

I felt like a stalker waiting outside Yvette's school for her to leave for the day, but when I saw her exit the side door and walk toward her car, hair blowing in the wind, I couldn't stop smiling.

"Is he gone?" I asked, pulling up to her as she was unlocking her car door.

"Don't scare me like that!" she said, holding her hand to her heart. "I thought I was about to be robbed or something. You're lucky I didn't have a chance to pull out my mace."

"This is Nashville, girl, not Detroit. Nobody around here is thinking about robbing you. Now, as I asked before, is he gone?"

"Yes, Terrence is gone."

"Out of your life?" I asked hopefully.

"Out of Nashville, Ajani. What are you doing here?"

"I needed to talk to you, to ask you something, and I didn't want to risk running into the good doctor. I may have to lay him out next time."

"Well, what's the question?" The way she smiled made me weak.

"Can you get in with me? It's cold out here, and I want to roll up my windows."

Yvette looked around before walking over to the passenger side of the car and sliding in next to me.

"Looking for someone?" I asked, moving several wisps of hair behind her ear.

"Just wanted to make sure the principal, Ms. Fisher, wasn't out here spying on me. I think that woman works for the FBI or something."

"Looks like the coast is clear," I said, sliding my hand into hers. "How have you been?"

"Okay, I guess. I'm kind of tired, though. The job is starting to get to me, and these wedding preparations are driving me crazy . . ." she stopped, no doubt correctly guessing that her upcoming nuptials were the last thing I wanted to chat about.

"I miss you, Yvette," I said, touching her cold cheek.

"I miss you, too, Ajani but I told you that last week."

"So have you had enough space yet, or should I give you a couple more months?"

"Is that really what you came to ask me?"

"No, not exactly. I wanted to know if you're available for a little getaway."

Yvette hesitated before answering, but I knew her interest had been piqued. "Where would we be getting away to?"

"Alabama. Fresh country air might do you some good. Give you clarity."

"Ajani, I am not a girl who camps," she said, looking mortified, as if the idea of fishing and sleeping outside was unthinkable.

"I'm not talking about camping. We would have all the amenities—kitchen, television, Jacuzzi tub . . ."

"Sleeping arrangements?"

"Three bedrooms. You can pick your favorite, and I'll sleep elsewhere."

"I don't know, Ajani."

"Yes, you do. When's the last time Terrence has taken you anywhere?" I asked. She looked at me, and I knew I had her.

"I'll leave work early. Pick me up Friday at noon."

Terrence

20

I couldn't help but stare at Wendy. Her low-cut, tight-fitting plum-colored halter begged for attention. She was gorgeous; I had to give her that. The way her caramel skin glistened, silky hair kissed her shoulders and sweet tongue wet her pouty lips, I wanted to forgo dinner and take her back to my place to do what we did best. Unfortunately, that wasn't an option.

This dinner had been Wendy's idea, and after much poking and prodding, I grudgingly agreed. In my opinion, she just wanted us to play house while Yvette was away, pretending that we had a real relationship, that we were more than bed buddies.

Lately, she'd been acting jealous and clingy. She wanted to come first; she very obviously wanted to take Yvette's place, and it was beginning to unnerve me. But with the threat of not having my piece of lovin' on the side, I decided to quiet her concerns and made reservations for dinner.

An hour and a half ago, I greeted Wendy at her apartment door dressed in a suit and tie and cradling a dozen roses in my arm. I smiled at her reaction and had been smiling ever since until, in the middle of dinner, she began dropping hints that she knew where I was last weekend. With all the "I talked to Yvette today" crap, it was obvious that she knew something and wasn't all that happy about it.

I didn't want to lie to her, but I didn't want to be honest, either, especially with the way she'd been acting lately. My going to Nashville and lying about it may have been the straw that broke the camel's back, perhaps causing Wendy to let our little rendezvous "slip" during one of her long-distance conversations with Yvette. And I couldn't have that, now, could I?

Wendy

I sat across from Terrence, trying to contain my anger. Nearly a week had passed since he had come back from Nashville, and he still hadn't said a word about his trip. As a matter of fact, he probably thought I didn't have a clue about his little surprise visit to Yvette.

"Wendy, what's the problem?" Terrence asked, looking irritated.

I looked at him as I sipped my red wine. Things had been going so well between us, and I couldn't decide whether to ruin what was supposed to be a romantic evening out.

"I'm just wondering if you are ever going to mention your trip to Nashville last weekend. Because if I'm not mistaken, you told me you were on call Friday through Sunday."

Terrence placed the linen napkin in his lap and picked up a fork before answering me, most likely trying to come up with a plausible excuse as to why he had lied to my face. "Yes, I did visit Nashville last weekend, and yes, I did mislead you, but for a good reason."

I folded my arms across my chest, ready to hear his "good" reason.

"I didn't want you to become upset or think that my visiting Yvette would negatively affect what we have," he explained, stuffing a heaping forkful of eggplant into his mouth.

"Oh, so you thought it would be better to lie to my face?" I spat out angrily.

"If you want to be honest about it, Wendy, it's really none of your business where I go and whom I go there with. I'm engaged to Yvette, not you, remember?"

His harsh words cut me like a knife. I sat back in the leather chair and felt tears stinging my eyes. "Okay, Terrence, since you brought it up, what do I mean to you exactly?"

Terrence wiped his mouth carefully and looked me straight in the eye. "Wendy, I like you, I really do, but I'm getting ready to marry your best friend. We have fun together. Why can't we just leave it at that?" Terrence asked, reaching across the table and caressing my hand, attempting to soften the blow.

"So that's all I am? The good-time girl? I guess I'm only good for a romp in the sack when Yvette's away."

"Wendy, don't pull this shit with me. You knew exactly what you were getting yourself into. Now all of a sudden you want to be my one and only? You're crazy!"

"I don't expect to be your one and only, Terrence; I'm not that naïve. However, I do expect a certain level of respect from you, and your traipsing off to Nashville and lying about it is completely *dis*respectful." I began to feel dizzy with anger. The restaurant began to spin, and an intense heat overtook my body, causing me to feel light-headed. "And why did you just up and decide to run there, anyway? Did I do something that made you have to see Yvette?" My voice weakly floated across the table in just above a whisper. I gripped the sides of my chair to keep from sliding onto the floor.

"I went because I thought Yvette was cheating on me. I wanted to see what she was doing."

Taking a deep breath, I asked, "Did you find what you were looking for?"

"The only thing I found was some college guy in her office doing an observation. I think I was just being paranoid . . ." Terrence stopped suddenly and looked at me. "Wendy, are you okay?"

I tried to sit up in my seat, but slumping down seemed to be a lot easier. "I'm fine. I'm just having some kind of anxiety attack or something. Probably all the stress you're putting me through."

"Drink some water. You look like you're about to pass out."

I sipped the ice-cold water and felt my temperature drop slightly.

"Our relationship is not supposed to be stressful, Wendy."

"I know, I know. I'm fine, okay? Let's just finish dinner and then you can take me home."

"Are these attacks something you get often?" Terrence asked.

"Every once in a while. As I said before, it's stress-related." The truth was I've never had an anxiety attack, and although I had no idea what was happening to me, I was sure I wasn't having one now. But if Terrence could lie, then so could I.

Yvette

21

I was thoroughly surprised when Ajani invited me to spend the weekend with him. After the run-in between him and Terrence I knew our separation was over, but I had not expected Ajani to invite me on a romantic getaway. But once I agreed to go for three days and two nights there was no telling what could happen, so I decided to make a much-needed trip to Vickie's to update my lingerie wardrobe. Not that I was anticipating anything, but a girl could never be too prepared.

I was at Victoria's Secret in Green Hills Mall, surrounded by pink silk and black lace, when Ajani's ex-girlfriend, the little slut who ruined my jeans, sauntered in, the most evil smile I'd ever seen plastered on her face. She wore a pink TSU t-shirt that was three sizes too small and jeans that looked as if they'd been painted on.

"Well, well, well, what do we have here?" she said to her buck-toothed friend standing next to her. "Tisha, remember when I told you that Ajani began doing charity work for the old folks' home?"

Her friend snickered as Lisa pointed to me.

"Can you believe Ajani brought this sweet little old lady to a Q party? I'm surprised you were able to stay awake 'til the end," she said, finally looking at me. "It's so nice to see you again."

"I think you know all too well that I'm not some charity case," I retorted, narrowing my eyes in disgust.

"Well, if you don't mind my asking, what is your relationship with Ajani exactly?"

"What business is it of yours?" I looked at her, one hand on my hip, the other holding a sexy red-and-black corset.

"Ajani and I have a history, and I don't want anyone to think that this little separation we're going through will last very long," Lisa responded, smiling sweetly.

"I see. So what you're trying to tell me is that you and Ajani are just on a break?"

"Exactly! You're a quick learner, aren't you?" Lisa said, clapping her hands twice. Her friend followed suit.

"Look, I'm not sure why you're over here, but I have some shopping to do and I'm not one for engaging in childish games."

"I just want to make it clear that Ajani is not available. He's my man, I'm his woman and that's just the way it is." Lisa turned on her three-inch heels and strutted away.

Watching her walk away in her disgustingly tight getup, I wondered what Ajani had ever seen in her. "If you think that you and Ajani are still in some kind of relationship, I suggest you let him in on that little secret because he tells me otherwise."

I returned the corset to the rack and picked up a fuchsia baby doll before Lisa turned around, her cute face contorted in anger.

"So you are seeing him?" she asked with the hiss of a python. "Don't you think you're a little old to be dating a twenty-one-year-old?" Lisa's eyes zeroed in on my diamond engagement ring. "Did he give you that?" She pointed at the ring with a shaky index finger.

Smiling, I held up my left hand and admired the way the ring sparkled under the Victoria's Secret lights. "Wouldn't you like to know?"

The two-hour ride to Pisgah, Alabama, had been a virtually silent one. Ajani seemed to be deep in thought, and I held my tongue about my run-in with Lisa earlier that day. We only spoke to comment on a song from his extensive CD collection or to ask if everything was okay.

Groceries were stacked on top of our luggage; firewood scented the entire truck, and wine bottles clanked as we drove over bumpy roads. From the moment I slid into Ajani's Chevy Tahoe SUV I wasn't sure I had made the right decision to accompany him this weekend. Being alone with Ajani at his father's getaway retreat spelled trouble for me.

Finally, Ajani pulled off a rural road and into a community that was so beautiful and peaceful that it immediately made me forget all the stress that plagued me for the past few months. Each home, some cottages and others mansions, faced a sparkling river. The homes were in restful tones of white, tan, blue and yellow, each one surrounded by pine trees, their scent permeating the air.

Ajani pulled into the circular driveway of a large yellow-and-white three-story home.

"It's beautiful," I said, getting out and feeling the brisk fall wind whip my loose hair around my face.

"This house has everything," Ajani said, searching for his keys in his coat pocket. He went to the back of the car and opened the hatch, pulling out bags of groceries. "Full kitchen, three bedrooms, fireplace, deck and, of course, the view."

"This is really wonderful, Ajani," I said, reveling in the crisp, clean air as we walked to the front porch. "Thank you so much for bringing me here."

"I thought the atmosphere would be conducive to talking—putting all our feelings out on the table—and seeing where it takes us."

We spent the afternoon unpacking, eating lunch and just talking. We were completely at ease with each other; it was as though we lived together and were accustomed to all those things that define a couple, that make two people have an instinctive rapport that binds them together. I liked the feeling, relished it, and was glad that I had agreed to come.

I had fully intended to tell Ajani exactly how I felt about everything—him, us, our budding relationship. But the thought made me nervous, and I needed to be in complete control for that. I decided to concentrate on the present and leave any such discussions for the future.

The hours passed almost unnoticed, and before Ajani and I knew it, dinner dishes had been washed, the TV volume turned down low, and darkness had fallen over the bluff. An extremely romantic mood fell as we relaxed on the couch, sipping champagne and wrapped in a red cashmere blanket. "Let's go sit on the deck," Ajani suggested, pulling my body close under the softness and warmth of the blanket.

"Ajani, the deck is cold. Why don't we stay inside and build a fire?"

"We won't be cold; we'll keep each other warm," he promised, kissing my lips gently and leading me out to the deck. I sat on a comfortable chaise while he quickly built a fire in the stone fire pit. He then slipped under the blanket with me.

"See, this isn't so bad, is it?" Ajani asked, wrapping his arms around my waist and nestling his head between my neck and shoulders. "Are you cold?"

"No, Ajani, I'm fine," I whispered. I was better than fine; I was perfect lying there in Ajani's arms by a fire and feeling as if I was falling in love.

"You'll never guess who I ran into today," I said, pressing my body closer to his.

"Who?"

"Lisa."

Ajani groaned and shifted uncomfortably. "So how did that meeting go?"

"It went," I replied sarcastically. "She wanted to know if you and I are seeing each other. She told me that the two of you are still together."

"You know she was lying, right?" Ajani asked, looking into my eyes.

"Of course I know she was lying. But you do know she's not over you, don't you?"

"That's an understatement. What did you tell her about us?" he asked.

"I didn't tell her anything. What we do and what we are to each other is none of her business. She did see my ring, though, and she thinks that you gave it to me."

Ajani laughed. "I'm sure she's in her room right now plotting to destroy you. I'm telling you, that girl is crazy."

"Is that why you two aren't together anymore?"

"Pretty much. Lisa is fun, but that's about it. We had a good time, but when she got too possessive, I ended it. But enough about her," Ajani whispered, nibbling on my earlobe. "I'm so glad you're here. I really didn't think you would agree to come up with me, especially after your fiancé showed up last week."

"Since I've been in Nashville, Terrence and I have grown apart. My best friend told me that she saw him having a very cozy lunch with someone that was not me."

"So he's cheating on you again?" Ajani asked, holding me closer. In one of our very late-night conversations, I had confided in Ajani that Terrence had been unfaithful.

"I'm not sure. I haven't asked him about it. My friend asked me not to."

"It's not like I'm trying to help Terrence out or anything like that, but are you sure that your friend is being completely honest with you?"

"Of course she's being honest with me. Why would she lie? What would she have to gain from Terrence and me breaking up?" I said staunchly, feeling slightly offended.

"Maybe she wants your man. Why else would she ask you not to mention anything to Terrence? I've heard some crazy stories about women concocting all kinds of devious plans to get at their girlfriend. Just be careful, that's all I'm saying."

"She asked me not to say anything because she wasn't sure if there was anything going on. It could have been nothing more than an innocent lunch with a coworker. Wendy would never do that to me, Ajani," I said, shaking off the memory of Wendy refusing to talk to me for weeks when she found out Terrence and I had become an item in college.

"I'm sure she wouldn't, baby; I was just giving you some food for thought."

"I hope you didn't bring me up here to talk about Terrence and Wendy," I said reprovingly.

"Actually, I brought you here to talk about us."

"Oh, really?"

"Really. Yvette, my feelings for you are getting serious, and after the run-in with Terrence, I need to know where your head is."

"Ajani, I'm not at all sure I understand what you want from me. Where do you expect this thing between us to go?"

"Honestly? I would love for you to break off your engagement to Terrence and have all your stuff shipped from Detroit. Then we could move in together and you could give me lots of babies."

I laughed, forming a mental picture of his ideal arrangement. "No marriage? Just us in your one-bedroom apartment with seven kids?"

"Of course we would get married. What kind of man do you think my father raised?"

"So are you proposing to me?"

"That depends. Is Terrence still a permanent fixture in your life?"

I turned slightly and caressed Ajani's face. "I can't break up with Terrence," I said, regret in my voice. "He has the stability I need."

"Then I'm not proposing to you." He laughed slightly, pretending he was joking, but I knew he was quite serious.

"If you can't marry me, what will you settle for?" I asked. I couldn't give Ajani everything he wanted, but I couldn't let him go, either.

"At the very least, friends with benefits," Ajani answered.

"That's all we can ever be, Ajani. I really like you; more than like you, actually. But we're worlds apart, and anything more than 'friends with benefits' would never work between us." I don't know when it happened, but Ajani had taken over my emotions, and I was feeling things for him that I had never felt for another man. He was everything that Terrence wasn't: sweet, romantic, attentive and sympathetic. He was as close to perfect as a man could be.

"You more than like me? What does that mean?" I felt Ajani's hands beginning to roam where they had never been. Slowly but urgently, my body began to ache as Ajani's touch heightened my senses. "Is love anywhere in the equation?" he asked, reaching deeper underneath the blanket. His hands circled my waist and he quickly pulled my snug-fitting, long sleeved t-shirt over my head tossed it near the sliding glass door.

"I feel as if I'm getting to that point, and it's a little scary," I admitted, nearly out of breath. In the time Ajani and I had known each other, something more than lust had grown between us. In a perfect world, Ajani and I were meant for each other. In a way, he represented everything that I wanted to be—aggressive, confident, and rebellious. More important, he made me completely happy. Ajani produced a feeling in me that I had never known. When we were apart, I felt tortured. I needed him, and that was the scariest realization of all.

Ajani unbuttoned my jeans and looked into my eyes as if asking permission to remove them. I wordlessly took his face between my hands and kissed him, enjoying the feeling of my pants being slowly pushed down to my ankles, eventually landing in a heap on the deck.

"You can still turn back, Yvette. It's not too late."

I didn't want to turn back. At that moment, I wanted Ajani more than I had ever wanted anything or anyone, and I intended to have him. "From the moment we met, I knew there was no turning back."

After removing his clothes, Ajani sat back on the chaise as I stood over him, shivering in the darkness. "Are you okay?" he asked, reaching out and softly touching my thigh. I nodded and brought my body down upon his.

We melted together seamlessly—minds, bodies, hearts and souls rolling against one another like the ocean. The wind blew and the fire had burned to ash, but I felt nothing except Ajani's skin, his scent mingling with mine. He pushed my hair back from my face, and one hand found my bare back and the other my bottom as Ajani guided me, our rhythms becoming one.

"It's snowing," he said, as several flakes fell and melted on our hot flesh.

I held on to Ajani, feeling nothing but pleasure, pain and warmth. "There is no turning back, is there?" I asked, as he exploded inside me. The love I felt for him was undeniable; I never wanted to let him go.

"As you said before, Yvette," Ajani responded, after catching his breath, "there never was."

Wendy

22

"Ms. Web, we need you at the desk in five minutes," my assistant, Vivian, called through the bathroom door.

"I'll be there, Vivian, I just need a minute!" I responded angrily. I was sick of her giving me minute-by-minute airtime warnings. I had told her I was on my way, and that should have been enough.

I looked in the mirror and sighed. Dark circles had formed under my eyes in the past few days, and the look of exhaustion I carried around with me was very noticeable. Thank God for the station's makeup artist.

Taking a deep breath, I opened the door to the bathroom and slowly began walking down the cramped hallway to the well-lit news desk.

"You look beautiful," Vivian gushed as I slid into the seat next to Rick Forest and read over my stories for the morning. My head swam and the exact same feeling that had come over me at dinner with Terrence hit me again, only it was stronger. It felt as if the temperature had risen to one hundred degrees and my legs, arms and neck had turned to Jell-O.

"Are you okay, Wendy? Can I get you anything?" Rick asked, touching my hand with concern.

"No, you can't get her anything! We go live in thirty seconds," the producer yelled from his glass box above the stage.

I watched as the cameraman held up five fingers for the countdown. Four, three, two . . .

"Wendy? Wendy?" Vivian called, frantically fanning my face with a newspaper. "She's awake, everybody; she's okay!"

I slowly pulled my hand out of her grasp and rubbed the back of my head. I felt searing pain, so I closed my eyes and rested my head on the cold tiled floor. "What happened?" I wondered, not remembering anything except the countdown to air.

"You fainted just as we went live. Fell right out of your seat and onto the floor. Someone is bringing my car around, so I can take you to the emergency room." Vivian offered, helping me into a sitting position. My head was throbbing relentlessly.

"Viv, I do not need to go to the hospital. I need to get back into my chair. Who's covering for me?"

"Rick's doing the entire show by himself, and yes, you do need to see a doctor. I have never seen anyone faint like that. I thought you were having a heart attack. You should see the phone lines. People are calling to make sure you're still alive."

"Great," I said letting Vivian lead me out of the station and to her car. "Now viewers are going to think I'm strung out on something."

"No, no. Rick announced that you're suffering from exhaustion. Everyone who has called has been very sympathetic."

Vivian drove the few miles to Riverview Hospital in record time. When we arrived, I was greeted by a patient advocate, who explained that the station had called ahead. A room and doctor were waiting for me.

"Good morning, Ms. Web, I'm Dr. Thompson and we've been expecting you," a tall, hazelnut-colored doctor said, shaking my hand gently. "I was actually watching the news when you took your little spill . . . pretty nasty. Can you describe the symptoms you were experiencing before you fainted?"

"Dizziness. My body got really hot, and my limbs felt like Jell-O," I explained, attempting to remain poised while wearing the flimsy hospital gown.

"Is today the first time you've experienced these symptoms?" Dr. Thompson asked, making several notations on his clipboard.

"No, I felt the same way about a week ago at dinner with a friend, but today was much worse."

"And when was your last menstrual period?"

"What does that have to do with me passing out?" I asked, slightly annoyed.

"Ms. Web, when dealing with women, we always like to rule out pregnancy as soon as possible. That way, if you're really ill, we can run the proper tests."

"Well, Dr. Thompson, I am definitely not pregnant. As a matter of fact, I just had a period."

"Was this period normal?"

"Normal?"

"Was it like all your other periods? Was it the type you're used to?"

I took a deep breath and resisted the urge to ask for another doctor. "No, it wasn't, if you must know. I just had about three days of spotting, but it was a period nonetheless, and I know that pregnant woman do not have periods."

"No, most pregnant woman don't, but early on there can be some spotting. I think we should test your blood just to be sure."

With a roll of my eyes, I consented to the blood test. After Dr. Know-It-All realized that I wasn't pregnant, maybe he would get to the bottom of the real reason I couldn't stay conscious.

An hour, three packs of graham crackers and four tiny cartons of apple juice later, the doctor came back in with that stupid clipboard in hand.

"Well, Ms. Web, I have your test results here . . ." He sat on the swiveling stool and scooted closer to me.

"Am I dying or what?" I joked, hoping that wasn't the case.

"No. Actually, Ms. Web, you're not dying, you're pregnant."

I laughed loudly, slapping my hand on my thigh. "Very funny. I guess you've got jokes because I gave you such a hard time earlier. What's my real diagnosis, doctor?"

"Ms. Web, Wendy, I'm not joking. You are certainly pregnant. You had just enough HCG in your blood to test positive. I'm sure you're very early in your pregnancy."

"Just enough? No, sorry, I think you better run the test again, and when it comes back that I'm not pregnant, you better pray to God that I don't sue you for pain and suffering," I demanded loudly, even though I knew that my threat was completely ridiculous. But I didn't care. I did not find this man funny.

"I had the lab run the test three times because you were so adamant about not being pregnant. We can do a vaginal exam or an ultrasound if you like. The last thing I want is for you to bad-mouth me on the news because you think I made a mistake."

I sat with my head in my hands as the doctor prepared the ultrasound machine. This couldn't be happening. I never missed my pill, not once. Obviously, the doctor didn't know what he was talking about, and I couldn't wait to see the look on his face when the ultrasound showed that my uterus is just as empty as it was the day I was born.

"Okay, this may be a little cold," he said, squirting a glob of icy blue gel on my stomach before placing the ultrasound wand on my skin.

He moved it up and down, and just as I got ready to blurt out, "Ha, I told you I wasn't pregnant," he smiled and pointed at the screen.

"See, right there? That thing that looks like a small kidney bean, that's your baby."

Ajani

23

I told Yvette that we were having dinner in, sort of luring her to my apartment after work with promises of my fried chicken and spending the rest of the night in bed. It wasn't the complete truth, but it wasn't a complete lie, either. Fried chicken *was* on the menu and we *could* spend the night in bed after my father and brothers left.

Their visit had been planned since shortly after Yvette and I returned from the bluff. I called my brothers after dropping Yvette off at her apartment and told them that she was definitely the one for me.

"This chick has got your nose open!" Dakari had laughed into the phone. "I need to meet her!"

"I want you to meet her, but—"

"But, nothing. Me, Jabari and Dad will be there next weekend." And that was that. I'd tried to convince them otherwise, coming up with every plausible excuse I could think of, but nothing worked. Once my father and brothers decided on something, it was pretty much a done deal and nothing you could do or say would change a thing.

I had broached the subject of meeting my family with Yvette several times, and her response was always the same. "You take women to meet your family when you're serious about them, Ajani, and I thought we agreed that 'a friend with benefits' is not serious."

Yes, that is what we agreed, but I had other plans for our relationship and, therefore, having her meet my family was an excellent idea, at least in theory.

"She's late," my father said, checking his watch for the billionth time since he'd arrived. He sat on the sofa looking as if he had come straight from the office. Dakari and Jabari sat on either side of him, one in jeans and the other in khakis, but nonetheless looking like the same person split in two.

"Five minutes, Dad. Why don't you cut her some slack?" I said. A soft knock on the door erased the irritation from my face and replaced it with a smile. "She's here. Please try to be as nice as possible."

"Oh, she's a big girl. I'm sure she can handle anything we dish out," Jabari said, a devious smirk on his face.

"That's enough, Jabari," my father warned.

I went to the door and opened it slowly. I expected Yvette to be upset, maybe even furious, that I had misled her, but I hoped she would be happy that she finally met the members of my family.

"How was your day?" she asked seductively. She was wearing a knee-length black trench coat, parted low at the collar and revealing a red lacy bra. She wore candy-apple red stilettos and furry pink handcuffs dangled from one hand. "What's wrong, Ajani?" she asked, pouting slightly. "Don't you like what you see?" Yvette untied the belt and let the jacket fall completely open.

"Yvette, I have people here," I said under my breath, reaching out and pulling the jacket closed. Her body looked so good that I was sorry my brothers and father were waiting in the living room. She deserved an all-night marathon and that's exactly what she would get when they left—if she wasn't too angry with me.

"People? What are you talking about?" The lust on her face was immediately replaced with a look of horror and embarrassment as she looked over my shoulder and saw my brothers smiling at her from the sofa. Even my father was trying to conceal his amusement. "Oh, my God, is that your father?"

"It's okay, baby, I don't think they saw anything," I whispered, making sure that her belt was tied tightly around her waist.

"This is like some kind of nightmare," Yvette said, holding her head in her hands. "If you think I'm going in there now, you're crazy."

"You can change. You left some clothes over here last night. Why don't you just put those on?"

"Because I'll still have this supreme embarrassment hanging over my head," Yvette said, bowing her head in shame. "Your father saw me in my underwear; I do not want to sit and eat chicken with him now."

"Come on, babe, do this for me. Please." I pulled Yvette by her trench coat and kissed her lips softly.

She rolled her eyes and sighed loudly. "Okay, Ajani, but I'm not happy, and we will be discussing this later."

Then she gracefully walked past me and into the living room. The embarrassment she claimed was not evident on her face. Yvette held her head high and smiled politely at Dakari, Jabari and my father. "I'll just be a couple of seconds," she said, quickly walking past them and into my bedroom.

"She's going to change," I explained, sitting in the leather chair next to the sofa.

"She doesn't have to go and put on anything for us," Jabari said, leaning across my father and giving his twin a pound.

"I didn't know women that age had bodies like that!" Dakari said. "No wonder you're so gone over her."

"Don't be disrespectful," my father said, glaring at my brother. "Show some class."

"She's embarrassed enough without the two of you acting like twelve-year-olds and going on and on about her impromptu striptease. Let's all pretend that didn't happen, okay?"

"It's certainly a surprise meeting all of you this evening," Yvette said, reentering the living room dressed in a mint-green wraparound sweater and boot-legged jeans. "I apologize for what happened a moment ago," she said, using her assistant principal tone. "I'm sure our introduction would have been less embarrassing had I been told that you were visiting." Yvette shot a look at me so fierce that I knew for sure I wasn't going to get the chance to make anything up to her tonight.

"No problem, no problem," my father said, before standing up and shaking Yvette's hand. "It's a pleasure to meet you, Yvette. My sons and I have heard so much about you."

"I've heard a lot about you, too, Mr. Riley."

"Mr. Riley is a bit formal, Yvette. I mean, there isn't that much age difference between us; why don't you just call me Anthony?"

His sly dig regarding Yvette's age wasn't lost on me. "She's thirty-four, not forty-four. That's a big difference," I said, coming up behind her and putting my hand on her waist.

"When you're our age, son, all the decades just sort of roll into one, don't they, Yvette?" my father laughed jovially.

"Dad, I don't think Yvette looks a day over twenty, right Jabari?" Dakari asked, looking Yvette up and down.

"Not a day. Actually, I was wondering if you had a sister?" Jabari asked, gazing into Yvette's face. "Maybe we could go out on a double date or something."

"No sisters. I'm an only child," Yvette responded, shifting her weight from one foot to the other uncomfortably.

"And what do your parents do?" my father asked.

Yvette's discomfort was palable, but she retained her poise. "I was raised by my grandmother."

"Your parents passed away then?"

"My mother is a recovering drug addict, Mr. Riley. When I was growing up, she was unable to care for me, so my grandmother obtained legal custody of me." Yvette looked him straight in the eyes, silently daring him to ask any more questions about her family. He didn't.

"I think we should eat," I said, taking her hand and leading her over to the table. Platters of fried chicken, yams, macaroni and cheese, and collard greens were piled high, with a huge pitcher of sweet tea in the middle. "Don't you guys have to leave soon?"

"No, we don't have anything to do, and why are you trying to rush us out of here, Ajani? I would really like the opportunity to get to know Yvette a little better," my father said, sitting next to me and smiling as if he were glued to the chair and wouldn't be getting up anytime soon.

We ate in silence, with Jabari and Dakari leering at Yvette, my father staring at the two of us curiously, and Yvette's foot tapping nervously under the table.

"So, Yvette, Ajani tells us that you're engaged. When's the big day?" my father asked, breaking the silence. The twins snickered over heaping plates of food.

"Um, in about two months, actually," Yvette answered, pushing a forkful of greens into her mouth.

"Now, does your fiancé know that you're seeing my son?"

"That's none of your business," I said, feeling myself become both angry and defensive.

"Of course it's my business. She's seeing you, but she's engaged. Ajani, from what I understand, your feelings for her go way beyond some weekend booty call. I just want to know what *her* intentions are." He smiled, but his words were vicious. It was obvious that attacking Yvette had been his plan all along.

"I'm not sixteen, Dad." I pushed back from the table and stood up.

"No, you're not, Ajani, but right now, with this situation you've gotten yourself into, you're acting like it. This woman sitting across from me that you claim to be falling in love with is getting married in two months, Ajani. Two months! Yvette," my father continued, looking at Yvette with sincerity, "I'm sure you're a very nice, intelligent, and obviously beautiful woman, but you're not right for my son, and I would appreciate it if you, as the more mature adult in this situation, put an end to it."

"If you wanted Yvette out of my life, then why would you give me the keys to the Gorham's Bluff house so I could spend time with her? It's like you want me to believe that you care, but in reality, you want everyone to be as alone and unhappy as you have been!"

"Mr. Riley, Anthony, Ajani is a grown man and we have an understanding. I have never lied to Ajani or misled him in any way," Yvette interrupted, obviously trying to defuse a potentially explosive situation.

"Yvette, he is thirteen years younger than you. His heart is in this . . ."

"My heart is in this, too. I hope you don't think I planned this. Do you think I wanted to fall in love with a college student when I'm only months away from getting married?" Yvette sat back in her chair and covered her hand with her mouth, no doubt realizing she just admitted to loving me. She had never said it before.

Yvette

I knew Ajani was embarrassed by his family's behavior at dinner, specifically his father's outburst. The way he sat in silence eating his chicken and not looking up from his plate, I could tell that he was furious. I was completely horrified that our time together had gone so badly. The fact that I'd admitted to being in love with Ajani was a mistake of epic proportions, but I couldn't take it back because it was the truth.

After his father and brothers left, no words were spoken between us. Ajani closed the door behind his family and took me into his arms, hastily removing my clothing, his eyes never leaving mine. We silently decided to work out all of our hurt, anger, embarrassment and uncertainty in the bedroom.

My tongue found his as Ajani carried me into the dark room. He placed me on the bed and kneeled down on the carpeted floor, slowly placing his head between my legs and finding my pearl instantly. I could no longer maintain the silence that floated between us as Ajani kissed and sucked, swallowing my juices to quench his thirst. I moaned loudly, twisting and turning, tangling myself in the navy-blue sheets. Ajani drank my explosion before removing his clothes and placing a condom on his erection.

All the negative things we felt disappeared as Ajani's strong body melted into mine. His hands touched every part of me, causing tremors to shake me to my core. As his center glided in and out of mine, it was as if he was driving himself deeper and deeper into my heart. With every thrust his purpose was clear; he did not want to lose me.

I lay in the bed next to Ajani with his arms wrapped around me and his head resting comfortably on my bare chest. His blue-and-white striped comforter was tangled around my waist, and the smell of sex hung heavily in the air.

"I'm sorry," Ajani whispered. "I really didn't think it would go like that."

I let my fingertips walk up and down his muscular back. "It's okay, sweetie, don't worry about it."

"I can't help thinking about the element of truth in all the things my father said. This isn't the relationship I want with you." Ajani sat up and turned away from me. "I think about you marrying Terrence every day and it kills me. I know it's inevitable and I know we have an agreement, but I am going to end up getting hurt. Hell, I'm hurting already."

"Ajani, this is difficult for me, too. I care so much about you and—"

"Do you love me? Are you in love with me as you said at dinner?" he demanded. I hesitated. Things were getting out of control, feelings and emotions were being mixed in with common sense and reality. Trouble was brewing but I couldn't lie to Ajani. Seeing the pain he was in tugged at my heart.

"Yes, Ajani, I am in love with you."

"But not enough to end the bullshit of a relationship that you have with Terrence?" Ajani rose from the bed, his voice rising a few octaves.

"It's not that simple," I answered weakly.

"I'm sick and tired of hearing that same old-ass excuse, Yvette." Ajani snatched on a pair of basketball shorts and looked down at me. "I don't know if I can do this anymore."

I closed my eyes and took a deep breath. "Do you want me to leave?"

"I want you to leave him! Call him," Ajani said, searching for his cellphone in the pile of clothes on the floor. "Call him right now and tell him that it's over between the two of you."

"I can't, Ajani. We talked about this and we decided that we could never have a real relationship. And now you're changing your mind?"

"I can't stand thinking about him touching you, kissing you, fucking you. It makes me sick."

"Then don't think about it. Let's just have a good time and worry about everything else as it comes along."

"So we'll be having this same conversation in two months, when you're in your wedding dress getting ready to marry some nigga who will never love you as much as I will."

"This is too much, Ajani. I'm not ready for this. I have to go," I said, jumping out of bed and hurrying to the living room to search for my clothes.

"Go ahead and do what you always do, run. When things get thick you're always out the door. You ran to Nashville when your man cheated on you; you needed space when you realized you had feelings for me. And now that you love me, watch the fuck out! Where are you running to now, Yvette?"

I looked at Ajani angrily as I zipped my jeans. "I'm not running, Ajani. I'm going home because we are too angry to discuss this rationally. I'll call you tomorrow."

"Don't bother."

I turned around sharply and faced him. "What's that supposed to mean?"

"It means that *I* need some space. It's my turn to think about what *I'm* doing with *you.*"

Terrence

24

"Terrence, I need to talk to you," Wendy said, coming up behind me and putting her hands on my shoulders.

Her behavior had been strange lately. After that episode at the restaurant, she had become quiet and withdrawn, wanting only to eat, sleep and occasionally have sex—and that was only when I started dropping hints that I wanted to visit Yvette in Nashville.

"Can't it wait?" I asked, pausing *Maternity Ward* with my Tivo remote.

"I think it's waited long enough."

Something in her voice made me turn around, and when I did, I saw the tears streaming down her face. She looked tired and beaten.

"What's going on?" I asked, getting up from the couch and taking her hands. I really wasn't in the mood for any theatrics, but how much sex would I get I if I acted like I didn't care?

"A few days ago, I passed out at work and Vivian took me to the emergency room," she sobbed into my chest.

"Why didn't you tell me? Are you sick? Don't tell me you've been walking around here sick for days and didn't say anything."

"I'm not sick," Wendy murmured, looking up at me. Her dark eyes were sad and uncertain, and something in them immediately told me what the problem was.

My mind flew back to all the times my body had become one with hers. She had told me she was on the pill and I believed her; I believed her so much that using protection never crossed my mind.

"You're pregnant, aren't you?" My voice sounded strained and hoarse.

Wendy nodded and then put her face into her hands.

"You told me you were on the pill." I was becoming angry. A little voice whispered in my ear that Wendy had trapped me, that this was her plan all along.

"I was on the pill, Terrence, but they are not one hundred percent effective. You're a doctor; you should know that."

"Of course I know that. But it's only in rare instances that a woman gets pregnant if she's taking the pill properly. Did you take some medication that would have compromised its effectiveness? Did you forget to take them?"

"No, I didn't do anything to cause this if that's what you're thinking. I'm just as surprised as you are, Terrence. As a matter of fact, the doctor ran the test three times before I would even consider the possibility of being pregnant." Her tears were drying up, and the look on her face had changed from sadness to confusion. I'm sure she had expected a very different reaction from me.

"If you are pregnant, the baby isn't mine," I declared flatly, getting up and walking to the other side of the room. At that moment, I couldn't stand being next to her.

"The baby is yours. Who else would be the father?"

"How about Mr. Baseball? You know, that guy you brought over as your little decoy for Yvette's benefit? You have probably been sleeping with him this entire time."

"No, I haven't, Terrence! I haven't even set eyes on Alonzo since that night, and even if I had, when would I have had time? I'm over here every second of the damn day."

"Not because you're invited," I spat out, before glancing over to an end table. A picture of a smiling Yvette looked back at me. The picture had been taken when we were happy, before things between us went wrong.

"So now all of a sudden you don't want me over here? Terrence, I can recall plenty of times that you've called my job looking for me. You wanted me with you just as much as I wanted to be here."

"Wendy, this is ridiculous. Arguing about how we got to this point isn't going to change anything. We need to come up with a plan. What are we going to do about this situation?"

She wiped her eyes and smiled hesitantly. "I thought this would be the perfect time for you to tell Yvette about us."

I laughed loudly; I couldn't help myself. Her solution was absurd. "Why would I do that?" I asked, trying to catch my breath.

"Because if Yvette knew the truth, the two of you could call off the wedding and then we could be a family-me, you and the baby."

I laughed louder. "Did you plan this, Wendy? Have you been plotting to get pregnant so that you could break Yvette and me up?"

"No! I just think that you would be happier with me. I'm here, Terrence, and I have been since Yvette left you for some job opportunity. I've been the one taking care of you. Cooking and cleaning and washing your clothes—I've been doing it all while you keep Yvette up on some pedestal. She's not an angel, Terrence, and it's about time you realized that."

"Obviously you know something that I don't, and since we're being all honest with each other, let me know. What has Yvette been doing?"

"Why should I tell you anything? Whatever I say about Yvette isn't going to change you. You'll still adore her and still consider me a booty call." The tears began flowing again, Wendy's chest heaving up and down with each sob.

"You're more than a booty call," I said, trying to reassure her.

"Don't play me like I'm stupid, Terrence. You can't sweet-talk me. Don't pretend you care about me or this baby while hoping I'll tell you who Yvette has been shacking up with."

Wendy stopped and shook her head. "Look, this isn't about Yvette. It's about us, and I just want . . ."

"I'm not making any decisions about *us* until you tell me what I want to know. Who Yvette has been shacking up with?" I folded my arms across my chest and waited.

Wendy drew in a deep breath and looked at me desperately. "I love you, Terrence. Why won't you see that I'm the one for you?"

"Who is Yvette down there with?"

"She's seeing some twenty-one-year-old college guy. Remember the guy who was in her office when you went to Nashville to see her? That's him, and she claims she's in love."

My mind quickly rewound to that day in Yvette's office. I remembered the guy quite clearly, but I refused to believe what Wendy was telling me. "You're lying," I said, sitting on the love seat across from the couch. "You're only telling me this because you want me for yourself. You have this fantasy of me, you and this baby becoming some kind of family, and you want your best friend, my fiancée, out of the way."

"I'm not lying, Terrence. She's been seeing him for several months now. He's trying to convince her not to marry you."

"Yvette would never cheat on me."

"She would and she is, and nothing you can say will change that fact."

"Get out!" I said, glaring at her contemptuously. "Get out of my house."

"You can't throw me out, Terrence. We haven't talked about the baby."

"We don't need to talk about the baby. I really don't give a shit what you do. I have let this go on too long as it is, and now you're lying about Yvette *and* claiming I'm the father of your baby." I shook my head. "What have I gotten myself into?"

"You will not leave decisions about this baby up to me, Terrence. I need help!"

Quickly, angrily I dug deep into my pocket and pulled out my wallet. "You want my help?" I hollered, my enraged voice filling the loft. "This is the only help I am prepared to give." Pulling three hundred-dollar bills from my wallet, I threw them at her one by one. "I am telling you that we will never be a family. I don't love you and I never will. Now take this money," I threw another bill, hitting her in the chest, "and get rid of that baby!"

Yvette

25

My life had become very lonely. Ajani meant what he had said about taking some time to think, because he hadn't called me since our spat a week ago. No flowers or little notes, either.

Jordan said she saw him at a party, some kind of luau where all the college girls wore string bikinis and the guys walked around with video cameras and liquor bottles.

"How did he look?" I asked before realizing that I sounded completely ridiculous and lovesick, but I didn't care. I missed him.

"As cute as ever. He had on this little fatigued Speedo and boots. It was hilarious, but I understand what the attraction is. He didn't leave anything to the imagination that night," Jordan laughed. I frowned.

"I'm just kidding, don't get so upset," Jordan said, walking over and patting my hand. "And where were you? I thought you and Ajani were joined at the hip."

"We had a fight. He said he needed some time to think."

"Did it have anything to do with Terrence?" Jordan asked.

"It had everything to do with Terrence. Ajani wants me to break off the engagement so that we can have a real relationship. I told him that just isn't a possibility."

"But I thought you two decided that you were both content with the way things were going," Jordan said, going to the copy machine and preparing the school's weekly parent newsletter.

"That *was* what we decided, but all of a sudden Ajani's asshole of a father starts ranting and raving and puts all this stuff into Ajani's head and poof . . ." I said, throwing my hands into the air. "Ajani says he needs some time."

"Can you blame him?"

"Of course I can. We had an agreement."

"Yvette, you're not dealing with a contract or suspending a student. You are dealing with a man with real feelings, and things change."

"Jordan, I am completely aware that things change. My feelings for Ajani have changed, but I can't lose sight of the bigger picture here."

"Which is?"

"Ahh . . ." I was becoming exasperated. "I feel as if I have to keep explaining myself over and over again. The bigger picture is that Terrence can give me the life I need."

"You don't love him," Jordan said, as if she knew everything about me.

"Terrence?" I asked, and she nodded. "Yes, I do!"

"No, you don't. You used to love him, but now you're settling for stability."

"Ajani cannot be a husband right now. He doesn't have a degree or a job. He's so immature at times that it drives me completely insane. For God's sake, his father pays his rent, his car note. His father buys the food in his refrigerator."

"Why do you have to have a husband now? I don't understand why you won't wait to find the right man?"

"I'm not twenty, Jordan. I don't have youth on my side like you and Ajani. I'm thirty-four and my time to wait is pretty much running out."

"So you'd rather marry the wrong man than wait for the right one to get on his feet?"

I looked at her but couldn't answer. As much as I hated to admit it, she was right and there was no arguing with common sense.

"Yvette, your office phone is ringing," Jordan said, pointing to the open door. I hadn't heard because I was distracted by the words of wisdom she had just given me.

"Thank you for calling Nashville Prep. This is Ms. Brooks speaking," I said, using the most professional voice I could muster.

"Yvette?" A voice barely above a whisper was on the line.

"Wendy? What's wrong? Are you crying?" Wendy was not a crier. The last time I had seen her cry was when we were fifteen and her grandmother had died suddenly. If she was crying now, something must be very wrong.

"Can you come to Detroit? I can't do this by myself," she begged, her words almost indistinct.

"Wendy, sweetie, relax and talk to me."

"I need you to come home. I can't believe this is happening to me!"

"What is happening?" My mind ping-ponged from one horrible scenario to the next.

"I'm pregnant."

My mind went blank. Wendy was the most careful person I knew. In fact, we used to joke that if she ever became pregnant it would be because of divine intervention. Wendy used every pregnancy-prevention method known to man. She once told me that a baby just didn't fit anywhere into the Wendy Web experience.

"Pregnant? I didn't even know you were seeing anyone seriously," I finally managed to get out, feeling completely out of the loop.

"I'm not," she said sniffling. "There is no one serious in my life right now."

"Well, who's the baby's father?" I was confused.

"Um, um . . . Do you remember the guy I brought to dinner that time?"

"Yeah, the baseball player, right?" I couldn't imagine that man being a father to Wendy's baby, not with the way he flirted with me right in front of her and Terrence.

"Yeah, Alonzo."

"Wendy, what are you going to do? Have you talked to Alonzo? Have you told him?"

"He doesn't want anything to do with the baby. He wants me to get an abortion."

"Is that what you want?" I walked over to the door separating my office from Jordan's workspace and closed it.

"What other choice do I have?" Wendy asked, sobbing into the phone.

"You can have the baby. Being a single mother isn't the scarlet letter that it used to be."

"I refuse to be anyone's baby mama, Yvette. I already scheduled the appointment to get rid of it. Will you come with me?"

I didn't understand how she could refer to her child as an "it". And to make the decision to abort so soon was slightly disturbing. I sensed there was a lot she was leaving out; nevertheless, she was my best friend and I had to be supportive.

"Of course, I'll come. I'll book a flight out tonight."

Ajani

26

"I knew you would come to your senses." I turned around and looked at Lisa sitting with her naked back against my headboard. A self-satisfied smirk was on her cinnamon colored face. This was a nightmare.

"Ajani, I have always known that we were meant to be together." She untangled herself from the covers and crawled forward, obviously intent on seducing me all over again. "Just look in the mirror," she said. "We were made for each other."

To pacify her, I looked at our reflections and had to concede that Lisa was perhaps right. In a different time and place we would have been a perfect match: same age, same family background. We even looked similar, but now . . .

Lisa wrapped her toned arms around my shoulders and smiled at the picture-perfect pair in the mirror. Her freckled face and long-lashed eyes gleamed with elation, while I looked somber, as if I had just made the biggest mistake of my life. And I probably had.

She softly kissed my neck, and I felt my insides turn to stone.

"I knew you would come running back as soon as you realized that Yvette couldn't give you what you needed."

I stiffened involuntarily at the mention of Yvette's name. I missed, loved, and hated her all at the same time. It physically hurt to be away from her, and that was the reason I had gotten myself into this mess with Lisa. Drowning your sorrows in Omega Oil never turned out well.

"Lisa, I was drunk. We had sex because I was drunk."

"Don't fool yourself. You're using that as an excuse, but we both know that you did exactly what you have been wanting to do ever since we broke up."

"I can barely remember anything from last night, Lisa, so I doubt that whatever the hell we did was premeditated on my part."

I tried to focus, hoping that I would recall a little more of what had transpired the night before. I could vividly remember downing half a bottle of Bacardi and then hearing my two frat brothers beat on the door to let me know it was time to head out. I slid into the car, talking loudly and feeling good until someone asked, "Where's that fine-ass chick you've been glued to?"

The night went downhill from there. When we got to the party, I headed straight to the bar and quickly slurped down two plastic cups of Omega Oil. Then I saw Lisa dropping it like it was hot on the dance floor. Her skirt was so short and her legs so juicy I wanted to take a bite out of them. That's exactly what I remember doing, crawling toward her on all fours and lifting her skirt with my teeth. Not my finest hour, but I had no idea it would lead to her in my bed, talking about getting back together.

"Please, boy," Lisa laughed, reaching for me. "You wanted it just as much as I did."

"What I wanted was to stop thinking about Yvette for a while and have some fuckin' fun. Everything just got way out of hand."

"You know what?" Lisa asked loudly, her voice becoming angry. "I'm sick of hearing about that stuck-up bitch, Ajani. You talked about her all night. It was ridiculous!"

"I talked about her because I wanted to be with her. Sorry to bust your bubble, Lisa, but I'm in love with her."

Lisa looked at me, her mouth open so wide it looked as if she was trying to catch flies. "You cannot be serious. You've known her for like five minutes."

"Amazing, isn't it?" I asked, unable and unwilling to hide the sarcasm in my voice.

"So what was I? Just some rebound booty call?" she asked, her voice changing from angry to hurt in seconds.

"That's exactly what it was, Lisa. As I said, I was drunk, and I'm sure you took advantage of the situation. I don't even remember what happened after the dance floor."

She stared at me, tears glistening in her eyes. "You know that's really fucked up, don't you, Ajani?"

I turned and looked at her, feeling the old Ajani rearing his ugly, male-chauvinist head. "You know me, Lisa. What else did you expect?"

Yvette

"What are you doing here?" a surprised Terrence greeted me when I walked into the loft. A fire was burning low in the fireplace, and the space smelled of steak and potatoes.

Terrence sat up on the couch and paused the television. He was wearing a pair of crumpled hospital scrubs, his appearance indicated that he had just finished up a rotation at work. It was very difficult to glean from the look on his face whether he was happy about my unexpected appearance.

It had been a while since I'd last visited Detroit, and while the house looked the same with its sage-colored walls and stainless-steel appliances; it felt different. It didn't feel like home; it wasn't where I belonged.

"Wendy called me yesterday. She's pregnant." I waited for a reaction from Terrence. I braced myself for his usual smart-alecky remark or even an expression of great surprise, but nothing came. "Did you hear me? I said that Wendy is pregnant." I walked over to the couch and stood over him after he un-paused the television. His eyes wouldn't meet mine.

"I heard you, but I'm not sure what you want me to say about it. Wendy is your friend, not mine."

"Well, if you're not going to say anything about Wendy, aren't you at least going to say how glad you are to see me?"

"Yeah, I'm really glad to see you," Terrence responded in a bored and insincere voice that made me wish I'd never opened the loft's door. There was a moment's silence, and then Terrence looked at me and said, "I do have something to say." He turned the TV off and got up from the couch. He maneuvered around the island and headed to the refrigerator, taking out the orange juice and drinking directly from a carton. "I find it strange that you come running back to Detroit when Wendy gets knocked up, but every time I ask you, your fiancé asks you, you're too busy."

"Terrence, she called me crying. Wendy never cries, and she said the father wasn't involved. He wants her to get an abortion. What was I supposed to do?"

"Who's the father?" he asked, his voice changing slightly. He glared at me from the corner of his eye.

"That guy she brought to dinner a few months ago, Alonzo, the one who plays for the Tigers."

Terrence snorted and put the juice back, slamming the refrigerator door. "I still don't understand where *you* fit into all this."

"She needs someone to hold her hand. She's pregnant and all alone. It's my job to be there for her."

"No, Yvette," he said, his eyes flashing. "It's your job to be here for me. Since you've been gone, my life has turned to shit. I need you here."

"What's so wrong with your life that can't wait to be fixed until after the wedding?"

"Are you even coming back after the wedding? It's less than two months away, and I haven't heard you making any plans to come back. Hell, I don't know if there will still be a wedding."

"Of course there will still be a wedding."

"The caterer called three days ago. She said that you still haven't finalized the menu for the reception."

Terrence stared me down, waiting for a response. I mentally kicked myself. The wedding plans had become secondary since I had begun seeing Ajani. When I was with him nothing else mattered. "I've been so busy. I'll get on it as soon as all this drama with Wendy is finished," I promised.

"It's always something with you, Yvette. Go ahead and go," he said, waving me toward the door. "I'm sure you're sorry you even had to stop by here on your way to save the world."

And so I left.

"It's so good to see you," I said holding Wendy in a tight embrace. I didn't realize how much I had missed her until I saw her tear-stained face. We had been through so much together; she was more than my best friend—she was my sister.

"Thank you for getting here so quickly. I don't know if I'd been able to do this alone."

Wendy grabbed her purse off the table in the entryway and we walked outside.

"I got here as soon as possible. Do you think I would have let you do this by yourself?"

"You've just been so busy lately . . ."

"You're the second person that's told me that today," I said, opening the passenger-side car door for her.

"Terrence?"

"Who else? He claims that since I've been gone his

life is in shambles." I turned the key and the car began its low rumble. "But enough about me and my nonstop drama. I want to hear about what's going on with you."

"Nothing much to say, really. Got pregnant, need an abortion." Her mouth laughed but her spirit was crying.

"You don't have to do this, Wendy. There are other options."

"No, there aren't. Having this baby would mean the end of my career, the end of Wendy Web. I'm not about to give up something I worked so hard for."

"Giving up everything for your career isn't always the best idea. Look at my life. I moved to Nashville for a promotion and now my fiancé is angry, probably cheating on me, and I'm in love with a college student. I'm not even sure if I can still marry Terrence without having a nervous breakdown."

"If you were in my shoes . . ."

"If I were in your shoes, I would have that baby and think about the rest later. There are women in this world who would give anything to have a baby."

"Well, I'm not one of those women," Wendy said, wiping her eyes and staring out the window.

"If you're not one of those women, why are you crying?" I asked gently.

"I'm crying because I can't believe how stupid I was to get myself into this situation. Pregnant by a man that doesn't even give two shits about me."

"I'm sure Alonzo cares about you, Wendy. He's probably just as scared as you are."

"Please."

We drove the rest of the way to the clinic in silence, with Wendy looking out the window and me thinking about Terrence's comment that his life is shit. If he knew the truth he would see that my life wasn't that far behind.

"The station would fire me if I have this baby," Wendy said, coming back to life after I pulled into a parking space at the clinic and killed the engine.

"No, they won't. You're the reason that people started watching Channel Four again. They can't afford to lose Wendy Web. Besides, there are wrongful-termination laws. You could sue and own the station if they fired you for having a baby."

She put her head against the headrest and closed her eyes. "What kind of mother do you think I'd be?"

"A great mother. That kid will be the best-dressed baby in the nursery," I joked, causing her to chuckle.

"Something inside me has been saying that aborting this baby is a mistake. I never thought I wanted a child, but now I don't know. I just keep imagining a little boy who looks just like . . ." A solitary tear fell down her cheek.

"Wendy, why don't you take a little more time to think about it? This isn't the kind of decision you make in haste."

"I'm not perfect. I haven't been an angel in the last couple of months, and I've been thinking that this is the universe's way of paying me back," Wendy said, looking sideways at me.

"A baby isn't punishment, Wendy. It's a blessing."

We sat, looking at the tall, mirrored building. We watched women go in and come out the clinic. Sad, happy, relieved, and confused faces kept me quiet and Wendy thinking.

We waited for at least two hours. Her appointment came and went without either of us commenting. I sat, speaking when she was ready and remaining silent when she wasn't. "Yvette, take me home," she said finally, turning to me with a determination in her eyes I had never seen. "Whatever this baby will bring to my life, I'm going to see it through 'til the end."

Yvette

27

I entered the loft as slowly as possible. I hated that I had to return, but Wendy had insisted she was fine, saying she didn't need me and wanted to spend a little time deciding the course of her life. Alone. That left me with a plane reservation for tomorrow afternoon and an angry fiancé to face at home.

The loft was quiet. The only light came from the bedroom. "Yvette?" Terrence called.

"It's me." I dropped my purse on the couch and sat down next to it. My feet were tired; my brain was exhausted. In some ways, I wished life could go back to the way it was before Nashville. That's when life was easy and uncomplicated. I wasn't happy, but things were simple.

"How did everything go?" Terrence asked, flopping down on the couch next to me and smelling of Zest soap and baby lotion. His white T-shirt gleamed, and his jeans were freshly pressed.

"Everything went well. Are you going somewhere?" I asked, touching his pants.

"In a bit. I've got a run to make, but I shouldn't be long." Terrence moved closer to me and laced his left hand through my right. I felt nothing.

"So how is Wendy feeling?"

I couldn't tell if he was genuinely concerned or being a smart ass. "She didn't go through with it. I don't think she ever wanted to in the first place. She was letting the baby's father pressure her into an abortion."

The warmth in Terrence's eyes slowly turned cold. I wondered why. "So she decided to keep the baby?"

"Yeah, said she wants a boy." I removed my hand from his and picked up the television remote.

"I can't imagine her as a single mom," he said quietly.

"Maybe she won't have to be; the father might come around. After he sees the baby, maybe he'll want them to be a family."

"Doubt it."

We had become strangers. "Your mother called a couple of days ago," he informed me, waiting for a reaction.

My heart fell and I didn't respond.

"I told her about the wedding. It was a mistake. I thought you would have told her by now."

"No, not yet. I was waiting . . ."

"Waiting for?" he prodded.

I shrugged. "I don't know. I guess I was trying to decide if I wanted her there." I stopped and looked deep into his eyes, hoping that he would give me a truthful answer to my question: "Why do you want to marry me?"

"Because I love you." His words were sincere.

"That's it?"

"That's it."

"Is that enough?" I asked seriously. "I feel as though I don't know you anymore; you're so different. Angry, bitter and it seems as if you're hiding something, so I do wonder if love *is* enough."

"No one will ever love you more than I do."

"Are you sure about that?" I asked, boldly challenging him and thinking about Ajani. "Someone could come along and sweep me off my feet, someone who would never cheat on me because he would appreciate just how special I am."

"And how do you know that?" He suddenly rose from the couch. His eyes had become angry slits.

"I *don't* know that," I lied, thinking about the way Ajani had loved me over and over again, thinking about the way we sat up for hours talking about any and everything. "But you've cheated on me before, Terrence, and what's to say you won't do it again?"

"*I* say I won't do it again. Yvette, you either trust me or you don't, but I'm not about to beg."

"I don't want you to beg, Terrence. I want you to care! I want you to understand that you have hurt me, and I may never be the same again."

"I don't want to keep reliving the past. We should be concentrating on the future!"

"Our future together?" I asked, hearing my cellphone ring as it sat on the couch.

"Our future together, just me and you. Leave everything bad behind us and start fresh."

I sighed. I wanted this to be over, but I didn't think I could end it. Too many years and too many dreams had been put into this life.

"Your phone's ringing." Terrence held my cellphone out to me. *Riley* blinked on the screen, but to my fiancé it could have been anyone.

The ringing stopped and I took the phone from Terrence.

"Are you seeing someone?" he asked, both sadness and accusation in his face. "Have you met someone in Nashville?"

"There's no one else, Terrence," I lied easily.

He looked at me for a long time and then reached down and kissed me. And again I felt nothing. "I'm going to run to the store. I want to cook up something nice for dinner, maybe some seafood linguini. There's a new gourmet market near the casino."

"Sounds good," I responded, managing a faint smile. Terrence grabbed his jacket and left, closing the door behind him, leaving me alone with my thoughts, regrets and sadness.

I opened my phone and redialed the last missed call.

"Yvette?" Ajani asked, calming me instantly.

"It's me."

"Where are you? Jordan told me that you took the rest of the week off work."

"I'm in Detroit. I come back to Nashville tomorrow."

A long silence ensued. "Ajani, are you still there?"

"I'm still here. I fucked up and I wanted to see you. I need to talk to you, but I guess what I need to say will have to wait until tomorrow."

"I miss you," I said, as confused tears stung the corners of my eyes.

"Yvette, we really need to talk. I'll see you when you get back."

Wendy

I knew he would be on my doorstep before the night was over, and he didn't disappoint me. Within an hour and a half of Yvette leaving my place, three heavy knocks at the door got me out of bed.

"What do you want?" I asked Terrence after opening the door.

He stalked in and slammed the door behind him. "Wendy, you know what I want."

I stood in the middle of my living room looking straight through him.

"Yvette told me you decided not to get the abortion."

"Little Ms. Perfect spilled the beans as fast as that big mouth of hers would allow, didn't she?"

"Don't get mad at Yvette for your stupid decision. We had an agreement, Wendy. What happened to that?"

"Emotions happened. My conscience happened. I'm carrying our child, Terrence. Did you think it would be that simple to get rid of our son or daughter?"

"Hell yeah, I thought it would be that easy. Wendy, this baby could ruin both our lives."

"Oh, Terrence, please! What this boils down to is your fear that I'm going to tell Yvette this is your baby and not Alonzo's."

"I'm not one hundred percent certain that you're going to keep this a secret."

"I shouldn't have to."

"Are you really going to keep this baby?" Terrence asked, walking closer to me and softening his tone, no doubt to lull me into falling for his madness.

"Yes, I'm going to have this baby. As scared and unsure as I am, I'm going to have this baby. So where does that leave you?"

"It leaves me nowhere. I already told you that I don't want anything to do with this entire situation—more so now that Yvette and I are going to try to fix the way things seem to be unraveling around us."

I looked at him skeptically. "You're completely clueless, aren't you?"

"What are you talking about?"

"I told you that Yvette was cheating on you, and you're still insisting that she can do no wrong. Terrence, you are completely delusional."

"You told me that so I would leave her to be with you."

"Keep thinking that, okay, Terrence? We'll see who the fool is when all is said and done." I walked over to the door and opened it. My hand pointed to the porch. "Now would you please leave? I'm tired and would like to get some sleep."

"I'm not going anywhere until we talk about this."

"There's nothing left to discuss. You made yourself perfectly clear when you threw your hush money into my face. You want nothing to do with me or this baby. I'm not stupid, Terrence. I get it, and if that's the way you want it, then that's the way it's going to be."

"I want more than that, Wendy. I want you to swear that you'll never tell Yvette anything about us. I'll give you all the child support you want, but if Yvette finds out anything—"

"Yvette and I have been best friends for a lot longer than you've been in the picture. I don't want to lose her now," I informed him. "Don't worry, Terrence, your secret is safe with me."

Yvette

28

Since my return to Nashville, things had changed a great deal between Ajani and me. The second I entered the baggage-claim area, I saw him waiting for me, his hands stuffed into his pockets and looking as if he hadn't slept in days. "I don't want to fight anymore," he told me, taking my hand and kissing it gently. "Let's go home." And that's what we did.

On the way, Ajani told me—in as much detail as he could remember—what had happened with Lisa. I wasn't happy about it; I was devastated, actually. But what could I say? We weren't a couple, and I was the one getting married. He had every right to see whomever he wanted, but accepting that fact didn't lessen the pain any less.

Ajani and I have been practically living together in my apartment ever since. As soon as we entered my apartment that night, Ajani began showering me with kisses and words of love. He told me that "space" was the last thing he needed. He ran a bath and proceeded to wash every inch of my body, as if to make up for his night with Lisa. Afterward we went straight to bed, and it seems as if we've been there ever since. That night left no doubt that there was something so strong between Ajani and me that we couldn't stand being apart. But the same old problems hung over our heads the next morning.

We'd talked about our issues a million times and had decided that yes, we were in love, but no, a serious, long-term relationship would never work. I could not get past the age difference and Ajani couldn't stand the fact that Terrence was still a part of my life. So we made a conscious decision to enjoy the time we still had together and whatever happened, happened.

Of course, we'd said the very same things to each other less than a month ago, but this time it was real. My wedding was four weeks away, and every time I talked to Terrence over the phone, his questions became more probing, more insistent. He obviously knew that something was going on, and I couldn't help thinking that Wendy had dropped a dime on my relationship with Ajani.

"Good morning," Ajani greeted me when I stumbled into the living room wrapped in the beige sheet from my bed. He sat Indian-style wearing purple and gold boxer shorts, his fraternity colors. He was positioned in front of the coffee table, with a PlayStation remote in one hand and a bowl of cereal in the other. It was times like this that the thirteen-year age difference practically screamed at me.

"Three o'clock in the afternoon is hardly morning," I said, looking at the clock on the cable box. "I can't believe you didn't wake me. I thought we were supposed to go to the mall this morning."

"We were, but after I tried to wake you and couldn't I figured you needed your rest. Especially after what I put on your ass last night." He laughed before slurping down the milk from the white ceramic bowl.

I sat on the couch and smiled, remembering the night before. Ajani and I had dinner with Jordan and her newest beau. We spent the evening holding hands under the table and finishing each other's sentences.

"My, my," Jordan chuckled, watching me feed Ajani a piece of strawberry cheesecake, "don't you two look in love?" I could feel myself blushing, but there was no denying it: Ajani and I were in love.

When we got back to my apartment, Ajani cleared off the dining-room table and we made love atop it. Then we made love from one corner of my apartment to the next—the couch, the kitchen sink, the wall in the hallway.

"That *was* fun, Ajani."

"Oh yeah? Because I was thinking about an encore." He crawled toward me and removed the sheet from around my body.

"I'm not your age, Ajani; my body needs time to recuperate. Can't you just wait until tonight?" I moaned as he kissed my neck, my collarbone and then my breasts.

"I don't want to hurt you, baby. Take all the time you need," he said, wrapping the sheet back in place and kissing my lips softly. "I need to finish this season, anyway. You know, I'm in the play-offs right now." He picked up the game controller again and pushed play.

I rolled my eyes but said nothing. It amazed me that such an intelligent, athletic, poised and passionate man could spend hours on end creating a fictional football dynasty. And he wasn't alone in his obsession. A week ago, he paid the cable company to install wireless high-speed Internet service in my apartment so he could play his campus friends and frat bothers.

"Ajani, you know I'm flying to Detroit next weekend to finalize the wedding plans?" I said, getting up and going into the kitchen. Saying anything about my wedding was to enter extremely sticky territory, and I didn't like the look on his face when I did.

He didn't answer. When I reentered the living room with glass of chocolate milk in hand Ajani had the headset on and was cussing out someone's defensive line.

"Baby, I'm hungry," I said, testing whether he could hear me.

"I figured you would be. I ordered a pizza about fifteen minutes ago, so it should be here shortly."

If he heard the being hungry part, then I knew he had heard the part about Detroit but didn't want to comment. I honestly couldn't blame him.

I left Ajani screaming at the television and went to shower. As I put on marine blue sweatpants and a matching hoodie, I couldn't help thinking that the time he and I had left was rapidly coming to an end. Every time I thought about saying good-bye for good I would become teary-eyed and be seized by depression. Ajani had raised the possibility of continuing our relationship even after I was married about a half dozen times. As tempting as it might be to engage in a clandestine Southern rendezvous while Terrence was on call at the hospital, it wasn't realistic, and I just wasn't that brazen.

Marriage was sacred, and there was no way I could continue seeing Ajani after my grandmother's minister had pronounced Terrence and me man and wife.

As I pulled my hair into a loose ponytail, I was startled by a loud knock at the door.

"It's probably the pizza," Ajani called from the living room. I heard him walk to the door, but before he could check the peephole, there was another knock, this one much louder. "This guy thinks he's the police or something."

I stood in the archway separating the living room from the back of the apartment watching the man I love turn the lock and then the doorknob. Half naked, Ajani pulled the door open. "Man, I'm sure your boss wouldn't like to hear about you beating on my door like th—" He stopped abruptly when he saw the person standing before him. Surprise shot across his face, almost instantly replaced with an unmistakable look of loathing.

"Knocking on *your* door?" a very familiar voice asked. In full-blown panic, I took one step forward and then two back. "Last I heard this door belonged to my fiancée, but I see that things have changed."

Ajani

"I knew something was going on between the two of you," Terrence said, brushing past me. Yvette stood in the hallway looking as if her world had come to a crashing end. I closed the door, resisting the urge to rip Terrence's throat out.

"Is this even legal?" Terrence laughed, turning to Yvette. "You could probably get picked up on charges of statutory rape if his parents found out, Yvette."

"I'm more of a man than you'll ever be," I said, snatching my T-shirt off the arm of the couch and pulling it on.

"Look, Terrence, I don't want any trouble. Obviously, there are some things we need to discuss and—" Yvette said, walking slowly into the living room.

"There are a lot of motherfucking things we need to discuss, Yvette! Let's start with why this little boy is answering your door in his underoos, shall we?"

"Don't raise your voice in here," I warned, stepping closer to Terrence and looking down on him. He was about three inches shorter and twenty pounds lighter me. Even though he wanted to come across as hardcore, I could see the fear in his eyes.

"I'll raise my voice anywhere I damn well please! You're standing in my fiancée's apartment, a month from our wedding, half-naked. How would you react in my situation?"

"Yvette and I both understand why you're upset, but you will still respect her and her house."

Terrence laughed nervously and then turned back to Yvette. "He's standing here talking to me as if he's your man or something. Please don't tell me this is more than sowing your oats before our wedding. I would like to assume he's like a bachelorette party stripper who has stayed way too long."

Yvette shifted from one foot to the other. I tried to catch her eye, make her look at me, make her tell Terrence that what we had was real, but her eyes were glued to the floor. "I'm sorry, Terrence, but Ajani and I have been seeing each other for a while now."

"Yvette, you don't have anything to apologize for. This guy cheated on you, remember? You, on the other hand, were just following your heart," I said, wanting this day to rewind itself and begin again, minus the good doctor's surprise visit.

"So you have feelings for him?" Terrence's voice cracked, and I could see his resolve weakening.

"I-I d-do care for Ajani a great deal," Yvette stammered, her eyes filing with tears. She looked from me to Terrence.

"She's in love with me."

"She's in love with you? So where the fuck does that leave me?" Terrence threw his hands up. "This is crazy, Yvette." He walked over to her and grabbed her by the arm forcefully. "Get your shit."

"What? Terrence, we need to talk about this," she said, tears spilling over onto her face.

"I said get your shit! I have let this go on long enough. You're coming back to Detroit with me, and your little prenuptial fling is officially over!" Terrence yelled, as he pushed Yvette in the direction of the bedroom we had made love in less than twelve hours before. She stumbled and fell to the floor and my mind went blank.

Before I knew what I was doing, my hands, without direction from my brain, reached out and grabbed

Terrence from behind. With greater force than I knew I possessed, I threw Terrence to the floor and stood over him with my fists clenched. "Don't you ever put your fucking hands on her again." My body was shaking with anger as I wrapped my hands around his slim neck and began to squeeze.

Terrence coughed and gagged under the weight of my grip. "Ajani, don't!" Yvette cried, getting up from the floor and clawing at my bare arms. "Please let him go. He didn't hurt me. I'm okay. Please don't do this," she cried, finally convincing me to let him go.

"Is this the type of crazy nigga you want to be with?" Terrence asked Yvette, his face slowly regaining its natural color.

"Are you okay, baby?" I asked, looking at Yvette.

"I want you to get your things together, Yvette. It's time for us to leave," Terrence said in an even voice.

"I'm not letting her leave with you."

"Ajani . . ." Yvette whispered. "I think you should go."

I looked at her, but I didn't recognize the person in front of me. "You think it's time for *me* to go?" I asked, confused. Didn't I just see him knock her to the ground, and I'm the one she was asking to leave? Something was seriously wrong with this situation.

"You heard her, man. Leave." Terrence looked at me with a maddening smirk, and I regretted taking my hands from around his neck so soon.

"Ajani, we both knew this wouldn't last forever."

I stared at her, but all I saw was the diamond engagement ring waiting on my dresser. I had bought it a couple of days ago because I never believed Yvette would really marry the man that was now holding her hand.

"I love you, Yvette. Doesn't that mean anything?" I asked, hating the fact that it sounded like begging.

"Should I play my violin now or later, Ajani? She asked you to leave, and if you don't I can always ask the police to escort you to the nearest precinct. You did assault me, and I'm not above pressing charges."

"Ajani, please don't hate me, but we've talked about this and you knew—"

I put up my hand and began gathering my belongings quickly. "I get it, Yvette, so you can save your excuses. I'm leaving, and I hope you and the woman-beater here live happily ever after."

Yvette

29

I fucked up. I chose the wrong man and I now wished I could turn back the hands of time. I missed him; I wasn't happy without him. Ajani was what I'd been looking for my entire life, and I was too stupid, too judgmental, and too immature to realize it. I decided that marrying Terrence just wasn't an option, not with the way I felt about Ajani.

After Ajani left, I sat and tried to imagine what being married to Terrence would be like after everything that had happened. I couldn't. All I saw was Ajani, a huge home and three kids who all looked just like him. My dreams had really changed.

Now I've resigned myself to telling Terrence that we weren't going to work. I spent the entire day in my office planning what to say. It had become painfully obvious to me that I could no longer live a lie. The wedding was off.

"Ms. Brooks?" Jordan said, entering my office. She looked somber, as if someone had just died. "Ms. Fisher wants to see you."

"Jordan, what's with the long face?" I asked, standing and going toward her. "Am I in trouble?" I joked.

Looking extremely uncomfortable, Jordan studiously avoided my gaze. "Um . . . well . . ." she stammered.

"What?" I was becoming alarmed. "Tell me before I go in there looking silly!"

"Ms. Fisher found out about you and Ajani. She knows how you met, and other details as well."

All the oxygen left my lungs and the room began to spin crazily. "How does she know?" I asked weakly, not recognizing my own voice.

"Someone told her."

I glared at her accusingly, the blood leaving my face.

"It wasn't me! I swear! You'd better get in there. Good luck."

Trying to breathe normally, I left my office and hurried to Ms. Fisher's office, hoping that Jordan had just been making a mountain out of a molehill.

That hope was immediately dashed when I entered and saw a familiar figure sitting demurely in a corner of the well-appointed office. Ajani's ex-girlfriend Lisa sat wearing her Sunday best and quietly crying, as if *her* entire world had come crashing down around her.

"This young lady has made an accusation that you are having an affair with her boyfriend." Ms. Fisher cut to the chase immediately, shooting me a no-nonsense look across her large oak desk.

Without realizing what I was doing, I closed my eyes, trying to decide which was the better route—to be honest or lie. "I don't understand what my personal life has to do with my professionalism here at the school," I answered, choosing, at least temporarily, to hedge, hoping to buy time.

"Well, you're right, Ms. Brooks. Normally, it wouldn't; however, Lisa tells me that you met this young man here, during school hours, while he was observing you for a required university class."

She knew everything. I looked over at Lisa and saw that her tears had stopped and a wicked smile replaced them. From the moment I met her, I knew she would be trouble, but I never expected this. Never.

"I-I—" I stuttered, desperate to save myself from the quicksand Lisa had thrown me into but not knowing how.

"Yvette, since you arrived at Nashville Prep you have been the consummate professional. Both staff and students love you, and I have never worked with a more competent assistant principal. Therefore, I wanted to hear your side of the story. I thought maybe there had been some sort of misunderstanding and wanted to hear from both of you."

A lump lodged itself in my throat. "Yes, I did meet Ajani here and we have been seeing each other, but it has never gotten in the way of my position," I admitted, deciding that lying would just make things worse. It was clear that I was in some pretty deep shit already.

Rejecting my explanation, Ms. Fisher said, "But, Ms. Brooks, it has. The relationship that you have with this young man has brought this young lady to my office in tears. She feels betrayed and frankly, Yvette, so do I."

I wanted to vomit. Looking at Lisa again, knowing betrayal was the last thing she felt. The vindictive little skank actually winked at me—as if it was all a big joke.

"Lisa, thank you for brining this to my attention. I hope that you will accept my sincere apology." Ms. Fisher escorted her out the door while I waited for the verdict to be handed down.

"Ms. Brooks, due to your serious lapse in judgment I am left with no choice but to ask you to take a few days off until the board investigation and hearing can be scheduled."

"But—" I began in disbelief. I had been sure that this fling would result in a slap on the wrist, a write-up, maybe even a good, stern talking to, but suspension?

"Ms. Brooks, there are really no other alternatives. Your behavior in this situation has been extremely unprofessional, and there are rules that were broken both here at Nashville Prep and at the university. I'm placing you on suspension until the board has an opportunity to review the charges."

I stood in the office, and the past few months flashed before my eyes. I had created this mess, and now my choices were biting me in the ass in a way I'd never expected. I couldn't believe that just a short while ago I had decided to give up everything for Ajani.

"There will be no need for a suspension," I said, feeling as if I was on the verge of a nervous breakdown. My hands and arms shook, and I could feel pools of perspiration forming in my armpits. "You'll have my resignation on your desk by the end of the day."

Head held high, I spun on my spiked heels and left the office. I walked past an open-mouthed Jordan and into what used to be my sanctuary. I sat down at the sleek black desktop computer and stared blankly at the dark screen.

I had worked so hard to get where I was—late nights at work, tutoring for free, making sure that I was the most dedicated and innovative employee Detroit and Nashville Prep had ever seen—and this was the thanks I got.

"What happened?" Jordan asked, rushing in and closing the door behind her.

"Lisa said that I was sleeping with her boyfriend, and Ms. Fisher told me that since I met Ajani at the school, my relationship with him was completely unprofessional. And then the witch suspended me," I spat out bitterly, despising Lisa and Ms. Fisher more and more with every word I spoke. "So instead of allowing myself to be humiliated any further, I resigned."

"You *what*?" she asked, shocked.

"I resigned. I hope you don't think that I would allow her to fire me and then put this shit into my permanent record. I'd never find another job."

"But don't you think you're being a little hasty? There is a possibility that she suspended you only until this blows over."

"Well, I'm not willing to take that chance." I booted up my computer, mentally preparing my statement for the board. Jordan stared at me helplessly, clearly not knowing what to say.

"But what are you going to do? How are you going to survive?"

"I have plenty of money in savings and I own the home my grandmother used to live in. And don't forget, I'm marrying Dr. Terrence Hall." I opened the word processing program and began to type furiously, resisting the urge to include words like 'stupid ass' and 'fat fuck' in my letter of resignation.

"So you're really going to marry him?" Jordan asked. Before I had been summoned to Ms. Fisher's office, my mind had been made up—there would be no wedding and absolutely no life with Terrence. But now, with no reason to remain in Nashville, it looked as if fate was making my decision for me. My relationship with Ajani seemed to have been doomed from the very beginning.

"What choice do I have now? I have no job, no place to live here because the apartment came with the position, and I told Ajani that we were finished . . ."

"But it's obvious that you don't want to marry Terrence and—"

"As I just said, I don't have any other choice. I really should have never come here."

"Don't say that, Yvette. You've been happy since you moved to Nashville. Admit it," Jordan knowingly.

"Look at what all this happiness is costing me," I said calmly, looking at her directly. "I hope you'll come to the wedding."

"I don't think there will be a wedding," Jordan predicted, watching me pull the finished letter from the printer with a flourish.

"Well, you're wrong!"

PART 3

Wedding Day

Terrence

30

"Where the hell is she?" I wondered aloud as I dialed Yvette's cell phone number for the fortieth time in the fifty minutes since she had disappeared. She wouldn't answer, and now the call just went straight to voicemail.

"You've reached Yvette Brooks. I'm unavailable at the moment. Please leave a . . ."

"I don't think she's coming back, Terrence," my mother said, rubbing my back in small circles, just as she used to when I was a kid. "The girls in the bridal party said they saw her run out of here in her wedding dress. She got into a cab and it sped off. It's been almost an hour, baby, and the guests are beginning to wonder what's going on."

"*I'm* wondering what's going on, Mama. I can't believe she would do this to me." Actually, I wasn't really that surprised, but my mother didn't need to know specifics.

Since Yvette's return to Detroit after that whole scene in Nashville, she had been less than the perfect fiancée. Where she was once bubbly and happy, she had turned cold and depressed. Sex was absolutely out of the question, and more than once I had been forced to choke the chicken to Internet porn. Sad but true.

I put up with it because I wanted to give her time to get over her little fling. She admitted that she loved the boy, but was committed to marrying me. So being the man that I am, I agreed to be patient and let it work its way out of her system on its own. I was supportive even when I shouldn't have been, and this is the thanks I got.

"Terrence, did something happen between you and Yvette that would make her run out on your wedding like this?" my mother asked, walking around to sit in front of me. She wanted to look me in the eyes; she could always tell when I was lying.

I sighed deeply, trying to buy some time so I could manipulate the story in my favor. There was no way I could afford to come out looking like the bad guy in all this. My mother had always loved Yvette, and although I was her only son, if I told the whole truth, I had no doubt that my mother's sympathies wouldn't lie with me.

"We've been having some problems lately," I murmured, looking at my mother. "When Yvette moved down to Nashville, she met someone."

My mother gasped, her hand clutching the freshwater pearls she wore. I continued my tale of woe, willing tears to form in the corners of my eyes. "He's a college student. She told me she loved him but wanted to work things out with me. I believed her, Mama. I thought we could get into some counseling, and we would be okay. I love her so much that I was willing to look past what she had done to me." I held my head in my hands and took a deep breath. While I wasn't as devastated as I wanted my mother to believe, I was still upset. Regardless of my many adulterous mistakes, I really did love Yvette and wanted nothing more than to make her my wife.

"Oh, baby," my mother said, wrapping her arms around me.

"Terrence, I'm sorry to interrupt, but the minister is wondering what's going on. He says that he has another wedding to perform in thirty minutes and it's across town," Wendy said, coming into the room.

I looked up from my mother's embrace and scowled at her. We hadn't talked since her decision to keep the baby and, frankly, I couldn't stand the sight of her.

"Terrence, I think it's time we announce that there won't be a wedding today," my mother said, sadness clouding her pretty face. "I can say something to the guests if you want."

"No, no, that's not your job, Mama." I turned toward the door. "Wendy, as the maid of honor, I think it would be fitting if you make the announcement. Shouldn't it be you who tells the guests that your friend has run off to God only knows where?"

"That's a good idea, baby," my mother agreed. "And, Wendy, make sure you apologize for the inconvenience."

Wendy stood with her mouth agape, obviously not believing my nerve. But before she could protest, I took my mother's hand and strolled past her and into the brightly lit hotel lobby.

"I'm sure she'll do a much better job than we would've, Mama," I said, as Wendy walked past me and headed for the ballroom, but not before she shot me a look that would put Medusa to shame. "Reporting the news is her job, after all."

Wendy walked to the front of the room and whispered in the minister's ear. Looking solemn, he whispered something back. Wendy shook her head and stood center stage in front of the microphone.

"May I have everyone's attention?" she asked, her voice cracking slightly. "May I please have everyone's attention?"

The restless guests quieted down, nearly all their faces showing curiosity and concern.

"First of all, I would like to thank everyone for your patience thus far." Wendy smiled nervously and cleared her throat before continuing. "I am sorry to report that due to unforeseen circumstances, there will be no wedding today. Again, I would like to thank everyone for your patience, and on behalf of Terrence, Yvette and their families, I would like to apologize for any inconvenience this may have caused." With that, Wendy turned off the microphone and walked away.

The clamor from the wedding guests was deafening. Some seemed angry and upset, while others reacted with a mixture of confusion and concern. Nearly everyone looked to the back of the room and directed questioning looks at me.

"What the hell is going on here?" someone in the crowd asked loudly.

"The groom is back there. It looks like we have a runaway bride on our hands," another guest said, chuckling appreciatively.

"What did you do now?" a woman I didn't recognize called out to me. She was clad in purple from head to toe and resembled a really bad imitation of Barney the Dinosaur.

"Just smile and be polite, Terrence. Show them that you're the victim here," my mother said, patting my arm.

I smiled sadly as I greeted the well-wishers turned sympathizers. For this performance, no coaching was needed; playing the victim was something I did extremely well.

Yvette

31

The line at the Northwest Airlines ticket counter reminded me of an amusement park queue. There had to be two hundred people waiting to finalize their travel plans. If I hadn't stopped off at Target to buy a jeans and a T-shirt and change my clothes, I would have had a better spot in line.

I had been waiting for an hour listening to crying babies with snot smearing their faces, men discussing golf scores, and women complaining to no one in particular about the slow-moving line.

I had absolutely nothing to complain about because I had absolutely nowhere to go. Since lining up with the one hundred and ninety-nine other people desperate to leave Detroit, I had kept my eyes glued to the departure screen. Atlanta, Chicago, D.C—none of them seemed far enough from my issues. I needed to get as far away as possible and I needed to do it ASAP because my cell-phone hadn't stopped ringing since I slid into that old man's cab.

The last time I checked, my service informed me that sixty-five new messages had been left, but there was no way I would be checking them anytime soon. When we pulled away from the hotel, I had already decided I would be unavailable indefinitely.

I had dialed Wendy's cellphone number four or five times without pressing the talk button. The curious cat in me couldn't help wondering what was happening at the wedding site, who was saying what—that sort of thing. But each time I dialed, something inside me said that if I talked to her I would be somehow persuaded to go back, and going back was the last thing I wanted to do. I needed time alone.

My life had been flipped upside down, and it was high time that I figured out what I was going to do with the rest of it. Under normal circumstances, I would have confided in Wendy, but this situation was anything but normal. Ever since I came back to Detroit with a broken heart and no job, my best friend had been the person following me around with *I told you so* stamped on her forehead.

Upon my less than graceful return to Detroit, Wendy had felt it necessary to tell me that I was the one who ruined my relationship with Terrence. "You just don't know what you have in that man, Yvette. He worships the ground you walk on, and you threw it all away." I was amazed that she could conveniently forget that he cheated on me, not to mention our stint in couples counseling before I moved to Nashville.

"I haven't thrown anything away," I told her a week ago. I glared at the best friend I had assumed would always be on my side. "Terrence and I are still getting married and—"

"And what about your career?" Wendy asked, cutting me off. "You worked so hard to get that assistant principal position, ruined your relationship with Terrence because of it and then end up getting fired over an indiscretion with a child."

"He's not a child, Wendy, and for the record, I was not fired; I quit before they fired me. I was placed on suspension, remember? And why are you trying to make me sound like some sick child molester or something? Yes, Ajani is younger than me—"

"A lot younger," she reminded me.

"Okay, so he's a lot younger than me but, damn, he's not a child. Ajani is a grown man and can—and does—make his own decisions. Age does not automatically mean maturity. Just look at Terrence."

"He may be able to drink and buy cigarettes, but you and I both know that he was off limits; we both know that your infatuation with him cost you your job."

I closed my eyes tightly, trying to block out that conversation.

"Can I help the next person in line, please?" the ticket agent said, looking at me. Her pretty chocolate face looked tired, but a slight smile graced her lips when I shot her a look of appreciation.

"Busy day?" I asked with a halfhearted chuckle.

"The busiest it's been in a while, and I still have three hours to go."

I watched as her fingers flew over the keyboard. Then she looked back up at me. "What can I help you with today?"

"I've been trying to figure that out since I got to the airport," I said, surprising the ticket clerk. "I need something that's leaving in the next thirty minutes."

Rhea, as her nametag read, looked at me and then at the long line behind me. She began typing furiously on the keyboard. A NWA supervisor passed by her workstation, a look of satisfaction on his pale baby face. He looked about the same age as Ajani. "The only thing leaving within the hour that's not completely booked is a nonstop flight to Phoenix. If you want, I can print your ticket out now and you should still have plenty of time to make it through security."

My heart began beating fast as I looked into Rhea's expectant and impatient face. I took a deep breath to calm myself. Of all the places Northwest Airlines flew, the only available flight was one to Phoenix, absolutely the last place I wanted to go with all this drama surrounding me.

"Ma'am, there is a line behind you . . ."

Rhea's boss was making his way back to her line. His very recent look of satisfaction had disappeared, replaced by irritation directed at the agent and me.

"Okay," I finally said, thinking of my mother and the beautiful home I'd purchased for her in Glendale, Arizona, a suburb of Phoenix. There were so many things that could go wrong if I showed up unannounced on my mother's doorstep. Other than the mortgage checks I sent once a month and an occasional holiday card, there had been virtually no communication between us for the past two years. Visiting her was not really on my list of things to do, but what choice did I have? The City of Sun was my only immediate refuge. "I guess I'll take it," I informed Rhea. The alternative to Phoenix was so much scarier.

Ajani

32

I don't know what made me suspend all reasonable thought and show up unannounced at Yvette's wedding, clutching the engagement ring I had for her and fighting back the tears burning the corners of my eyes.

After that horrendous, Terrence-inspired scene in Nashville mere weeks ago, I should have known better. A woman who would marry a featherweight like Terrence was clearly not a woman I should be hankering after.

But no matter how hard I tried or how many willing women crossed my path in the four weeks since the nightmare in Nashville, I still could not stop thinking about Yvette. She had become a permanent fixture in my heart, and I desperately wanted her.

So I put on a pair of jeans and a T-shirt, put my suit into a garment bag, got on a plane to Detroit, and barged into her bridal suite. I practically begged her to come back with me, and naively thought that if I kissed her, she would respond, would remember what we once shared. Well, she responded, but still said no.

Since meeting Yvette, I seemed to have developed a taste for punishment. Why else do I keep coming back for more? Why else did I come to Detroit? But I needed her and knew deep down in my heart that she needed me, too.

I sat in the back of the ballroom waiting for the ceremony to get underway. After leaving Yvette's room, I tried to leave the hotel but felt compelled to stay. Even though I told her I wanted to watch her ruin her life by marrying Terrence, that couldn't have been further from the truth. I needed to get away from the situation, but instead I sat in the back of the elegantly decorated ballroom. I was there for nearly an hour and then Wendy, Yvette's best friend, stood at the microphone and informed the two hundred plus guests that the wedding would not be take place. After she stepped from the mike and left the room, nearly every guest turned and looked toward the back of the room where Terrence stood. He was within steps of me.

Our eyes met and his pitiful demeanor turned vicious in a flash.

"What the hell are you doing here?" he asked loudly, moving closer to where I sat.

"I was here to witness Yvette make the biggest mistake of her life," I said, laughing in his face. "But it seems she has finally come to her senses."

"Have you talked to her? Do you know where she is?" Terrence demanded.

"If I knew where she was do you think I would be sitting here shooting the shit with you?"

"Gentlemen, gentlemen," Wendy whispered, coming up behind me and placing a calming hand on my shoulder. "I don't really think this is the time or the place to have this discussion."

"Wendy, would you shut the hell up and mind your own business," Terrence said, his aggravation boiling over.

"Look," she hissed, matching Terrence's attitude with one her own, "I'm trying to save you the embarrassment of getting your ass beat in front of two hundred of you and Yvette's closest friends."

I laughed loudly, enjoying Wendy's display of spunk and the spark of fear in Terrence's eyes. "You better listen to your girl."

"There's a room next door. Why don't the two of you go and deal with this problem there."

"I don't have shit to say to him," I said, feeling like a middle-school student being forced into peer mediation.

"You saw Yvette before she disappeared. Did she tell you where she was going?" Wendy asked, looking directly at me.

"I knew you had something to do with this!" Terrence screamed hysterically, causing many of the guests to stop and stare, mouths agape.

Wendy quickly took Terrence and me by our hands and led us into a small conference room next door to the ballroom. "Now you have your privacy."

"You really don't want to be alone with me, do you, Terrence? Scared I'll pick up where I left off in Nashville?" I asked, deliberately provoking him.

"I know this is entirely your fault," Terrence sputtered, ignoring my challenge. "You came here, got inside her head and now she's gone. Is Yvette somewhere waiting to meet up with you for your happily ever after?" Terrence hollered, apparently not caring how irrational he sounded.

"She's not waiting for me. I went up to her room before the ceremony that wasn't and she told me that although she did love me, I lack the resources to take care of her the way you can. Sounds to me like she was going to marry you only for your money. But when she thought about it, really thought about what her life would be like with you, even the big bucks you rake in as a doctor couldn't keep her from bolting."

"I cannot believe this is happening," Terence wailed, hanging his head. "So if you're not the one who caused her to run out of here, then it must have been you," he said, turning his wrath on Wendy. "You must have told her about us."

I looked from Terrence to Wendy and back again. I was shocked, even though I had warned Yvette that her best friend might have a hidden agenda. I was right.

"Don't blame this on me," Wendy yelled at Terrence, who was now feverishly pacing across the carpeted floor. "I told you I wouldn't say anything to Yvette, and I haven't. She probably just decided that she couldn't go through with the wedding because she doesn't love you anymore."

Her words seemed to further enrage Terrence. "You told her because you want me all for yourself," he shouted at her, spittle flying from his mouth, his face contorted with anger. "You have this deranged fantasy that you, me and this baby will get together and become some kind of family."

I sat down in a cushy burgundy armchair and listened to their heated argument, completely stunned, my mouth hanging half open in surprise. They had obviously forgotten I was still in the room as they kept bickering about their love affair gone terribly wrong.

"I cannot believe you are still talking about this baby as if it isn't yours. You are not the man I thought you were, Terrence."

"So let me get this straight," I interrupted. "You and you," I said, pointing to each of them, "have been sleeping together the entire time Yvette was in Nashville." Laughing, I rubbed my hands together, not bothering to hide my glee. This news was too good to be true. "And now you're pregnant."

They looked at me, startled. My voice had reminded them that I was still in the room and that I heard every private word they had uttered.

Yvette

33

I pulled the red Ford Focus rental in front of my mother's off-white stucco ranch. With rust-colored rocks instead of a lush green lawn and a seven-foot cactus, the home I'd been funding for the past two years looked pretty much as I'd imagined.

After folding the map of the Phoenix metro area and returning it to the glove compartment, I sat in the car for nearly thirty minutes after finding the house. I was trying to decide whether I really wanted to go knock on my mother's door. While contemplating my options, I dredged up the courage to check my voicemail.

Messages from an angry and confused Terrence filled my ears and shattered my newfound peace. Wendy called begging me to contact her. "You need to get back here to fix this!" she pleaded at the end of her message.

The last voicemail was from Ajani. His voice was low, sexy and deeply concerned. "Yvette, I'm worried about you. Everyone here is going crazy, and I found out something that I've got to tell you. Please call me as soon as you're ready."

Not unexpectedly, Ajani was the only person who left a message showing any concern for me. He was the only one to actually worry about *me*.

Finally I snapped my cellphone shut, took a deep breath and stepped out into the Arizona sizzle, which greeted me with full force. The sun was so hot that, in the seconds it took me to walk from the car to the front door, I thought my skin was going to burn off my body.

I rang the doorbell twice before the door was opened. "Are my eyes deceiving me?" my mother, Nina Dupree, wondered.

"No, Mama it's really me," I answered nervously. She looked so much better than she had two years ago, just before she begged me to sponsor her last stint in rehab. Back then, her cheeks were sunken, dark circles shadowed her eyes and her hair was matted and smelled as if it hadn't been washed in months. Clothes that used to fit snugly hung loosely on her sickly frame. "You look wonderful," I told her honestly.

"Your old lady cleans up pretty nice, doesn't she," my mother laughed, spinning around like a schoolgirl. Although she wanted to make light of her physical change, she did look beautiful. Her face was full, her cheeks pink and the large green eyes that were identical to mine emitted a spark of happiness and contentment I had never seen. She reminded me of the Nina Dupree I had seen only in pictures taken back in the 70s with a dark, curly afro, miniskirt and bright smile.

"Now are you going to stand on the doorstep all afternoon, or are you going to come in, have a glass of Sun Tea and tell me what in the world you're doing here?"

I entered and paused in the small foyer. I was a stranger in my own mother's home. Even though I paid most of the bills, I had never set foot in her house. Until just a few hours ago, there was no need to, but now I needed her to finally be the mother she should have been a long time ago.

"Give me a hug, Yvette, you're standing there like you don't know me." My mother pulled me into a tight hug. The warmth of her arms caused the dam of tears I'd been holding back to burst free and flow down my cheeks.

"I knew something was wrong, Yvette," my mother said, holding me at arm's length. "Why else would you show up on my doorstep out of the clear blue with absolutely no luggage?"

"I'm fine, Mama, just stressed. Tired from the plane ride," I lied, as she led me into a simply decorated living room. We sat on the couch, and she took my hand in hers.

"You know, Yvette, I may have been MIA while you were growing up, and we haven't had much of a relationship now that you're grown, but you are still my child. I know when you're upset about something."

I looked at my mother and laughed slightly. "Everything that's wrong with my life is something that I brought on myself."

"Are you and that doctor on the outs? He told me that you two were getting married this month. Do you have cold feet?"

"Cold feet? I wish it were that simple." I wanted to change the subject, needed to. "Can you take me on a tour of your place?" I asked, standing up and heading down a long hallway.

She guided me with the flourish of a model showing off a new car. The kitchen was first, small but well equipped and so clean it could easily pass a white-glove test. The back yard contained more cacti and a large, covered patio with chairs and a table. A small pool stood in the center of the yard, its bright blue water gleaming in the sun. Back inside, one bedroom was painted aqua and contained a bed, dresser and a mirror; the other was painted stark white with the words of Maya Angelou's poem "I Know Why the Caged Bird Sings" on the walls stenciled in black cursive letters.

"This one is my art studio," she said, smiling widely.

"I didn't know you liked to paint," I said, admiring a woman rising from the ashes like the phoenix. Done in yellow, brown, red and orange, the painting was the most beautiful thing I'd ever seen. "Is this you?"

"It's my rebirth. From the depths of hell to paradise."

I looked at the painting again. "You're doing great out here, Mama. I'm so proud of you."

"I couldn't have done it without you. I'll never be able to repay you for all you've done for me. I owe you everything."

"You don't owe me anything. I'm your child and you're my mother; it's my responsibility to take care of you."

"Yvette, you've always thought like that, and for a long time our situations were reversed. I was like a child and you were so responsible and mature, too mature and responsible sometimes. So I think you have that backwards. I'm supposed to take care of you and now that I'm able, why don't you tell me what's really going on. Why are you really out here?"

"I just needed some time away. I couldn't think in Detroit. I needed a refuge, somewhere no one would think to look."

"Well, you sure picked the right place," she laughed. "No one even knows I'm out here, right?"

"Not a soul."

"Good, don't need to share my paradise with anyone."

"Well, Mama, I hope you can spare just a little bit for me. I need it to heal my heart."

"Only you can do that, Yvette. After all, it's your heart to heal and only you know what medicine you need."

Yvette

34

Nearly two weeks had passed since I'd arrived in Phoenix. My cellphone rang constantly, although fewer and fewer messages were left. Terrence called almost every day begging me to come home, telling me that we could work out anything. I believed him, but I really didn't want anything to work out. I was unwilling to sacrifice myself any longer trying to make what Terrence and I had work. Being with him was old and familiar, but being with him was also filled with drama and stress—two things that I'd gotten used to doing without.

Wendy had also been calling my cellphone, but somehow she had gotten my mother's phone number and called Phoenix twice. My mother told her both times that she hadn't talked to me in over a year.

Calls from Ajani were the only ones I had difficulty not returning. He called twice since I'd been in Phoenix, and both messages he left showed nothing but concern for my well-being. "Just call me and let me know that you're okay," his message from last night urged. "I won't ask you any questions about where you are and why you're there."

I replayed the message at least six times before deleting it. I missed him terribly, but I wasn't ready to go back; actually, I didn't know if I would ever be ready to go back.

On my fourth night at my mother's, I finally began sharing bits and pieces of my life. Prom, college, graduation, planning my wedding, the moment I found out that Terrence was cheating on me and finally the day I moved to Nashville.

"Why did you stop there?" she asked, handing me a bowl of freshly popped popcorn.

"Because moving there is why I'm here."

"What's so special about Nashville?"

"I met a man in Nashville."

"So you cheated on Terrence?" she asked, a knowing smile on her face.

"Cheated, fell in love and lost my job," I confirmed.

"All in six months? Weren't you a busy bee?"

"I didn't go down there looking to meet a man," I said, "especially one as young as Ajani."

"How young is he?"

"Twenty-one. He was supposed to be observing me for a college course, but things got way out of control."

"Is he the reason you're unemployed?"

"Pretty much," I said, thinking back to my last day at Nashville Prep. Lisa had sat outside the school in her car, smiling as I drove away, the contents of my desk in a box in the backseat.

"So," my mother said, dropping down on the couch and picking up the remote, "you fell in love with a twenty-one year old, got fired and left your fiancé to come stay with a mother you haven't seen or talked to in years." Mother stuffed a hand full of popcorn into her mouth. "Yvette, you may not believe this, but we are more alike than you think."

Aside from physical features, I couldn't imagine in what ways she considered us similar. "How are we alike, Mother?"

"We both let Carrie guilt us into doing things we really didn't want to do. And we both run when life gets tough."

"I don't think I let Grandma run my life. I mean she's been dead for a while now, and I made the mess that I'm in all by myself."

"Yes, you did, but why were you with Terrence in the first place? Why did you continue your relationship with him after he cheated on you?"

I sat quietly, knowing that the only reason I stayed was because I knew it was what my grandmother would have wanted.

"You know, my mother always had the best intentions, but somewhere along the way you and I took on her wishes and dreams as our own."

"But—"

"When I was finishing up high school, I wanted to go to art school. Got accepted and everything. My plan was to become a famous artist, travel the world, maybe even open up an art gallery somewhere, but that dream died when Carrie found out that the school was in San Francisco. She put a guilt trip on me that kept me in Detroit. I enrolled in a community college and . . ."

"And got pregnant, had me, got strung out and left," I finished her story with the version my grandmother had preached to me my entire life.

"Close. I went to college, met your father and fell in love. We wanted to get married, or so he said. But after I told him I was pregnant, he left me faster than I could blink. Just up and disappeared one day. After I had you, *that's* when I got strung out."

I knew my father had died about ten years ago, but I never knew all this. "Strung out over someone who wasn't even man enough to take care of you and his child?"

"I was running, Yvette. I wasn't rich, didn't have anywhere to go, so that drug, that pipe, was my escape. It made me forget that I hadn't followed my dream. My man left me, I had a baby that I had no idea how to take care of and an overbearing mother who wouldn't allow me to breathe. Losing love and not living for yourself will make you do some crazy things."

"But I'm not on drugs, Mama."

"No, you're not, but you are doing a different kind of escaping. You ran to Nashville because Terrence cheated on you, then you ran back to Detroit because you fell in love with another man, a much younger man, and lost then your job because of it. Now you're here, running from it all."

I took a deep breath and concentrated on the television screen. "I'm just not ready to go back yet."

"Well, when will you be? Are you planning on waiting until all your money runs out?"

"I'll leave when I figure out what I want to do. Are you trying to kick me out? Do you want me to leave?" I asked defensively.

"No, Yvette, I don't want you to leave; I want you to stop running. I want my child to do what it took me thirty years and a lot of rehabilitation to learn. There comes a time when you have to stand up and face the music, however difficult it may be."

Wendy

35

The banging on the door wouldn't stop. I'd parted the heavy brown curtains at my living-room window and looked outside the minute it began. I did not recognize the drunken, unkempt man standing on my doorstep, but when he began screaming "Wendy!" in a slurred, angry voice, I knew Terrence was my unwanted visitor.

"I know you're in there!" he called, banging on my door. "Stop being a coward and let me in! I need to talk to you, and I'm not leaving until you hear what I have to say."

I peeked out the window again and his tired, bloodshot eyes met mine. I jumped back as if I'd been burned, and it honestly felt as if his eyes, as devastated, angry and bitter as they appeared, were burning a hole into my soul.

"If you don't leave right now, I'm going to call the police!"

"Fuck you!" he screamed hysterically just as Randy, my neighbor and all-around nosey ass across the street, opened his front door and stuck his head out. I watched as Randy squinted his blue eyes and then began dialing his cordless phone furiously.

"Let me in!" Terrence demanded again.

"Wendy, is everything okay?" Randy called, quickly walking across the street towards my little situation. While I didn't want Terrence inside my home, I didn't want my business all in the street either, and that's what Randy was known for.

"Terrence, I'm going to let you in because if I don't, all our shit will end up on the seven o'clock news." I turned the deadbolt and slowly opened the door, stepping aside to let him in.

"Have you talked to Yvette?" he asked immediately. Terrence smelled worse than the bum that slept outside the news station and looked just as bad.

"When was the last time you took a shower?" I wondered, then noticed that he was still wearing the tuxedo shirt and pants he'd worn the day of the wedding—two weeks ago. The bow tie hung loosely around his neck and he had grown a dirty, rough, and matted beard.

"That's none of your business," Terrence responded indignantly, turning to the oval-shaped mirror on the wall and straightening his tie. It was a pretty sad display.

"You're a complete mess."

"I didn't come over here to talk about health and hygiene, Wendy. Now I asked you a question . . ."

"I haven't seen or spoken with Yvette. I've called her cell and her mother's house, but I haven't gotten a response from her and her mother hasn't spoken to her. It's like she's fallen off the face of the Earth," I told him, sitting down in an armchair.

"You're lying! It's not like Yvette to run off and not tell you where she is. I know why you don't want to tell me. You want to keep me all to yourself."

I snorted loudly. He was completely off his rocker. "It's official, Terrence . . . you've lost your mind."

"Let's get something straight right here and now, Wendy. I don't love you and I never will. The worst thing I could have done is sleep with you, and the fact that you're pregnant is sickening."

"The fact that you're standing in my living room smelling like a fifth of scotch and open ass is pretty sickening, too." I stood up and folded my arms across my chest. "I think it's time for you to go."

"Are you still going to have this baby?" he asked, completely ignoring my request to leave.

"I most certainly am, but I thought we already had this discussion."

"I can't believe you're still going to go through with this after all the trouble it's caused."

"What trouble?" I demanded.

"Because of you and this pregnancy crap, Yvette has gone to God only knows where. Because of you, I've probably lost her forever."

"No! Let's get something straight right here, right now. I am not the reason you lost Yvette. Yvette is the reason you lost Yvette. She never trusted you after your little infidelity episode, and meeting that boy didn't help things, either," I reminded him. "You need to get yourself together, Terrence, take a shower and head back to work. You'll need to keep your job with the child-support suit I'm going to put on your ass."

"I'm going to get her back, you know," Terrence slurred, staggering slightly.

"Sure you are," I responded, my voice thick with skepticism.

"You don't believe me?"

"I'm not stupid, Terrence. The only reason Yvette would ever come back here is to pack up the rest of her stuff and hightail it back to Nashville. I mean, she hasn't even contacted me, and we've been friends forever."

"Why would she call you after you admitted to seducing me and then purposely getting pregnant?"

"I already told you that I didn't tell her anything about us! If she knows, it's because Ajani told her!" I felt a sharp pain surge through my lower abdomen. "Terrence, can you just get the hell out of here?" Another pain, this one stronger than the first, caused me to sway, falling onto the coffee table before hitting the carpeted floor. "I should have never started this mess," I said weakly, the pain now nearly blinding me. "I should have let Yvette have you."

"Get up off the damn floor, Wendy. I know this is just another one of your theatrical stunts." Terrence rolled his eyes but came closer to me, the doctor in him both curious and responsible.

"Terrence," I panted, "my stomach . . . the baby . . ." The pain was unbearable.

"Don't play with me, Wendy," Terrence warned, kneeling down, the stench of his unwashed body causing me to gag involuntarily.

"I'm not playing, Terrence," I cried, tears falling hard and fast down my cheeks. "Please call someone . . . I think I'm losing the baby!"

Yvette

36

I hurried down the sterile hallway of Detroit's Riverview Hospital, my heels clicking loudly. The air smelled of cleaning solution and sick people, reminding me of the last time I had seen my grandmother, hanging onto life in this very same hospital.

Wendy's scared and desperate voice kept replaying in my head as I walked. I tried to ignore it, not wanting to return to my past, but I couldn't. No matter what damage I had done to my life, Wendy was still my best friend. When she needed me, I had to be there.

A few hours before, I was sitting outside the airport in Phoenix debating whether or not to get on the plane. "You're ready," my mother had insisted. "You have to stop running, Yvette. Face your life head on. Break the cycle, create your own destiny." She sounded like one of those annoying motivational speakers, but I knew she was right. I couldn't spend the rest of my life acting as if the past six months hadn't happened.

The numbers on the hospital room doors got smaller and smaller as I neared Wendy's private room. I felt my cellphone vibrate inside my purse, and I decided that it was time to stop running. I answered without checking the caller ID.

"Hello?" I said, willing my voice to sound steady and confident.

"Wow!" Ajani's deep voice came on the line. "Wow, Yvette. I really didn't expect you to answer."

I couldn't speak. There were so many things that I wanted, needed to say, but at the same time, my mind was blank.

"Are you okay?" he asked.

"I'm fine, Ajani. How are you?" I managed to choke out. At the sound of his voice, tears began to sting my eyes.

"Better now that I know you're okay."

There was a pause. Ajani felt both familiar and like a complete stranger. I knew I still loved him, probably always would, but I wasn't sure that we were right for each other anymore. So many things had changed; I was different and I didn't know if Ajani could handle it. But then again, maybe we were never right for each other.

"Where are you?"

"In Detroit. Something happened to Wendy; she called and said she needed me."

"Wendy, huh? Have you been speaking with her this entire time?"

"No, I haven't spoken with anyone. Wendy left me a voicemail. I didn't want to come back, but it's time I stop running away from my problems," I said, stopping three doors down from Wendy's room.

"So you're going to see Terrence?" Ajani sounded strange, almost as if seeing Terrence was exactly what he wanted me to do.

"Yeah, I guess I will."

"Then I don't need to be the one to tell you anything. Sounds like you'll find out for yourself."

"Find out what?" I pressed, suddenly nervous.

"I don't want to be the one to tell you, Yvette."

I decided to let whatever he was talking about drop for now.

"You know, we have some unfinished business of our own," Ajani reminded me.

"I know."

"So do I get to see you?"

"Ajani I—"

"I just want to talk to you," he said, cutting me off.

"We can just talk on the phone. I think that if we see each other . . ."

"You won't really hear what I have to say over the phone, Yvette."

I weakened, knowing he wouldn't take no for an answer. "I'm different, Ajani; so much has changed."

"I'm different, too, Yvette."

I leaned against the cream-colored wall and shut my eyes. "Can you come here?" I asked quickly before I could change my mind. "I'm moving into my grandmother's house until I decide what's next."

"I'll be wherever you want me. I can be in Detroit by tomorrow morning."

"I'll see you then," I responded, closing my phone and smiling in spite of myself.

I continued down the hall, this time slowly and quietly; I needed the few extra seconds before facing Wendy.

Also, I wanted to think about Ajani and our meeting tomorrow.

"Wendy, I'm sorry . . ."

I heard the voice faintly at first, coming from a room two doors down from where I was standing. Then louder, more insistent, the speaker choking out the words almost in a sob, reminding me of the way Terrence had apologized after he'd been caught cheating.

"I was angry in the beginning, but after all this ..." the vaguely familiar voice whimpered. I stopped just before I reached Wendy's room door.

"Don't try to act as if everything is okay, Terrence." Wendy's voice could be heard loud and clear in the hall. "You're the reason that I'm in here."

Confusion settled over me. Why was Terrence in Wendy's hospital room? Why was he apologizing?

"I know that I haven't been perfect, but this has all been a huge change for me. First, Yvette leaves, then you and I get together and then you tell me that you're pregnant and I'm the father! How did you expect me to feel?"

Gasping, I slid down the wall and onto the ice-cold linoleum.

"I expected you to at least take care of your responsibilities and not treat me as if I were some street whore," my best friend responded bitterly.

"I thought that if I accepted the fact that you were going to have my baby, then Yvette would never come back," he whined.

"She's never coming back," Wendy said, her voice softening noticeably.

"I know that now, Wendy, and I'm ready for us to be a family."

I sat on the floor, my back resting against the hard wall. It all made sense now—the way Wendy always took Terrence's side, the day she told me that she'd seen him having lunch with another woman. It was obviously all in her plans: She had always wanted him, and when I left for Nashville my best friend decided to move in for the kill.

"I don't want to be your second choice. I don't want you to be here for me and this baby because you don't want to be alone."

"That's not what this is about," Terrence insisted.

"Then explain to me, Terrence, what is it about?"

I stood on wobbly legs and looked around, having no idea what my next move would be. There was no doubt in my mind that a confrontation was necessary, but as the bile rose up bitterly in my throat, I wondered if I would be able to . . .

"I want to be with you," Terrence said. I forced myself forward and peeked into the room. Wendy sat resting comfortably in the bed, a manicured hand on her belly. Terrence leaned over her, wearing an expression that I had never seen grace his features—genuine remorse.

Without knowing what was pushing me forward, I stepped into the room, startling them both. They exchanged surprised glances, probably wondering how much of their intimate conversation I'd been privy to.

"Is everything okay?" I asked Wendy, not bothering to look Terrence's way.

"I can't believe that you're here. When I called I never really thought that you'd come."

"Obviously," I responded, unable to hide the contempt in my voice. "I hope that the baby is okay."

"Yes, the baby's fine. I had a really stressful morning and felt some sharp pains in my stomach. My doctor wants me to stay away from upsetting situations for a while," Wendy explained. Terrence remained silent.

"Then maybe I shouldn't be here."

"No," Terrence said, rising from his seat slowly. "Maybe I'm the one who needs to leave."

"Oh, come on now, Terrence, why should you be the one to leave? After all, this is your baby we're talking about, right? I'm sure that you want to be with Wendy right now."

The room grew eerily quiet. Although I was angrier than I had been in a long time, a sickly sweet smile never left my face. I refused to embarrass myself.

"Yvette, I'm so sorry . . ." Terrence began, but I lifted my hand to silence him.

"I expected this from you, Terrence. Infidelity is just in your nature, but not from Wendy. I can't believe you would do this to me."

"We didn't plan it," Wendy said.

"I think you did. Everyone in this room knows that you've always wanted Terrence; hell, you've always wanted everything I have." My voice exuded calmness and confidence, but inside a roaring fire raged.

"Don't go putting this on me, Yvette," Wendy retorted. "You were the one who decided to move away.

You're the one who decided to have an affair with a college student. Whatever Terrence and I did was a direct result of the choices *you* made."

"Are you *serious*?" I asked. Her audacity was stunning. "Wendy, we were best friends. You betrayed me; you slept with my fiancé."

"Yes, I did. I slept with your fiancé and you slept with Ajani."

"And the entire time you made me feel guilty about what was going on . . . 'Terrence is a good man, you're making a mistake,' " I mocked. "Now you're pregnant with his baby . . ."

I looked from Terrence to Wendy and back again. "I feel so stupid."

Both stared at me silently, something passing for guilt on their faces. "I hope that the two—I'm sorry, the three of you—are very happy together," I said and turned to leave.

"Why can't we just talk about this?" Terrence asked, finally finding his voice.

I whirled around, ready to strike. "What is there to talk about, Terrence? You and Wendy have made it perfectly clear that my opinion isn't necessary in this little drama!" My voice was becoming louder, more shrill, so much so a nurse paused outside Wendy's room before moving on down the hall.

"And what if I had decided to marry Terrence? Would the two of you have kept sleeping together, raising your little illegitimate family on the side?"

"No!" they both exclaimed in unison.

"This is too much," I said, feeling sick to my stomach. "This is like some disgusting nightmare. The past month has been like something I can't wake up from, and the two of you," I said, pointing a trembling finger from Terrence to Wendy, "deserve each other."

Yvette

37

Ajani walked slowly up the porch steps. He looked better than I remembered, older somehow, as if in these past few weeks the weight of the world had been resting on his shoulders.

"How are you?" I asked, letting him in. He walked past me, making my spine tingle.

"I'm good. How are you?" Ajani stood looking as if all he wanted to do was to reach out and touch me.

"I'm-I'm-" I stuttered, unsure of myself. "I really don't know how I am, actually. I think coming here may have been a huge mistake."

"I take it you've seen Wendy?" Ajani sat down on the couch and watched me curiously. "Is everything okay?"

"You knew, didn't you?" I asked, sitting next to him. "That's what you wanted to tell me yesterday over the phone. You knew that Wendy and Terrence had been sleeping together."

"I found out after you left the wedding. They were arguing and blaming each other, and it just all came out somehow."

"But you wouldn't tell me . . ."

"I didn't want you to think that I was making it up so that you would come back to me. Something that big deserved to be uncovered on its own."

"Well, it did. I heard them discussing their fling in Wendy's hospital room after she almost lost her baby . . . their baby."

"I'm sorry, Yvette," Ajani said me sincerely.

"It's not your fault; they were the ones who decided to betray me," I said sadly. "Wendy and I have been friends for a very long time. You know this was not the way it was supposed to be? I moved to Nashville to get clarity, to find out if Terrence was really the man I was supposed to marry—"

"If you think about it, Yvette, Nashville eventually did exactly what it was supposed to do. You found out that Terrence is a cheater and Wendy is a liar."

"But, Ajani, I'm more confused than ever. I have no job, no fiancé, no best friend."

"You've got me," Ajani said, his eyes boring into mine.

"Ajani, look at what my life has become."

"What? What has your life become? You've been given the opportunity to start over, make your own path, really be happy."

"It's too late to start over!" I yelled at him, angry and frustrated at the same time.

"No, Yvette, it's too late not to!"

I closed my eyes, hearing his voice echo in my ears long after he had stopped speaking.

"Where did you go after the wedding?" he asked gently, moving closer to me.

"My mother's. I knew that no one would look for me there."

"And how'd that go?"

"She's doing well. I should have gone to her a long time ago. I learned so much while I was there, so much about myself and why I am the way I am."

"I was worried about you," Ajani said, touching my face. I wanted to savor his touch, I wanted to feel him remove my clothes and place his body on top of mine, but I couldn't . . . "I still love you, Yvette."

"Don't say that, Ajani."

"Why not? It's the truth. I love you and I want to be with you. I need you."

"As difficult as this is for me to say, Ajani, I need to choose myself. For the first time in my life, I need to listen to me. I need to slow down and find out what being Yvette Brooks is all about. It's time for me to stand on my own two feet for a change."

"I get all that, Yvette, but—"

"I love you, Ajani, but I have to learn how to love myself, too."

"So should I just go back to Nashville and pretend that we never met?"

"No, that's not what I want you to do."

"Then what?"

"I want you go to back to Nashville and finish school, get a job and live your life."

"And where does that leave us, Yvette?"

"It leaves us with six months that I will never forget. It leaves me loving a man who has changed my life forever."

"This is crazy, Yvette. So we're done?"

"We're done."

Ajani stood, smiling that one-hundred-watt smile at me. "We've been done before, Yvette," he told me, his confidence returning.

"I know, but this time is different."

"Sure it is, Yvette. You'll keep in touch, won't you, come to my graduation and all that?"

"Of course. Nothing could keep me away."

"I'm going to hold you to that," Ajani said pulling me up. I wrapped my arms around his neck and inhaled his fresh, clean, masculine scent. "Don't forget me," Ajani said, pressing his mouth against mine for one last kiss.

"Ajani, I could never, ever forget you."

EPILOGUE

"Are you nervous?" Jordan asked me quietly. I stood at the open French doors looking out into the crystal-clear Caribbean Sea and marveling at how wonderful my life was turning out to be. Just three months ago, I watched Ajani walk across the stage to receive his degree, and now I was only minutes away from becoming his wife.

When Ajani and I last saw each other, I honestly thought our relationship was over. I had vowed to change, I vowed to get to know myself, and ending things with Ajani was to be only the first step in that transformation. I sold my grandmother's home and left Detroit and the memories of my life there and relocated to Denver, where jobs were plentiful and no one knew who I was, much less what I had been through.

A few months later, I received an invitation to Ajani's graduation. He never called or contacted me, but the invitation said it all: He was growing up and he wanted me to be a witness to his own new beginning.

I was tempted to toss the invitation, wanting to forget everything that Ajani was reminiscent of, but something stopped me. I kept the invitation and logged on to the

Internet to reserve my plane ticket and a hotel room in Nashville before I lost my nerve.

Ajani looked more handsome and mature than I remembered. He wore a suit and tie, and his black gown was adorned with gold cords, indicating that he was graduating with honors.

I sat in the packed gym stadium having second thoughts about being there. Ajani didn't know I was there, but just as I stood to leave the stadium, his name was called. He walked across the stage and shook hands with everyone, all the while scanning the audience. As if by luck or by fate, our eyes met, and without caring about how it looked or what others would think Ajani hurried from the stage and into the audience, where I waited for him nervously.

"Of course I'm nervous. Wouldn't you be?" I replied, turning from the picturesque view and looking into Jordan's smiling face.

"Yeah, I guess I would be, but it's been a long time coming," Jordan said, holding my hand. "You look beautiful."

"I feel beautiful," I said, looking down at the knee-length, white halter dress I was wearing. I held a small bouquet of red roses, my ponytail was held back with a sparkling tie and my feet were bare. "I can't get over how different it is this time around," I said, more to myself than to Jordan.

"This time it's right," Jordan said, going to the French doors and beckoning me forward to follow.

"This time it's perfect," I agreed.

We walked through the French doors and onto the sandy Bahamian beach.

"There she is," Ajani said, smiling from ear to ear. He was flanked by his two brothers, Jabari and Dakari, and all three were wearing jeans and white linen button-down shirts. "Hurry up, girl! Let's get this show on the road!"

"I'm coming, I'm coming, Ajani. You can't rush perfection."

"You look great," he whispered, taking my hand and kissing me softy. "Are you ready?"

"Are *you* ready?" I asked jokingly.

"I've been ready since the day I met you." He kissed me again, and a warm rush of joy spread through every inch of my body. This was real happiness; this was life at its best.

"This is disgusting!" Jabari said, rolling his eyes skyward. "Can the two of you just tie the knot already? I'm trying to get my party on, and if that waitress passes by with anymore rum punch, you're going to have an extremely drunk groomsman on your hands."

"It is my understanding that you have written your own vows," the minister said, looking at Ajani and me with an amused smile.

"Yes, and Yvette will go first," Ajani volunteered.

I looked at him and smiled indulgently. "Okay, since I don't seem to have a choice . . ." I stood tall and looked into Ajani's eyes.

"I can't believe that I am actually standing here, so close to becoming your wife," I began, immediately feeling tears form in the corner of my eyes. "The first time we met, I knew that you were someone special, someone I had been waiting for my entire life. But my world was so complicated then, and I couldn't envision spending the rest of my life with you. Now, Ajani, I cannot imagine spending the rest of my life without you.

"I promise to love, honor and keep you all the days of my life. I promise to always put our love first, give you lots of babies and to make you the happiest man in the world. I promise to make you feel as special as you make me feel."

Ajani took a deep breath and squeezed my hand before speaking. "Yvette, you are amazing. You are everything I never thought I wanted in a woman but everything I need. You are the first thing I think about when I wake up and the last thing I think about at night. You are my best friend, the one I want to grow old with, and the one I want to take care of. You are my everything, and it is because of you that I am complete."

I looked into Ajani's eyes and smiled, peace and happiness filling every inch of me. This was real, this was right, and I couldn't believe that I was finally here.

The minister cleared his throat, "By the power vested in me by the Commonwealth of the Bahamas, I now pronounce you husband and wife. You may kiss your bride."

As our small bridal party applauded, my husband wrapped his strong arms around me, pulled me close and kissed me until I was dizzy.

ABOUT THE AUTHOR

Maryam Diaab was born in Detroit, Michigan and received a degree in Arts and Sciences from Tennessee State University in Nashville, Tennessee. She currently works as a fifth grade Reading and Language Arts teacher in the Metro-Detroit area where she lives with her husband and two sons. Her fist novel, *Where I Want To Be*, was published by Genesis Press in January 2008. *Things Forbidden* is her second novel.

Visit the author at www.maryamdiaab.blogspot.com.

2008 Reprint Mass Market Titles

January

Cautious Heart
Cheris F. Hodges
ISBN-13: 978-1-58571-301-1
ISBN-10: 1-58571-301-5
$6.99

Suddenly You
Crystal Hubbard
ISBN-13: 978-1-58571-302-8
ISBN-10: 1-58571-302-3
$6.99

February

Passion
T. T. Henderson
ISBN-13: 978-1-58571-303-5
ISBN-10: 1-58571-303-1
$6.99

Whispers in the Sand
LaFlorya Gauthier
ISBN-13: 978-1-58571-304-2
ISBN-10: 1-58571-304-x
$6.99

March

Life Is Never As It Seems
J. J. Michael
ISBN-13: 978-1-58571-305-9
ISBN-10: 1-58571-305-8
$6.99

Beyond the Rapture
Beverly Clark
ISBN-13: 978-1-58571-306-6
ISBN-10: 1-58571-306-6
$6.99

April

A Heart's Awakening
Veronica Parker
ISBN-13: 978-1-58571-307-3
ISBN-10: 1-58571-307-4
$6.99

Breeze
Robin Lynette Hampton
ISBN-13: 978-1-58571-308-0
ISBN-10: 1-58571-308-2
$6.99

May

I'll Be Your Shelter
Giselle Carmichael
ISBN-13: 978-1-58571-309-7
ISBN-10: 1-58571-309-0
$6.99

Careless Whispers
Rochelle Alers
ISBN-13: 978-1-58571-310-3
ISBN-10: 1-58571-310-4
$6.99

June

Sin
Crystal Rhodes
ISBN-13: 978-1-58571-311-0
ISBN-10: 1-58571-311-2
$6.99

Dark Storm Rising
Chinelu Moore
ISBN-13: 978-1-58571-312-7
ISBN-10: 1-58571-312-0
$6.99

2008 Reprint Mass Market Titles (continued)

July

Object of His Desire
A.C. Arthur
ISBN-13: 978-1-58571-313-4
ISBN-10: 1-58571-313-9
$6.99

Angel's Paradise
Janice Angelique
ISBN-13: 978-1-58571-314-1
ISBN-10: 1-58571-314-7
$6.99

August

Unbreak My Heart
Dar Tomlinson
ISBN-13: 978-1-58571-315-8
ISBN-10: 1-58571-315-5
$6.99

All I Ask
Barbara Keaton
ISBN-13: 978-1-58571-316-5
ISBN-10: 1-58571-316-3
$6.99

September

Icie
Pamela Leigh Starr
ISBN-13: 978-1-58571-275-5
ISBN-10: 1-58571-275-2
$6.99

At Last
Lisa Riley
ISBN-13: 978-1-58571-276-2
ISBN-10: 1-58571-276-0
$6.99

October

Everlastin' Love
Gay G. Gunn
ISBN-13: 978-1-58571-277-9
ISBN-10: 1-58571-277-9
$6.99

Three Wishes
Seressia Glass
ISBN-13: 978-1-58571-278-6
ISBN-10: 1-58571-278-7
$6.99

November

Yesterday Is Gone
Beverly Clark
ISBN-13: 978-1-58571-279-3
ISBN-10: 1-58571-279-5
$6.99

Again My Love
Kayla Perrin
ISBN-13: 978-1-58571-280-9
ISBN-10: 1-58571-280-9
$6.99

December

Office Policy
A.C. Arthur
ISBN-13: 978-1-58571-281-6
ISBN-10: 1-58571-281-7
$6.99

Rendezvous With Fate
Jeanne Sumerix
ISBN-13: 978-1-58571-283-3
ISBN-10: 1-58571-283-3
$6.99

2008 New Mass Market Titles

January

Where I Want To Be
Maryam Diaab
ISBN-13: 978-1-58571-268-7
ISBN-10: 1-58571-268-X
$6.99

Never Say Never
Michele Cameron
ISBN-13: 978-1-58571-269-4
ISBN-10: 1-58571-269-8
$6.99

February

Stolen Memories
Michele Sudler
ISBN-13: 978-1-58571-270-0
ISBN-10: 1-58571-270-1
$6.99

Dawn's Harbor
Kymberly Hunt
ISBN-13: 978-1-58571-271-7
ISBN-10: 1-58571-271-X
$6.99

March

Undying Love
Renee Alexis
ISBN-13: 978-1-58571-272-4
ISBN-10: 1-58571-272-8
$6.99

Blame It On Paradise
Crystal Hubbard
ISBN-13: 978-1-58571-273-1
ISBN-10: 1-58571-273-6
$6.99

April

When A Man Loves A Woman
La Connie Taylor-Jones
ISBN-13: 978-1-58571-274-8
ISBN-10: 1-58571-274-4
$6.99

Choices
Tammy Williams
ISBN-13: 978-1-58571-300-4
ISBN-10: 1-58571-300-7
$6.99

May

Dream Runner
Gail McFarland
ISBN-13: 978-1-58571-317-2
ISBN-10: 1-58571-317-1
$6.99

Southern Fried Standards
S.R. Maddox
ISBN-13: 978-1-58571-318-9
ISBN-10: 1-58571-318-X
$6.99

June

Looking for Lily
Africa Fine
ISBN-13: 978-1-58571-319-6
ISBN-10: 1-58571-319-8
$6.99

Bliss, Inc.
Chamein Canton
ISBN-13: 978-1-58571-325-7
ISBN-10: 1-58571-325-2
$6.99

2008 New Mass Market Titles (continued)

July

Love's Secrets
Yolanda McVey
ISBN-13: 978-1-58571-321-9
ISBN-10: 1-58571-321-X
$6.99

Things Forbidden
Maryam Diaab
ISBN-13: 978-1-58571-327-1
ISBN-10: 1-58571-327-9
$6.99

August

Storm
Pamela Leigh Starr
ISBN-13: 978-1-58571-323-3
ISBN-10: 1-58571-323-6
$6.99

Passion's Furies
AlTonya Washington
ISBN-13: 978-1-58571-324-0
ISBN-10: 1-58571-324-4
$6.99

September

Three Doors Down
Michele Sudler
ISBN-13: 978-1-58571-332-5
ISBN-10: 1-58571-332-5
$6.99

Mr Fix-It
Crystal Hubbard
ISBN-13: 978-1-58571-326-4
ISBN-10: 1-58571-326-0
$6.99

October

Moments of Clarity
Michele Cameron
ISBN-13: 978-1-58571-330-1
ISBN-10: 1-58571-330-9
$6.99

Lady Preacher
K.T. Richey
ISBN-13: 978-1-58571-333-2
ISBN-10: 1-58571-333-3
$6.99

November

This Life Isn't Perfect Holla
Sandra Foy
ISBN: 978-1-58571-331-8
ISBN-10: 1-58571-331-7
$6.99

Promises Made
Bernice Layton
ISBN-13: 978-1-58571-334-9
ISBN-10: 1-58571-334-1
$6.99

December

A Voice Behind Thunder
Carrie Elizabeth Greene
ISBN-13: 978-1-58571-329-5
ISBN-10: 1-58571-329-5
$6.99

The More Things Change
Chamein Canton
ISBN-13: 978-1-58571-328-8
ISBN-10: 1-58571-328-7
$6.99

Other Genesis Press, Inc. Titles

A Dangerous Deception	J.M. Jeffries	$8.95
A Dangerous Love	J.M. Jeffries	$8.95
A Dangerous Obsession	J.M. Jeffries	$8.95
A Drummer's Beat to Mend	Kei Swanson	$9.95
A Happy Life	Charlotte Harris	$9.95
A Heart's Awakening	Veronica Parker	$9.95
A Lark on the Wing	Phyliss Hamilton	$9.95
A Love of Her Own	Cheris F. Hodges	$9.95
A Love to Cherish	Beverly Clark	$8.95
A Risk of Rain	Dar Tomlinson	$8.95
A Taste of Temptation	Reneé Alexis	$9.95
A Twist of Fate	Beverly Clark	$8.95
A Will to Love	Angie Daniels	$9.95
Acquisitions	Kimberley White	$8.95
Across	Carol Payne	$12.95
After the Vows	Leslie Esdaile	$10.95
(Summer Anthology)	T.T. Henderson	
	Jacqueline Thomas	
Again My Love	Kayla Perrin	$10.95
Against the Wind	Gwynne Forster	$8.95
All I Ask	Barbara Keaton	$8.95
Always You	Crystal Hubbard	$6.99
Ambrosia	T.T. Henderson	$8.95
An Unfinished Love Affair	Barbara Keaton	$8.95
And Then Came You	Dorothy Elizabeth Love	$8.95
Angel's Paradise	Janice Angelique	$9.95
At Last	Lisa G. Riley	$8.95
Best of Friends	Natalie Dunbar	$8.95
Beyond the Rapture	Beverly Clark	$9.95

Other Genesis Press, Inc. Titles (continued)

Blaze	Barbara Keaton	$9.95
Blood Lust	J. M. Jeffries	$9.95
Blood Seduction	J.M. Jeffries	$9.95
Bodyguard	Andrea Jackson	$9.95
Boss of Me	Diana Nyad	$8.95
Bound by Love	Beverly Clark	$8.95
Breeze	Robin Hampton Allen	$10.95
Broken	Dar Tomlinson	$24.95
By Design	Barbara Keaton	$8.95
Cajun Heat	Charlene Berry	$8.95
Careless Whispers	Rochelle Alers	$8.95
Cats & Other Tales	Marilyn Wagner	$8.95
Caught in a Trap	Andre Michelle	$8.95
Caught Up In the Rapture	Lisa G. Riley	$9.95
Cautious Heart	Cheris F Hodges	$8.95
Chances	Pamela Leigh Starr	$8.95
Cherish the Flame	Beverly Clark	$8.95
Class Reunion	Irma Jenkins/ John Brown	$12.95
Code Name: Diva	J.M. Jeffries	$9.95
Conquering Dr. Wexler's Heart	Kimberley White	$9.95
Corporate Seduction	A.C. Arthur	$9.95
Crossing Paths, Tempting Memories	Dorothy Elizabeth Love	$9.95
Crush	Crystal Hubbard	$9.95
Cypress Whisperings	Phyllis Hamilton	$8.95
Dark Embrace	Crystal Wilson Harris	$8.95
Dark Storm Rising	Chinelu Moore	$10.95

Other Genesis Press, Inc. Titles (continued)

Daughter of the Wind	Joan Xian	$8.95
Deadly Sacrifice	Jack Kean	$22.95
Designer Passion	Dar Tomlinson Diana Richeaux	$8.95
Do Over	Celya Bowers	$9.95
Dreamtective	Liz Swados	$5.95
Ebony Angel	Deatri King-Bey	$9.95
Ebony Butterfly II	Delilah Dawson	$14.95
Echoes of Yesterday	Beverly Clark	$9.95
Eden's Garden	Elizabeth Rose	$8.95
Eve's Prescription	Edwina Martin Arnold	$8.95
Everlastin' Love	Gay G. Gunn	$8.95
Everlasting Moments	Dorothy Elizabeth Love	$8.95
Everything and More	Sinclair Lebeau	$8.95
Everything but Love	Natalie Dunbar	$8.95
Falling	Natalie Dunbar	$9.95
Fate	Pamela Leigh Starr	$8.95
Finding Isabella	A.J. Garrotto	$8.95
Forbidden Quest	Dar Tomlinson	$10.95
Forever Love	Wanda Y. Thomas	$8.95
From the Ashes	Kathleen Suzanne Jeanne Sumerix	$8.95
Gentle Yearning	Rochelle Alers	$10.95
Glory of Love	Sinclair LeBeau	$10.95
Go Gentle into that Good Night	Malcom Boyd	$12.95
Goldengroove	Mary Beth Craft	$16.95
Groove, Bang, and Jive	Steve Cannon	$8.99
Hand in Glove	Andrea Jackson	$9.95

Other Genesis Press, Inc. Titles (continued)

Hard to Love	Kimberley White	$9.95
Hart & Soul	Angie Daniels	$8.95
Heart of the Phoenix	A.C. Arthur	$9.95
Heartbeat	Stephanie Bedwell-Grime	$8.95
Hearts Remember	M. Loui Quezada	$8.95
Hidden Memories	Robin Allen	$10.95
Higher Ground	Leah Latimer	$19.95
Hitler, the War, and the Pope	Ronald Rychiak	$26.95
How to Write a Romance	Kathryn Falk	$18.95
I Married a Reclining Chair	Lisa M. Fuhs	$8.95
I'll Be Your Shelter	Giselle Carmichael	$8.95
I'll Paint a Sun	A.J. Garrotto	$9.95
Icie	Pamela Leigh Starr	$8.95
Illusions	Pamela Leigh Starr	$8.95
Indigo After Dark Vol. I	Nia Dixon/Angelique	$10.95
Indigo After Dark Vol. II	Dolores Bundy/ Cole Riley	$10.95
Indigo After Dark Vol. III	Montana Blue/ Coco Morena	$10.95
Indigo After Dark Vol. IV	Cassandra Colt/	$14.95
Indigo After Dark Vol. V	Delilah Dawson	$14.95
Indiscretions	Donna Hill	$8.95
Intentional Mistakes	Michele Sudler	$9.95
Interlude	Donna Hill	$8.95
Intimate Intentions	Angie Daniels	$8.95
It's Not Over Yet	J.J. Michael	$9.95
Jolie's Surrender	Edwina Martin-Arnold	$8.95
Kiss or Keep	Debra Phillips	$8.95
Lace	Giselle Carmichael	$9.95

Other Genesis Press, Inc. Titles (continued)

Last Train to Memphis	Elsa Cook	$12.95
Lasting Valor	Ken Olsen	$24.95
Let Us Prey	Hunter Lundy	$25.95
Lies Too Long	Pamela Ridley	$13.95
Life Is Never As It Seems	J.J. Michael	$12.95
Lighter Shade of Brown	Vicki Andrews	$8.95
Love Always	Mildred E. Riley	$10.95
Love Doesn't Come Easy	Charlyne Dickerson	$8.95
Love Unveiled	Gloria Greene	$10.95
Love's Deception	Charlene Berry	$10.95
Love's Destiny	M. Loui Quezada	$8.95
Mae's Promise	Melody Walcott	$8.95
Magnolia Sunset	Giselle Carmichael	$8.95
Many Shades of Gray	Dyanne Davis	$6.99
Matters of Life and Death	Lesego Malepe, Ph.D.	$15.95
Meant to Be	Jeanne Sumerix	$8.95
Midnight Clear (Anthology)	Leslie Esdaile Gwynne Forster Carmen Green Monica Jackson	$10.95
Midnight Magic	Gwynne Forster	$8.95
Midnight Peril	Vicki Andrews	$10.95
Misconceptions	Pamela Leigh Starr	$9.95
Montgomery's Children	Richard Perry	$14.95
My Buffalo Soldier	Barbara B. K. Reeves	$8.95
Naked Soul	Gwynne Forster	$8.95
Next to Last Chance	Louisa Dixon	$24.95
No Apologies	Seressia Glass	$8.95
No Commitment Required	Seressia Glass	$8.95

Other Genesis Press, Inc. Titles (continued)

No Regrets	Mildred E. Riley	$8.95
Not His Type	Chamein Canton	$6.99
Nowhere to Run	Gay G. Gunn	$10.95
O Bed! O Breakfast!	Rob Kuehnle	$14.95
Object of His Desire	A. C. Arthur	$8.95
Office Policy	A. C. Arthur	$9.95
Once in a Blue Moon	Dorianne Cole	$9.95
One Day at a Time	Bella McFarland	$8.95
One in A Million	Barbara Keaton	$6.99
One of These Days	Michele Sudler	$9.95
Outside Chance	Louisa Dixon	$24.95
Passion	T.T. Henderson	$10.95
Passion's Blood	Cherif Fortin	$22.95
Passion's Journey	Wanda Y. Thomas	$8.95
Past Promises	Jahmel West	$8.95
Path of Fire	T.T. Henderson	$8.95
Path of Thorns	Annetta P. Lee	$9.95
Peace Be Still	Colette Haywood	$12.95
Picture Perfect	Reon Carter	$8.95
Playing for Keeps	Stephanie Salinas	$8.95
Pride & Joi	Gay G. Gunn	$15.95
Pride & Joi	Gay G. Gunn	$8.95
Promises to Keep	Alicia Wiggins	$8.95
Quiet Storm	Donna Hill	$10.95
Reckless Surrender	Rochelle Alers	$6.95
Red Polka Dot in a World of Plaid	Varian Johnson	$12.95
Reluctant Captive	Joyce Jackson	$8.95
Rendezvous with Fate	Jeanne Sumerix	$8.95

Other Genesis Press, Inc. Titles (continued)

Revelations	Cheris F. Hodges	$8.95
Rivers of the Soul	Leslie Esdaile	$8.95
Rocky Mountain Romance	Kathleen Suzanne	$8.95
Rooms of the Heart	Donna Hill	$8.95
Rough on Rats and Tough on Cats	Chris Parker	$12.95
Secret Library Vol. 1	Nina Sheridan	$18.95
Secret Library Vol. 2	Cassandra Colt	$8.95
Secret Thunder	Annetta P. Lee	$9.95
Shades of Brown	Denise Becker	$8.95
Shades of Desire	Monica White	$8.95
Shadows in the Moonlight	Jeanne Sumerix	$8.95
Sin	Crystal Rhodes	$8.95
Small Whispers	Annetta P. Lee	$6.99
So Amazing	Sinclair LeBeau	$8.95
Somebody's Someone	Sinclair LeBeau	$8.95
Someone to Love	Alicia Wiggins	$8.95
Song in the Park	Martin Brant	$15.95
Soul Eyes	Wayne L. Wilson	$12.95
Soul to Soul	Donna Hill	$8.95
Southern Comfort	J.M. Jeffries	$8.95
Still the Storm	Sharon Robinson	$8.95
Still Waters Run Deep	Leslie Esdaile	$8.95
Stolen Kisses	Dominiqua Douglas	$9.95
Stories to Excite You	Anna Forrest/Divine	$14.95
Subtle Secrets	Wanda Y. Thomas	$8.95
Suddenly You	Crystal Hubbard	$9.95
Sweet Repercussions	Kimberley White	$9.95
Sweet Sensations	Gwendolyn Bolton	$9.95

Other Genesis Press, Inc. Titles (continued)

Sweet Tomorrows	Kimberly White	$8.95
Taken by You	Dorothy Elizabeth Love	$9.95
Tattooed Tears	T. T. Henderson	$8.95
The Color Line	Lizzette Grayson Carter	$9.95
The Color of Trouble	Dyanne Davis	$8.95
The Disappearance of Allison Jones	Kayla Perrin	$5.95
The Fires Within	Beverly Clark	$9.95
The Foursome	Celya Bowers	$6.99
The Honey Dipper's Legacy	Pannell-Allen	$14.95
The Joker's Love Tune	Sidney Rickman	$15.95
The Little Pretender	Barbara Cartland	$10.95
The Love We Had	Natalie Dunbar	$8.95
The Man Who Could Fly	Bob & Milana Beamon	$18.95
The Missing Link	Charlyne Dickerson	$8.95
The Mission	Pamela Leigh Starr	$6.99
The Perfect Frame	Beverly Clark	$9.95
The Price of Love	Sinclair LeBeau	$8.95
The Smoking Life	Ilene Barth	$29.95
The Words of the Pitcher	Kei Swanson	$8.95
Three Wishes	Seressia Glass	$8.95
Ties That Bind	Kathleen Suzanne	$8.95
Tiger Woods	Libby Hughes	$5.95
Time is of the Essence	Angie Daniels	$9.95
Timeless Devotion	Bella McFarland	$9.95
Tomorrow's Promise	Leslie Esdaile	$8.95
Truly Inseparable	Wanda Y. Thomas	$8.95
Two Sides to Every Story	Dyanne Davis	$9.95
Unbreak My Heart	Dar Tomlinson	$8.95

Other Genesis Press, Inc. Titles (continued)

Uncommon Prayer	Kenneth Swanson	$9.95
Unconditional Love	Alicia Wiggins	$8.95
Unconditional	A.C. Arthur	$9.95
Until Death Do Us Part	Susan Paul	$8.95
Vows of Passion	Bella McFarland	$9.95
Wedding Gown	Dyanne Davis	$8.95
What's Under Benjamin's Bed	Sandra Schaffer	$8.95
When Dreams Float	Dorothy Elizabeth Love	$8.95
When I'm With You	LaConnie Taylor-Jones	$6.99
Whispers in the Night	Dorothy Elizabeth Love	$8.95
Whispers in the Sand	LaFlorya Gauthier	$10.95
Who's That Lady?	Andrea Jackson	$9.95
Wild Ravens	Altonya Washington	$9.95
Yesterday Is Gone	Beverly Clark	$10.95
Yesterday's Dreams, Tomorrow's Promises	Reon Laudat	$8.95
Your Precious Love	Sinclair LeBeau	$8.95

Order Form

Mail to: Genesis Press, Inc.
P.O. Box 101
Columbus, MS 39703

Name ______________________________
Address ______________________________
City/State ____________________ Zip ____________
Telephone ____________________

Ship to (if different from above)
Name ______________________________
Address ______________________________
City/State ____________________ Zip ____________
Telephone ____________________

Credit Card Information
Credit Card # ____________________ ☐ Visa ☐ Mastercard
Expiration Date (mm/yy) ______________ ☐ AmEx ☐ Discover

Qty.	Author	Title	Price	Total

Use this order form, or call 1-888-INDIGO-1

Total for books ____________
Shipping and handling:
$5 first two books,
$1 each additional book ____________
Total S & H ____________
Total amount enclosed ____________

Mississippi residents add 7% sales tax

Visit www.genesis-press.com for latest releases and excerpts.

A Caroline Grade Mystery

The Paper Route Treasure

by Marcia Hoehne

LION PUBLISHING
A Division of Cook Communications

Published by Lion Publishing Corporation
850 North Grove Ave. Elgin, Illinois 60120, USA
ISBN 0-7459-2801-3

First edition 1994

Cover art by Robert Papp
Cover design by Jeff Barnes

The characters and situations in this book are entirely imaginary and bear no relation to any real person or actual happening.

Library of Congress Cataloging-in-Publication Data

Hoehne, Marcia
The paper route treausre / Marica Hoehne.—1st ed.
—(The Caroline Grade mysteries)
Summary: Caroline and Chad, two friends who are in the Gifted and Talented program at school, help Mrs. Ames unscramble codes and solve word puzzles to find a treasure.
ISBN 0-7459-2801-3
[1. Buried Treasure—Fiction. 2. Gifted children—Fiction. 3. Christian life—Ficion.] I. Title. II. Series: Hoehne, Marcia, Caroline Grade mysteries.
PZ7H667Pap 1994
[Fic]—dc20 94-32678
CIP
AC

*For Scott,
who lent me his
paper route*

Chapter 1

I'VE BEEN WATCHING you, Caroline Grade."

In a squat, I jerked to my right, toward the voice. I had to pivot on the balls of my feet, lost my balance, sat down on the twenty-seven newspapers stuffed into the fanny part of my head-hole style delivery bag, and let the lid of Mrs. Laura Ames's pretty wooden newspaper box slam on my fingers. When I came to rest, the first thing that struck me was that Mrs. Ames had said my name right. That's GRAH-dee, not GRAYD. It's German.

I looked at Mrs. Laura Ames. She's old, but she's not wrinkled up into a little puckered lady. Her hair is the color of expensive pearls, and it's thick and permed into soft curls around her face just like women my mom's age wear. She stands straight. That day she had on a silky summer dress just the color of Mrs. Peacock in the Clue game. It swirled softly around her calves.

"I've noticed that when you collect you seem competent and trustworthy," she said.

I almost laughed. When I deliver, it's something else again, huh? But I smiled and said, "Thank you."

"You never miss my paper. You've never slammed the lid on the box once since I told you about my insomnia."

Some wholly wild giggles were building up inside me. Never slammed the lid except for just now, right? This old woman was so elegant and serious. Did she have any idea she was funny? I found myself wishing, hoping, she did.

"When I handed you that twenty and said I'd lost my glasses but here's a ten, you spoke up right away. It wasn't a mistake. I was testing you. You passed."

Maybe I nodded, but maybe I was too shocked.

"You're the accelerated girl who uncovered that burglary ring last winter, aren't you?"

I nodded. Evidently Mrs. Ames read her paper. She must have seen the article on the Gifted and Talented program that was published toward the end of sixth grade, in June. There was a big picture of me and Chad Neumann and Mr. Schreiber, the director of the program. I didn't mind being interviewed about the G & T program, but I hadn't wanted the reporter to mention that Chad and I had solved a bunch of burglaries. Nevertheless, a couple lines about the burglary ring wound up in the G & T article, and that's how Mrs. Ames got her information.

"Everything I know about you tells me you have a good character," said Mrs. Ames. "And I consider myself a good judge of character."

I'm not sure what to say to things like that. I mean, I'm used to having adults be pleased with me.

A smile tugged at Mrs. Ames's plump lips. It struck me that one reason she didn't look really ancient was that her lips hadn't disappeared. "You can probably get off your newspapers now."

I hadn't even stood up. Maybe I'm just not aware enough of what my body is *doing* half the time; maybe that's my problem.

"My couch is a much more comfortable place to sit," she said.

CHAPTER ONE

I struggled to my feet and ended up turning onto all fours, then settled onto my haunches and rose straight up like an elevator, twin pouches of papers banging my stomach and swatting my seat. My mom says wearing this head-hole bag is worse than being pregnant, but it beats carrying forty pounds on one hip.

Mrs. Ames was still talking. "On a day like this, you can take a lemonade break, papers or no papers. Come in." Laura Ames reached out and pushed her heavy front door open wide. "I'm in need of your help and I've decided you are to be trusted."

"When my husband Arthur died in January, he left this note." Mrs. Ames took a sheet of paper from a corner desk and strode toward me. I was sitting on her couch in her huge, blessedly cool living room—she calls it a great room; I mean *great room* is the name of it—paper sack slumped at my feet, worrying a little about sweating on her nice upholstery, drinking a slippery glass of delicious lemonade, the kind where the ice clinks in the glass and it's decorated with lemon slices perched on the rim. She handed me the paper. "I can't read the whole thing, but I think I know what it means."

I expected old, scrawled handwriting. But what I saw thrilled my little mathematical, word-loving heart. This is what Mr. Arthur Ames's note said:

THə
o abbreviate limited
bkumm
youngster (plural)
conjunction plus
steal, but nicer
plural possessive

BY
-15
10 15 25
not out
first clue
anyooil
tnuh

"Wow," I said, looking over the whole list. "I think I can read the first word. It looks like *the*. I think he just used the phonetic spelling from the dictionary."

Laura Ames nodded soberly.

"And these last four—do you have a pencil?"

I just have to write stuff down; it gives my head a rest from thinking. Laura Ames got a pencil from the same corner desk.

"'Not out' is 'in,' right?" I scrawled 'in' on the paper, next to the phrase 'not out.' "'First clue' is 'the.' This next one is a funny way to spell 'annual'—an-yoo-il?—and the last one is 'hunt' backwards." In a column next to the last four clues I now had scribbled:

in
the
annual
hunt

"*Annual!*" cried Laura Ames. "*That's* what that says. I just couldn't make sense out of 'any oil' with an extra o."

"I'd love to work on this," I told her. "I could do stuff like this all day. But I've got to get the papers delivered." I didn't really want to leave Laura Ames's air-conditioned house and trudge back out into the heat of late July and lug a ton of evening papers around the neighborhood, but I've been well-trained to stick to duty.

"I understand," she said. "I'd appreciate it greatly if you could come back."

"I could . . . copy the note and take it with me," I ventured to suggest.

For the first time the shadow of a frown crossed Laura Ames's face. Two nuggets of flesh sagged on her jaw for just seconds and then disappeared. "I said I trusted you, and I meant it. But there is someone I don't trust. Right now I have my reasons for not wanting the note to leave the house."

Hmm. *That* was sure interesting. "Mrs. Ames." I got up from the couch without a reminder this time, held the paper sack like a tent, and eased my head through the neck hole. "You said you couldn't read the whole thing, but you thought you knew what it meant."

My long hair was trapped under the paper sack, pulling my head back. Mrs. Ames lifted it out and laid it around my shoulders. "Yes, I did say that." Now the sack was choking me because I had more papers in back than in front. Mrs. Ames shifted some. There are things about carrying a paper route that I haven't quite smoothed out yet. "Caroline—do they call you Caroline?"

"Yes. Sometimes friends call me Caro. But then kids start calling me Syrup. Actually, I'm a Caroline type." I decided to shut my mouth at this point, but I really am a Caroline type. It's a plain, serious, earnest name that drags out behind me just a bit longer than it should.

"Caroline." Mrs. Ames is almost as tall as I am, and she looked me in the eye. "Since you were able to find burglars, how would you like to try your hand at finding treasure?"

LATE AFTERNOON IS the hottest time of day."

Mom came in the back door from work with my seven-year-old brother Danny, who was pushing his thick, blond bangs straight up in sweaty spikes. Mom had picked him up at day-care, where she was lucky enough, she says, to find a part-time, summertime slot for him. Mom works part-time in the fabric department at Shopko, but she complains that it's getting much closer to full-time than she wants. She doesn't like her job.

"Oh, you made a casserole, honey. Bless you." Mom took a hair clip from her Shopko shirt pocket, scraped her grown-out perm back from her face, and fastened it in a tail behind her. "Don't tell me the air conditioner's on the fritz again?"

I sighed. I am not a heavy sigher like my mom, but this time it just came out. *Bless you* is not something my mom says unless she's responding to a sneeze, and I thought maybe she was trying to say something sort of supportive to me because I've become a Christian. Then she went on with a typical Mary Grade negative comment, this one about the temperamental air conditioner. The moment was over.

My sister Samantha, who's sixteen, burst in

wrapped in a beach towel, her long brown hair, which is just like mine, streaming down her back. "Oh good, supper's ready. I gotta eat and get to work." Sam's a checker at a grocery store. She disappeared down the hall to our room. "Hey Caro," she yelled, "it actually doesn't smell half bad."

"Dad gonna be here?" I wrinkled my nose experimentally at the casserole. It was just hamburger, onions, rice, potatoes, carrots, and celery, sliced where necessary, tossed in the dish raw, covered with a can of some sort of cream soup, and baked. Assembled rather than cooked. My real accomplishment was putting it together without breaking something, slicing my hand off, or burning the house down. I do not claim to be a cook.

"Well, let's see, what's today? Monday? He's at the elevator."

Dad got a part-time job at a grain elevator, which mostly sells huge sacks of exciting things like animal feed to farmers and salt pellets for water softeners. His regular job at the paper mill isn't going too well. He says the workers don't get the pay or fringe benefits they used to. I'm afraid he works all the time because he's wondering how to put me through college. Well, Sam too, since she'll be going a lot sooner than me. It makes me feel kind of funny—guilty, maybe—that he plans so seriously for something I hardly think about.

The phone rang. Sam and Danny yelled "GOT IT!" and lunged for the nearest phones. "Hang up, Sam," Danny said. "Hey, Mom, can I eat at Paul's house?"

"Well, I don't know. . . ."

"Aw, please? Hurry up, Mom; there's another call."

"Fine, you can go." Mom's been worried lately because Danny doesn't have many friends. He seldom does much except play in his room with his Legos, so I suppose she didn't want him to pass up an invitation.

Danny slammed down the phone, the other call rang immediately, Sam screamed "GOT IT!" and Mom picked it up.

"'Bye, I'm goin' to Paul's. I'm taking my bike."

Mom raised her chin above the mouthpiece. "Wear your helmet."

"Yeah, yeah."

"Hey, Caro, can you throw some of that on a plate quick?" Sam hurried in, dressed in her navy pants, white blouse, and grocery store name tag. "I've gotta get out of here." Sam shoveled her food down while Mom told some salesperson she wasn't interested. "Hey Mom, can I take the car? I'm gonna be late!"

"I'm sorry, we're not interested," Mom said into the phone. She tossed the keys across the kitchen to Sam. "If you hadn't stayed at the pool till the last minute . . ."

Sam grabbed a can of pop from the fridge and slammed out the screen door. Mom looked at the door, then at the phone as if to say, Why am I listening to this? She slammed the phone down. For a split second the room was quiet and Mom and I looked at each other.

"Can you dish me up some of that?" Mom began picking up sale catalogs and junk mail which were strewn on the snack bar and setting them in a pile on the dining table behind her. My newspaper stuff was still on the counter too—thick sheets of paper they put at the bottom of the bundles to protect them when they toss them out of the delivery truck, strips of yellow plastic they bind the bundles with, my paper sack. There were also potato and onion peels, celery leaves, and the plastic wrap and styrofoam meat tray from the hamburger. I scraped a bunch of stuff into the garbage and set Mom's plate on the snack bar. "Want to eat here with me?" she asked.

The phone rang and I got it. "May I please speak to Caroline?"

My nerves began to vibrate. Only the third time in my life I'd heard the voice of Mrs. Laura Ames, and I recognized it.

"It's important," I mouthed to Mom. "Can I take it in your room?"

"Never mind." Mom picked up her plate. "I think I'll eat there." And she left.

"Would it be an imposition if I asked you to come over tomorrow?" Laura Ames asked. "We could discuss the code I showed you. And the clues. And the secret."

Clues? Secret? Mrs. Ames has a way of getting people to listen. "All these things have to do with treasure?"

"You're a quick study." Mrs. Ames sounded pleased. "Would you come, maybe in the morning if you're not busy? We'd have a lot of time before you'd have to deliver papers."

A plan was forming in my mind. In fact it was more than a plan. It felt wholly like a desire, even a need. "Mrs. Ames, when I—uh—solved the burglaries," I said self-consciously, "I didn't do it by myself. A friend helped me. Chad."

Like I said before, Chad Neumann is one of the other kids in the Gifted and Talented program. We had seen more of each other in the seven or eight weeks since school got out than I ever expected we would. It kind of got started when we ran into each other at the swimming pool. (I'm a horrible klutz at sports, but I can actually swim.) Then we went to the library, the nature center, and Burger King, and pretty soon we were calling each other up, and before we knew it we were a lot better friends than just school friends. After our experience with the burglary ring, I just couldn't see solving clues and hunting treasure without him.

"Chad's a really good friend," I told Laura Ames, "and we worked as a team. Would you mind—could I bring him? If he's free? He's got this saying that eight heads are better than four." I was suddenly so embarrassed that I closed my eyes and nearly dropped the phone.

To my amazement Mrs. Ames's voice came back with a hint of laughter in it. "I'm not sure I should say this, since I don't know your Chad, but he sounds like just the kind of person I may need. By all means. Bring Chad. Say ten o'clock?"

I dialed Chad Neumann's number immediately. "A matter of utmost urgency has come to my attention, via a telephone discourse with an elderly female consumer of the daily periodicals I market," I said as soon as Chad answered. He just lives with his mom (his dad died when he was little) so there was no danger I had the wrong family member on the line.

"Do you intend to imply to this astonished party that the woman *eats* your current events publication?"

I imagined Chad grinning into the telephone. I imagined his freckles, his dimples, his short, dark hair lying perfectly on his head. I tried to focus instead on a verbal comeback. Chad knows I hate the word "consumer" used to mean a person who buys things. It sounds like we're all a bunch of fat people just sitting around going "Ssslurrppp!!" whenever some new product comes on the market.

"I intend for you to fix your attention on the principal idea in my opening sentence," I retorted. "Which is that our attention to a situation of grave significance has been begged by the aforementioned lady."

"Attention duly fixed. Who is she and what does she want?"

Lapsing into regular English, I told Chad about Mrs. Laura Ames, her request to meet with us, and her mention of a treasure.

"You think she's really got something?"

"She showed me a code her husband left her, made up of funny words and math symbols. I could read part of it. She hinted that she's got a general idea what he's up to, but can't unscramble his specific instructions. I want to help her, and I was hoping you'd . . . come too?"

I couldn't keep my voice from going up at the end, like a timid little question. I wanted Chad to understand that I really wanted to help Mrs. Ames, not just amuse myself with breaking codes, or prove I was smart by finding treasure. And I wanted Chad to feel the same way. But I wanted him to understand all this without asking me *why* I felt I should help a paper customer I really didn't know all that well.

It was because I'm a Christian. See, if Mrs. Ames specifically asked *me* to help, and if it turned out she needed help with just the thing I seemed able to do best, then maybe this was a "calling" type of thing our teacher, Mr. Schreiber, mentioned to us once. He said a "calling" is something God wants us to do. Of course, God might not have been calling Chad to take part in this thing with Mrs. Ames. But I really hoped he was. All of these thoughts flashed through my mind in no more than two seconds and I ended my recruitment effort by quoting Chad's own line back to him. "Eight heads are better than four, you know."

"I admit my inquisitive mind has been fully engaged by your intriguing proposal," Chad returned. "Unless the chain falls off my two-wheeled, pedal-powered vehicle again, I'll be at your house at 0945 hours."

"Affirmative," I signed off. I couldn't even get off my stool to go get a plateful of the rapidly cooling casserole before the phone rang again.

"Caro?" It was my best friend, Erica. "Can you go to the mall tomorrow morning? You get your paper profit today, right?"

Uh-oh.

This was not just a simple matter of telling Erica tomorrow morning was a bad time. You remember I said I was doing stuff with Chad more than I thought I would? Well, this meant I was doing stuff with Erica *less* than I thought I would. If you've ever had a friend that was jealous of another friend, if you've ever been afraid to tell a friend the truth about where you were going and who you'd be with because you didn't want to hurt their feelings, you know what I was going through.

"Do you realize school starts in a month?" Erica said. "Yesterday I realized that whether they call it middle school or not, this year we are starting junior high. *Junior high.* I decided it's time to get my look together once and for all."

Erica knew very well I wanted to do the same. A lot of my paper route profit goes in the bank for Caroline's Marvelous Future, of course. But some is spending money, and I really wanted to get some new clothes. While I'm waiting for that marvelous future to get here, I sure wouldn't mind a more marvelous present.

"Caro?"

"Sorry, I was daydreaming. Erica, can we maybe go Wednesday? Tomorrow morning I'm busy."

"Busy with what?"

Lies sashayed through my mind. I had to baby-sit Danny. That was the most natural and believable. (He doesn't go to day-care every time my mom works.) Or how about—I'm grounded? No, I'd have to paint a full-blown fictional scene to explain that one. (The fact is, I don't get in much trouble. At least, not intentional trouble. I am too much of a parent-teacher pleaser.) Or I could agree to go and then tomorrow plead major stomach upset. By this time I was disgusted with myself. But what truth should I tell? I shouldn't tell Mrs. Ames's business to any more people. Uneasily, I thought that I had chosen to tell Chad and now was not going to tell my best friend, Erica.

"Well, see, Chad and I have got something really important to do that just came up."

There was one of those loaded silences on the other end of the phone. Naturally I tried to fill it with nervous chatter.

"It's kind of complicated. We have to help somebody, but I really can't tell that other person's business. Anyway, Chad and I just found out about this—"

"And it's real important," Erica finished. "Yeah, right. You don't have to make excuses to me, Caroline. Just say you can't go."

Yeah right, indeed. If I'd said that, you think she wouldn't have asked why? But I didn't want to get mad at her. Our friendship was just getting back on steady ground. See, back during the burglary business, Erica and I had a bad experience where she got stuck someplace and I had to figure out how to get her free. It made her feel really helpless and stupid and mad at herself, and I think she sees our friendship differently now. I'm afraid she thinks Chad and I belong together because we're both gifted. This makes *me* kind of mad. I don't want to be stereotyped, and I don't want it to be true that Chad and I have only unusual intelligence or weird minds in common.

"Look, maybe it's time to be honest," Erica said.

"You're seeing an awful lot of Chad lately. Maybe you'd just rather do stuff with him."

"Erica—I think we can have more than one friend. Just because I do stuff with Chad doesn't mean I don't like you. I'm sure not going clothes shopping with him. You're my best friend!" But when I said that, I wondered if it was true anymore or if it was just a reflex statement.

"Is Chad your boyfriend?"

Talk about time for honesty. She had just asked the question that was wholly mixing me up. On the one hand, if I said yes, Erica might feel better. Everybody knew people had room for both girlfriends and boyfriends. But if I said yes, it might get back to Chad, and I didn't know how he would take it. Besides, I didn't know if it was true. I didn't know if my feelings for Chad were just friendship (By the way, I hate that phrase 'just friends.' There is nothing *mere* about friends.) or if I wanted Chad as a boyfriend. I had paused too long.

"I don't know."

Erica's pause was shorter this time. "Fine. Look, maybe you can call me sometime about going to the mall."

"Erica, I said we could probably go Wednes —"

The phone clicked in my ear, followed by the buzz of the dial tone.

Chapter 3

THE NEXT MORNING Chad and I rang Laura Ames's doorbell at ten o'clock sharp. Laura Ames answered the door wearing up-to-date stonewashed denim shorts and a white top with a rose silk-screened on the front. Her perm looked bouncy and she wore makeup. This was definitely not your average old lady.

"As I've told Caroline, I think I know what Arthur wants me to do." She sat us down on her couch in the great room, across from the fireplace and the TV. "But if I can't read his writing, so to speak, the whole thing will be just an exercise in frustration." She sat down on the love seat next to the couch where Chad and I sat, and handed Chad the coded note from her husband. Chad immediately held the note as if to share it with me, and we bent our heads over it. I did have a fleeting thought that this show of togetherness would help Mrs. Ames decide that Chad should be trusted. Then I concentrated on Arthur Ames's clues:

THə
o abbreviate limited
bkumm
youngster (plural)
conjunction plus
steal, but nicer

plural possessive

BY

-15

10 15 25

not out

first clue

anyooil

tnuh

"Become," Chad said, pointing to clue three.

"Youngster plural should be kids or children," I put in. "Could we have paper and pencil?" I asked Laura Ames.

"Could we have a dictionary?" Chad added. He looked up the abbreviation for limited while I wrote down 'children' next to 'youngster (plural).' Laura Ames looked on with interest.

"Conjunctions are those little words that join phrases and stuff, right?" Chad asked. "Like, and, but, or, if."

"Yeah. Mrs. Timmers went over that last year." Mrs. Timmers was my regular sixth grade teacher. I'd had her in the afternoon, and special Gifted and Talented (G & T) classes—literature, geometry, and biology—with other teachers, in the morning. Chad and I got to know each other in the G & T program; he was the only kid who shared all three classes with me. He was in seventh last year.

"Wow, you mean Mrs. Timmers actually taught you something?"

I snickered a bit. Mrs. Timmers was kind of a character, but she hadn't turned out all bad. "Due to the mixed nature of her influence on me, and the complexity of my feelings toward her, I would prefer not to ridicule her at this time." The truth was, meanness just didn't feel good. It pinched, or something.

"Fine. I have no particular need or wish to dwell on the unfortunate woman's quirks."

At that moment, in stereo, we remembered Laura Ames and our heads shot up to look at her. She was grinning broadly. "The longer this goes on, the more sure I feel that when I came to you kids I came to the right place."

You kids. She had already accepted Chad and me together!

"Conjunction *plus!*" I shouted. "Plus means *and.*"

"And isn't 'steal, but nicer,' *take?*" asked Chad. "What have we got so far?"

I held out the paper as best I could to include both Chad and Laura.

The
old
become
children
and
take
plural possessive

BY
-15
10 15 25
in
the
annual
hunt

"Plural possessives," Laura mused. "Our, their. Well, it should be *their*, to go with *children*."

"Right!" I yelped. I guess I was half surprised that Laura was going to contribute. I shouldn't have been.

Sometimes I feel funny talking about giftedness because I don't know how it sounds to people, but one thing I noticed about myself is that I really don't know how much other people know or what they can do. I mean, I've been told all my life that my intelligence is much higher than average. So does this actually mean I have no experience of *average?* Do I overestimate or underestimate most people? Do they get insulted? Is my ability to relate to them limited? I don't know.

"Let's look at the math ones," Chad said. "What's 'by minus fifteen?'"

"Well, b is the second letter of the alphabet so that could stand for two," I started out. "And y is the twenty-fifth—oh, I don't think it's two twenty-five minus 15. The digits don't line up right."

"Try counting five letters backwards from y," Chad said. "That's t. And of course one back from b is a—"

"And we've got 'at,' " I finished.

"Oh, you *do* work well together." Mrs. Ames clasped her hands in excitement. "Ratio Ames, eat your heart out!"

This stopped us cold.

"What?" I said. "Was Ratio what you called your husband?" That didn't sound right even while I was asking. She'd called him Arthur up to now. Besides, she'd never hinted that she and her husband were—*opponents*, or anything besides friendly. Unless there was a lot more to this story than met the eye.

"No. Ratio is Arthur's nephew." Laura unclasped her hands and relaxed. "Well, *our* nephew I suppose you'd say. But we can talk about all that later." She looked back at the paper. It was clear Chad and I would have to solve this puzzle before we'd get any more info. It was not at all clear why the Ameses' nephew would have a first name that basically meant *division problem*. Unless he was a math freak? Even a—oh good grief—a *gifted* math freak? What was going on here?

Chad was muttering about the '10, 15, 25.' He decided to try letters first this time before we tried any funny number crunching, and we came up with *joy* .

"I knew it, I knew it," Mrs. Ames was murmuring, mostly to herself, I think. "This is the proof." She turned to us. "Now there's nothing left but that curlicue thing, right? What does that mean?"

Of course she meant the swirl, with the arrow going counterclockwise. Around? Spin? "*Turn!*" I cried. "Children take *turns.*"

"Read the whole thing to me," Laura commanded.

"It's kind of like a verse or something, almost a poem." I read it aloud,

"The old become children
And take their turn
At joy in the annual hunt."

"Yes!" Laura Ames exploded. "I knew it. Arthur is sending us on a treasure hunt."

"How do you know it's a treasure hunt?" I asked.

"Why does it say *annual* hunt?" Chad said at almost the same time.

"Oh, you bright, bright children." Mrs. Ames clasped her hands again, and for a second I thought she was going to drumroll her white Nikes on the carpet. "Those questions are connected. They virtually have the same answer."

I glanced at Chad, but he didn't return the quizzical look I was giving him. I guess he couldn't. Today was his first introduction to Mrs. Ames, while I was mentally comparing the slightly wacky Mrs. Ames of today with the regal Mrs. Ames of yesterday.

A sense of calm seemed to settle over her. "When our son Alan was a child, Arthur devised a treasure hunt for him every year."

"You mean he had to find toys or presents or stuff?" Chad asked.

Laura Ames hesitated, then smiled a smile that looked like some kind of surrender. She was about to trust us a little farther than she had before.

"Yes, but not just your run-of-the-mill toys or presents. One year it was a convertible with a roof that really went up and down, lights, horn, radio, upholstered seats, turn signals, the works. Arthur never would tell me how much it cost. Alan was nine that year."

"There were toys like this?" I screeched.

She gave the faraway, almost sleepy, smile again. "Well, not for everyone. By the time he was a teenager it was cash, a stereo system that filled a whole room—and finally, a real Caddy."

Chad whistled. I didn't know what a Caddy was, but since Chad seemed to I didn't ask. (Now I know it's a Cadillac.)

"So you're rich," Chad said. "And you mean your husband is sending you on a *serious* treasure hunt."

"I guess it's time to tell you the secret," Laura Ames replied. "The secret that no one ever knew except Arthur and me. And," she sighed. "Ratio Ames."

"Not your son Alan?" I asked.

Mrs. Ames looked at me with the faraway smile again. It had a sadness in it. "Alan died in Vietnam."

"Oh. Oh," I said. "I'm sorry."

She acknowledged this with a nod. After a moment she said, "The secret has some background information. My husband, Arthur A. Ames, was an architect, and the business he owned is called Ames Architectural Associates. Arthur wasn't given a middle name at birth. He added the initial A so he could call himself Triple A, A^3 and the like. I half believe he chose his profession because it started with A. I'm lucky he didn't choose his wife that way."

"Was your husband really into math?" Chad asked. "Was he—well, gifted?" Chad must have known, as I did, that this was a touchy question. Most people see specialness in their loved ones, and lots of people get kind of huffy and argue that *everyone* is gifted in some way.

"I'm really not in a position to judge if he was outstanding," Mrs. Ames answered. "He was well educated in math, certainly. The important thing to know about Arthur is that he had fun in life, he knew how to create games, he never took himself or his financial affairs too seriously. Yes, we did have money, because Arthur was first-rate at what he did. But we didn't accumulate the wealth we might have, because Arthur's way of handling money was—unusual."

Chad and I sat at attention. We could feel the secret coming.

"Arthur put some into savings and investments, as most people would," Laura told us. "And he designed us a nice but not extremely fancy home." She spread her hands briefly to indicate the definitely nice great room we were sitting in. "But investments really weren't fun for Arthur. He could see the numbers on paper, but he didn't *feel* rich. No, Arthur kept hundreds of thousands of dollars in cash, jewels, gold, and silver. Cash and jewels really appealed to the little boy in him. For much of our lives these things were right in the house with us. But Arthur never felt unsafe. Until perhaps two years ago no one on earth knew about this except Arthur and me. No one would have expected it. But naturally the time came when he confided in his crony, Ratio Ames." Laura turned her gaze right on us. "I know there isn't money and jewelry in the house now. I know Arthur wants to send me on a treasure hunt to find it." She sighed and her forehead curls riffled slightly. "And I strongly suspect Ratio Ames intends to find it first. So are you with me, kids? Will you help me find a treasure of cash and jewels?"

We were hooked. Bent forward at the waist, almost falling into Laura Ames's lap, Chad Neumann and I nodded, in stereo.

Chapter 4

"MAYBE IT SEEMS crazy for me to trust you. On the other hand, I should ask if you trust me." Laura skewered us with her eyes. I saw they were a deep marbly blue, kind of a color you could fall into and wonder if you'd ever hit bottom. "Do you think I'm a bit touched in the head?" She flicked her pearl-colored curls with one hand. "I realize how this sounds."

"I trust you," I said. I'm not sure I was using any of my allegedly huge brains to make this judgment. It would have been awfully hard for me not to please a grown-up. I was also nervously aware that deciding whether to trust Mrs. Ames was not an answer I could find in a schoolbook or on a homework sheet. It was a part of life that my teacher, Mr. Schreiber, calls fuzzy furry stuff—things we have to use our judgment on that might not have very clear answers. I thought grateful thoughts toward Mr. Schreiber at this moment. He was the first person to tell me there was greater help for me in the world than just my own brains. He has everything to do with why I became a Christian.

"I'm in." Chad, with his dimples wholly hidden, looked a shade skeptical, but I think he followed my lead. I felt a shade nervous about that. My responsibility to have good judgment had suddenly grown. Maybe he reasoned we had nothing to lose even if she was wrong about a treasure. Meanwhile, the chance that she was right was tantalizing.

"I don't wish to insult you, but I must ask directly that you keep this confidential. The reason is naturally obvious."

"You can trust us." As I said this I felt a little jab somewhere inside. I'm fairly careful with secrets, but I did have some mouth trouble a while back that led to trouble with the burglars. I decided then and there I would work extra hard at keeping Laura Ames's confidence. There was no reason I couldn't—No. I'd given up talking like that. I would just say it was my goal, with God's help, to discuss Mrs. Ames's business with no one.

"Exactly what I said to begin with: you are to be trusted." Mrs. Ames sounded satisfied. "Actually, I have far more to lose if I don't trust you. Alone, I'm no match for Ratio when it comes to solving the clues. His chances of beating me to the treasure are simply too great."

With that, she walked over to the corner desk, took another paper from one of its drawers, and handed it to Chad and me.

This is what it said:

CLUES I
Mind over matter
7/31/11:59:59 ↛ 8/1/12:00:00
Oh say can you rhyme?
piano
storage

"Oh say can you rhyme?" Chad murmured.

"It should be 'Oh say can you *see*,' " I thought aloud. "So do we rhyme 'see'? Be, me, knee . . ."

"Yeah, that's it." Chad straightened up in enthusiasm and his dimples popped in briefly. "Take it alphabetically. Fee, gee, he, key. Hey, key is a treasure-type word."

"Key goes with piano, too." I looked up at Laura, who had gone to the kitchen and now was bringing in three glasses of lemonade on a tray. "Do you have a key to a storage closet in your house?"

Laura set the lemonade down on her glass-topped coffee table. "Wow, you kids really are fast."

I kind of wiggled, feeling uncomfortable. I liked Mrs. Ames, and I didn't want her to feel stupid when she wasn't. I even didn't want her to let us jump to conclusions. The truth was, too much of that would make me like her less. "You can't just—" I began. Oh, how should I say this without sounding bossy? "It seems hard when you look at a whole list like this and say to yourself, 'I don't get it.' You have to take it in pieces. You look at each clue by itself and try to work it out."

Laura was shaking her head. I figured it was because she was doubting me, doubting herself. Her head-shaking bounced the curls around her face, kind of taking them apart. I was just about to decide my strongest feeling for her was pity.

Still shaking her head, Laura said, "No. I'm certain the treasure's not in the house."

She'd already told us that. I'd forgotten, and I guess Chad had, too.

"And I don't have a storage closet that locks. In fact, I think I know what the first line, 'Mind over Matter,' refers to. Arthur wants us to figure out the clues, not tear the place apart with a crowbar. If we thought the treasure was here, that would be all too tempting."

Chad and I were quiet. Laura Ames was no

pushover after all. And in case we'd forgotten, she'd have good contributions to make to our clue-solving, whether she thought she was smart or not.

"Has this Ratio guy got these clues or something?" Chad asked. "What's the story with him, anyway? You said he plans to beat you to the treasure. But a couple times you made it sound like Arthur planned the hunt for more than one person. I'm kind of mixed up here."

Laura nodded. She crossed her legs and propped her elbow on the arm of the love seat, as if to settle in. "I told you Ratio's our nephew, didn't I? His real name is Horatio. Maybe that's part of his problem," she said dryly. "He's always been a misfit, nearsighted, cruelly homely, overweight." She sighed. "He was orphaned at age nine, and three years later our Alan was killed. After that, Arthur felt it was only right and natural that we play as big a role in Ratio's life as possible. Had he not been living with his godparents, I expect we would have taken him in. I don't think either he or his godparents particularly liked their living arrangements, but there was no graceful way to suggest a change. Besides, the godparents had been named guardians by Ratio's parents and their wishes had to be respected, etcetera, etcetera. I don't think Ratio's father, who was Arthur's brother Walter and much the stuffier of the two, thought playful Arthur would be a good influence." She paused. "And has he got clues?" Laura sighed again. "Oh yes, Ratio has got clues. Mine and his, I suspect."

"Yours and his . . ." Chad repeated.

"Oh yes. There are two sets. You see—well, *you* figure it out. Read the verse you worked out again."

I grabbed the paper and read aloud,

"The old become children
And take their turn
At joy in the annual hunt."

CHAPTER FOUR

"Who are the old who are becoming children?" Laura Ames asked, and for a moment she sounded for all the world like our literature teacher, Mrs. Heimer. She was so much nicer, though, so much more dignified, so much more respectful of us. I felt a kind of longing. I guess that was the very beginning of my fondness—love, I guess—for Laura Ames.

While I was longing, Chad was answering. "You and Ratio?"

"Right," Laura pronounced. "Do you see? Arthur meant to send Ratio and me into the treasure hunt as partners."

"Just how old *is* Ratio?" I asked. A nephew was a fairly young person in my experience.

"About forty," said Laura.

"Oh, well then," I said, understanding why the verse included Ratio.

"That's old," Chad confirmed.

Laura Ames laughed.

"So did you work together to start with? If he has your clues, why don't you have his?" I think about a thousand questions flew through my mind all at once, but these were the two I grabbed onto.

"Arthur died in January." Laura Ames settled back on the love seat as if to tell another chapter of her story. "His will stated that on July 20, I was to invite Ratio Ames to dinner at four-thirty sharp. During the meal Federal Express arrived with the verse you just decoded."

We didn't know quite what to say. "No kidding," Chad finally managed.

"Arthur was a little more than merely playful," Laura Ames admitted. "He was a wonderful, refreshingly sane man, but by the world's standards he was a bit—eccentric."

"Like—weird, you mean," Chad said, as if

checking his understanding of the situation.

"No doubt that's exactly how you young people would put it. Anyway, there were two copies of the verse, which again seemed to leave little doubt that Ratio was to be part of the hunt. I suspected a treasure hunt because that's what he was known for, because I knew he had money that hadn't yet come to me, because it seemed reasonable there would be an inheritance for Ratio too. We mulled over the verse right there at the table and I wasn't making much headway. Ratio claimed he wasn't either, but I didn't believe him for a second."

"Why?" I said. I had heard the shade of bitterness cloud Laura's voice.

"I wouldn't trust Ratio Ames any farther than I could throw him!" Vehemence lighted Laura's eyes. "I loved my husband, but he wasn't much judge of character, at least not where Ratio was concerned. He never saw that Ratio despised me because I didn't have the odd brilliance that he and Arthur shared. He never saw that Ratio was jealous of our marriage because he craved Arthur's undivided attention. Not that some of Ratio's needs weren't genuine; he probably never got the nurturing he needed from anyone else." Laura's voice quieted, then grew brisk again. "Besides, his name is *Ratio*. That's more than a nickname for Horatio. He called Arthur 'Cube,' which is short for 'A cube.' I never took algebra, but I'm sure you kids understand."

"Sure." Chad and I nodded. Arthur's initials were AAA, which in math means A times A times A, which you can write as A^3, which you say 'A cubed.' Only when you have to say it a lot, you drop the 'd' and say 'A cube.'

"Ratio and Arthur were nuts about puzzles of all kinds, mathematical concepts, things I probably don't even have words for. They read *Scientific American.* They were on the computer endlessly."

"Computer?" said Chad.

"The computer room is next to the master bedroom." Laura gestured vaguely toward the fireplace wall. "The computer." Laura sighed. "That's another thing. Anyway, do you see why I'd have trouble believing Ratio couldn't make hide nor hair out of that note? For all I know he translated the whole thing on the first reading. I really don't have a good sense of how hard or easy something like that would be for someone of Ratio and Arthur's caliber. Do you understand what I mean?"

I thought of my similar feelings about gifted and regular people. "I do understand."

"There was another note, in plain English, enclosed with the two copies of the verse," Laura told us. "It said we were to meet again the following evening—that was Tuesday the twenty-first—at four-thirty for dinner."

"Did Federal Express come again?" Chad asked.

"It did." Laura nodded. "This time we got two separate envelopes. These were called our first set of clues. My set is what you have there." She gestured at the paper that sat between us on the couch. "The atmosphere at the table got quite interesting indeed, when Ratio and I opened those envelopes and avoided looking at each other and tried to plot how we would proceed."

"What happened?" I'm always interested in how people 'plot how they're going to proceed.'

"Ratio couldn't look me in the eye because he's a snake," Laura declared. "He was afraid I'd see it in his face that he had no intention of making this a joint hunt. He just decided he'd solve those clues and get that treasure. He figured I'd never know whether he'd found it, or if it was just that I *hadn't* found it." Laura sighed. "I couldn't look at Ratio because I was afraid he'd see my dislike of him, my distrust, and it would turn him against me further. I tried," Laura interrupted herself with a hopeless lifting of her hands. "I tried to honor Arthur's love for Ratio, to honor his wish that we work together. I showed Ratio my clues as a good-faith gesture. Until then, I wasn't even sure the two sets were different. He didn't show me his, though. Oh no. He argued that we should glean all the information we could from our own first, so that when we combined our clues we could share our insights as well as the clues themselves. A clever argument, but I don't believe him for a minute."

"So he's got your clues," Chad said.

"Not just from that little bit he saw. No, if he'd been able to memorize them on the spot, he wouldn't have needed to sneak to the computer room while I was cleaning up after dinner and copy and print out my clues."

"You caught him at this?" Chad asked.

"No. I didn't even suspect him of it till later. I thought Ratio had gone to the computer room, and I thought I heard the printer going, but he and Arthur had used it so much that this didn't seem strange. If anything, I worried that Ratio was somehow getting treasure hunt information *off* the computer. Now I feel certain he copied my clues." She sighed. "So often I wanted to give him the benefit of the doubt, for Arthur's sake, for his *own* sake, but I can't anymore. If my better judgment doesn't prevail, I may make a mistake as large as Arthur's. Damn him," she fumed, "for betraying Arthur's trust."

"No, Laura!" I broke in instantly, then felt a flood of embarrassment. Not only had I admonished Mrs. Ames, I had called her Laura. "Please don't say that."

Mrs. Ames seemed startled. "I—I'm sorry, Caroline. I didn't mean to offend."

"It's not that," I said. "It's that damning somebody is really serious. It's—well, I'm sorry, but it's horrible to want somebody to be damned." My voice was rapidly fading out. "God doesn't want anyone to be damned. I mean, that's why Jesus died."

Mrs. Ames and Chad were staring at me. Mrs. Ames looked amazed but thoughtful, white lights glinting in her wide-open, marbled blue eyes. I didn't have the guts to look at Chad. I felt relieved that he'd assume I'd been talking to Mr. Schreiber, that he'd know this just hadn't come out of the air.

"Your intelligence spans more than just schoolwork," Laura Ames observed.

"It's not intelligence," I said. "I mean, not that there's no intelligence in it. There definitely is. But I mean—Jesus is in my life, not only my head."

By now I was just about on fire. I had not come here to discuss my becoming a Christian, so how had we gotten to it all of a sudden? I knew becoming a Christian is something we're supposed to get fairly open about, but I was still the deep-inside kind. I mean, I'd been a Christian since July ninth and it was now only the twenty-eighth so give me a break! I don't know if that's right or not, but it was how I felt.

"Again, I apologize." Laura Ames looked at me steadily. "That's an interesting viewpoint, and I certainly respect it."

Hey, maybe this wasn't so bad after all.

"So, you were saying Ratio had made a copy of your clues." Chad turned back to Laura a bit slowly, I thought. "There's no way he would have saved the file, is there? I mean, so you could call it up on the screen and prove he had put it on the computer? Not that it would do you that much good to be able to prove it."

Chad's voice took on a talking-to-himself tone. "And it would be a stupid thing to do."

"It would, wouldn't it?" said Laura Ames cheerfully.

We looked at her in surprise.

"That's one of the things about Ratio Ames. He's fiendishly bright, but he's got a stupid streak a yard wide. I've got a story to tell you as a case in point, but right now we could go to the computer and see if he's shot himself in the foot again." She got up from the love seat. "Shall we?"

THE COMPUTER ROOM had no furniture in it except the huge, pale wood computer desk and shelves along one wall. The wall to the left of the desk was taken up by a closet, and centered in the wall to the right was a large window. The tan wall behind us held only a painting of apples spilling out of a basket.

"I know next to nothing about computers," Laura said, as Chad pulled off the plastic covers and pushed two switches. Some lights came on and we heard the start-up hum. The monitor lit up and flashed some words on the screen, beeped a couple times, and gave Chad a prompt.

"Well, I'm no expert," said Chad.

"Where is Matt Boles when we need him?" I asked. Matt Boles is the G & T program's computer whiz. Or he was. He's going into high school now and is taking college courses.

"We don't need to know *that* much." To Laura, Chad said, "If you want to learn to use this thing, what you have here is an IBM compatible."

I laughed. "I thought he'd have an Apple!"

"Why?" Chad looked at me. I pointed to the painting.

Then Laura Ames laughed. "I understand now, for

the first time. No wonder Arthur was so amused by the apple painting in here. It's kind of a conversation piece no matter which kind of computer he's got."

I was having wholly good feelings about all this. Maybe Chad would help Mrs. Ames by getting her acquainted with her computer. Maybe there was a 'calling' type of thing here for both of us. It made me feel good about God and it made me feel good about Chad. I was suddenly very sharply aware of his presence next to me.

He continued, "I can find out pretty fast what software you've got by making the computer list it for me, or by looking at your husband's program disks and manuals."

I shifted my attention from the study of Chad's fingers on the keyboard to the shelves directly above us. Several thick manuals sat there.

"You have WordPerfect, DOS of course—hey, you've got a lot," Chad said. "That might make it harder to find Ratio's file, if he made one. He could have stored it anywhere."

"He hasn't got Windows," Laura said, "if that means anything to you. He and Ratio went around and around about that. Arthur was for. Ratio was against."

"Ratio won," observed Chad.

"That he did," returned Laura.

There was a slight pause.

"So we use DOS," Chad murmured. He leaned over the keyboard and typed "edit." Then he pushed a few more keys until a funny box came on the screen. (Chad has more computer experience than I do, since he's got one at home and we don't.)

"Now what would Ratio Ames name the file that contained Laura's clues?" Chad asked.

"Clues," I supplied.

"He can't be this stupid," Chad muttered, typing

the word. Then he cast a sidelong glance at Laura. We were taking quite a few liberties, it seemed, with the information she'd given us.

Sure enough, a little gray box came up that announced "file not found."

"We're wasting our time," Chad said, but he went into WordPerfect and checked for a file there. "There is nothing named 'Clues,' and there's no reason to start guessing other file names. He had no reason to save your clues in a file."

"I think I'm relieved he didn't, then," Laura said as we exited the computer room. "I truly don't want Ratio to be that stupid. Oh, I shouldn't talk." Laura suddenly addressed herself in a scolding voice. "I'm the one who can't solve her own clues and can barely find the ON switch on the computer."

"Oh, but you're smart," I said, following Laura Ames down her beige-carpeted hall, through her slate foyer, and back to her great room. I wasn't patronizing her. Obviously someone who spoke as well as she did was intelligent.

"Oh bosh," said Laura Ames.

I was speechless, at least for a little bit. It wasn't just that Laura Ames thought she wasn't smart; I've found out that lots of people think that about themselves. It was that 'oh bosh' was such a grandma-phrase, as if she was pulling back into a little-old-lady role to prove her own point.

"In my day if young women were smart, it kind of came to a natural end when they finished school." Laura talked while she made sub sandwiches for lunch and showed us out to the terrace. We ate at one of those round tables with a huge yellow umbrella stuck in the middle of it. "Frankly, I went to college to meet someone of my station and marry. It was understood that I wouldn't work. We thought of it that way then; if you weren't employed you didn't work, never mind how heavy your load in the household." She paused thoughtfully as the breeze riffled her hair, then chuckled. "You know, the only person who wouldn't have been surprised if I'd worked would have been Arthur. He never did things the expected way."

Our sandwiches tasted as good as ones from a sub shop, and we munched silently for a few moments, enjoying the breeze blowing the humidity away.

"Anyway, it seems we were discussing Ratio Ames." Laura looked at us directly, her reverie over. "About his stupid streak? Early Sunday morning I was up with my insomnia, pacing the hall outside the bedrooms—did you notice when we came out of the computer room that there are three windows right there? They look directly out onto the front entry."

Chad and I shook our heads. I felt a flash of guilt that I hadn't noticed the windows. I don't mean guilt about not being helpful enough to Mrs. Ames. I mean guilt that I hadn't done service to my brains or something by being more observant. I think it's guilt toward other people. I'm always afraid if I miss something people will think, "Here she is with this Gift and she's not using it to the full."

I quickly prayed not to feel guilty about things I don't have to feel guilty about. It's bad enough to feel guilty about the things I just plain do wrong and should feel guilty about. Jesus forgives those. But it's the stupid kind of guilt—Dr. Schiff, the school psychologist, calls it 'false guilt'—that makes Erica furious with me. She thinks if I'm going to get all worked up over things I can't help, then I must think I should be able to take care of everything in the whole world, and therefore I think I'm too important. What if she's right? Yuck.

But I'm getting off the track. Back to Mrs. Ames and Ratio.

CHAPTER FIVE

"So it was early morning and I was pacing the hall, not being able to sleep, and I heard the cover on the paper box clump."

Instant guilt. She'd asked me not to do that because if the cover slamming down woke her up she'd never get back to sleep. But I *hadn't* let it slam.

"I feel bad now that I thought it was you," Laura Ames said to me. "But who else should I expect to be in my paper box? Not Ratio Ames, certainly. But I peeked out and there he was, all hunkered down on my front entry with his round fanny sticking up, shuffling the sections of my Sunday paper."

Chad and I laughed at her description.

"Rather than attract his attention, I just watched what he was going to do. He put my paper back together so meticulously, kneeling there on the bricks, creasing all the folds with the heels of his hands so it would look like no one had touched it, pushing up his glasses, wiping his hands on his shirt when he skinned them on the bricks. All except for the one section he left out. Then he put the paper back in the box, let the cover slam again, and left with the section he'd taken out. Walking. I assume he parked a ways away."

My eyes were riveted on Laura.

"By this time I was really wide awake and retrieved my paper as soon as he was gone. I had to look through it three times before I found anything missing! Finally I saw the date on the business section. It was July 19th, and of course Sunday was the 26th."

"You mean . . ." I groped. I actually felt a bit responsible, as if I'd delivered this defective newspaper.

"Yes. Ratio had taken out the business section and replaced it with one from the previous week. I immediately guessed there was something in Sunday's that he didn't want me to see, and later I asked my neighbor if I could see hers." Laura shook her head. "It almost worked. If he hadn't been so stupidly clumsy when he made the switch, he might have got away with it."

Stupidly *clumsy?* Ouch.

"He probably reasoned that the business section wasn't one of my favorites and that I wouldn't recognize the same one two weeks in a row. And I almost certainly wouldn't have noticed the wrong date—who checks the dates on sections of the paper? And he didn't just take the business section out without a replacement; I might have noticed it was missing and called for a complete paper." Laura shook her head. "No, he was thinking, all right. He just couldn't carry out his plan without—well, like I said—without shooting himself in the foot."

"And what did you find in your neighbor's business section?" Chad asked. "What didn't Ratio want you to see?"

"The bankruptcy column," said Laura Ames. "It's published every Sunday and it's common knowledge that many people like to read it. Well, there was Ratio's name. He's twenty-some thousand dollars in debt and he's worth only about two thousand."

Chad whistled. "Looks like he could use a nice-size treasure right about now."

"And the funny thing, for Ratio anyway," Laura said, "is that this little caper of his has made me more suspicious of him, not less. If he was trying to hide his bankruptcy from me, it's obvious he was afraid I'd suspect he was going after the treasure. Do you see what I mean by a stupid streak? He can think, but he can be so awkward at carrying things out that he loses more than he gains."

An awful thought swept through me. Does awkwardness equal stupidity? Did Laura Ames remember that our whole relationship had started with me falling down on my own pack of newspapers, and then not having the sense to get up until she told me?

"Not to be rude or anything, but should we get back to the clues?" Chad asked. "If Ratio is out there trying to find the treasure, shouldn't we get going?"

I felt kind of cut off, suddenly, wholly alone with these doubts I was having. But Chad was right. Both of us tend to sit around and think and talk smart, but we feel doubtful when it's time to act because we're not real practical types. But this was action time.

We spread the clue paper in front of us as best we could so everybody could see. A hunk of mayo-covered lettuce immediately fell out of my sub, and I wiped it off the clues with a napkin.

> CLUES I
> Mind over matter
> 7/31/11:59:59 —/→ 8/1/12:00:00
> Oh say can you rhyme?
> piano
> storage

"Can we copy these down and take them home?" Chad asked.

This time Mrs. Ames said yes. We jotted them down fast although I could see that Chad was careful to get them accurate, just like I was. We might have thought we had figured something out quick, with our key-unlocking-a-storage-closet business, but now we realized there could be more to these clues than it seemed. The first conclusion we had jumped to had been just too easy. As we finished our writing I kept wanting to duck my head in embarrassment at my conceit.

"There is one other thing," said Laura Ames. I

looked at her, with her alert expression and marbly-blue eyes, and I wholly understood then that if she needed us for her treasure hunt, we needed her just as much. "These lists of clues, mine and Ratio's, each came with identical notes attached, again in plain English. The note said we are to eat dinner again, this Friday the 31st, only this time Ratio is to bring the food and not expect me to cook. And at this dinner, I have no doubt, we are going to get our envelopes labeled Clues Two."

Chapter 6

A PAPER ROUTE SHOULD be easy, right? I mean, you just deliver one paper to every house on your list and you've got it. And I suppose it *is* that easy, in a way.

But it's only easy on paper. Ha ha. When I actually had to start doing it, my sister Samantha put my two-pocket sack on me, stuffed the front and back halves to the bursting point with newspapers, and almost fell down laughing.

"I can't believe Caroline K-for-Klutz Grade has a paper route! You look like a double-sided kangaroo!" That may not sound very nice, especially from someone who wants to be a sociologist. I mean, shouldn't she care how teasing might affect my social behavior? But the point here is, she saw the big problem, the klutz factor, right away. I guess it's pretty amazing that I didn't.

To make my knees bend when I climb someone's front steps I have to push the bag away from my stomach and stick my legs out to the side as if I'm riding a horse. Not that I've ever ridden a horse. I have to squish across soggy lawns to avoid horse-size dogs who growl and circle the cement blocks they're chained to in the driveway, and whose chains just might be too long. On windy days when doors are locked I have to come up with clever ways to secure newspapers. I've held them down with garden hoses, roller skates that I hoped the homeowners wouldn't trip over and sue me for using, and loose bricks that really shouldn't have been falling off the house. I'm sure when fall comes there'll be lots of handy ears of Indian corn and rotting jack-o'-lanterns sitting on porches just waiting to end their lives as newspaper weights.

Anyway, on July 28th, after Chad's and my long talk with Laura Ames, I was delivering my papers while mulling over the clues. I have this tendency to second-guess. I mean, I think I figure something out and then decide the answer could be totally different and I start over again. Did 'Oh say can you rhyme' really mean we should be rhyming the word see? Maybe we should be rhyming the following word on the list, which was piano. I couldn't think of a single word that rhymes with piano. And what rhymes with storage? Porridge?

"Young lady, don't forget me!"

Oh good grief. An old woman who should be getting a paper was sitting in her front yard and I was walking right past her.

"Sorry." I sounded kind of breathy as I handed her her paper. Probably full of air and not much else in her opinion. "I was—daydreaming." I use this explanation a lot with my friends and family. I mean, it's true, but newspaper customers who don't quite trust kids to deliver the thing in the first place are not impressed. Maybe this sounds awful, but when I know people are not impressed with me I always wish for a way then and there to let them know I'm a smart person. I guess I grew up feeling that if people don't know that about me, they can't *see* me. Funny, my sister Samantha thinks people can't see her either, because they're too busy looking at me.

CHAPTER SIX

Well, I walked on, sweating in the heat and trying to look around me so I didn't miss any houses, trying to perfect the art of throwing papers between the screen and storm doors. I don't mean to be a complainer, but there *is* a trick to it. You can't open the screen door too wide, and you must toss the paper high and quickly shut the screen door almost on your hand before the paper hits the ground. Otherwise the sections fan out all over the front stoop and you have to put it back together and start over. Simply place the paper between the doors and it slides out the bottom before you can shut the door on it. Fail to give the screen door a good slam and it means you didn't shut it fast enough and the falling-apart paper is now wedged between the door and its frame. The screen door is not shut, the wind will come along and not only blow the paper away but blow the door off its hinges, the angry customer will call the newspaper, and your supervisor will call *you*. Start over. Pick up paper, smooth crumpled edges, put back together (some sections may be upside down by this time), open screen door no wider than hand, toss paper straight up against inner door, slam outer door while quickly pulling throwing arm out. Yell ouch and suck your thumb. You caught it in the door.

When I delivered Laura Ames's paper I half expected her to be waiting for me, but she wasn't. I quietly lowered the lid on her pretty wooden paper box in case she was catching up on her sleep. I looked her house over: one story, all red brick, lots of roof showing, semicircle window over the front door matching a big arched window where the dining room is. It's a very nice house, on one of the two streets of very nice houses which are kind of around the corner from the four streets of ordinary houses where we live. (We live in a small neighborhood on the outskirts of a small village called Orchardville, Wisconsin. In other words, we live out in the sticks, but if you're actually in our neighborhood you can't tell.)

Yes, Laura Ames's house is nice, I thought, as I turned away from the house to finish my route. But not nearly as nice as you'd expect a person with a treasure to have. From the looks of his outward possessions, no one would ever guess that Arthur Ames's most serious hobby—even since he's been dead!—has been treasure hunts.

No one would ever believe that Chad Neumann and I, and Laura Ames were about to go on such a hunt. Not Mom, not Dad, not Sam, not Erica. And, I thought, arriving at my back door and finally pulling my sweaty paper sack off over my bedraggled hair, it didn't really seem that I should tell them.

The phone rang as soon as I got into the kitchen. Sam pulled the can of pop from her mouth almost in mid-gulp and screamed, "GOT IT!" even though Danny was nowhere around, which meant he was building Legos in his room. I don't fight her for the phone that much, although you do find out who your family's getting calls from if you're the one who answers the phone.

Sam covered the mouthpiece. "It's an old lady," she whispered urgently. "Wants to know how her paper ended up in the birdbath."

"Sam*an*tha!"

She laughed and ducked out of my reach as I grabbed the phone. "Hello?"

"Caroline, did I give you a chance to finish delivering?"

So Laura Ames wasn't napping after all. I was half expecting her call, though. She and Chad and I had agreed we had to figure out how she was going to handle Ratio Ames when he came for dinner on

Friday. Was she going to treat him as the enemy? Was she going to pretend to work with him?

Standing there in the kitchen with the phone almost slipping from my sweaty hand, the feeling came over me that my being a Christian now should have something to do with the advice I gave Mrs. Ames. My heart pounded. I didn't know yet what I thought she should do, and right now I felt funny speaking freely about either treasure hunts or something that sounded Christian. My mom was standing at the counter assembling a gigantic ham, cheese, and vegetable salad in a punch bowl, and my sister was hanging around to see if some adult was actually displeased with Caroline.

"Can I take this in your room?" I asked Mom.

"Hurry back, I could use a hand setting the table."

"Gonna take your scolding in private, huh?" Samantha said. "Mom, you better pay attention to this. Everybody thinks she's perfect, but who knows what sloppy, mistake-filled, double life she's got going when nobody sees?"

"I'm here," I said to Laura Ames, flopping on the bed and picking up the phone in Mom and Dad's room.

Laura got right to the point. "I've thought it over. As much as I distrust Ratio, I'm not going to be hostile when he comes. Family was always more important to Arthur than any money. If I declare war on Ratio I'll be just as disloyal to Arthur as he is. It would crush Arthur to know we were fighting over his treasure."

I could see what Laura Ames meant. Maybe this was a good Christian answer, and now I wouldn't have to try to wrestle one into words. I suddenly thought of my Gifted and Talented teacher, Mr. Schreiber. There are (or were, last school year) five people in his special morning classes: Tommy Trenton (mad scientist), Matt Boles (computer nut), Mi Lee Yang (artist and writer), Chad Neumann, and me. Though we were all there mainly to develop our gifts, Mr. Schreiber let us know he cared a lot more about *people.*

He didn't just scold or punish when Tommy T. magnetized Matt's computer disks after Matt made up a personal and wickedly clever computer profile on him. He didn't let Mi Lee Yang stay quiet and aloof and separate from everybody. He got everybody together and held a whole discussion about our relations in the G & T room, and somehow we all came out feeling we understood a little about being in everybody else's shoes. Mi came down off her throne a little bit and began to speak to us. Matt deleted his offensive computer file. Most surprising of all, Tommy T. actually bought Matt three new floppy disks.

Mr. Schreiber would approve of Laura Ames's decision, I thought. Even though our main purpose was to find a treasure, Laura would not betray Arthur, or even Ratio, to get it.

One thing bothered me, though. "You don't mean you'd just let Ratio get the treasure, do you? Help him even though he's cheating you? That seems—" *Stupid* was what I wanted to say, but I didn't.

"Oh no," said Laura. "If Ratio insists on being my enemy, just letting him win would make an even worse mess of Arthur's wishes. I'm only saying I'll try appealing to his sense of fairness and his love of Arthur first."

"Sounds great," I said. Again I was glad that Chad was in G & T with me, that he was familiar with Mr. Schreiber's ideas. We hadn't talked about Laura and Ratio's upcoming dinner, but surely Chad would agree with what Laura was deciding? At least, since he knew Mr. Schreiber, he would understand the thinking?

CHAPTER SIX

It wasn't long before we did have a chance to talk. I had barely hung up the phone when it rang again. Still being in Mom and Dad's room, I picked it up.

"Francis Scott Key!"

I had to pause to gather my words. "I'm sorry sir, the correct answer to the question 'Who made the first star spangled banner?' is Betsy Ross. Ah, gotta watch those trick questions, Mr. Neumann. Too bad you didn't win our ten trillion dollar grand prize, but we do have some lovely parting gifts—"

"Ah, too bad yourself, because I'm indubitably on the trail leading relentlessly to the zillion dollar treasure!"

My mood changed instantly. "You found something?"

"Francis Scott Key," he repeated in a reasonable tone. " 'Oh say can you rhyme' is like a double clue. It points to Francis Scott *Key*, and it tells you you're looking for a word that rhymes with *see*. Again, key. The following clue, piano, confirms it. An important word in the puzzle is definitely *key*. To find the treasure we're going to have to unlock something with a key."

"Hey, that's pretty good." I heard my voice come out soft, kind of thoughtful. I was amazed at my own feeling, actually. Six months before, when we were working on the burglaries, I would have been nervous or even jealous that Chad had figured this out before me. Now, at least this time, I was just admiring. Respectful, I guess. It felt good. "What about the clue with numbers? It looks like dates and times, right?" I fished my copy of Laura's clues out of my shorts pocket. I figured it should be carried on me at all times so I could keep working on it. There was the second clue:

7/31/11:59:59 —/→ 8/1/12:00:00

"Yeah, it looks like July 31, eleven fifty-nine and fifty-nine seconds, is not going to turn over to midnight, August 1. What does that mean? The world's going to end then? He's going to stop time?"

"Stop time! Deadline!" I shrieked. "The treasure hunt does not continue past July 31!"

Chad was silent a moment. "Arthur doesn't give us much breathing room, does he? They're supposed to get another set of clues that day at dinner!"

"That must mean it's their last set."

"Yeah. But why is there a deadline? Does the treasure disintegrate then, like Cinderella? Why couldn't we find it or get to it after July 31?"

I had no answer for that one.

"We'd better call Mrs. Ames."

"Yeah. We better tell her Friday night's gonna be a beast."

"Wait a sec. Caroline? Ah—there's something I've been meaning to ask you. About what you said to Mrs. Ames today. About—now don't cleave my head from my very neck with your incisors—about *damn?"*

Oh what would I say to him? That it's not the word itself that's bad, that it's a perfectly legitimate word in the dictionary, not to mention the Bible, but the problem is we flash it around like a weapon: *damn* this, *damn* that, not realizing we're asking that things be thrown into killing fire?

"I mean, you must have been talking a lot to Mr. Schreiber lately. I'm not sure exactly what I'm asking, but what did he say—"

"Caroline!" The door to Mom and Dad's room crashed open and Sam stood there. "Don't you remember Mom asked you to set the table? She's plenty mad. Hey, since it's actually quiet on your end of the line I guess you're not playing Word Wars with the boyfriend, huh?"

CHAPTER SIX

Embarrassment ran through me like a spilled hot liquid, and I squeezed my eyes shut.

"Erica!" Sam yodeled, "I'm about to grab her by her neck chain and haul her to the scullery. She'll call you back!"

"Uh, I'll call you back," I repeated stupidly into the phone, careful not to say Chad's name. I could hardly spit the words out, and I sounded like a cross between a spy, a breathless lover, and a kid who was too embarrassed to ever inflate her lungs again.

"Sa*man*tha," I screeched, the instant the phone hit its cradle. "The next time you have a call, I will think up the most exquisite, humiliating, torture never before unleashed on earth. I will—"

The phone rang again.

"GOT IT!" Sam lunged and landed practically upon my body as I snatched up the phone.

"Caro?" It was Erica. "I'm so glad I finally got through. Did somebody disable the call waiting? Your phone's been busy for ages—"

"Is *this* one the boyfriend?" Sam cackled. "Nah, can't be. Your mouth's still shut."

"Boyfriend?" said Erica. "Then you *are* going with Chad?"

"Erica." I tried to fight my way to a sitting position.

"Then the *other* one was the boyfriend!" crowed Sam.

"I've got to help in the kitchen or I'm dead. I'm sorry; I promise promise promise I'll call you back as soon as I can."

With Sam pulling on my arm, about to fall on the floor, I had no choice. I winced as I hung up the phone on my best friend Erica.

Chapter 7

I BIKED OVER TO Erica's the next morning, Wednesday. I didn't want to because (1) I was nervous, and (2) I should be studying the clues. I'd called Laura about the deadline, and she, Chad, and I had agreed to work as much as we could on the clues, calling each other as often as necessary. We also agreed to meet at Laura's at five o'clock Friday. That was only half an hour after her dinner with Ratio would start, but we'd have no time to lose.

It seemed we had got just about as much out of Clues I as we were going to, though, I soothed myself as I pedaled along. This going to Erica's was okay, because there really wasn't much we could do except wait for Friday, and Clues II. Or so I thought.

As I pulled into Erica's yard and approached the door, my stomach flared with nervousness again. But if I put this off, I'd just get nervouser about the time we'd eventually have to get together. This was the morning I'd originally suggested we go shopping, I reminded myself. And here I was, to spend it with her. I was *not* ignoring her.

She answered the door right away and led me into the living room. I had that relieved feeling you get when you haven't seen somebody for a while and they still look familiar. Erica was still the short, bouncy blonde she's always been, lively but not too noisy or idiotic, practical but not too fussy for fun. "Any chance you can go to the mall today?" She was striding ahead of me, leading me to her room. I was about to say I'd ask my mom about the mall question. Really I was. But I was stopped short by the sight in her living room.

There was a woman there taking apart the piano. She was holding a white piano key, which I guess is a lot longer than we think it is, in her hand. In the space on the keyboard where it should have been was just a piano-key-shaped hole.

"The keys come out?" I cried.

The piano person looked at me and smiled pleasantly, a thin woman with thin, pale hair that flowed closely over her shoulders and back the way water would. "They sure do."

"What are you doing? I mean what kind of person are you?" Boy, that didn't sound right. "I mean . . ."

She turned back to her work. "I'm a piano technician. I'm basically tuning the piano and checking it over. Something that should be done periodically." Her voice faded out as she seemed to really get into the act of putting the piano back together.

"Erica, the keys come out," I said. Erica was standing in the doorway leading out of the living room, wishing, I'm sure, that I'd forget the dumb piano and follow her.

I hadn't seen Laura Ames's third bedroom. What if it had a piano in it? Since keys could be removed from pianos, were there inner spaces where things could be hidden in pianos? Things like wads of bills? I couldn't ask the piano technician, who I think was afraid I was going to turn out to be a pest. It was just too weird a question.

"Caro?"

CHAPTER SEVEN

"Coming!" I tore my eyes away from the piano woman, who was now using a screwdriver on the piano, but my attention stayed with her even after we got to Erica's room. I knew that even if Laura had a piano, she was sure the treasure wasn't in her house. But would we be led to another piano somewhere? Totally off the track, I even began to wonder if I should take piano lessons. I mean, some people were wholly amazed that a gifted kid didn't play an instrument. I didn't know if my parents would get a piano, but if Mrs. Ames had one maybe she'd let me—

"Caro, are you really that hot on looking at the stupid piano?"

I looked at Erica. It was like I suddenly remembered I was with her. "Uh—no! No. Should I call my mom about the mall?"

"You *do* want to look at the piano. Caro, listen. Tell me the truth, okay? *Why* do you want to watch the piano tuner? That's all I want to know. Just—*why?*"

I was still looking at Erica, trying to decide what to say. Of course that wasn't making her feel any better, so I ended up telling her a dangerous bit of truth. "I wanted to know if you could hide stuff in a piano. You know, if there's room?" Now would I end up telling her about Laura Ames? Well, why not? I never had secrets from Erica. She wasn't going to steal the treasure.

"Why do you want to know that? You don't have a piano."

"I know." I sighed.

"Am I really so boring that you'd rather watch the piano get taken apart than talk to me?"

"No! I was . . . wondering about lessons. Really. Maybe I should take piano lessons."

"Yeah, right."

"I was!" Already this conversation had gone too far wrong. Now we could start yelling "was not," "was too," and all we'd really remember when we gave it up was that we were on opposite sides. I walked farther into Erica's room and sat down on her bed. Erica's room is pink and white and ruffly, and I probably don't fit into it even though I'd secretly kind of like to. I had certainly spent enough time in her room. Instead of sitting down with me, she stayed standing with her back to the bookshelf.

"Tell me, Caro. When you saw the piano half apart, did you suddenly get all interested in the insides? I mean, did you want to see the hammers and strings or how they went together or how they vibrate or something?"

"No. Well, kind of. Well—oh, this is really tough to explain."

It *was* tough. Because I realized Erica saw a big divide between us. She wondered if I thought she was boring. She wondered if, because I was a gifted kid, I could at any moment get all interested in weird taking-apart and putting-together problems with nuts and bolts, computer chips, cells, atoms, or any things that could be called *parts*. She was worried because she wouldn't be able to get into that. And I couldn't tell her that I was interested in the piano's innards because it had to do with a treasure hunt—because I just couldn't. I trusted Erica, but Mrs. Ames was trusting *me* to keep her secret, and I had to. This idea of trusting Erica but still not being able to tell her something was new to me, so it made me confused. And the biggest reason it was all so tough to explain is that people just don't say all this stuff. They don't say, "Hey, I see you're worried about being boring, but forget it because I like you." They don't say, "We're not as different as you think just because one of us is called gifted." They don't say, "How can you make me feel like I can't fit in with you just because the school hung some label on me?" Instead they yell, "Was not!" "Was too!"

"Why do you have to give me a mixed-up answer? Why can't you say, 'Yeah, I think the piano's insides are a scientific marvel,' or 'No, they're not that cool."

She knew I was keeping something from her. So what should I say? What answer was true? What answer helped our friendship? "Hey, why don't we just go to the mall, okay?"

Well, we went. I could afford one outfit and was careful to pick one out that would make me look like a wholly regular kid. Erica liked it. She said the butterscotch-colored top went with my "melting caramel" eyes, and she made me buy a matching ponytail thing for my "molasses" hair. Looking at clothes was cool, and it gave us—me, at least—a good feeling that seemed to flow over my skin and soothe the uneasy stuff. But while I was helping Erica with her "new look" I kept thinking that I really should be talking to Mrs. Ames about pianos, and that I really couldn't wait to get home to call her. And I wanted to call Chad. I wanted to see him that afternoon, and I wanted to say something that would make him smile so his dimples popped in. Good grief, what did all this mean?

"Caro, can I ask you something?" Erica asked as we walked through the mall.

"Sure," I said, but immediately felt nervous. Was this going to be a test question to see how honest or revealing I'd be? That thought made me feel a flash of anger at Erica, and at myself.

"Do you like Chad as a boyfriend?"

It was a perfectly proper best-friend type of question. I admired Erica for being brave enough to ask it at this moment. I mean, she must have been scared she'd get a beating-around-the-bush type of answer to this one, too.

I figured I owed her.

"I don't know. I mean, that's really really the truth! I *don't* know." I started walking faster, as if I imagined she was stalking ahead of me and I had to catch up. I felt my hair sail farther out behind me the way it seems to do in malls, as if you're outside on the street after all. "But you know, I think I do." Now I had to slow down. I couldn't say this deep-dark-confession type of stuff at high speed. Erica stayed even with me. "Just the way I think about him lately—I mean, how he looks, and I want to see him a lot, and I think about stuff besides his br—"

Oh good grief. I was going to say besides his *brains,* of course, but I was so embarrassed I just shivered. And was I only starting to think about Chad as more than just a smart kid I had to compete with? That was just as bad as people thinking about *me* as nothing but a smart student! Had I, who should know better, done this to Chad? The idea gave me a fierce, odd protective feeling for him that was absolutely, wholly new.

"I mean I think about him as a whole person, a lot of different things about him, you know?" I rushed on, before Erica could think I was hiding some feeling I was having. "Yes," I summed up, quieter, feeling like this whole thing with Chad was getting gigantic and powerful just because I was talking about it. "I would like to have Chad as a boyfriend."

"Wow." Erica's voice was quiet and awestruck, which I appreciated. "That sounds pretty exciting."

"Erica, I know you keep secrets, but I've got to say it anyway. Please, please don't say anything. Especially to Chad, especially where he might hear. It would be so easy to say the wrong thing and have him find out."

"I won't. I promise."

I knew she meant it, and she wasn't at all mad that I made her promise. It's really pretty much of a compliment to be begged not to repeat the deep, dark secret only you have been told.

A little smile stayed on her face for the rest of the day. I didn't feel so smooth and easy about my own friendships, though. What if it turned out that I liked Chad as a boyfriend but he didn't like me as a girlfriend, and we'd start to feel stupid and finally avoid each other? Well, at least I had some sign now that my friendship with Erica was hanging together. She had my secret, and I had a new regular-kid outfit that she liked.

The thing is, there's more to the story. It wasn't only Chad that was Erica's rival. Erica might have smoothed over her worries about Chad and me, but she didn't know a thing about Paige Halsey.

Chapter 8

IT ALL STARTED with Paige on the hot humid first of July. That was a Wednesday, but I had it in my head that it was Thursday and had biked to the library in Orchardville that night thinking it would be open. Circling around the empty parking lot and coming out the exit, I found I could see into the church across the street.

This was a smallish white church with a steeple and slanted roof like you've probably seen in pictures. The double doors stood open like welcoming hands. I was suddenly struck with curiosity, I guess because my teacher, Mr. Schreiber, believes in God. I mean believes like he thinks God is actually important. I'd gotten curious about God when we went through the stuff with the burglars, and I'd started reading about Jesus. Anyway, I could hear the lively, conversational voice of the pastor, and I was just—kind of captured by this voice. I expected a pastor's voice to be either shrill and scolding or low and zombie-like, but really what would I know since I've hardly been to church in my life.

Well, I crossed the street and kind of snuck up to the open doors from the side so I wouldn't be seen so easily, and there in a pew on the left sat none other than my Gifted and Talented teacher, Mr. Paul Schreiber.

The hot pink lab coat he wears at school was missing. I don't mean I was stupid enough to think he'd have it on, but I mean the absent lab coat really made me aware that I was seeing his life outside of school. Judging from the side of his face that I could see, he looked the same: brown hair, brown beard, a little bit tanned. Listening.

Still sitting on my bike, I pushed my wheels along the sidewalk so I could see the right side of the aisle. That's when I saw Paige Halsey, a regular, blending-in girl in my school. Paige is such a regular kid I can't even decide if her hair's blonde or brown; I mean, she *fits in*. And behind Paige was an empty seat.

I was conscious of how sweaty I was, how I was wearing jean shorts that were getting tattered and I wasn't sure they were supposed to be worn to church. I studied the inside of the church like crazy, trying to decide if it was big enough for me to risk going in, or if I'd feel like I'd just entered somebody's living room. But I felt like those doors were open for me, and I chained my bike to a two-hour parking sign and slid into that empty pew behind Paige.

"No one reaches God except by following Jesus," the pastor was saying. "That's what's so hard for many people to understand. They feel they have to find their own way to God, some way that feels right to them. But God reached out to *us* when he sent Jesus. They don't have to find their own way at all!"

I wanted to hide somewhere, but the presence of Mr. Schreiber and Paige Halsey kept me pinned to my seat. If they believed what the pastor was saying, then I could listen a little longer.

"Some people feel it's snobbish to say that only Jesus leads us to God. They feel it's not accepting of other people's beliefs."

The pastor wasn't old or young, just caught somewhere in those medium adult ages that are all the same. He was a tall blond man with a tall forehead, too. He put his hand in and out of his pants pocket in a casual way that pushed his suit coat open, and I could see small wrinkles and bulges of his shirt tucked into his waistband. He seemed normal enough. As his sweeping gaze moved in my direction I looked away.

"Those people need to see that God didn't mean to make it hard or confusing for us to find him. He doesn't play favorites. He doesn't say that some people must come to him this way and others must reach him that way. Simple belief in his son Jesus makes each and every person acceptable to him."

Maybe it was my gaze on the side of his face, but whatever it was, something made Mr. Schreiber turn around. When he saw me, surprise jumped through his eyes. Then a kind of softness came onto his face, and he raised the fingers of his left hand above his pew and flicked them at me in a falling-dominoes wave.

"Some people feel life is too hard and God doesn't help us. They wonder how he can just watch terrible things happen, like crime or sickness. They need to see that God gave us his son, who is also God and who had done nothing wrong, to die horribly on a cross to pay the death penalty for our crimes! This is a more loving thing to do for the world than any of us could bring ourselves to do."

Suddenly my attention was riveted to the pastor, and I was soaking up what he'd said.

"And people need to know that God does care about all the wrong. But he is patient with all of us who are doing wrong today, because he wants people to turn their lives around even more than we want them to."

The pastor ended with a prayer. The idea that God had done much more for the world than people had done really stuck with me. Not only was God more powerful, he *cared* much more. I sort of put this thought together with the stories I'd been reading about Jesus—stories about healing awful diseases, and talking to crowds of people when he was exhausted. Most people would have gone home for supper and a nap.

Of course Paige Halsey had to turn around when we filed out. Just like Mr. Schreiber, at first this huge jerk of surprise crossed her face. "Caroline. Hi." Her voice was really friendly. "I never saw you here before."

"I never was. I just sort of—came in."

"It's really nice to see you," Paige said.

I'm very seldom tongue-tied, but I didn't know what to say.

"I mean, usually during the summer you see the same few people, but there's always a group you won't see again till fall. I think it's kind of cool to run into those people unexpectedly." Paige smiled up at me, her brown eyes warm and shiny.

"Yeah, so do I." I started smiling as I realized then and there that I thought the same thing.

"Hey, Mom." Paige plucked at the sleeve of the tiny Native American woman next to her, who was talking to someone in the pew ahead. "I want you to meet a girl in my class."

Seconds later my sweaty hand was clasped in both of Mrs. Halsey's. Then Paige pointed out her dad, who was blondish like Paige and wore glasses and looked serious, and her two sisters, who looked younger and very Indian like their mom and who were darting between people, heading for the door.

"I'd love it if you'd come back," Paige said. We

stood outside with her family, bunched around her car giggling while organized-looking Mr. Halsey poked in every one of his pockets for his keys.

Paige's sisters, Leigh and Claire, played tug of war with a new bumper sticker, which Claire finally peeled off its backing and plopped crookedly on the tailgate of their minivan.

"What does it mean?" I asked Paige. On the bumper sticker was a fish shape with ΙΧΘΥΣ printed inside it.

"I think it means fish. The fish shape is a Christian symbol. See you soon?" she added as Mr. Halsey finally got his door open. She waggled her fingers at me, and her brown eyes and turned-up mouth looked really hopeful.

I couldn't help but nod. As I waved good-by to the Halseys I wondered why I had never really known Paige before. Maybe school wasn't a place where you could always see what people had to offer.

Twirling the combination lock on my bike chain, I felt that little bubble of happiness that sometimes stays with you even after you forget why it came in the first place. Then I realized someone was watching me.

"Caroline."

Mr. Schreiber. I'd know his voice anywhere. His car was parked only a few yards from my bike.

"I was really happy to see you tonight."

I knew he meant *in church*, not that he would have been unhappy to see me someplace else.

"Do you mind if I ask whether something special brought you in?"

He was standing right in front of me at my own height (I'm five eight), looking at me with his brown eyes that just pull honesty right out of you. So this is what I said: "I wanted to find out if it was true."

He studied me for a minute. "And what did you

find out?" he asked softly.

I thought of the time last school year when he told me he believed in God because he couldn't believe the order and beauty of the universe happened by accident. I thought of what the pastor had said about God doing so much for the world that he had allowed Jesus to take the death penalty for crimes in our place. I thought that nobody could deny those crimes were real; I mean, they're mostly the very same horrible wrong things people complain God doesn't care about! I thought about Jesus healing people, and actually *walking* from one town to another to talk to them about God, and spending his time with people who weren't cool, and I thought that if he were here today he'd visit hospitals and prisons and bars and inner cities where proper people don't want to go.

"I think it's true," I said.

He nodded. "You're more fortunate than I am. I didn't think it was true till after college, and then it was even longer before I *believed* it was true."

I suppose I looked at him funny. "What do you mean? Isn't thinking the same as believing?"

"Well," said Mr. Schreiber, "when I *thought* it was true, someone could have asked me whether I believed Jesus really died for our sins, and I would've answered 'yes.' Then I would have forgotten about the subject. I began to *believe* it was true when I began to *live* like it was true. I started praying. I don't mean boring stuff full of 'thees' and 'thous.' I mean I talked to him like I would to anyone. When I had to make decisions, I thought about God watching and caring. In fact I told Jesus how sorry I was that he had to die for all the sins I committed. That's when believing became real to me."

I nodded.

"May I ask? Have you made a decision to follow Jesus, Caroline?"

I nodded.

And you know what? It was a lie.

Mr. Schreiber made a few more chit-chat remarks to me and I kept nodding. I managed to get my stupid combination lock open, and he drove away and I pedaled away thinking how I'm just a goody-goody student who pleases teachers, so I tell them what they want to hear.

I hadn't really made a decision to follow Jesus, not right then. I guess I had suddenly wanted to belong to a group that had both Mr. Schreiber and Paige Halsey in it. Anyway, it was thinking about the stupid lie and the fact that I told it to Mr. Schreiber, of all people, and the fact that it was about God, that made me finally decide to pray to Jesus and tell him I'd been really stupid and I was sorry. I thanked him for forgiving my sins, and for being so big that my brains are really little in comparison, and I told him I was going to follow him. By this time it was July 9, so that's the day I became a Christian.

And by then I'd already seen Paige again. And we're starting to talk on the phone.

Erica is going to have a fit.

I haven't told my parents much about this. I just asked them why we've never gone to church. They did try to be honest.

"Maybe we should go, but when it comes right down to it, I don't see what it really has to do with anything." Mom chuckled kind of self-consciously as she loaded the dishwasher. (Kitchen chores are good for one thing: they give you a time to ask your mom stuff.) "Besides, they'd try to get me on some committee, and I'm busy enough, thank you."

"Never was much interested," was Dad's reply. "And they want too much money." Dad is sensitive about money. Growing up, his family of nine kids lived on a really tight budget, and he's concerned about sending us kids to college.

I worked up my courage and announced I was a Christian.

"Well, that's your privilege," Mom said, and it sounded like she meant, 'Well, that's a stage you're going through.'

"As long as you're thinking carefully. Make sure you're thinking for yourself," Dad said.

"Wooowww," said Sam, in this wholly mystified way. "That must be something really smart kids—I mean, you hear about genius kids who understand philosophy and stuff—"

On the whole, they took the announcement as if I'd said I'd become a vegetarian or something. It's for sort of strange people, they'll tolerate it, and it's fine for me but they don't want it for themselves.

The question I came back to a lot was, what would Chad Neumann say?

Would he say, "I find it intriguing that you've embraced this unusual system of thought, but I must inform you it's not compatible with my outlook on life"?

Would he say, "That's kind of weird"?

Would he say, "Sounds like you've been talking to Mr. Schreiber," and would he mean, "When and why has he been talking to you and not me?"

I didn't wholly like any of these.

But we needed to talk about treasure in pianos, and pretty soon we'd be into a heavy search for cash and jewels, so I was pretty sure I'd find out what Chad Neumann would say.

Chapter 9

THE FIRST THING I wanted to do when I got home from the mall that Wednesday, July 29, was call Laura Ames to ask if she had a piano. But Samantha met me at the driveway.

"*There* you are!" Fists on hips, she stood next to a boulder-pile of newspaper bundles. The reason the whole curb looked like an avalanche scene was that along with that day's papers, two different kinds of inserts for the Sunday paper had been dropped off. "Inserts" are pages and pages and pages of store ads and coupons, and maybe your comic page and TV listings buried in there somewhere. These must be "inserted" into the Sunday papers in the pitch dark early morning by the bleary-eyed carrier. They're what make your Sunday paper fat. (Okay, sometimes a bleary-eyed sister or parent helps me.) Anyway, here they were, all two hundred and ten or so of them, needing to be hauled someplace where they wouldn't get in the way for the next four days. The little blue or pink slips attached to the bundles flapped in the stiffening breeze.

"Fun's over." Sam eyed my clothes bag from the mall. "You're real lucky I'm going to help you drag these things into the garage, and then stay with

Danny, like I did all day, while you do your papers. And *then* . . ." Sam paused dramatically. "*Then* I'm going swimming at Sasha's. The one day in about the last eighty that I don't have to work at the store, and I had to spend the whole time answering your phone calls and making sure my little brother didn't get crushed by a falling Lego satellite or something."

"My phone calls?"

"Not now!" Sam screamed. She swung a leg at me and picked up a bundle. "Come on, start carting."

We hoisted the inserts to the garage and piled them along the wall, going back and forth between there and the curb a bunch of times.

"Well, these things'll about amputate your fingers." Sam had carried two bundles by grabbing the plastic binding stuff like a handle. She dropped them on the garage floor and kicked them the rest of the way.

"Hey, easy on the merchandise. Yeah, that plastic is like a knife. Just pick up the bundles in your arms." I came puffing across the concrete floor after her.

"By the looks of your face, that's not a whole lot easier."

She smiled a shade wickedly. "Or are you just concentrating on putting one foot in front of the other?"

Unfortunately my foot chose that moment to stub itself against a stack of papers. I sprawled forward and my paper bundle practically sailed through the garage window. That would have been a better fate than my head met. It bounced smartly off the exposed-beam wooden garage wall.

"You okay?"

"You're exactly right, you know." I rubbed my head hard, stirring my hair up like an electric mixer might. "I was concentrating on walking."

Sam roared.

"That's what you do," I persisted. "If your arms are carrying a heavy load, for example, you don't think about the tired, achy arms. You think about the legs walking smooth and fast toward the goal."

Sam doubled over and stamped the floor.

"It's the principle of distraction," I expounded. "Employed for decades to relieve the minor pain of headaches, illness, and early labor. The theory is that concentration on pleasant activities or properly functioning parts decreases the discomfort of ill or overworked parts."

Sam was still laughing. I figured I might as well pour it on. I mean, what did I have to lose?

"It's the scientific study of coping techniques. It's the concept of fixing your mind on what's going right, applied to a wide variety of life situations. Got that? Theory applied to life situations!"

Sam got herself under control, giggling and wiping her eyes. "It didn't *work*."

"It did too," I said to her back as she left the garage. "I forgot all about my tired arms. I just didn't stop my legs soon enough."

"Hurry up or I'm going for my swim now!" she called without turning around.

"I'll bet you were thinking about your fingers all the way up the driveway, weren't you?" I reached the doorway of the garage just in time to see three junior high boys from next door digging a basketball out of our bushes. Or at least they had been digging for the basketball. Now they were giving me strange looks. I went into the house and headed for the phone.

"No way." Sam blocked my path, threw my sack over my head like a lasso, and began weighing me down with papers. "You can discuss the principles of concentration or distraction or whatever with the boyfriend later. And when you're done passing these things out, you can make a salad to go with supper. Fruit or vegetable, nobody cares, but edible would be a plus."

I delivered fast until, puffing and lumbering, I got to Laura Ames's house. Then, instead of putting her paper in her wooden box and not banging the cover, I rang her doorbell.

"Laura, have you got a piano?" I burst out before she had the door all the way open.

"A piano?" Laura, in crisp plaid shorts and a white top, looked me up and down. "You look more like you should be begging for water after a trek through the desert."

I suppose I was pretty sweaty, and one hand lifted to the top of my head told me my hair was still beaten to a froth. Several thoughts began to fire at once: (1) At least Chad isn't here. (2) Chad should be here. If Laura's got a piano with money in it . . . I pushed all this aside and breathed in, trying to sound like a normal person. "Yes. A piano."

"As a matter of fact I do, in the third bedroom." Laura watched my face. "You want to see it now?"

I hardly needed to croak out a yes. Laura stepped aside, led me to the right, down the hall, and into the third bedroom. Painted a pale orange—I guess you call it peach—it was about as empty as the computer room. But alone on one wall next to a window was a dark brown piano with a matching bench that looked like a thousand other dark brown pianos. Of course I went straight to it, stripping off my paper sack as easily as if it were empty.

I grabbed the lid of the bench on the side that had the hinges on and almost tipped the whole works over. When I finally got it open I found piano music—big surprise, right? Most of it was lesson books with titles like *Miniature Melodies for the Young Pianist*, with loose, brownish pages and covers torn off.

"Those are from when Alan took lessons," Laura said, behind me. No wonder she'd saved them. Immediately I stopped pawing through the bench and began lifting the edge of each book with two fingers to look underneath. I couldn't blame her for thinking that if I got my hands on them in a serious way, those ancient books might just crumble to a fine powder that only an archeologist could identify.

The bench had nothing else in it. "Did you or Arthur play the piano?" My breathing got a bit faster. "Or Ratio?"

"Oh, not me," said Laura. "But Arthur was a jack-of-all-trades. He ran his hands over the keys now and then, playing something that sounded ripply but not like any melody I knew. I remember Ratio plunking a little too."

I watched Laura with interest.

"He'd plant himself right in the middle of that bench, fanny hanging over the edge, and set all his fingers on the keys one by one. When he was sure they were all sitting right he'd play his chord. Then he'd move all his fingers to the next keys, check each one at a time, and play that chord. He might not have been much else at the piano, but he was correct."

"Did Ratio or Arthur have a favorite song?" I ran my fingers up the keyboard, trying to hold them curved and flexible, but my ripply notes sounded like they came out of either a horror movie or a kindergarten. I deliberately tried to sound like Arthur and not like Ratio, even though Ratio's fingers got the right answers. I also hoped some hidden drawer would spring open and reveal itself to be stuffed with cash or diamonds. I suppose I've read too much Nancy Drew.

"I can't really say they had any favorites that I know of," Laura answered. "You think that would be a clue?"

I guess I still hoped playing the right tune might make some hidden panel slide open or something. I got down on my back to look at the underside of the keyboard, as if I was going to work under a car.

"The treasure's not here, Caroline," Laura said softly.

"Maybe in a different piano." I got back up to all fours and poked my fingers down the opening where I could see the strings showing, looking like a harp in there. "Maybe this piano will show us how to look in a different piano." I stood up, and with several tugs managed to roll one end of the piano a couple feet from the wall without wrecking anything.

"Oh, that'll be so dirty," said Laura, but in the same instant she ran to help me. The wooden beams and slats in back of the piano were coated with dust, and I had to take a serious sneezing break. I bent down and poked around. A person could easily have wedged rolls of bills or a box of something in here, but they hadn't. No way had anything disturbed the dirt.

"If there's a different piano we need to find," said Laura, "first we'll need the rest of the clues to find it."

"I saw a piano technician at my friend's house today." I knelt under the keyboard again to stick my hand down the slot where I could see the strings. "She had the piano half apart." I stuck my hand farther behind the panel than I'd got it before. My hands are big but my arms are thin and I got in up to my wrist. I suddenly remembered hearing about a girl who stuck her arm up a Coke machine when her can didn't come out. Her arm didn't come out either, until somebody called 911 to free her.

"Ah, Laura?" I said casually, wiggling my hand a bit. There seemed to be just this very minor jam-up where my wrist had turned the corner at the top of the panel. "Maybe we should check the encyclopedia for a diagram on how pianos fit together." That's it, Grade. When real life gets hairy, retreat to a book. "We can see if there might be hiding places inside."

"All right, it's worth a look, but shouldn't you be getting on with your papers?"

Papers! I'd forgotten. Not *really* forgotten, just sort of temporarily.

"Ah. Yes I should." I pulled my arm, big time. Just the right snap of the wrist should make my hand come flying up out of the slot and unhook my wrist from the piano's jaws. Instead I just got a red, ragged scrape on my tendon. My mind groped for what to do. It hit on Jesus.

Lord, along with forgetting my papers, I forgot to pray. I realize I mostly pray only when I need something—

"Caroline? Are you finding something down there?"

"I hope so." *—but I'm just getting used to talking to you. Can you please get my hand out of this piano so 911 doesn't have to? And thank you that Chad's not here.* "You're right, I've got to get going," I said rather loudly to Laura. "I'm coming up." The phone rang and Laura left the room.

Lord, getting your arm stuck in a piano is a lot stupider than having it happen with a Coke machine. I mean, you see a kid getting eaten by a Coke machine, and you understand right away why it happened. But how do explain this? 'You see, I'm sure there's a million bucks hidden in front of the strings, just above the pedals.' Yeah right.

Laura stepped back into the room. "Caroline, the phone's for you."

I pulled mightily.

"Caroline? I admire your persistence, but we'll have to wait for the next set of clues. We're not going to take the piano apart."

Oh we're not, are we? I yanked my arm. Just when I thought it might pull out of my shoulder and send me hurtling backwards like a bowling ball, my hand came out of the piano. My wrist, red-striped and skinned, wholly looked like it'd been raked by teeth.

Thanks, Lord. No 911.

"Your sister sounds quite upset."

Sam was on the phone? My heart sank.

"*Care-o-line. Grah-dee.* No, skip the last name; right now we share nothing, not even a last name, do you hear me? In the last fifteen minutes, *five,* count 'em, *five,* of your customers who haven't got their paper yet called up to bellow at *me.* Listen, Mega Brain, it's like matching, okay? One paper, one house. Did you trip and fall down the sewer? Did you get wound up in somebody's hose and get gangrene?"

"I got bit by a piano."

Pause.

"Caroline, are you all right?"

Her voice hadn't softened a bit, but what could I say to this? "Yeah. I am."

"Then deliver those papers. *Get!*"

I got.

Chapter 10

WHAT IS ALL this with you and that old lady?" Samantha asked.

It was finally Friday, July 31, late afternoon. Sam was in our room getting ready for a date. I'd delivered my papers, and now I was sitting on my bed basically fidgeting because I knew Laura Ames and Ratio Ames would be having supper soon, and because Chad and I would be going over at five when Ratio might still be there. Actually, I'd just got back from riding around Laura's house on my bike, hoping to spy Ratio, but no luck. It was still too early.

"Does that lady have something to do with why you say you're a Christian?"

Was I finally going to *see* Ratio Ames, in all his flesh—wait. Sam had asked me a question. "No. Mrs. Ames is just a good friend, that's all."

"Well I can understand how you know her because of your paper route." Sam peeled off one pair of jeans and began to pull on another. Actually, the floor around her was covered with pants. "But how does Chad Neumann get into the act?"

Fortunately an answer came to me right away. "Oh, you know how it is. Everybody in Orchardville knows everybody else."

Sam yanked the jeans off and picked up yet another pair. "My theory is that you and the woman wage wicked, wise-guy, witty games of Word Wars." She changed her top. "Not bad, huh?"

"Alliteration," I said.

"Alliteration!" Sam cried. "The repetition of the same first sound or first letter in a group of words. The woman waged wicked wise-guy witty Word Wars."

"Mrs. Heimer taught us," I said. "Lit class."

Sam smiled at this. She changed her top one last time, twisting her shoulders in front of the mirror left and right to check how it looked. I wondered if she was thinking the same thing I was, which was that she, being older, should learn things first, and that my explanation of how I could possibly know about alliteration was my respectful acknowledgment that I was really too young. In other words, when we have a tie, Sam wins on maturity.

I was sort of relieved that Sam had gone by four-thirty. By that time my nerves were sizzling. And by that time I had a new problem.

"*Where* is it exactly you're going?" Mom asked.

"To Mrs. Ames's house. Chad's coming too." If someone else's mother let him go, she can let me go, right?

"Does this have something to do with school? I mean, I realize school is *out*, but—" Mom seemed to be groping around. "I'm just questioning why this older adult is interested in you two. You can't be too careful these days, you know."

I was going to have to ask Laura Ames what I should tell my parents. Even if it was okay to say she's got a fortune in money and jewels stashed someplace just waiting for somebody to stumble on it, they'd think Laura Ames was nuts or something.

"Is she intelligent?" Mom asked.

Oh, that would explain it all, wouldn't it? The world is so short on intelligent beings that when we find each other we just have to form a club or something.

"Yes," I said truthfully.

"Well, I guess I can understand that."

"We're working on solving some puzzles." True, of course, but I wasn't happy about the impression I was giving. We were not just two weird kids and a grandma person getting together to play nerdy games.

"Go ahead then." Mom finally waved her hand in dismissal. "Of course I've heard of Arthur Ames, and I'm sure his wife must be okay. You guys enjoy yourselves, but be sure you're polite to Mrs. Ames. Just because you might be on the same level brain-wise doesn't mean you treat her just like any young friend of yours."

"Sure, Mom." I was halfway out the door before she had finished, before she could give me a curfew. How was I going to tell Mom (Dad was working at the grain elevator) that we *had* to stick with Laura Ames from now on until the treasure was found?

I biked to Laura's and got there just as Chad was pulling up. Seeing the green rattletrap car in the driveway sent a zing through my stomach, but then I looked at Chad. The heat and humidity had gone away over the last couple days, and Chad was wearing gray sweats. I watched him brake and swing his back leg over the rear wheel as he stopped. I had this crazy wish that he was on tape so I could rewind it and watch him again.

"Obtaining clearance from my opposite sex parent for this caper required a significant quantity of complex explaining," Chad greeted me.

I decided to analyze his eye color. It's blue-gray-black: murky, inky, and secretive. Then I began to wonder if he'd passed me in height. He used to be a shade shorter; was he now a shade taller? I quickly hoped so, then dashed into my overdue reply.

"Acquiring consent to remain late will prove to be a further challenge—"

Laura's door flew open. She was dressed in lemon yellow sweats, and I suddenly began to view sweats as a uniform of action. But she looked kind of white. Her lips were pressed together and the skin above them was wrinkled like crepe paper. Suddenly Ratio's bespectacled, pumpkin-size head loomed above her left shoulder.

Maybe Chad and I somehow looked like we'd definitely arrived to stay. Maybe Ratio saw a connection between Laura's sweats and Chad's, because he suddenly seemed to understand the whole situation. His globe-shaped body squeezed past Laura's and popped out the door. A flush crept out of a fat fold in his neck and spread up his face like a stain. He turned on Laura.

"All that claptrap." His voice was surprisingly high, and trembly. "About honoring Cube by working together. All the phony sniffling about *me* avoiding *you*. All the insinuations that I'm a double-crosser." Ratio's arm and pointing finger sprang toward Chad and me like an arrow out of a bow. The fat under his arm swung like a hammock. "Then who," he roared, "are they?"

"Well, Ratio." Laura followed him outside. "It's not too late to cooperate—"

"Kids?" He swung his massive body around to stare at us. "You had to resort to junior high kids? What, you ask the school to send you the local spelling bee champs?"

"That's enough, Ratio. I'm telling you, we can work together."

"Bull. Why should I *honor Arthur's memory*," he mimicked, "when he just wants to exploit my intelligence to help you get the money?"

"I'm certain there'll be a share for you, too."

Ratio drew himself up to his full five feet nine. "The old," he said peevishly, "become children and take their turn at joy in the annual hunt."

Laura seemed dumbfounded. "Yes?"

Ratio rolled his eyes and turned completely back to Laura. "I hate to say it, darling aunt, but 'the old' obviously refers to you. There's no mention of me. You think I'm just going to be the handy brains that puzzle it out for you?"

He thought he wasn't old? I couldn't believe it.

"Ratio," said Laura. "The note said *children*, and *their*. How do you explain the plural if Arthur wasn't referring to both of us?"

"Oh for the love of—" Ratio threw up his hands. "It's a matter of writing style, like the 'editorial we.' It doesn't necessarily literally refer to two or more people. You can't be expected to understand."

I sure didn't.

"Or you." Ratio sneered at Chad and me.

It was too much like he'd read my mind, and maybe I flinched. Ratio smiled. He turned to Laura once more.

"I'm the one," he said. "*I'm* the one who knows how Arthur's mind worked. I'll find that treasure wherever it is, without leaving a trace. And you'll never prove a thing since you'll never find the hiding place anyway."

"How can you do this to Arthur?" It was like Laura's last, best hope, the only thing she could say. "How can you?"

"I think the question is," Ratio said shakily, "how could he do this to me?"

I had the funniest feeling Ratio wasn't talking only about money. I thought he was asking how Arthur could die and leave him. He got in his car, cranked it until the back end fired three times, and drove away in a cloud of exhaust.

"Well," said Laura.

Chad and I waited.

"Well," she said again. "Come on in, kids. Wait'll you see these clues."

Laura set out a whole buffet. Cheese and crackers, slices of sausage, watermelon wedges, and a pitcher of lemonade sat in line on her glass-topped coffee table. "I just ate, of course," Laura said. "Ratio brought two take-out perch dinners. But you probably haven't." She got out paper and pencils for each of us, and two calculators. There was every indication we were going to be here for the long haul. We sat cross-legged, Laura Ames too, around the food and spread the list labeled Clues II between us.

CLUES II
My words are not perfect,
oh what shall I do?
pass_ _ _ _
homophone of anagram of partner's name
island (3 letters)
single, cabinet, or computer
rental
my favorite literary technique

For a minute or so, no one spoke.

"Kind of makes you wish Ratio wasn't being such a twerp, doesn't it?" Chad mused.

"Well, where do you suggest we start?" Laura asked, munching a cracker.

"The beginning," I said. "Maybe he had a reason

for putting the clues in a certain order."

Chad was laughing before I finished the sentence. I had said something to make his dimples pop in already! But it was hardly a clever statement. In fact it was pretty dull—hey, what was happening to my concentration?

"His goose is cooked," Chad was chortling. "That's all she wrote. He's dead in the water. Done before he started. Skydiving without a parachute."

"Chad?" I queried. If Ratio's defeat was this certain, we were suddenly not in as big a hurry. What did he see that I didn't?

"Unless." Chad frowned. "It's too easy. It's too lucky. Ratio knows how important the computer was. He'd know how good the chances would be that something would be on there."

"Chad?" I tried again.

"Maybe we should let him be. He's percolating," said Laura.

"The computer." Chad jumped up. "Let's go."

I leaped up too. Laura got up more slowly, holding the edge of the coffee table and kind of unfolding herself piece by piece.

"How do you know—" I began, grabbing the sheet of clues that Chad had left half in the cheese dip, following him into Laura's foyer and down the hall into the computer room. "Oh, of course!"

The first clue read 'My words are not perfect, oh what shall I do?' To get perfect words, you go to WordPerfect, do you not?

Chad turned the computer on and in seconds had a blue box on the screen, followed by another blue box, followed by a green one. "Eureka!" Chad's expression of triumphant discovery abruptly changed. "I mean," he said darkly, "eureka. This is not what we wanted."

"Show me," I said. Laura Ames bent her head close too.

"Each of these," Chad pointed to a list of numbers on the screen, "tells when a backup copy of the hard disk was made. Of course people make backup copies so if something goes wrong inside the computer, they've still got all their files stored on floppy disks."

Laura Ames nodded.

"The next to last backup was done on January third. That's what the digits 0103 in the middle of that number mean. First month, third day." The number Chad was pointing to went like this: CC30103A.DIF.

"Then Arthur made that backup," Laura said. "That was three weeks before he died."

"The letters DIF mean he backed up only the files that had changed since the backup before that." Chad paused. "Did I say that clearly?"

"You mean," Laura said, "he wouldn't copy everything that's inside the computer every time he made a copy. Sometimes he'd copy only the things that had changed since his last backup."

"Right."

"That makes sense. I don't know much about computers, but maybe this old dog can learn a few new tricks yet."

Chad's finger advanced to the next number on the screen, which was CC30721A.FUL. Looking at the four digits after CC3, I suddenly knew what it meant. "A *full* backup was made on seven-twenty-one. July twenty-first."

"Bingo," said Chad.

"So that second night we had dinner here, when we got the first set of clues . . ." Laura began.

"And you thought Ratio was in here copying and printing out your clues . . ." Chad continued.

"He was also in here copying your entire hard

disk onto a set of floppy disks for himself," I finished. "All he has to do is put those disks into another computer, and he's got everything we've got."

Chapter 11

WOULD HE HAVE had time to do that?" Laura asked. "I mean, copy everything that's inside the computer?"

"Sure," Chad replied. "Fifteen minutes or so would be more than enough."

"I doubt he's got a computer. Ratio has never had much in the way of income."

"I've wondered about that." I looked at Laura. "What does Ratio do for a living?"

"That's been a mystery to me for the last twenty years," Laura said tartly. "He sold a couple of oddball inventions a few years back. Plastic widgets that do obscure jobs I never knew needed doing. He's always boasting about patents he has pending, and he falls for every get-rich-quick scheme he's ever seen advertised in lousy magazines. None of it ever came to anything."

"We can be sure he's got the use of a computer somewhere," Chad said. "A treasure is at stake. We'll have to get into WordPerfect and figure out what Arthur's got for us there."

"First we better solve a few more of these." I tapped the paper the clues were printed on. I had this uncomfortable feeling that Chad was getting ahead of me—not showing off exactly, but showing himself to be really smart and competent. "They may tell us what we're hunting for in the WordPerfect files."

"Right," Chad said. If he'd been planning to go ahead without figuring out more clues, he didn't show it. I was getting angry at the competition that always springs up between smart kids, and at myself for feeling we had to compete. It's like pushing and shoving with thoughts and words instead of arms and bodies. I had the feeling it was something that shouldn't be in me now that I'm a Christian, but I didn't know how to take it out.

"Here, you sit at the computer." Chad got up and motioned Laura Ames to take the desk chair. That was really nice of him, and I was reminded that I really liked him, and it would be just too stupid for words if brains and clues and competition messed things up.

Laura sat down in the desk chair on wheels, ready to be the one who would actually press the keys when we decided what we wanted to do with WordPerfect. After a dash back to the great room to get the paper and pencils, and then another dash back to the great room to get the food, we set to work.

"Homophone of anagram of partner's name," Chad muttered. "Does Arthur mean WordPerfect will find anagrams and homophones for us?"

"You have certainly got me there." Laura Ames shook her head and I thought she was looking a shade old and helpless again. "I have to confess I don't even know what anagrams and homophones are."

"Anagrams are words that you can make out of other words by rearranging the letters," Chad said. "Like you can change the letters around in *teach* and get *cheat*. And homophones—"

Chad's eyes met mine. For some reason he didn't continue. His eyes were murky, inky, and secretive.

"Are homophones the ones that sound the same and are spelled different, or sound different and are spelled the same?" Chad's eyes never left mine.

"Well, I've had some Greek, so I can help there," Laura chirped. I could tell she straightened in the chair. "Homo means same, and phone means sound. Same sound."

Chad and I exchanged sort of a smile before our eyes slid apart and we looked at Laura. Having to recite a lot of things that you know, all in a short time, can sure get weird.

"You took Greek?" I said to Laura.

"In my day the classics were very proper studies for young ladies." I could almost hear the little sniff that Laura didn't quite add, and I could almost see the well-bred young lady she had been, although the lovely French twist with escaping tendrils that I pictured in my mind was still gray. I guess old people were young once after all, but it's all so impossibly long ago.

"No anagrams listed here." Chad was searching the WordPerfect reference book. "The closest I can find is antonyms."

I sighed. That meant we couldn't make the computer scramble the letters in a word and show us all the new words they could spell.

Muttering, Chad picked up his pencil and surrendered to the idea of finding anagrams by hand. No doubt he realized there were 119 ways to arrange the letters in RATIO, not counting the word Ratio itself. Many of these arrangements would not make sense, like words that began with RT, for example, but he'd have to write most of them down and look at them in order not to miss any words.

"At least we know one thing," Laura said. "My partner's name is Arthur."

Chad turned white and dropped his pencil. His

freckles stood out like pepper. There was not a dimple to be seen. Chad no doubt realized there were 719 ways to arrange the letters in ARTHUR, not counting the word Arthur itself. Of course some of those would be duplicates since two of the six letters were the same, but—never mind. It was still bad enough.

"Not a chance," Chad said calmly. "This means your partner in the treasure hunt, and that's supposed to be Ratio. Trust me."

I looked up island in the dictionary, while Chad wrote down things like *roait, roita, roiat.* I didn't learn a thing except the definition of island (surprise, surprise). I sure didn't find any three-letter word that meant body of land surrounded by water.

"*Artio, artoi, aroit,*" mumbled Chad.

"Let's try the atlas," Laura suggested. "We'll look at the names of some islands. Maybe that's what he means."

"Great idea." Soon I was sprawled on the tan carpet at Mrs. Ames's feet, running my finger over the pages and pages of blue water and pin-prick sized islands.

"There *are* no anagrams of Ratio!" Chad complained.

I was lost in the South Pacific. "Pitt Island? Bounty Islands?" Some islands were tiny specks of ink on the oceans, wholly in the middle of nowhere. Could people actually be living on these? I mean, right now, this minute?

"At least not in English," Chad groused.

"There are actually places named Bora Bora and Pago Pago," I told Laura.

"Oh yes," she said. "My brother was in that part of the world during World War II. I'm sure he got his fill of islands and malaria and things like that."

"He got *malaria?*" I'd heard that people got

malaria in the tropics from mosquito bites, but I didn't expect to know somebody who did. Well, know somebody who knew somebody who did. It's funny how just plain people sitting next to you might have experienced the strangest or scariest or most important historical stuff in their lives, and you might not even know.

"Taori!" Chad shrieked, as if it were *eureka* in another language. "Atiro orati oitra itaro?"

I burst out laughing and hit my head on the atlas. For a few minutes we did nothing but just laugh away the tension. It made me feel sorry for Ratio Ames. Wherever he was (he lived in a ratty little rooming house in the city, according to Laura) he was working on the clues alone.

"Arthur didn't mean for us to do this." Laura finally caught her breath and gestured toward the atlas. "We can't be meant to find the name of an island somewhere in the world. It's like looking for a needle in a haystack."

"No kidding," said Chad. He was not speaking of islands.

I was paging ahead in the atlas as she was speaking. There was Antarctic, there was Arctic, there was—the United States. There was the coast of Florida. There were little islands called—

"Keys!" I yelled. I jumped up. "The Keys are islands! Key has three letters! He's giving us the word *key* again!"

"I'll bet that's it," said Laura.

"How many times does he have to give us *key*?" Chad asked.

"Maybe several, if we're supposed to understand that it's important." My voice sounded brisk and busy. "We should have both pages of clues with us." This led to a search by Laura through her bedroom for her sheet called Clues I (Could it be her room looked like mine?) and when she found it we laid both sets of clues and our solutions out in front of us:

CLUES I	
Mind over matter	concentrate on thinking more than searching
7/31/11:59:59 —/→ 8/1/12:00:00	deadline is July 31
Oh say can you rhyme?	Francis Scott Key key (rhymes with see)
piano	key
storage	?

CLUES II	
My words are not perfect, oh what shall I do?	go to WordPerfect
pass _ _ _ _	?
homophone of anagram of partner's name	in progress
island (3 letters)	key
single, cabinet, or computer	?
rental	?
my favorite literary technique	?

CHAPTER ELEVEN

Writing stuff down is a good rule to live by. Something happened in Chad's and my heads in the next moment that made us start to shriek in unison. What we shrieked sounded something like this:

"Allitfiletion!"

"I beg your pardon?" said Laura Ames.

"Fileration!"

"You're getting a mite clearer," said Laura Ames. "Maybe one at a time."

I nodded to Chad.

"File," he said, calmer by now. "That's the answer to 'single, cabinet or computer.' You know, *single file, file cabinet . . .*"

"Absolutely," said Laura.

"I'm not sure it's such a brilliant revelation," Chad added. "I mean, we've already guessed we need to find a file in WordPerfect." He looked at me, signaling my turn.

I took a breath. "Arthur A. Ames, architect, owned Ames Architectural Associates."

"Yes," said Laura, waiting.

"His favorite literary technique even starts with his favorite letter."

"Alliteration," Chad supplied.

"Sure enough," said Laura wonderingly. "Why, that dredges up memories of some English class; must have been eons ago."

Munching crackers, we looked at the sheet of clues again. There were suddenly only three question marks in the solutions column instead of five, but what did *alliteration* tell us? Did the name of the computer file use alliteration? Nah, that was stupid. File names can have only eight letters. Well, what if the words were short?

"Should we try a file name like AAA?" I asked Chad. "Or A cube, or something?"

Chad shrugged as if it was worth a try. He guided Laura Ames step by step in turning on the computer, starting the WordPerfect program, and asking for a list of all the files in the general directory. There were only two that started with A, and they were obviously files that existed just to make WordPerfect run right, not files created by Arthur Ames for the treasure hunt.

"Do we look in a different directory?" I asked.

"I think I'd better get back to my anagrams," Chad said.

"I have to agree with Chad." There was a gentle finality in Laura Ames's voice that told me we should follow her. "Remember, we're not to search wildly. We're to think."

Think. Right. We not only had to solve these things, but figure out how they fit together. What I didn't think, what I didn't know, was that we were so close, but so far away.

Chapter 12

YOU HEAR A noise?" Chad asked.

Stuffed with cheese, sausage and crackers, lying at Laura Ames's feet writing down arrangements of R-A-T-I-O that began with I and O, I jumped and looked up. My neck cracked. "What kind of a noise?"

"I didn't hear a thing." Laura gestured to the computer. She meant she couldn't hear with it running.

"Kind of like a board falling on concrete," said Chad.

We scrambled to our feet and ran for the hall.

"Kind of like Ratio slamming the paper box . . ."

"Sneaking around . . ."

"Shooting himself in the foot . . ."

We flew to the three windows outside the computer room that looked out onto the front entry. One to a window, we pressed our faces against the glass, fogging it, leaving handprints.

The only thing we saw was a car backing out of the driveway. It was definitely not Ratio's loud greenish rattletrap. It was a navy blue Cadillac. A Caddy.

"Oh, that's just the Armstrongs turning around." Laura gestured straight ahead toward the next-door neighbors' property. "They often do that when they want to park on the street."

"The sound I heard wasn't a car running," Chad said as we backed away from our windows. "But I suppose it could have been anything. The neighbors." He shrugged.

I looked toward the neighbors'. There were people in the driveway carrying grocery bags to the house. A wheelbarrow loaded with dirt sat off to the side. A guy walked to the garage carrying a paint can. Plenty of potentially noisy activity going on.

"We better get back to the anagrams," Chad said. "I think we're almost there."

Back in the computer room, Chad picked up his paper. "Okay. This is it. The anagrams are: *a riot, a trio, to air, air to*, and *orait*, which isn't a word, but the word *orate* would be its homophone."

"Now we work out homophones of all these and hope that something makes sense," I said. We all grabbed paper and pencil. There just weren't any other ways to spell *a riot* or *a trio*.

"*Air to* could be *heir to*," I said.

"*To heir*," Chad was murmuring. "*Two heir*. That's it!" he shouted. "Two heir! That's the proof there are two heirs!"

"That's it, then," said Laura Ames. She braced her hands on the arms of the desk chair as if to hoist herself to her feet. "I'm going to get Ratio Ames on the phone once and for all and tell him not to act so crazy. We'll put our clues together and each receive our share of the treasure, just like Arthur wanted."

A little needle of fear went through me. I looked at Chad. He was already looking at me, doubtfully. This is funny to say but I felt a little thrill. His face was cute and familiar, he had wondered what I thought, and we both were worried.

"If you give him your clues, he'd have an easier time cheating you," said Chad.

"He might have the same kind of a clue," I put in. "He might already know there are supposed to be two heirs, and maybe he doesn't care."

Laura looked from one of us to the other. Her face was pretty, and livened up with strokes of makeup, but she looked troubled, and her jaw looked saggy and soft again. "I thank you for your caution," she said, and despite how she looked I could see the regal Laura Ames taking command. "But I'm going to call him."

"Laura—" I realized I didn't want things to suddenly change. I wanted the three of us to find Arthur's treasure, and I didn't want Ratio Ames with us.

My saying her name kept Laura in her chair only a moment longer. She pushed herself up with a grunt. I watched the back of her yellow sweat pants as she walked out of the room.

"She cares about Arthur, and even Ratio, more than money," I said to Chad.

"She should, shouldn't she?" Chad answered.

"Yeah, but that's a lot easier to say than do, isn't it?" I looked at Chad and my heart started to pound, because I was talking with Chad the way I might talk to Mr. Schreiber. "I mean, what if she comes back in here and says Ratio is going to join us? Besides not trusting him, won't you feel kind of let down? Like it's not going to be as much fun anymore?"

Chad nodded.

"Me, too. And that's probably not the right way to feel."

"Hey—I've been meaning to ask you something. What you said about being a Christian—"

"There's no answer." Mrs. Ames came back into the computer room and looked again from one of us to the other.

"If you say he hasn't got a computer, then I'd

guess he's using one somewhere," Chad said.

"Or—" This horrible thought leaped into my mind. "He's solved all the clues and is searching." I suddenly felt itchy to move.

"If you—" Chad began, "want to try him every once in a while—well, maybe you should."

Laura, her mouth in a straight line, nodded and sat down again at the computer. "What's our next step?"

"Let's read the clues we haven't figured out." I took the sheets of clues and held them between the three of us again. "Storage. Pass and then four blanks. Rental. What goes in the blank after pass?"

"I don't know," Chad said, "but say the other two together. Storage rental. Rental storage."

"Oh my goodness," Laura Ames burst out. "We weren't meant to really *solve* those two clues, just put them together. The treasure may well be at a storage rental place."

"Oohh." I let my breath out slowly. I really didn't have any experience with places like that, but I remembered seeing rows of garages and sheds, with a sign saying something like EZ Storage Rental, near the highway on the way to the mall. "Now we know what the key is for," I said.

"And the deadline," Laura declared. "The rental period must expire today."

We looked at Laura.

"Of course." Laura's face softened as she sank back into her thoughts. "Arthur would never put the treasure where we might lose it permanently. If we don't find it by tomorrow, I imagine the rental place would call me to extend the rental period or come and get the stuff."

"It's six thirty-six." I twisted my neck to read Chad's watch.

"A lot of those places are open twenty-four hours," said Chad.

"The one Arthur chose has to be," I added. "Arthur obviously expected Laura and Ratio to find the treasure today even though they wouldn't have all their clues till 5 p.m."

"Today." Laura's voice was still dreamy. "He chose today."

We fastened our eyes on Laura again. She was staring past us at the window wall.

"He must have selected this time so carefully," she mused.

"Is today special?" I made my voice soft.

"He knew he had only a few months." Laura's eyes looked a little wet and I was nervous that she'd cry. "I suppose he thought if he planned the hunt six months in the future, he'd for sure be gone."

We just watched her.

"He had to allow time for the will to be read. And then today was the end of a month, so convenient for the rental, just the day before . . ." She stopped.

"I think," Chad's voice cracked and he cleared his throat. "I think Ratio's not the only one who knows how Arthur's mind works."

"And speaking of Ratio," I said, "since he has the deadline clue, he knows if he finds the treasure in the next few hours—before time expires and the owner calls Laura—he could get it all."

"And he thinks if he doesn't," Chad put in, "he won't get any."

We paused.

"Okay, let's read these solutions again, from the top." I offered the sheets of clues one more time, and this seemed to jog Laura back to the present. "We have to figure out how they fit together."

"Mind over matter. We have to think, not just run

around like crazy," Chad began.

"Deadline July 31."

"A key is very important."

"We have to find a file in WordPerfect."

We also knew there were two heirs, somehow there would be a group of words that began with the same letter (alliteration), and pass____ was an unsolved clue. This was not a very tidy package.

"WordPerfect," Chad pronounced patiently.

"Pass blank," I said, reading the next clue down.

"Two heir," said Chad.

I took my turn. "Key."

"File," said Chad.

We looked at each other. Was the file named *key?* Would it tell us where the key was—

I thought Chad was opening his mouth to tell Laura what keys to press on the computer, but instead he said, "Rental. Alliteration. Could the name of the storage rental place use alliteration?"

"You kids have got it!" Laura Ames leaped from her chair and dashed out of the room. I had a horrible feeling she was going to call Ratio; I had a moment's thought that she moved really great for an old lady, and almost that fast she was back, waving the phone book. "You kids know how businesses sometimes name themselves AAA in order to get listed first in the phone book? They do it so that people looking in the yellow pages see them first, ahead of their competitors."

This was new to me, but Chad and I nodded. Was that what Arthur had done with his architectural firm, I wondered, but it wasn't the time to ask.

"Let's look up the rental places!" Laura exclaimed, plopping down in the desk chair with the phone book.

This part was as simple and straightforward as could be. The very first listing in the yellow pages under *Storage—Household and Commercial* was AAA

American Self-Storage. The ad said units as small as three feet by six feet could be rented, and people could have access to their storage units twenty-four hours a day.

"We could call before we go there," Chad said. "Remember, Arthur said thinking, not running."

"Good idea," Laura said. "But for that very reason we'd better make peace with the rest of these clues first."

"Yes!" Chad and I crowed together, then laughed. We felt sure we were about to open our computer file.

"Mrs. Ames," Chad said, enjoying this moment, "let's go into WordPerfect and look up a file called *key*."

Laura Ames turned on the monitor and hit all the buttons at Chad's direction. Soon we had a huge list of files in white letters on the blue screen.

"Press *find*," Chad said. The phrase *enter word pattern* came up on the screen. "Now," Chad said, "K-E-Y."

In a flash we had three file names in front of us. *Fastkeys* was the first and just plain *keys* was the second. Alone in the right hand column was the simple word *key*. And next to the word was a date and time.

"We've got it," Chad told Laura. "This file was created on January third at 1:22 p.m. The same day your husband backed up his hard disk. Put the cursor on the file name."

Laura pushed the arrow buttons on the computer keyboard until the file name *key* was highlighted in red.

"Push number one to retrieve the file."

I think I held my breath. In less than an instant, directions on how to find the key to the storage unit Arthur Ames had rented were going to flash on the screen. In less than an instant. Hey, this was taking a lot longer than an instant. Nothing on the screen was changing. Then we saw the cursor blinking at the bottom of the screen, prodding us to enter something. To the left of the cursor was this phrase: enter password.

"Password!" Chad shrieked, while I had my mouth open to shriek the same thing. "Now we know what *pass blank* means. It's a clue that the file is protected by a password. And following Arthur's clue pattern—" Chad stopped and looked at me.

What a time to feel a flash of anger. But I did. Chad seemed to be developing a habit of just throwing me a couple lines of dialogue here and there. I didn't need his charity. But we know what I did next, don't we?

"Following Arthur's clue pattern," I said carefully, still looking at Chad, "the clue directly after the one about *pass* will tell us something about the password."

"Homophone of anagram of partner's name," Laura Ames read.

There was an odd moment of silence. Then Chad, his fingers already curved like they were sitting on a keyboard, reached in front of Mrs. Ames and typed. The letters of the password did not appear on the screen, but I knew what they said anyway: *two heir.*

And still that crazy screen didn't change. Just that last maddening line. It now read, in caps, ERROR—FILE IS LOCKED.

And at that moment the phone rang.

Chapter 13

THE WAY LAURA Ames rushed out of the computer room, she must have hoped the call was from Ratio. It really began to hit me then that Laura must care something about him. I mean not just care for him as a general human being, and not just care for him because Arthur had. I thought she must actually feel a little fond of him, maybe even a shade responsible, as if he really had become sort of their son when Alan Ames and Ratio's parents died.

But it wasn't Ratio. "Caroline," Laura Ames called.

She showed me into the master bedroom, right next to the computer room. Her room was *not* messy like mine. The bed was king-size and the comforter, with its broad swipes of peach, gray, green, and aqua, looked like it had been decorated with a painting roller. The bed sat against a sea-green wall below a pretty semi-circle window, and centered in the ceiling smack over the bed was a skylight. It would not have surprised me one bit to learn that Arthur A. Ames, *a*rchitect, had been an *a*mateur *a*stronomer as well. I reached for the slender receiver of Laura Ames's fancy white and gold telephone, which sat on her pretty white bedside table. Then I saw the picture of Arthur Ames and picked that up instead.

Arthur was round, but not fat, with silver-framed glasses and a full head of white hair. In his blue suit he looked wholly normal, but the twinkle in his eyes and the one-sided smile were eager and teasing. I thought about how he'd started everything Laura, Chad, Ratio, and I were doing, and murmured, "You didn't really die all the way yet, did you, Arthur Ames?"

Finally I picked up the phone. This only goes to show how completely we'd been living Arthur Ames's treasure hunt. I should have been expecting this call, and I just wasn't.

"Well, *there* you are. Caroline, it's time to come home," said my mom, without introduction, without even 'hi.' She's direct like this when she's made up her mind about something and she's steeling herself for an argument.

"Oh, but it's only six-fifty," I countered, glancing at Laura's clock. "And tomorrow's Saturday." I didn't really expect this to work. Besides, in summer most every day is the same.

"And I'm working on Saturday, and it's your turn to watch Danny, in case you forgot."

"Oh."

"The phone's been ringing for you, too. First Erica, then somebody named—what was that—Paige Halsey? I don't have any idea who that is. And then Erica again."

Paige had called? I felt a flash of excitement, of having missed something. And Erica. I had to reach Erica. I had to stop letting her down.

"We'll see you in about fifteen minutes, then," my mom said, preparing to hang up.

"No! Wait." I sighed. I was going to have to get Laura Ames. "Wait right there. Okay, Mom?"

"What is going on over there?" I could tell by her wondering tone of voice that she didn't really expect an answer, that she figured our activities were just too mysterious for words. "Hurry up, okay?"

I ran back to the computer room. They just couldn't have opened the key file without me. Although they should, if they could. Ratio Ames might be sitting in front of some other computer with the right password. For all we knew every second counted.

"What should I tell my mom?" I dashed into the computer room and met Laura's eyes. I wanted so badly to dash back to the phone and hold my mom off. I wanted so badly to beg Chad and Laura not to go any farther without me, even though they should. "My mom wants me to come home."

"I'll talk to her." Laura Ames got up. "It's my responsibility now to answer the questions, explain why I'm keeping you."

I took a big breath to calm myself. Right now the most important thing was to get permission to stay. I motioned to Chad, and we followed Laura. Did I want to hear another adult sort of win out over my mom? Did I want to keep Chad from trying another password in my absence? Did I just plain want to hear how Laura Ames was going to explain all this?

At any rate, Chad followed me. And I'd noticed that there was something called Burn Protection flashing on the computer screen. It meant the screen hadn't been used in several minutes. It meant Chad and Laura had waited for me.

"I realize you know little about me and I realize this is going to sound strange," Laura Ames was saying into the phone. "But my late husband has left me a number of cryptic instructions of the kind that Caroline and Chad are gifted in solving."

Wow. Laura Ames had probably defeated my mom already, unless Mom felt her control slipping away and decided to insist.

"I don't mean to disrupt your family life, but if I may, I would so appreciate being able to keep them a while. Without going into all the details, I'm afraid deciphering my husband's instructions must be done as soon as possible. Several of his last wishes, things of great importance, are at stake."

Chad and I sure weren't the only ones who could play Word Wars. Laura Ames did it so smoothly, so confidently, and she did it for real-life purposes instead of just to act smart. I guess I felt a little silly, and a little envious too.

"Time is really of the essence, and though we may run late we expect to finish this evening. I guess I'm begging your indulgence, asking you to please let them remain here until we've reached our solution. I guarantee the children will be with me, and that I will drive them home when we're finished. Provided, of course, this is all okay with you." The pause was short. "Fine, then. I do greatly appreciate it, and please don't worry. Good-bye." Laura Ames delicately hung up the phone.

"Hey, that was totally cool." Chad laughed and his dimples showed. "You know, my mom's gonna need an explanation too."

"Of course she is," said Laura, and she immediately picked up the phone and told Chad's mom exactly what she'd told mine. Chad and I were grinning with all this new freedom, but there was a streak of something in it that was kind of a spoiler. To be wholly honest, something in me was sorry my mom could be beat.

But there was no time to dwell on that interesting thought. Back to the computer. We were trying to find the password that would let us into the file called *key*.

"Instead of 'two heir,' we could try 'to err,' " Chad said, but when he typed it in he got the same rude capitals: ERROR—FILE IS LOCKED. "Well, 'to err' is what we just did," he observed. By this time Chad and I were each hanging over one of Laura Ames's shoulders, six eyes mesmerized by the blue screen.

Chad typed 'orate.' Response: ERROR—FILE IS LOCKED.

"It's got to be a homophone of an anagram," Chad cried.

But there was one we hadn't tried. I reached around Laura Ames's shoulders. If 'two heir' was wrong, well—it still seemed the whole purpose of this hunt was to find what Laura, and possibly Ratio, were *heir to*. I typed 'heir to,' and then 'enter.'

Instantly the screen cleared. In place of a page of instructions on how to find a key, we were given a plain blue field that seemed at first to be wholly empty. Then we saw the cursor blinking under one word high in the upper left hand corner. The word was 'keystone.'

We began to make noise.

"What? A one-word file?" shrilled Chad.

"What is that supposed to mean?" I shouted.

"How'll that help us find anything?" Chad asked the screen.

"That's no answer, that's just another clue." I slapped my hand to my forehead.

"Hurray!" yelled Laura Ames.

Everybody shut up. Chad and I sort of knelt on each side of Laura to see her better. In fact, we kind of pushed her chair on wheels away from the desk to see her better. Her straight, triumphant little smile pushed her cheeks into two shiny balls. Her marbly blue-gray eyes sparkled.

"You guys don't know what a keystone is?" Her smile grew.

Like she needed to ask. "No!" we howled. "What's a keystone?"

"Thinking time is over." Laura got up from the chair. "Action time is here. If you would turn off the computer, Chad."

Chad, half-looking after Laura Ames as she rapidly left the room, pressed several keys and the screen went dark, the humming sound died. I hurriedly pulled the plastic covers on and we took off after her. There was no doubt at that moment who was in charge.

"We'll need a ladder." Laura's voice sailed back to us from about the kitchen door area. Chad and I trotted through the great room, around the snack bar, into the laundry room and went out into the attached garage. Laura Ames stopped still and we nearly ran into her. "Ratio," she gasped.

Well, it wasn't Ratio we saw there. It was a long ladder next to Laura's car, lying at an angle on the concrete floor. It was pretty easy to tell that the ladder should have been propped next to the other one standing against the garage wall.

"How much do you want to bet," Laura said wryly, turning to Chad, "that this is your board falling on concrete?"

At that moment I felt kind of slow-moving and stupid. Maybe Chad did, too.

"You mean Ratio came back?" Chad said. "While we were in the house? Why did he need a ladder?"

"I'm afraid we're about to find out. Grab an end." She picked up the front end of the ladder, and Chad and I ran over to carry the rest.

Like an engine and two train cars, we went out the front of the garage, past the huge rounded-top window of the dining room, and up onto the low brick patio-type area that led to her front door. The door was topped by another semi-circle window, and the whole door and window were framed by an arch made of stone.

CHAPTER THIRTEEN

"See that?" Laura pointed to the top of the arch of stones. "The very center?"

Chad and I craned our necks up. The yellow-orange sun coming down the sky stabbed my eyes, but I could barely make out that the stones at the very top of the arch were shaped like pieces of pie with the tips cut off. The center stone, the one Laura wanted us to look at, was bigger than the others, broader and taller.

"That, my friends," Laura said, pausing dramatically while pushing her end of the ladder upward, "is called a keystone."

I had to let go of the middle of the ladder suddenly, before my graceful fingers got tangled and broken by its rapid turning to the vertical. I grabbed its sides, thrusting feet and more feet of this ladder toward the sky, stubbing my thumbs on the rungs as they rose. Chad propped his end down on the bricks at the proper angle, and Laura's end came to rest, with a thunk and few inches to spare, at the top of the stone arch.

Now it was time to face what someone had to do with this ladder, right? It was seriously beginning to look like someone was going to have to climb it.

"Chad, you can do it," Laura Ames encouraged, but Chad wasted no time getting started. I thought I knew how Chad felt: If Ratio Ames could do it—

But *could* Ratio do it? Had such a big guy climbed the ladder alone, without Laura to hold it at the bottom the way she and I were doing now? Or had he chickened out, dropped the ladder, and fled?

At least Laura didn't ask *me* to climb the ladder, I thought, as I stood uneasily right smack under Chad's potentially falling body. I would have sweated so hard with fear that I would have slid right off. Because I'm a klutz, that is, not because I'm a girl. Girls can climb ladders too. Or did we all just say that, and in real life would it always be boys who climbed ladders? Holding tight at the bottom, I felt the movements of Chad's solid weight travel down through the wood and I hung on with all my strength.

Chad got to the top of the ladder. Carefully he let go with one hand and reached slowly toward the keystone.

God, all my strength isn't enough to hold this ladder, I found myself praying. *Thanks for holding the ladder with me. Thanks for standing at the foot of the ladder with me.*

"Can a key really be in a stone?" I asked Laura Ames.

"Well, in the King Arthur stories there was a sword in a stone," Laura replied. "Oh my, did you hear what I just said? In the King *Arthur* stories?"

By the look of Chad's arm I could tell he was reaching up behind the keystone, but the sun burned his movements out of my vision. All I could really see was pink gum on the bottom of his shoes, and grease from his bike chain on one leg of his sweatpants. Maybe Chad was the one on the ladder, I thought suddenly. But up there he was much more defenseless than I was.

"There's some caulking stuff here," Chad called down. "It's pretty loose." Like bird droppings, the sticky whitish material suddenly plopped down on the bricks. "There's a hole," he added. He leaned forward to reach up higher behind the stone and his weight shifted suddenly on the ladder. My heart lurched. Then he brought his arm down. He actually half turned on the ladder and looked down at me.

"Be careful, Chad," I said.

To which he replied only, "Caro. Catch."

I held my cupped palm as far up as it would go. Even though I felt like I was gazing into fire, that heavy, notched piece of metal landed straight in my hand, and I held out to Laura Ames the key to the treasure.

Chapter 14

"WE WON," I said.

We were in Laura Ames's car rolling down the highway toward AAA American Self-Storage. I was the first one to remind us that it had been a competition, the first one to remind us of Ratio, ever since that light, floaty feeling had come over us when the key landed in my hand. (Or maybe it came over us once Chad had both feet on the ground again.)

We had the key. Ratio didn't.

"May that be a lesson to him," Laura remarked as she braked in front of a red, white, and blue sign proclaiming AAA AMERICAN SELF-STORAGE. She turned in at the concrete entrance and drove through an open gate in a chain link fence. "Even the smartest person in the world can't get along alone."

There it was again—my favorite true statement, told to me by some of my favorite people: my teacher Mr. Schreiber, the school psychologist Dr. Schiff, and now Laura Ames. No matter who we are, we need t thinking and help and love and guidance of o people. And of God. And Jesus, and the Holy When I think of God now, I'll always think of parts of him.

The sun was hanging really low. T

turned blue, and the clouds in the west were striped pink and lavender. Laura's car cruised slowly down the wide, paved aisles, between the storage sheds and garages and extra-tall warehouses. A man came out of a small office and approached the car. Laura braked and rolled down her window.

"Ah, Mrs. Ames," the man said with a smile when Laura gave her name. His cap shaded his face, but I could see he looked old, although not as old as Laura. "Yup, Art sure did rent a unit. He mentioned you'd be coming the end of July. That's how long he paid for, at any rate. Nice guy, Art. It was really too bad to hear about his passing; he was a good friend to me. He named this place, did you know that?"

The guy was probably surprised when we laughed. *AAA American Self-Storage*? We almost should have known.

"Art was quite a character." The man chuckled. "Wanted a key with no ID on it so it wouldn't give too much away at once. I remember the unit he rented, though. One of the smaller ones. Number twelve. Maybe you can point Mr. Ames in the right direction. He got here just ahead of you. Sure was in an all-fired hurry."

For an instant I thought he actually meant Arthur. But then the terrible truth hit me—Ratio. I hadn't thought I had anything in my mouth, but I suddenly felt as if I'd swallowed a tennis ball.

"Which way?" Laura gasped. When the man pointed straight ahead, the car leaped forward so fast she might have run over his toes.

"Drat it all," fumed Laura. "Of course, we have the ey." She sighed. "Well, fine. At least once more, I'm oing to try with Ratio, face to face."

Laura rounded a corner, and there it was. Number ve. A smallish but very strong-looking, blue storage shed with about a six-foot tall door. She slammed on the brakes, we leaped out, and at that same moment Ratio burst around the corner, from the side of the building. Well, *burst* is a little too energetic a word. When he ran he toddled from side to side, and he was seriously huffing and puffing.

"Ah-AH!" or something like that he cawed, as he charged toward the door of the shed. His face was so puffy his cheeks almost pushed his glasses off, although his glasses seemed useless anyway since his eyes were squeezed to slits. He would have been funny in a movie, and that thought made me feel horribly sorry for him.

When he saw us he gave away one look of surprise, but then his face rumpled in contempt. "You're still too late!" He never slackened his pace toward that door. Was he planning to break it down?

Chad and I started forward. Behind us, Laura called, "Ratio."

And then some trick of light—maybe it was the white arc light fluttering to life above us, maybe it was a last long ray of sun—made me see the glint of metal in his hand. The sparkle that couldn't flash when I'd had to gaze into blazing sun and catch blind the key Chad tossed to me. Ratio had the lock open before Caroline K-for-Klutz Grade even got her mouth open. Then he dived onto the concrete floor of the shed as if to scoop up what was there, as if to fall down in worship. I suddenly felt sick. His shirttail yanked out of his jeans, and a roll of white fleshy back stretched across the doorway.

"He won," I whimpered as Laura's hand came down on my shoulder. Her other hand came down on Chad's.

"Let him." Laura's urgent whisper brushed my ear. "You can't fight him physically. You can't stoop to his level."

I actually felt weak, watching him grovel on the floor. From the back he looked like he might be eating from a trough. *Help me God,* I prayed, *never to look like this in front of you.*

"If we attack, he feels justified in his behavior," Laura advised softly.

Suddenly Ratio's arm sprang up and a light came on in the shed. He pushed himself backwards into a squat. He hoisted himself to his feet. He was screaming.

"Clues, words, riddles, sermons! Talk, talk, talk. Traitor!" Waving his arms, Ratio rotated his planet-like body toward us and launched a sheet of paper into the air. It dipped and rocked crazily and hit the ground not far from my feet. "Take it! It's yours!"

I reached for the paper. Some lines of verse were written there, in handwriting rather than computer printout. Stunned, I read them out loud:

"The LORD will be the sure foundation
  for your times,
a rich store of salvation and wisdom
  and knowledge;
the fear of the Lord is the key to this treasure.
  Isaiah 33:6."

"Har-dee har har," mocked Ratio. "Take it to the bank, Laura."

Or something like that. I barely heard him. All my thoughts were spinning to the edge of belief and crashing over.

Keys and treasure were in the Bible? Arthur knew that? There was really no money? I couldn't believe it. In fact I couldn't believe it so much I began edging around an imaginary circle, hoping to work my way between Ratio and that shed.

"There's more," I said, and I began to read:

"But store up for yourselves treasures in heaven,

where moth and rust do not destroy, and where thieves do not break in and steal. Matthew 6:20."

Even Ratio made no noise this time. I was beginning to feel like Arthur was looking right over our shoulders. I was willing to take all his words to heart, I really was, especially because they were God's words. But I couldn't accept Arthur as a tease, a cruel practical joker. I sidled closer to the row of storage units, a bit bolder this time. Ratio had begun to pace and swing his arms oddly, flinging them out to the side and then almost slapping them together in a clutch.

"There's still more," I said.

"Haaoouup!" Ratio barked, like a seal. I think it was a laugh. I guess he was waiting around to watch when we finally gave up.

"So if you have not been trustworthy in handling worldly wealth, who will trust you with true riches? Luke 16:11."

Ratio's face contorted. "When was I not trustworthy in handling worldly wealth, Cube?" he howled. "When did I even get a chance to handle it?"

I saw it then. In the corner of the storage unit that was in my line of vision, only steps away. Ratio hadn't looked far enough. He'd dived to the floor, grabbed the paper, and had his fit.

Ratio hadn't seen the second keyes humming like
Arthur's next line set all read it. I was afraid
guitar strings. I didn't something in me thrilled
Ratio would und I hadn't announced I was going to
at the risk aid, "Be ye therefore trustworthy. AAA."
a look at Chad. His face was straight, but
es were wholly ablaze. Laura shifted one
ot slightly.
If you have not been trustworthy in handling

worldly wealth, who will trust you with true riches? Be ye therefore trustworthy.

Hard to do, isn't it, unless, as Ratio said, there's some wealth to practice being trustworthy with.

Ratio, pacing with his back to us, stopped, rigid. His bulky body turned back. Turned faster than I thought it could.

I sprang for the open storage unit then, feeling that no matter how long and horsey my legs were they would never get me there. I crashed through the doorway onto the concrete, ripping the knee of my jeans, Ratio barreling after me. Would he just keep coming like a runaway blimp and crush me? Would he *try* to hurt me? He had me trapped now, could lock me in, get me and the key out at his leisure. Laura and Chad couldn't free me. Not with the fake key Ratio had put in the keystone after he took the real one. But of course I still *had* Laura and Chad. And God. I was not alone, like Ratio. Laura and Chad could get the owner. Where was he anyway? Probably in his apartment. I remembered faintly from the yellow pages ad that the owner lived on the grounds.

Ratio filled the doorway. I screamed and Chad shouted "Hey!" Feet came thundering. With an
"[illegible]ooff!" air whooshed out of lungs. *Chad!* At the cost
of two [illegible]gernails and half the skin of my hand, I
scraped the [illegible] across the concrete and under my
chest, cupping [illegible] across the concrete and under my
Finally, I was Grad[illegible]'d recovered a fumbled football.
tackled by the Crusher. [illegible]hlete, and I was about to be
But the smothering, squ[illegible]
ears registered scraping, whi[illegible] [illegible]ght never fell. My
that weren't mine after all. They c[illegible] grabbin[illegible]ds—sounds
I wrecked the rest of my hand grabbin[illegible] [illegible]nd me.
rolled onto my side, raked hair out of my [illegible]
Chad, stern and dimpleless, staring Ratio dow[illegible] I

CHAPTER FOURTEEN

Ratio, afraid of Chad?

But yes; he lay in the doorway of the shed, collapsed into his own overstuffed body as if it were a too-soft chair. His chins quivered. Sweat showered him. I blinked, sort of realizing his exhaustion in slow motion, realizing how much running around he'd done today, how out of shape he was. How old he was. There was no sound except Ratio's desperate panting for air. It came to me not only as the sound of defeat, but as a kind of last gasp for life.

Chad turned to me. "You okay, Caro?"

I allowed myself a two-second look into his murky, inky, secretive eyes before I sat all the way up. I was ripped, disheveled, bleeding, and my skinned hand stung like crazy, but I shoved back the hair that had fallen in my face again and answered, "Yeah." Smiling, I held up the key in my hurt hand, and the tattered paper with Arthur Ames's messages in the other. And then Chad Neumann reached out his own hand and helped me up.

"There's one more thing on the paper." My voice was trembling now. Chad and Laura snatched me deliberately out of the shed, into the open, away from any place where Ratio Ames could imprison me. "It's marked 'Last Clue.' "

Ratio began struggling to his feet, but in one beat Chad and Laura were reading over my shoulders.

LAST CLUE
ΙΧΘΥΣ All are Greek, some are Roman.

I had seen those Greek letters before. (Of course, so had Laura, who had studied Greek.) I had seen them on a bumper sticker on the back of the Halsey's car. They had something to do with Jesus, and that's when I knew for sure Arthur Ames had been a Christian. And the Roman numerals were there, too, clear as day.

I handed the key to Laura Ames. My voice still wobbling, my body chilly with cold sweat, I said to her, "Take this and unlock unit nine."

Chapter 15

UNIT NINE HELD two brown drawstring bags, like mail sacks, sitting on the floor. Chad and I moved up to protect Laura, who had opened the door and switched on the light. Chad murmured that he'd run for the owner's house and a phone at the least little snort from Ratio. But Ratio didn't follow.

Each sack had a paper with a name on it pinned neatly to its side. The larger one was labeled 'Laura,' and the smaller one, 'Ratio.'

She wouldn't have had to tell him.

Not that I thought for a moment she wouldn't, but it hit me like a falling rock that she wouldn't have had to. Ratio sat slumped against the other shed, [illegible]sts clenched, jaw clenched, face bent upwards. [illegible]d somehow I knew there were tears oozing out [illegible] his squeezed-together eyes, getting trapped by [illegible]ms of his glasses that dug into his flesh. Ratio [illegible] was right now accepting that Arthur had forc[illegible] up Ratio's sack. Silently she walked

Laura [illegible] unit twelve, the bag hanging at her side the di[illegible]ed care. She braced her left hand on her [illegible]vered thigh, bent her knees, and held the bag [illegible] to Ratio, the way she would have to a child. She [illegible]oked him right in the face.

Ratio's head moved toward her, then snapped away as if she was a light too bright to bear. He scooped his arm forward and captured the sack in a hug, raised himself to a crouch, and scuttled around the corner of the shed the way he had come.

Laura stood slowly, looking after him.

In a little while she turned toward Chad and me and walked back to where we waited.

We sat bunched around the doorway of unit nine, using the shed as a shield. Laura pulled her drawstring bag open.

A hundred dollar bill drifted out.

Laura spread the mouth of the bag wide. In one motion the three of us bent our heads forward to peer in, and saw a whole lettuce salad of bills. A big enough salad for a Friday night all-you-can-eat fish fry buffet. During the supper rush.

We actually ran the money through our fingers, gasping and laughing softly. Tossing the salad. It sounded crinkly and scrunchy, and the papery smell made our noses wrinkle in the cool summer air. In the corners of every bill we saw '100.' My fingers got tangled up with Chad's a few times, under the money.

"Oh, there's something else here," Laura murmured. Wiggling h[illegible]r fingers down, she pulled it up out of the money and set it [illegible] the concrete floor of the shed.

It was a velvet [illegible], a little bigger than a child's pencil case, and the [illegible] of the champagne I saw bubbling in a glass last N[illegible]ear's. Stroking its fuzzy softness (with my good hand[illegible] bu[illegible]ouldn't get it dirty) was almost beautiful enough, [illegible]ned to let Laura lift the lid.

Even Chad gasped at the jewelry in[illegible]

Laura lifted a sparkling ring that ha[illegible] all the way around the band! I knew from a TV [illegible] that this was called an eternity ring. But she did[illegible] on right away. She set it in *my* hand, and in case I didn't dare put it on she said softly, "Try it, Caroline."

Lifting my eyes to hers, receiving a nod, I fumbled the circle of diamonds onto the ring finger of my left hand. I could have tipped my hand back and forth under the shed lights forever, watching the fire and the sparks, but I began to feel stupid in front of Chad. I took it off and gave it to its owner. The look on Laura's face when it glided over her own finger, as slow as it would at a wedding, was like a picture of something tremendous found and something unbearable lost. I looked away.

She took a string of pearls out of the box, and they clicked faintly as she held them out to us. That necklace is why I said Laura Ames has soft permed hair the color of expensive pearls. They were just the color of her hair, and they were real. I had never thought I'd be able to tell the difference between real and fake, but I could.

"Let me put them on you." My voice came out shy. Laura nodded, and I undid the clasp and fastened the pearls around Laura Ames's neck. They rested elegantly against her lemon yellow sweatshirt.

At the sight of the rest of the jewelry, Laura actually cried out. Without even picking a piece up, she turned the velvet box back toward Chad and me. There, sitting in a circle, just like it would go around a neck, was an emerald and diamond necklace that had all the jewels and dangling parts connected like the teardrops of a chandelier. The center green stone was as big around as a dime. There were earrings—emeralds set in crowns of diamonds—to match.

When I could finally tear my eyes and fingers away from the sparkle and glitter of the stones, I saw that Laura Ames was crying.

"You wanted me to get these things right now," she whispered. "You actually picked a time, *six months after your death*, that would be accurate within a few hours."

Of course she was talking to Arthur. I asked again, timidly, "Is today special?"

"August first is my birthday," Laura said. "I see by young Chad's watch that it's only three and a half hours away." She paused. "I'm seventy-two in case you're curious." A small wet explosion of a chuckle escaped her.

"But where will I ever wear these things now?" She dabbed at her eyes with a crumpled Kleenex. "I'm sorry, Arthur, but I don't even want them. I just want you."

I couldn't believe what she was saying. It confuses me when people who are lucky enough to get spectacular things don't seem to want them. I feel like they're scorning all the people who're drooling over the stuff, exclaiming how they'd never have a bad day again if they could just get their hands on a fortune. "But they're beautiful, Laura, please, you have to want them," I said.

She looked at me. "Yes. I got you two involved in this, didn't I? How can I belittle the fabulous things you worked so hard for? And this," she gestured at the jewelry, "this is Arthur's last gift to me, his grand finale. How can I reject it? I have to be trustworthy with it, don't I? But still, it makes my heart ache for him. You'll understand some day."

I thought of something Paige had told me. She said Jesus had given us such a huge priceless gift there was nothing to do but accept it. And I thought of what she said about your heart hurting for him, for what he had to do, at the same time. "I think maybe I understand a little bit already," I said, but I shouldn't have. It just made Chad look at me questioningly, and it just made Laura Ames smile a little smile, like an old woman who, even though she loves you, knows better.

Full darkness had fallen, but as Laura reached to

take the velvet box she turned it, and the arc light caught an edge of thick paper I hadn't noticed before. The paper peeked out of a pocket in the satiny material on the underside of the lid. "Laura, wait, don't close it. There's something else."

Laura found the pocket as I pointed, and she drew out an envelope made of heavy parchment with kind of a puckered surface like I saw on a wedding invitation once. Of course, written across the front in Arthur's handwriting was the word *Laura*.

She looked at it with a soft, dreamy face, lips parted—the way she should have looked at the real treasure. I realized with a sharp pang that to her the treasure was the worldly wealth and this envelope was the true riches, and there was no way she was going to open it now. Her flashing jewels, worthy of a pirate's treasure chest, her bag of hundred dollar bills—these Chad and I were allowed to know about, to see, to touch, even to try on. But the true riches were so private, so priceless, that they couldn't bear more than a few moments out of their keeping place until the time they would be opened by her alone. Laura Ames slipped the envelope tenderly back into its pocket.

The cool breeze that had seemed to die down sprang up again. Even dressed in our sweats and jeans we shivered as we helped Laura Ames up from the concrete. We shut the lights off in the two storage units, put the jewelry case back inside the drawstring bag of money, returned the key to unit nine, and drove away. Such ordinary things to do after finding a fortune.

"What'll the owner do about the key to unit twelve?" I asked. My voice seemed in the way. Talking was such an ordinary thing to do, and sound just seemed like the wrong thing to have around us.

"He'll change the lock," Laura said, driving along in the dark that seemed so extra dark now that we were away from the AAA American Self-Storage floodlights.

"Ratio got ahead of us." Chad put into words what we were all piecing together in our minds. "He knew the key would be in the keystone before we did, snuck up there, took it, and put just any old key in its place. No wonder the caulking stuff Arthur used to plug the hole was so loose. The ladder fell when he was putting it back, or he dropped it and ran. The car we saw turning around in your driveway might have scared him away."

We drove on in silence for a while. Then Laura said, "Poor Ratio."

I looked at Chad when she said that. I suppose to see his reaction; maybe just to see him. He made a wrinkly face at me like, *Poor Ratio? Ratio is a bug.*

Yeah, I know, I wanted to tell Chad. He's a bug who scuttles away when the light shines on him. But he's a sorry human bug. And it was Ratio Ames scuttling away like a bug with his money bag that made me think maybe that stuff, that Scripture, about worldly wealth and true riches being different things is more than just nice, holy talk. Because Ratio had worldly wealth, but he didn't have true riches. He was a miserable, sorry, buggy person, and at this moment, with his eyes blinded by the shine of whatever was in his drawstring pouch, he didn't know it. Yes, indeed, *Poor Ratio.* And I could only pray that Ratio, now that he had his worldly wealth, would be therefore trustworthy.

Chapter 16

I WAS TRAPPED IN layers of dark. My eyes wouldn't open. Some kind of stick was poking my leg, then my arm. "Caroline."

Caroline. Oh yeah, that's me. Dad's voice.

"Come on, up you go, late night or not, it's paper girl time."

Some things never change. Parents and sisters go off to work. Trucks drop humongous bundles of fat newspapers in *your* driveway that parents and sisters will drive over if you don't go out and get them. Little brothers get up *voluntarily* at the same ridiculous time morning paper carriers do, in order to spill cereal and puddles of milk for everybody to step in, and to watch disgusting monster robot cartoons, and to build Lego towers, and to start bawling that their towers are so tall and detailed and great that they can't bear to dismantle them even a hair so they can get their doors open to come out of their rooms.

It was much more humid than the night before. I dragged on my shorts (although I couldn't use my skinned right hand and had to yank them on little by little with just my left), and stuck a pen in my pocket. I stuffed my hot sweaty paper sack (left-handed) to the bursting point with newspapers. Even though the

Saturday papers are not too fat, there are about eighteen more papers on weekends than during the week. I walked around my route with them, looking for clever places to stash them when the customers have their outer doors locked (because those who are not up to go to work or walk the dog are sensibly in bed). I put them under flowerpots, or rolled them up and stuck them through the door handles.

When I came to Laura Ames's house I pulled out my pen and with my left hand scrawled 'Happy Birthday Laura' above the headline of her paper. I put it in her pretty wooden paper box and begged the lid not to slip out of my klutzy fingers and bang down and wake Laura after it had probably taken her hours to fall asleep. Then I looked at her house and wondered if last night had really, truly happened. I mean the money part. It had been like an extra-special companionable time around a campfire, sitting there in a little circle on that concrete in the doorway of that shed, the kind of time that seems to belong so deeply to the night that the next morning you suspect you came back to regular ordinary earth from somewhere else. Or maybe even that you dreamed.

But I guess I hadn't dreamed. Because when I got back to the kitchen with my empty paper sack, the weight of the world news off my shoulders, the phone rang.

"GOT IT!" Sam and Danny yelled.

Sam was still home, dressed in her grocery store navy and white, drinking some kind of diet breakfast milk shake. Danny must have emerged from Lego Land long enough to spill his latest breakfast on the floor, because it crunched under my feet. But I was closest to the phone, and *I* got it.

"Caro?"

I liked how Chad knew my voice, even with just

one 'hello.' I liked how I knew his.

"Never mind, guys." I twisted the receiver away from my mouth. "It's for me." Fortunately Sam had to leave for work right then, and I chose not to notice that Danny, peering hard through his bangs, carefully walked his sloshing bowl of cereal to his bedroom.

"I trust you recall," Chad said, "our attempts to foil a league of prowlers during the winter immediately past?"

The burglary ring? I sure wasn't expecting that topic. But of course I remembered. "Unquestionably."

"Although I should properly call them *your* attempts. Really, when it got down to the end, you did it all."

What was this? Why was he bringing up something that happened way back when, and leaving me alone in it? But at the same time I was touched. I mean, I knew it was hard to say that another kid might have got ahead of you in something, might have done better or been more successful. "No," I said. "All that stuff would have turned out completely different if it hadn't been for you."

"Well, anyway. Back to the bandits. I further trust you recollect what they stole?"

"Well yeah, a lot of things. Cameras, VCRs, computers, fancy CD players and stuff. My mom's antique music box." But wait. Somehow I knew Chad didn't mean any of these things.

"And?"

I took a breath. "And a fake pearl necklace and a real diamond ring."

"Do you recall inquiring," Chad asked, "whether a professional burglar would be fooled by fake pearls?"

I took a deep breath and let it out. "They were pretty fantastic, weren't they?" My voice sounded too soft and dreamy, and I rushed on. "I mean, maybe the jewelry didn't mean anything to you; that's okay. But now I just can't imagine seeing real pearls and not knowing they're real."

"They *were* real, weren't they?"

Yes, Chad. The money and the jewelry did really happen.

"When Laura brought out the diamond ring, and when I saw the sparkly necklace," I told Chad, "I thought of the diamond ring that Graci Mertens brought to school last year." Graci Mertens was a girl in sixth grade that my teacher made me tutor in math. "I've hardly seen any real jewelry in my life, but every time I do it's shocking. Sometimes good shocking, like last night, and sometimes bad."

Thoughts began to churn in my mind. If the shock could be bad, maybe this was what people meant about wealth not always being good or making people happy. (Really, that's always been hard to believe. I mean, stuff is great, right?) What I'm saying is, when an expensive thing makes you feel shocked in an uncomfortable way, maybe that means somebody hasn't been trustworthy with it.

"Uh—Caro?"

"Yeah?"

"I've been meaning to ask—have you been seeing Mr. Schreiber around a lot this summer or anything?"

Oh boy, here they were: the questions about being a Christian. Too bad I couldn't say yes, I've seen Mr. Schreiber a lot, and sort of blame his influence in case Chad thought talking about Jesus was dumb. But I had only run into Mr. Schreiber twice. At church. I told Chad the truth.

"Then he hasn't been talking to you that much? Well—what about the time you were talking to Laura about—damn?" Chad took a breath. "Then you said something about Jesus being in your life, not just your head. It's something I can picture Mr. Schreiber saying or thinking, I guess." He paused. "What did you mean?"

I was all busy thinking what I was going to say. But just in time the thought came into my head that maybe it was just as hard for Chad to ask the question as it was for me to answer it. Not only because the subject makes people feel funny, but because Chad was admitting he thought Mr. Schreiber and I were in on something that didn't include him. He was admitting again that something was going on that his brains hadn't quite caught up to. And when a gifted kid doesn't have his brain, he's naked.

"I just mean I believe in Jesus, that he died to pay for my sin, the stuff I do wrong. But I don't think it's enough to just say you believe it in your head." Mr. Schreiber's words outside the church, where he'd stood with me while I was unlocking my bike, came back to me. "Being a Christian means following Jesus, and following Jesus must mean your life changes from when you didn't follow him, right? One thing that changed in my life is I go to church when I can. That's what I meant when I said Jesus was in my life, not just my head."

He didn't say anything, and I started to sweat. Paige told me once she'd lost a friend because the person thought her Christian family was weird. It began to scare me how much I didn't want to lose Chad.

Then he said one little word, one little syllable.

"Wow."

It was a very respectful 'wow,' with a sense of wonder mixed in. I felt like a refreshing breeze had begun to blow over me. Chad's 'wow' didn't sound sarcastic, like 'Oh man, this is heavy, you're crazy.' It sounded like, 'I'm thinking about what you said but I don't know how to take it yet, and I don't know what to say.'

"Listen, Caro," he said. "That's really interesting." He snorted. "That sounds stupid. Hey, I mean it. It is. Okay?"

Of course it's okay. It's very okay. And that's what I said: "Okay."

"Arthur Ames was a Christian, wasn't he? With the Bible verses and that."

"I think he must have been."

"So are true riches, and the treasure in heaven, stuff like salvation and wisdom and knowledge? Like in the first verse you read off the paper?"

Chad sure had a fantastic mind. "Oh, there's so much I don't know," I said. "But those have got to be some of them." *And my friends*, I wanted to say. *My friends and family are true riches.*

As soon as Chad and I got off the phone it rang again. Danny must have been lost in a Lego maze because he didn't even yell "GOT IT!"

"Caroline?" came Paige's voice. "I just called to say hi. Because I missed you." And all the way through the phone call so many things made me happy. Paige's voice had become a voice I recognized. She hadn't called for a special reason, but just to say hi. She had missed me and actually didn't mind saying so.

I fixed lunch for Danny and me and he actually managed to escape from his room and come out to eat it. Then he showed me the bridges he built in his Lego city that he could crawl under to reach the door. I couldn't believe it when he asked me to help him build a skyscraper, and then when I knocked half of it over hitting my head on it, he didn't even throw a fit.

The phone rang again. "Caro?"

Erica. I began to sweat a little. She shouldn't have

had to call me. It was amazing that she would call me. I should call *her.*

"Uh, Caro, are you doing anything today?"

If I said I was busy would she ever ask again? "I'm not allowed to have friends over when I baby-sit, but let's just talk on the—"

The back door swung open. "Hi, hon." Mom came in, already dressed in her shorts and top, her brown hair cut shorter again and newly permed. Was it that late already? "Oh, great, I can actually feel the air conditioning."

The phone line began to click, meaning another call was coming in. I heard a faint moan from Erica.

"Ignore it," I said to her. "Let's go to Burger King for supper."

I caught Mom's eye and pantomimed, pointing to the receiver, mouthing ER-I-CA, clenching my hands together and begging PLEEEEEASE, until Mom laughed and nodded.

"You can go too? Great," I said into the phone. I took a deep breath, really savoring the next phrase. "I've got so much to tell you."

Chapter

LAURA AMES, LOOKING like a queen in a silky silvery dress with a scoop neck, emerald and diamond necklace sparkling at her throat, matching earrings shining on her ears, raised her glass of fruit punch in a toast. Seated with her around her dining room table, Chad and I raised ours, too.

"To Chad and Caroline," she said. "Without whom Arthur's wishes would never have been carried out. But more than that, without whom I would be missing out on two new, dear friends."

It was with only the tiniest wiggle of embarrassment that I smiled, glanced at Chad, looked away, and sipped my punch. Chad's freckles, dimples, and cap of dark hair looked all shiny from a shower, and his white shirt was crisp. (I was wearing a sort of buff-colored sundress, and my hair was French-braided.)

Fragrant steam from the shish kebabs we'd cooked on Laura's grill—chunks of steak and vegetables roasted on skewers—drifted up my nose. Cream-colored envelopes, with our names written on them, sat half tucked under Chad's and my white, gold-rimmed plates.

"I called Ratio today," Laura said.

"You did?" Somebody said this, but I'm honestly not sure if it was Chad or me. Both of us kind of jerked in our seats and quickly turned to Laura in surprise. Both of us knew very well that in kid society people could declare themselves sworn enemies forever over a whole lot less than Ratio had done.

"I invited him to dinner. Not tonight, of course." Laura gave a little smile.

"What'd he say?" asked Chad, pushing shish kebabs off his sword onto his plate with his fork.

"Barely a word," said Laura. "He wouldn't tell me whether he'd come or not. I'm not sure what he's feeling right now—genuine hate, or maybe shame. But he didn't say no. And he stayed on the line and listened."

"You forgive him, don't you?" I looked right at Laura and she turned her marbly gray-blue eyes to mine.

"Yes," she said simply. "I forgive him."

The phrase *true riches* flashed into my mind. Forgiveness must be one of the true riches. Not that you had to know how to handle money first to get something like forgiveness. But being mean and careless and selfish and foolish with money and things could hurt people, and make you lose true riches, like love, and forgiveness, and friends.

"Why don't you two open your envelopes," Laura said.

I automatically looked at Chad, and he was looking at me, and we gave just these tiny shrugs and smiles and picked up the cream-colored envelopes with our names on them. I matched my speed pulling on the flap to Chad's, so I wouldn't get mine open first. Then I saw what was inside, and I forgot everything else.

It was not a card. I thought it would be a thank-you card. For helping her, or something.

Instead it was two hundred-dollar bills.

"Oh, you don't have to pay us," Chad said immediately, looking at Laura with his fingers still poking into his envelope.

She answered swiftly. "No, I don't. And I'm not. You're not my employees; you're my friends. I'm giving you a gift because I want to be generous. I'm giving it to you because what fun is a treasure hunt if you don't get some of the treasure?"

"But—it's so much. We didn't expect—" I burbled.

"And that gives me all the more pleasure, that you didn't expect it. I thank you for your polite protests, but one of the privileges of old age is that we get to be crotchety and insistent. So humor an old widow of an eccentric treasure hunter, and accept my gift with no more resistance. In Arthur's words," her voice dropped and her head extended toward us, "be ye therefore trustworthy."

I would. I really would. This would be the most wisely invested two hundred bucks in the history of American currency.

I looked at Chad in time to see him raise his punch glass. "I'd like to propose a toast," he said gallantly. "To Laura Ames, neither crotchety, cantankerous, crabby, nor cross, an example of alliteration, a master of Word Wars, from whom the remaining company at this table have much to learn."

I lifted my glass, wondering what my line was. Oh yeah. "I'll drink to that!" And we did.

"And what, pray tell," Laura said, taking her glass from her lips, "is Word Wars?"

Chad and I just laughed. We'd tell her someday, if she didn't catch on sooner, but not just now. For now we'd eat and laugh and talk and enjoy our friends—some of our true riches, our real treasure.

Clues

ARTHUR AMES'S CLUES TO THE TREASURE

While Caroline, Chad and Laura Ames were working on Laura's sets of clues to the treasure, Ratio Ames was, of course, trying to solve his, too. Here is what *all* the clues looked like.

CODED POEM (Delivered to both Laura and Ratio at dinner on July 20)

THə	phonetic dictionary spelling of 'the'
o abbreviate limited	old (Ltd. is a more common abbreviation for limited, but ld. is also accepted.)
bkumm	become
youngster (plural)	children
conjunction plus	and

steal, but nicer	take
plural possessive	their
↶	turn
BY -15	at (5 letters before y, 1 letter before b)
10 15 25	joy (10th, 15th, & 25th letters)
not out	in
first clue	the
anyooil	annual
tnuh	hunt (backwards)

The old become children
And take their turn
At joy in the annual hunt.

CLUES I (Delivered to Laura and Ratio
at dinner the next night, July 21)

<u>*Laura's Clues*</u>	<u>*Ratio's Clues*</u>
Mind over matter	$\frac{\textit{my-end}}{\text{substance}}$
7/31/11:59:59 ↛ 8/1/12:00:00	Don't wish Laura happy birthday.

Oh say can you rhyme?	skeleton
piano	lock and
storage	mpdlfs, or knbjdq

Arthur wanted Laura's and Ratio's first, second, etc., clues to correspond with each other. For example, Ratio's first clue is a word and picture play on Laura's first clue, 'Mind over matter.' Caroline, Chad and Laura were correct in believing they were to think (mind) before they took action (matter). The second clues were meant to show a deadline of July 31, the day before Laura's birthday. Had Ratio been able to say "Happy Birthday, Laura" before they found the treasure the hunt would have been over. The rental period at the storage company would have expired.

Laura's third clue was 'key,' a word that rhymes with 'see.' 'Key' is also hinted at by the name of the Star-Spangled Banner's composer, Francis Scott Key. Ratio's third clue, 'skeleton,' refers to a key that can open many different locks. Their fourth clues, 'piano' and 'lock and' also suggested the word 'key.' Can you solve Ratio's fifth clue? (Try now, if you like. For a hint, turn to the last page.) If Laura and Ratio had combined their fifth clues, they might have realized much earlier in what type of place the treasure was hidden!

CLUES II (Delivered to Laura and Ratio during their third and last dinner, on July 31)

<u>*Laura's Clues*</u>	<u>*Ratio's Clues*</u>
My words are not perfect, oh what shall I do?	WP is my WP

Pass _ _ _ _	_ _ _ _ word
homophone of anagram of partners name	_ _ _ _ _ _ the throne
island (3 letters)	You and I sing off
single, cabinet, or computer	That's a name
rental	You'll have to call the place.
My favorite literary technique	Now what would *I* name a business?

Caroline, Chad, and Laura are of course correct in thinking that Laura's first clue means they should look for something in WordPerfect. Ratio's first clue stands for 'WordPerfect is my word processor.' A lot of time could have been saved if Laura and Ratio could have combined their second clues. Their third clues told them that the password was a homophone of an anagram of Laura's partner's name, and that the password was a two-word phrase with four letters in the first word and two letters in the second. (See Ratio's clue.) Not having the use of Ratio's third clue is probably what slowed Laura and the kids down the most. Without Laura's clue, Ratio simply had to guess that 'heir to' the throne was a sensible answer.

The fourth clues again pointed to 'key,' and the fifth clues told them that key was a name (Ratio's clue) of a file (Laura's clue). The next clues, 'rental,' and 'you'll have to call the place' suggest that Arthur was telling Laura and Ratio to look in the phone book for help. He probably expected them to call the storage rental business and ask if a unit (actually units) was rented in his name. From their conversation with AAA's owner, we suspect Caroline, Chad and Laura didn't call ahead, even though Chad suggested it. Whether Ratio did, only he and the owner know.

The last clues, of course, were meant to help Laura and Ratio figure out *which* storage rental business Arthur had used. Not only was AAA American Self-Storage a name Arthur might have chosen, according to its owner, he actually did!

How did Ratio find the key before Caroline, Chad, and Laura did, but still not arrive at the storage business any sooner?

First of all, since he'd replaced a useless key in the keystone for Laura and the kids to find, he wasn't in as big a hurry.

Second, using his own clues, Ratio didn't have too much trouble figuring out that 'key' was a file name in WordPerfect, and 'heir to' was the password that would open the file. He found the word 'keystone' an hour or more before his opponents. But Ratio ran into trouble on place clues.

His place clues were: 'mpdlfs, or knbjdq,' which he figured out meant 'locker,' 'you'll have to call the place,' and 'now what would *I* name a business?' He also had Laura's CLUES I place clue: 'storage.' But Ratio had only his own head to work with. He thought 'storage' was just a synonym that was meant to give Laura the word 'locker.' Thinking only the word 'locker' was important, Ratio spent a lot of time checking out public lockers in the bus station and the mall before he thought of looking up *storage lockers* — rental places—that began with A. By the time he did, Caroline, Chad, and Laura had caught up.

Arthur's LAST CLUE, which was on the paper Ratio pulled from storage unit twelve, looked like this: ΙΧΘΥΣ. These Greek letters spell 'ichthus,' a word meaning 'fish.' Early Christians used a fish as their symbol, and we often see these fish symbols on bumper stickers, key rings, or other items today, sometimes with the Greek letters inside. The clue Arthur wrote to go with the Greek letters, 'All are Greek, some are Roman,' helped Caroline see that the first two letters, IX, were also Roman numerals that stand for nine. She then guessed that the second key, also found in unit twelve, would unlock unit nine.

If you like math, logic, and word puzzles, there are many books that contain them in your school library, public library, or bookstore. These puzzles can give you hours of fun and fascination as they sharpen your thinking skills. So get out your paper and pencil, pull up a chair, and enjoy!

Marcia Hoehne

*Hint: To solve Ratio's fifth clue, substitute for each letter in 'mpdlfs' the letter that comes *before* it in the alphabet. Then substitute for each letter in 'knbjdq' the letter that comes *after* it. Your answers should agree. A bit easier to read, isn't it?